The Chronicles of Merkadiah: The Rise of the Gryphon

Edgar Lewis

The Chronicles of Merkadiah: The Rise of the Gryphon

Copyright © 2018 by James Smith

Published by Sibling Rivalry an imprint of
Dead Pirate Media Group, LLC.

ISBN 978-0-578-25003-8

Cover Design by Julliet Bookishgrove

For those who believed I could

Acknowledgements

There are many people that need to be thanked for making this book possible. First my cousin Ricci for always believing and pushing me to get this finished. Additionally, I would like to thank James and Pat for helping create my own version of Grivon's furnace, and for giving it the fuel needed to keep it burning.

A special thank you to Rita, you made me realize I could do it! A big thank you to my best friend Paige, you read so many drafts! Another big thank you to my first official fan Cameron. Thank you to Chris, Aaron, and Daniel for being my sounding board as I slaved away on this. Thank you to Nathaniel for putting up with all you have during the time I worked on this. Thank you to Deborah and Robert for your brutal honesty.

A huge thank you to my wife Alesia, without you being patient and inspiring confidence; I don't think I would ever have gotten this far. A big thanks to Anne, Gail, and Juliette for helping edit this. An additional thank you to Juliette for the awesome cover!

Thank you to my aunt Linda, for always seeing something in my stories. Last but surely not least, thank you to my eighth grade English teacher Mr. Brittan, for inspiring the desire to write.

Glossary

Aridaunt: Liege Lord of one to five fiefs. They are recognized in public by their white robes and faceless alabaster masks. An Aridaunt carries an honorific given at his own discretion and carries two votes in the Senate.

Aurora: This small microchip is implanted in the pineal gland. With proper training, a person can use it to create an Aurora Field, teleport without a transporter, and be sent to rejuvenation after sustaining life- threatening wounds and illnesses. If the heart stops or brain function ceases, the person bearing an Aurora dies.

Autocrat: The leader of the Senate and Merkadiah. Even though he has no real political power he can present laws, policies and issue two decrees a year. The Autocrat wears whatever color of robes he wishes and a purple mask carved from amethyst. The Autocrat carries two hundred forty votes.

Aurora Level: This is an abstract number used to help Kartah define how long they can maintain their Auroras. Every time the field stops an object from harming the person it surrounds, several minutes are deducted from this number, and the color of the field changes.

Blue Star: A large blue celestial body the Pantherines and many citizens of Merkadian believe to be Earth. It is the third star in the Gryphon Constellation. In actuality, it is an Einstein-Rosenburg Gate used for space travel.

Depublic: When the Autocrat takes his seat, he promotes one Kofah to the rank of Second Depublic and the former Second Depublic becomes the new First Depublic. Depublics sit on the right and the left hand of The Autocrat. Each Depublic is responsible for the management of four Kofahs. Depublics wear green robes and masks carved from large peridots. Each Depublic carries one hundred twenty votes.

Depublic Guard: An elite force of Kartah charged with the guarding of Depublics, The Autocrat, and important Aridaunts without Senate duties.

Kartah: A highly trained warrior from one of five different Guilds. Each Guild has its own unique set of forms and teaching techniques. A Kartah serves either directly under a politician of rank. Kartah are used to settle personal disputes between two or more parties in a tradition of dueling. Each party involved in the dispute selects a predetermined number of Kartah –no more than three; and whoever has at least one Kartah left standing is the winner of the dispute. Kartah are also used as bodyguards, police officers, and when the need may arise soldiers. Kartah wear blue robes and alabaster masks while in the Senate, or in the presence of their Liege Lord.

Kofah: A Kofah is responsible for a select number of Aridaunts. This number varies from Kofah to Kofah. They wear red robes and masks carved out of large garnets. Each Kofah carries fifteen votes Mutiny, the : A revolution against the Xóa Empire that brought about the use of Kartah to handle disputes instead of wasting lives on war.

Network Terminal: These computer terminals keep the denizens of Merkadiah connected over light years of distance. The Network also functions as a limitless data bank of history and entertainment.

Pantherine: A large humanoid cat creature. They are split into four tribes defined by their markings. The Chisis, graceful cheetah humanoids, are fast runners. They once populated the planet Felonius. Secondly, are the Leonis, proud lion humanoids with full manes and traditions of honor. They once populated Tygrano. The third tribe are the Lepridis, regal leopard humanoids. They once populated Rhokahl, the forested moon of Felonius. The fourth tribe of Pantherines are the Tigris. A regal tiger humanoid, these elegant tacticians once populated the jungle world of Felion.

Pantherines Bane: A thick, black, sticky liquid that when exposed to air immediately combusts and burns until the liquid is consumed by itself. This highly explosive substance is used by Pantherine soldiers and is also used against Pantherines.

Queen: A queen is a female Pantherine.

Selmar: A highly volatile crystal found growing naturally on the planet Merk. It grows at a rate of four centimeters a minute. This substance is highly combustible when propelled at high speeds at an object, or when it is quickly compressed. Selmar is used to make mortar shells, grenades, and batteries. It is found in the bottom of extinct volcanos on the planet Merk. It was once found in a meteor on Earth, sparking a new gold rush and bringing Darrian D'Gaul and his colonists. It is sold to unknown buyers who pay well for the crystal.

Selmar Tube: A sixteen-centimeter cylinder with a timer or motion sensor. A piece of selmar crystal is put into it and is then capped with the timer or sensor. At the bottom of the tube is an area for additional tubes to attach or for use with Pantherines Bane.

Teleportation Station: A transportation device that allows for almost instantaneous transportation. Powered by selmar, this device was created after the colonists landed to reduce the need for starships.

Therian: The result of the union of a Human and a Pantherine. Therians often pass along their genes for hundreds of generations and are usually outcasts from both races. Therians often die before reaching a year old due to abandonment, or their mothers killing them right after birth.

Wergare Clones: In their basic form these creatures have no real resemblance to one person. They are the product of years of research to provide the ultimate "expendable soldier." Wergare Clones can be purchased in either male or female and can resemble anyone you wish, even a Pantherine. Wergare are not given Aurora, but a Controller. Wergare Clones eat very little and require no long-term care as they become unstable after three weeks and die.

On a midsummer night, under the Moon of Sekhmet, the stars will fall on her children. From the Blue Star, the children of tyrants will come, and war will soon follow. The war will be swift, and the children of Sekhmet will fall into the hands of oppressors. Sekhmet will rise and herald the Winged God, but before the blessing, three demons will arise, one with wings, one with a horn, and one with ears black as night. The Winged God is not whom he seems to be.

Prologue

Elder Leon Trey sat in front of his star viewer eating his leftover antelope meat. He ran a large paw through his mane as he gazed at the stars. Grousing to himself about how the other elders refused to believe in the old scrolls. How they refused to believe in the prophecy that spoke of the Winged God. An Avatar that would one day bring peace to the four tribes of the Pantherines and would one day guide them back to their home, The Blue Star.

Home, Leon sighed. The Blue Star, the planet of the Elders, the Great Scions, and the Wise Ones: A home that he or others would never know. For now, they lived in a solar system of endless planets and only populated the one called Merk.

He was so lost in his thoughts about the home he would never know, and of the prophecy, that he didn't notice the thousand tiny sparkles that we're moving in the heavens. Taking another bite to eat, he pondered his life, and all the hopes of the four tribes of the Pantherines.

The ground shook when the first star impacted. Leon looked through his star viewer and saw hundreds of stars crashing to the ground. Standing too quickly, he bumped his head on the low ceiling in his hut. Cursing, he pulled on his cloak and ran out into the dark village square.

When he arrived, the rest of his village was outside watching the stars fall; nevertheless, he was more interested in the one that fell close enough to make his hut shake. He looked to the western horizon and saw an orange glow and smoke pluming from several meters away. Leon knew that he should signal the elders in the other Leonis villages but was more excited to be the first to see the Winged God.

Making his way from the village, he shed his elder robe and sprinted off into the night. He arrived sooner than he thought, and he could hear the echoes of his villagers shouting and talking as more stars streaked through the open sky. Coming to a stop, he sniffed the air through his mouth. His whiskers twitched, and he sneezed at smelling the acrid smoke floating from the star.

Curiosity kills. Leon's mother's words echoed through his head giving him caution. He crouched low and slinked toward the glowing object. When he reached the star, he noticed it was made of metal and was the size of a small village. A tight lump formed in his throat as he approached the mass.

The smell was worse now making his whiskers bristle, causing him to sneeze again. He was so busy recovering from the sneeze, that he did not hear the soft footsteps coming from behind him. A deep voice boomed in his ear. Turning around with claws extended and his fur standing on end, Leon almost clawed the face of Chief Elder Morah.

Morah, a beastly Leonis, stood glaring down at Leon with his rare beautiful blue eyes. When he gazed at you, you felt as if you had just dived into a frozen lake. The knot fully formed in his throat, and he was unable to speak. Instead, a stammering of grunts came out of his mouth. Chief Elder Morlah held the look of death in his eyes. Apparently, he was somewhere he shouldn't have been.

"Leon," roared Morlah, "instead of taking control of your village, you came out here, naked, to see a fallen star? How cub-like of you. You may be a young elder, but you cannot come running naked to see every new star that falls. This is the tenth in this month alone and it was just another piece of junk from Sekhmet. Why do you insist on letting your infatuation with ancient scrolls govern your reason? You are the least wise among the Council of Elders. How you ever proved yourself to Chief Elder Vhrothy as a worthy contestant is beyond my understanding. The question I have for you is, what do you plan on doing?

"Do you plan on letting your village descend into chaos, or do you plan on taking charge of the chaos that you have caused in not being anywhere remotely close to the village. Did it ever occur to you that the Tigris, Lepridis and the Chisis are reading the same…?"

Morlah was distracted from his long lecture as a hatch popped open and several strange creatures without fur carrying long metal objects step out from it. Leon and Morlah watched Chief Elders from the other three tribes arrive from their territories to the star. The hairless creatures parted for another creature with similar features and strange skin on its torso and legs to come to the foreground.

The strange being that stood before them was smaller than Morlah and held a long silver rod in its left hand. What appeared to be large wings billowed from behind it. It smiled a devious smirk as he saw the frightened faces of the cat creatures in front of him. Leon looked the creature up and down, seeing the skin on his belly, arms and legs which were the color and texture of obsidian. The darkness seemed to suck into the skin itself. Morlah took a step back when the creature opened its mouth.

"I am a human from the Solaris System and have come to claim this system as part of the Human Empire Xóa. My name is Darrian de Gaul. Please take me to whoever has ownership of your pets."

Leon was somewhat surprised to hear the creature speaking in high speech. Before he could ponder the meaning of such a thing, quick movement out of the corner of his eye drew his gaze back to his superior.

Morlah took several steps back, extended his claws, and shook his tail back and forth before pouncing on the hairless creature. At first, he clawed at the demon's face, but the creature was too quick. Morlah was pushed off the human's shoulders. Backflipping, he regained his footing for another attack. This time he concentrated on the torso of his adversary.

His claws broke on the obsidian skin of the demon. Morlah let out a mournful howl as he fell to the ground, his large paws bleeding. The interloper smiled as the silver rod shifted into a long thick curved grass thresher. Then with calm that Leon had only seen in warriors, the demon cut off Morlah's head. Leon stood shocked and confused and before he knew what he was doing, he spoke the words no one dared, "Are you the Winged God?"

The demon in front of him smiled and said, "Yes, I am."

Part I
The Chaos Guild

Seven Hundred Fifty Years Later

Preamble

"All historians know that deciding where to begin is the hardest part of any text. To tell the history of Elysium, one must begin where The Gryphon himself first began, in the Chaos of Guild on Tygrano, in the Merkadian Solar System. One must also know the name of the first Gryphon and how he came to power in order to understand the events that brought this galaxy to its knees," -Introduction to, The History of Elysium, by Shelah Barrim.

The Senate liaison materialized in a storm of blue and yellow sparks. The storm settled as quickly as it began, and a tall dark-skinned man stood drinking in the stone walls of the room. A squirrely technician scurried from around the terminal and bowed. "Mister Jericho, we are honored to have a man of your esteem visit.

Where can I take you?"

Taking a moment to observe the tiny man, Jerimiah bellowed, "Get up you fool! Take me to The Guild Master immediately!" The man stood up and nodded. Before Jerimiah could say anything, he had scampered out the door of the teleportation chamber. A flash of anger enveloped him, and he stalked after the wily technician.

This was already proving to be a bad assignment. The Guild Master was already proving to him he did not care about the future. A young man dwelled here who should have died long ago as a child. Now he was a man and about to be unstoppable. Hallways and stone walls seemed to blur by as his twitchy guide had to stop and wait for him to catch up. Great men rarely hurried for any reason, and though this assignment was thrust upon him at the last minute, an aide to The Autocrat was never hurried.

After several minutes of striding and catching up, the guide stopped in front of an opulent cherry door that seemed out of place with the drab stone walls and metal doors he had passed. The little man rapped soundly on the door and hurried away. Jerimiah watched as he rounded a corner and nearly toppled what appeared to be an aide of some sort.

The door creaked open and before Jerimiah stood a stout bald man with age spots splattered across his shining scalp. He looked both ways and motioned for Jerimiah to accompany him into a posh office.

The Chronicles of Merkadiah:
The Rise of the Gryphon

Thick green carpet squished beneath Jerimiah's feet as he strode toward a short white leather chair in front of a desk that matched the door he had just walked through. The Guild Master flopped into his tall black leather chair. He scooted forward putting both elbows into well- worn spots in the lacquer and clasped his hands together.

"How may I help you Mister Jericho?"

Jerimiah was stunned at how well the voice flowed out the tiny purple lips and into the atmosphere. He swallowed to wet his lips a little bit and then spoke, letting his baritone voice fill the room with its own presence.

"The Autocrat came to me late last night and said that a student by the name of Grivon D'Gaul is studying here. Is that true?"

The Guild Master seemed taken aback by the question. He scratched his ear and took a sip of water from a glass that sat to his left. After several seconds he spoke, "Yes."

"I see and why did you let him stay here, or let him live for that matter?" The Guild Master once again seemed caught off guard by his question.

"Under laws passed at the time the Guilds were established, it is unlawful for a Guild to refuse refuge to a child whose parents can no longer care for him or wish to care for him. Guilds are to be de facto orphanages. Additionally, we cannot refuse a child given to us based solely on the surname, or by whatever biases we have. Only if we don't currently have room."

This man is sly, Jerimiah thought. I wonder if he could dislike the boy. Rumor had it he had just came of age in the last month, and while physically he was a man, that did not mean he was one.

"Tell me, why did you not kill him at the first opportunity?"

The Guild Master took another gulp of water, "Students aren't allowed to participate in duels to the death until they are level five, or the age of fifteen, whichever comes first."

"Tell me, did it ever occur to you to try and slip him some poison, or something to that effect?"

"Well, no, that sort of thing is the tool of a politician," The Guild Master sneered.

"I see. I want to see the boy, and I want a full tour of this facility. I trust you have accommodations for me. I'm sure you are aware I will be staying longer than just a few hours."

"Yes, and I will conduct the tour myself. Where would you like to begin?"

Jerimiah mulled the question over in his mind, letting it knock against different thoughts like it were some sort of marble. All the while he bore a hole in the listless blue eyes of The Guild Master, trying to garner a weakness of some sort. Something he could exploit. Having been a lobbyist for twenty years had given him a few talents most people didn't possess, and reading others through their eyes was just one of them.

"Why don't we begin with the common teaching area and work our way toward where young master D'Gaul is being taught today."

"Very well, if you will follow me," The Guild Master said as he stood.

Grabbing an alabaster mask from a drawer in his desk he secured it and bid Jerimiah to follow him.

"You will notice that here we don't allow the students to show their faces," to Jerimiah's surprise, his guide's voice wasn't muffled. "Each student eats in his or her own private chamber," The Guild Master continued. "Students stay sequestered from the others unless they are sparing or dueling. We find this keeps them more focused on their studies, and less focused on trivial matters like gossip, dating, and other frivolous activities non-Kartah youths like to partake in. This isn't a run of the mill academy this is a training school for future leaders."

He is taking this tour to heart. I would be willing to bet he tells me all the laws and regulations about the guilds I already know, Jerimah thought.

The Guild Master led him through a winding maze of corridors and courtyards droning on about the need for discipline or the lack of need of leisure activities. It was all very boring and not what the overall goal was for. The Autocrat had told him that he had unilateral control to change how The Guild operated to insure the swift expulsion or destruction of Grivon.

After what seemed like hours of walking and listening to the pompous man's droning, they arrived at a large courtyard filled with students in black hooded robes and alabaster masks sparring with sabers. There were over a dozen sparring circles, each three meters in diameter and two students in each one. Each circle was guarded by an instructor and filled with alabaster dust to give a defining space. The corridor in which they stood echoed with the clanging of metal bouncing off metal.

The Guild Master and Jerimiah stood watching for several minutes before the squat man said, "These are level twenty-five students. They are all around the age of thirty and have been taught how to spar with edgeless weapons.

The Chronicles of Merkadiah:
The Rise of the Gryphon

As much as Grivon wants to be among those in there, the laws passed since he began first level training forbid a student of age eighteen to progress past level twelve.

Tomorrow Grivon will be testing to become tenth level." Jeremiah stroked his smooth chin in quiet contemplation. Perhaps I could use this desire to excel to my advantage, but how? Before he could say anything, the ringing of metal suddenly stopped as a student dropped his sword and gripped his wrist. He could hear frantic whispers, and then one of the instructors pulled a saber from his side and cut the student's hand off.

Blood sprayed the instructor and the other student in the circle. An indigo light enveloped the student and he was gone, only his hand remained on the alabaster dust.

"Why did that instructor do that?" Jeremiah demanded.

"Weak students are often maimed as a teaching tool. The first time you have the opportunity to redeem yourself by being sent to our rejuvenation clinic under the guild. As you well know Kartah are given access to rejuvenation clinics on each planet in the solar system. Each guild has its own infirmary and rejuvenation clinic to treat its students.

If you are proven to be weak a second time, you could be killed or sent to rejuvenation again. If you go to rejuvenation a second time, all the students in the guild are gathered in the teleportation chamber, and line each wall.

"When the disgraced student shows themselves, they all turn their backs on them in shame and they are sent to Ormah with enough money to find lodging and food for a week. It may seem barbaric, but it keeps all the students sharp."

"And yet you haven't done this to Grivon? Why?"

The Guild Masters eyes narrowed at the question, "You really think it is easy to expel someone like Grivon?"

"From what I just witnessed, yes."

The Guild Master grunted and motioned for Jeremiah to follow him. The next several hallways were filled with people in white uniforms pushing hover carts filled with food. Savory smells wafted into Jeremiah's nose making his mouth water and stomach rumble.

"Where are they going with those carts?" Jeremiah asked.

"They are going to the student quarters. It is almost time for the mid-day meal. Would you like to eat before we continue?"

"Yes."

Stopping at an opening in the left wall, The Guild Master motioned his hand to show Jerimiah a large mess hall for instructors. Several rows of buffets were filled with steaming food, cold vegetables, and chilled fruits. The two men walked to one of the bars and picked up a plate. Jerimiah filled his with some kind of grilled meat, fruit, and vegetables.

The Guild Master mostly filled his with meat and some starchy looking grains and smashed roots. In total silence they walked to a door at the end of the room that opened as they approached it. Behind it sat several rows of tables and instructors sat in sporadic clusters talking, laughing, and eating.

As they sat down to start eating, The Guild Master pulled off his mask and said, "Someone will be along with drinks in a moment. Everyone here either drinks plain water or a special tonic to enhance brain function, electrolyte retention, and mental focus.

I prefer water. The tonic is more for the students, and instructors that actually want a hands-on approach to teaching their student."

The Guild Master shoveled a large fork full of his food into his mouth, just as a blonde woman dressed in white set down two large glasses of water. Jerimiah thanked the woman as she left. He took a sip and was instantly refreshed. Giving The Guild Master a wry look he took another sip before trying his food.

Everything tasted magnificent. Perfectly seasoned and the right temperature. He could live here just for the food.

"So why do you all eat in here?" Jerimiah asked as he ate a mouthful of vegetables.

"As I said before. Student's aren't allowed to see one another's faces or the faces of their instructors. Keep in mind no one has ever seen the face of The Autocrat, or the other members of the Senate, at least not the everyday person. Why should the students among the guilds be any different? It prepares them for the facelessness of politics that await them upon graduation," The Guild Master shoved another fork full of food into his unsightly maw.

Jerimiah took another bite and said, "That is a valid point. How do the students unwind after a day of training?"

The Chronicles of Merkadiah:
The Rise of the Gryphon

The Guild Master put his fork down and scratched his head, "I suppose they read or find something to entertain themselves on The Network. I decided long ago not to filter the outside world from the students. A lot of them find enjoyment in music, or in art. Others find solace in self-expression through poetry."

"And Grivon?"

The Guild Master took a long draught of his water before speaking, "I have seen reports of him hacking into private libraries looking for books on combat and history. He has a thirst for knowledge unlike that of anyone else his age."

"Fascinating," Jerimiah mumbled through a full mouth of food. If Grivon had a single-minded focus, then it could be problematic to get rid of him easily. "Does he have any friends or cohorts that you have noticed?"

"Yes, he has two…well I don't know if you would call them friends. One I would, but the other I don't know. There is something unsettling about him. The one I would call his friend has been progressing in levels rather quickly lately. I think he may be teaching her somehow, but I have yet to figure out how. After the seventeenth hour, everyone is confined to quarters until I shut off access to The Network at the twentieth hour."

"Do you patrol the halls at night? Perhaps they are sneaking out," Jerimiah postulated.

"Perhaps, but the laws forbid me to use surveillance near student quarters or the courtyards near them," The Guild Master wiped his mouth with the sleeve of his robe, and stood, "If you are finished I will take you to where Grivon should be right now," The Guild Master said securing his mask to his face.

The walk was uneventful and filled with boring facts about laws that Jerimiah already knew or didn't care about. After almost an hour of walking through the labyrinthine hallways, they came to a small door in a wall. This door looked like the passage to a linen closet but instead opened into a small rectangular room with an observation window.

"You can see him, but he can't see you," The Guild Master chortled.

Jerimiah stepped close and observed. The boy was average height, possessing an almost Adonis-like body. Sweat shimmered in silver rivers running down his chest and stomach as he fought against seven clones in white body suits. His instructor stood stoically in the corner of the closed-off sparring room. His arms folded across his chest in a manner that showed not only disinterest, but disgust. Jerimiah could tell by the look in the instructor's eyes; he loathed his student.

On the other hand, Grivon's pale green eyes were alive with purpose as he cut a clone diagonally across the chest. As blood spattered across Grivon's chest, Jerimiah caught a glimpse of euphoric delight flashing in the boy's eyes. The instructor rolled his eyes as Grivon backflipped and thrust his sword out to catch another clone in the neck, sending a sharp spray of blood across the viewing window. A clone seemed to come out of nowhere and Grivon narrowly escaped losing his arm.

Instead, he counterattacked in a twirl relieving the clone of its own head. Four more still remained and Grivon danced into the middle of them. One of them swung and managed to cut off the thick silver braided ponytail that trailed down the middle of his back. In a roar of rage Jerimiah was glad he could not fully hear, Grivon whirled around in a fast spin. The four clones advanced for a second, but then crumpled to the stone floor as thick gashes appeared in their necks and blood flowed down soaking their white unitards.

Grivon flung the blood from the sword and sheathed it in a scabbard propped against the wall where his instructor stood.

A hidden door opened and several men in blue uniforms rushed in to remove the seven bodies and clean the blood on the floor. Jerimiah witnessed a soundless conversation as Grivon stood still with his back to the window and the instructor gesturing wildly every so often.

The Guild Master looked up at Jerimiah and said, "This is what we are dealing with. A student who is only limited by his own ambition. While he isn't all-powerful, he is definitely stronger than most students in his age category."

Jerimiah nodded and began heading for the door. He needed time to process everything. He would need an idea that would accomplish both what he was sent to do and make some drastic changes to not just this guild, but all of them. The Guild Master led him back to his office where a dwarf-like man stood. He appeared to be waiting for them. Small and bald save for a single black braided ponytail similar to Grivon's, he had a long catfish mustache and thin goatee. He wore a green tunic and black pants.

The tiny man leaned against the wall staring daggers at him through slanted eyelids. His coal eyes searching Jerimiah. *In all the places, in all the worlds, I never thought I would see him again!*

12

The Chronicles of Merkadiah:
The Rise of the Gryphon

Jerimiah hoped the man wouldn't recognize him. Once upon a time they had been friends, but they hadn't spoken in nearly four hundred years. If Phoy Yin was here, that could only mean one thing. He wanted to take the boy and train him.

Chapter One

Grivon D'Gual

"The best way to make a student excel is to cause psychological and emotional duress."-
Chaos Guild Training Axiom

I

Grivon D'Gaul stood in a crowded room full of small children. Each child was with one or both of their parents. They were being examined by old men and women in black robes and were told they needed to answer questions. Afterwards, each child was given a practice sword.

The dream phased from the room with the children to another room with a weary woman and a man with a strong, set jaw. Grivon knew them as his parents. They were leaving him there with other children. Suddenly, his parents were being ushered away from him by men in black robes. He watched in horror as his parents were led away, and he heard the words that haunted him still, "Never forget, you're full of greatness."

Grivon jolted awake, covered in a cold sweat, panting as if he had just finished a marathon. Sitting up in his bed, he looked around his quarters. His muscular chest reverberated with the strained effort as his eyes darted about the room. Glancing at the clock port on his console, he strained to see the blue lights on the Network terminal but could only tell that it was sometime early in the morning. Laying back on his pillow, he looked up at the stone ceiling of his room and rested his hands on his soft wavy hair.

He thought long and hard about his dream, feeling it was more a memory more than anything else. The memory wipe

The memory wipe they had given him ensured that he would no longer have these dreams, but it did not seem like it was working. Now, he would have to go and see the health administrator, but that could wait. For now, he needed rest. His tenth level assessment was only a few hours away.

This test would put him ahead of the others in his age category, the majority being level six. Unfortunately, this had created a lot of jealousy. The only other students at the guild that were close to being as advanced, were

The Chronicles of Merkadiah:
The Rise of the Gryphon

Steven Anthony and Barbarah Watts. Each of them was level eight and rising fast, perhaps from his tutoring them in secret.

Barbarah and Steven were Grivon's best and only friends. Being a year younger than them sometimes made even his best friends jealous, but he never mocked them, nor rubbed it in. Eventually, sleep found him again.

II

The morning alarm jarred Grivon awake. Morning light cascaded through the high window in his room. His eyes shot open, and with a groan, he began his daily rites. Sitting on the side of the bed, he pulled on his shorts and then his solid black robe.

To accompany his robe was a featureless alabaster mask; the only markings on the mask were black letters and numbers, printed under the left eye on its cheek: his Guild name and level. "The Gryphon, Level Nine", it read.

Each student was required to wear a mask to hide their identity. In theory, the masks prevented the students from becoming promiscuous. If nobody could see your face, how could they know if you were attractive, read the student handbook. The theory was to ensure that the students could focus on their studies.

However, the students found ways around this rule and would show their faces in secret outside the guild. This loophole was the reason Grivon knew what his friends looked like.

Grivon let out a deep breath as he attached his saber. His was ornate with a spiked guard and decorative writing on the blade. The sword held a secret, if one was to press a concealed button on the handle, a dagger could be summoned from the pommel, a second touch would retract the blade.

A saber identified its owner as a Kartah, but Grivon wasn't even close to being one. He bought his with his monthly allowance and was allowed to wear it, which he did with pride. When he finished dressing, he began his morning practice. He would practice every day for several hours, and when he did, he would think about one of two things: his future and his past.

His past was often at the front of his mind. The thing he thought about most, was the day he met his friend Barbarah. Barbarah the blonde-haired, green-eyed, beauty that he hoped to spend his life with. Every time he saw or even thought about her, he got butterflies in his stomach. It always felt as if he was about to fall apart when he was around her. Though at the same time, he felt as if he could do anything.

The memories freely flowed as he swung the sword in the motions of the form he was practicing. As he spun to complete the form, he flowed into another one, and his thoughts drifted into bittersweet memories of the day he first saw Barbarah's face.

III

It was a frigid day in his favorite courtyard. He sat on a stone table in the middle of a sand garden, his sword on his lap, reflecting on the dreams he had been having.

As he sat with his eyes closed, he heard a swishing sound. Keeping his eyes closed, he knew someone was watching him. He opened his eyes and saw the most beautiful pair of emerald orbs he had ever seen.

She stood looking at him through her mask. With her hands placed firmly on her hips as she looked him over. Her eyes were paralyzing. She was an angel.

"You're the one they call the Gryphon, aren't you?" she asked.

"Yes, I am lady Unicorn," he replied.

"My name is Barbarah Watts and I want to talk to you."

"Aren't you already?" he quipped.

"You don't have to be an ass," she said with defiance.

He sighed, "Call me Grivon. Grivon D'Gaul. What do you want?"

"Well, I have seen you here for the last week reflecting, and I was curious what the infamous Gryphon was thinking." She asked.

"Why do you want to know?" Grivon growled. "We've never talked before. Are you here to mock me too?"

Soft peals of laughter escaped from her, "You're a hard person to talk to you know. No," she gave a brief pause. "I want to know more about you."

He sighed, if she were that fascinated, he would oblige her and then she would leave him alone.

"I came here when I was four and my parents left me. I have had dreams about it for the last few weeks, and it is almost more than I can handle. In fifteen years, I have advanced more than anyone else. No one wants to talk to me let alone look at me so why should you be any different?" his voice cracked with emotion. Barbarah cupped her hand to his cheek and looked deep into his eyes. She put her hand inside his hood and ran her fingers through his hair. Then she reached down to rub his ear. For the first time in ages, he smiled.

"Look, you are one of the smartest and strongest among your age, and more importantly your name has a meaning."

"What do you mean by that? It means gryphon, so other than that what else could it mean?"

She looked both ways, and leaned in toward him and barely whispered, "Meet me at the fountain in the main courtyard after the mess hall closes and bring three practice swords. I want to spar with you. Don't let any of the Guild Lords see you or follow you."

Her response had taken him aback. She was interested in learning from him?

IV

Grivon arrived at the fountain early. The purple liquid within bubbled and frothed. He stood with three wooden practice swords and nervously scanned the courtyard for Guild Lords. He felt as if his stomach would fall through to the ground, his palms were sweaty, and he almost dropped the swords. Just about the time he was about to leave, she showed up.

"Follow me to a place where the Guild can't touch us, and where we can see each other's faces," she whispered behind her mask. Grivon blinked and asked in a worried voice hinting at the edge of expectation, "How do you know of such a place?"

She winked at him, her eyes sparkling, "Let's just say that I like to walk a lot."

Grivon understood the meaning and looked away. His mind filled with images of him kissing her, holding her head gently to his chest as he stroked her hair. He wondered what color her hair was, what her face looked like. He was worried about The Guild Lords catching them together, expelling him as well as her; but this was worth the risk of seeing her face. Grivon felt a soft hand on his left shoulder and heard the words,

"Come on. We will need some sleep tonight."

Barbarah grabbed his hand and led him to the fountain and out a hall into the open courtyard. She led him to a stone wall on the east side, she looked around, checking her surroundings, then pressed a red stone in the wall. A large section of the wall sank in and made a door that slid into the tall stone wall that revealed a passage into a starlit veldt.

As they exited The Guild's courtyard into the field, the stone door slid back into place and Grivon looked up into the star-filled sky to the constellation he was named after. If you were to look at the star charts and drew a line between each star, it made a rough shape of a gryphon with a bright blue star as its eye. Grivon turned his attention to Barbarah and began to follow her on into the night. They walked for several minutes before either spoke.

"Have you ever heard of the Prophecy of Felonis?" Barbarah asked, reminding him of Professor Gates his history tutor. Confused, Grivon did not give an answer at first. He thought for a few moments and shook his head.

"The prophecy talks of an Avatar of the Pantherines. They call him the Winged God. He is supposed to come and eradicate the threat to the existence of the Pantherines. It is said that when we first came to this system before the Mutiny of the Empire, the Pantherines dwelled on the planet Merk long before we got here and had a unique system of government and a way of settling disputes. This is like the way we resolve things now, but when humans got here, we forced the Pantherines to the outskirts of the system and began to regulate them.

"The prophecy warns of them trusting people and that Sekhmet will rise to lead them. If this prophecy is true then, what is the god of the Pantherines?" She asked.

"It would be a gryphon," he said, thinking of a lion-bodied eagle.

"Exactly, and you are him."

"Figures," he said, thinking of such things made him bored.

"Your name alone speaks volumes, and you, with the right motivation, could unite them under the guise of the Winged God and overthrow this horrid government," she said excitedly. "You know as much as I do that the Senate is corrupted by activists and that the Kartah often take the law into their own hands most of the time.

I mean the fact that you alone could change the course of history, and possibly the system, is just mind-blowing. This is far enough." She stopped walking and talking.

Grivon had been walking beside her, with his head hung low contemplating destiny, his legs felt as if he had been walking for hours. It

18

was probably the fact that this young woman was making a lot of fuss over something as menial as his name.

His hands were cramping from holding the practice swords, so when she had said that this place was good enough, he dropped them in a pile at his feet. He then looked to his side and saw that she had taken off her mask. If it had felt like his stomach was going to fall to the ground earlier, the feeling was stronger now.

The bright light from the double moons illuminated the veldt letting him have a look at his new friend's features. Barbarah's hair fell down to her waist, the moonlight made her golden hair shimmer. This curtain of hair framed her face with high cheek bones, a short-sloped nose, and large almond-shaped eyes.

Her face spoke of exhaustion, of things she desired, and a life that was less than ideal. A look that told him that he would never want to consider the eyes of another for as long as he lived.

She shed her robes revealing a toned body defined by a tight-fitting body suit, the color undeterminable in the moonlight. Grivon's stomach tightened with nerves to the point of nausea. He couldn't move past her beauty. With a sigh, trying to calm his nerves, he removed his mask, revealing his face. Barbarah watched as Grivon removed his robe exposing a similar body suit molding around his well-trained muscles. He took her breath away.

She composed herself and motioned for him to toss her a practice sword, catching it with her left hand. The movement intrigued him, as he raised an eyebrow. He picked up a practice sword and began running through the basic attack form. She watched for a moment before starting to stretch and loosen her arms and legs.

The third moon rose over the trees and revealed the color of her body suit, a red-based purple that complemented her hair and eyes. Her curves flexed as she stretched out her muscles and warmed up. He felt as if he were drowning, and he liked it. The same way he liked the seething he felt in the monthly tournaments. That passion made him the champion of this cycle and led him to a perfect winning record in the last three seasons. All he had to do was summon the thought of the fifth level assessment. How, even though his age was still four years less than the recommended age, he took the assessment and passed.

He was told to fight a clone, which turned out to be one of himself. The duel proceeded as normal. The clone proved itself to be a tough opponent, and with a lucky strike, Grivon broke off the clone's mask. The alabaster visage shattered on the floor of the stage and to his horror there stood a clone of himself. It had been the most traumatic thing he had ever seen. He forgot all his forms and blocked the assault with sloppy instinctive parries. Neither before, nor after, had he been so close to dying.

His heartbeat hard in his chest just thinking about the affair. His mind's eye flashed with an image of him cowering at the corner of the stage on one knee. In an instant of clarity, he jammed the blade into the clone's gut and twisted the hilt.

Then in a flawless motion he pulled the blade free cutting the doppelganger almost in half. Blood and entrails sprayed his face, the stench and exhaustion making him pass out. When he had awakened, he vowed to never lose his wits again and began practicing his forms religiously.

After coming out of the infirmary, he was pelted with an insult beyond all insults and it was summed up into one word, "Freak."

Everywhere he went everyone chanted it. It was the mantra of all the students at his level and those in the levels beyond. He had become little more than an animal for their amusement. If he were a freak to them, so be it. That title would give him the fuel he needed to become what they could not.

"I'm ready when you are," Barbarh's angelic voice jarred Grivon from his memories. "I just want to spar, so go easy on me."

He nodded and walked to stand about a meter from her taking the stance of the Kathaga Form. His right hand gripped the hilt, and his left hand rested on top of his right wrist with the blade pointed at the ground. Barbarah took the stance of the High Thay're form. This was a form for left-handed people, but many right-handed people used it for added balance.

The two looked at each other. Green eyes watching green eyes, they began to circle each other still holding their stances. Suddenly, her arm flinched, and he struck at her middle. Agile as a cat she blocked his blow and kicked him in the chest. The force knocked him back, but he focused his momentum and backflipped into a more defensive stance. Grivon held his practice sword in front of his face and danced into a swirl and slashed, aiming at hers. She blocked the strike.

They parried each other for several minutes and then she said, "Is that all you've got, freak? I was expecting more from you."

He didn't speak. His heart shattered, dropping to his stomach. That horrible name! It caused his blood to boil and he fed it. The rage burned like a furnace, and he stoked its flames with all the hate and pain stored in every fiber of his being. How dare she! His mind roared.

She seduced him out of the Guild and built his ego only to destroy it in a sparring match. He ran straight toward her and faked right. She anticipated his move and blocked left. He swirled around and kicked her in the stomach. When she hit the ground; her breath was driven from her lungs. He raised his sword above his head and struck hard down into her torso.

The wood hit solid, and it drove breath further from her lungs. He stooped and pulled her to her feet with the small amount of slack afforded by her body suit. Holding her close to his face, he spat in hers. Then he raised his practice sword and struck the side of her head. She went limp in his hands, and he threw her into the grass.

Looking down, he frowned hoping she was still alive.

It was not his intention to hurt her, but that word made his sight go red and act on impulse. Stooping to the ground, he felt for a pulse. Her heart was beating. She was just knocked out. Standing up, he stomped back to the guild.

Grivon finished practicing his forms. The memory sent a bitter pang through him. Especially how, when three days later she came and apologized and told him how she wanted to "push" him. He chuckled to himself at the thought of what she meant. It still hurt, but he used it to stoke the inferno that roared within, even if he was angry with himself.

V

Walking over to his desk that was underneath the windowpane, he saw a bowl of fruit native to the planet he was on. He picked up ovular fruit with a hard-pink hull and small black bumps. Quickly, he peeled the hull and ate the green pulp inside it. It was a sour fruit, but a good one that would sustain him until his assessment was over.

Grivon walked down the crowded hall to the outer courtyard focusing on one thing: his smoldering aggression. It fueled his concentration and centered him. The emotions that swirled within added more fuel, and when

21

he applied it to combat, it frothed out in a fierce explosion that put his opponents off balance.

He was so deep in thought; he didn't feel the soft tap on the shoulder. It was Steven, his only other friend. Sliding in silently beside Grivon, they continued in silence until Barbarah slipped up on his other side. His stomach tightened with a mix of happiness and anxiety. Turning to look at her, he winked.

Her eyes flashed seductively, making his heart flutter. He was feeling depressed after calling upon his own regrets to fuel his practice; a push she called it. It still made him chuckle even at this moment in time. It had been three years since she had "pushed" him, and he began studying things that the guild didn't know about, let alone approve of.

Specifically, the Prophecy of Felonis, he spent three years learning all he could about the Pantherines and their unique culture, spending countless hours studying the anthropological records of them. What he had found was that the Pantherines were made up of four tribes that constantly fought each other, and that each had a special weapon unique to their tribe along with a universal tribal weapon called a Kadar.

As the crowd moved through the small halls, they passed by the Guild Master's private suite and office. When Grivon walked past the office, he saw that the Guild Master had a couple of visitors; one tall dark-skinned man with a shaved head that was beginning to grow stubble; and the other, a short man with olive skin, a smooth bald head, and a long catfish mustache that hung almost to his mid-abdomen.

An odd sensation came over Grivon as he walked past the shorter man. He didn't know that he was standing still until someone behind him pushed him forward. "Out of the way, freak," was all that was said, and the person was gone. The comment was almost enough to cause him to start a fight, but after he took a moment to think he instead used the words to fuel the furnace and center himself even further.

Now he was several feet behind his two friends and began to move through the mass of bodies as they made their way to the arena.

VI

The arena was a funnel-shaped outdoor theater, where assessments would often take place. Some of these assessments were oral, some were physical, and some were a mixture of both. Still, others were of whatever torture The Guild Master and your Guild Lord wanted to put you through. Sometimes the participants were killed.

Especially if they ran the Gauntlet.

The Gauntlet was the final test. In the time Grivon had been at the Guild, he could only remember there being six people to pass the Gauntlet. Most of the time nobody passed it. If a person passed it, they could choose any job they wanted. Most wanted to be Kartah, and the rest became politicians. Still, others would become high-ranking officers in the Security Force. Grivon, Steven, and Barbarah wanted nothing more than to be Kartah.

By the time Grivon caught up to Steven and Barbarah, they had saved him a spot in the upper seats. He sat down between them and sighed. Barbarah looked around and whispered in his ear something that would stick with him forever.

"You're going to knock them dead today. By this time next year, you won't be here."

Barbarah always wanted nothing more than to support her friend. She tried the first time she sparred with him, but it backfired. Instead of boosting his confidence, it only succeeded in making him angry. She never told him that he had beaten her within an inch of her life. At least he wasn't like other men.

They didn't want to spar or help her learn. All they wanted to do was to run their hands over her curves and kiss her lips. Sometimes she let them, but other times she fought them hard, only to have her ribs cracked and be left broken.

She was glad that her mask was a little loose so that no one would see her tears, but Grivon always did. He was the one person in the whole Guild who wanted nothing more than to just be with her. It was funny, he always noticed when she was sad. Like he was looking into her soul with his pale green eyes and understood her on a level no one else did.

Not even her Guild Lady could predict her mood, but Grivon could. Steven was too focused on himself and his family to care about her.

Barbarah reflected on the day after her first encounter with Grivon. She had gotten back to her quarters just before morning. Her stomach cramped worse than anything she could remember, and she was bleeding out of her normal cycle. After sending a sick message to her Guild Lady, she then climbed into her bed and let the built-in rejuvenator heal her.

When she woke up that afternoon, she used her refresher and looked in the mirror. In her reflection, across her face, a large dark bruise, almost black, making it hurt when she touched it.

"Quiet please," the booming voice of the Guild Master broke Barbarah from her reflection.

"I have an announcement to make." The Guild Master was a medium-sized man who usually wore black robes with an alabaster mask as well, but today he was only wearing his robes. The students in the arena leaned forward to see an old, balding man with grey wiry hair, brown eyes, liver spots on the top of his head, and two large moles on his face.

As the Guild Master began to give his long-winded announcement, Grivon began to think about two things. First was the day Barbarah told him why she called him a freak. Once again, he was brooding, sitting on that same stone table. He felt her presence long before she got close to his face. "Go away; I don't want to talk to you. I was hoping that you would be expelled before the end of this week," he grumbled, his eyes sealed tight.

"I wasn't trying to hurt you. I was trying to push you. I was trying...to make you see how talented you are. You're very gifted. Most men here are bastards and will take what they want. I wanted to spar with you, so I can learn to be a better fighter. My Guild Lady doesn't teach me anything that I don't already know and if I mention an assessment, she changes the subject.

She makes me read the books and practice forms that I already know, so I seek out the boys with a higher level than myself. I tell them I want to spar, and they see it as some sort of euphemism for carnal favors. Sometimes I give in I mean, I do have desires as I'm sure you do, who doesn't? Most of the time that is not what is on my mind. I try and fight them off and sometimes succeed.

"Then there are other times..." Barbarah broke down in tears.

Grivon still had his eyes closed, wondering why she was even talking to him still. When he heard her begin to cry, he realized she needed someone to listen to her. That was when he opened his eyes and did what she had done only a few days before. He cupped her cheek in his hand, feeling behind her hood to rub her hair and caress her ears. Barbarah shuddered at the touch, and they locked eyes.

"Meet me here tonight and bring two practice swords with you because you will break them. What level are you?" Grivon asked.

"I'm level four why?" She replied.

The Chronicles of Merkadiah:
The Rise of the Gryphon

"I needed to know which level you are, so that I can properly instruct you. That way I'm not trying to teach you something you already know.

You're also left-handed, correct? I will begin to teach you some left-handed forms. Of course, don't be followed."

Grivon sighed at that memory. She really had wanted to be his friend, and for some reason, he had always felt that since that night they sparred, she had deeper feelings for him. Something beyond friends, something that gave him chills that ran up his spine anytime he thought about it.

Looking over at her; he saw her tears.

He couldn't blame her for crying about things she had gone through and the indignities she suffered. She was unlike anyone he ever met; being one of only a hundred girls at the guild and the only one over level three at the age of twenty-three. Grivon wanted to take her pain and suffering onto himself, so Barbarah would no longer feel those things.

He used the wrongs done to his closest of friends to fuel the smoldering furnace within. Stoking it with his hatred of the others to turn their wrongs against them. To think they thought she was promiscuous and that she wanted nothing more than to give in to base lusts. It burned him, and he wondered who they were. If he ever found out who had done these things to cause a beautiful person so much pain, he would personally kill whomever had done it, all of them.

For a while, Grivon suspected Steven but was unsure. He figured Steven was the kind of person to take what he wanted and was empty hearted enough to do those things, but in the end, it was all just speculation.

Barbarah noticed Grivon was staring at her. Smiling, she winked at him. His eyes considering her very core. She knew she couldn't hide her feelings from his eyes, but there was something different in them today.

There was a red gleam to them, an unrequited emotion that built inside his mind. She knew that he was ready for this assessment. One day he would be her avenging angel and would set all wrongs right. There was no doubt in her mind that he was destined for greatness, but she often worried that the feelings they shared might lead to disaster.

Even though neither one of them ever said it, Barbarah always knew he loved her. She also knew from the first time they looked into each other's eyes; she was his and he was hers. Steven knew of their feelings and was envious enough to do something crazy. She was afraid he would kill someone just to have her.

But in the end, it was all just unsubstantiated fear. Besides, Steven was her only other friend. She leaned back and sighed, wishing she could leave the planet with Grivon. As she was just about to sit back and listen to the droning old man in the front, she heard something that made her both happy and a little scared.

"And lastly," droned the Guild Master "Mister Jeremiah Jericho here is now the recently created Senatorial representative for this Guild. He has been sent here to make sure that I comply with the new Senate laws mandating that the Chaos Guild be put under review. One of these laws is the elimination of the need for our masks: so now each of you remove your masks and show one another the faces you've been hiding."

In a loud swish, all the students removed their masks and began chattering. Barbarah, Steven, and Grivon already knew what each other looked like but were able to see one another in full daylight, no longer just the light of moons. Grivon and Barbarah looked at each other and couldn't take their eyes off one another.

The Guild Master moved his arms to quiet down the rowdy masses, "In addition to no masks, I have been directed to have a ball next month so, all of you young men and ladies can have time to get to know each other.

Of course, with two hundred boys and only a hundred ladies, there will be some competition, but remember, no fighting outside of sanctioned events. Now, on to other business; will Grivon D'Gaul please come down here and cite the rites to begin his assessment?"

As Grivon stood, the response was less than warm. People jeered as he began his descent to the bottom of the arena. He listened to the insults and fed them to the inferno. It felt like it was ready to envelop him, but he could not be consumed by it.

He thought of the form he would recite in front of the Guild now that they could see his face. Deciding upon the High Thay're form, he smirked. He would do it right-handed and then when the assessment began, he would do the one that no one had ever seen before.

As he approached the bottom of the arena, he saw the man with the catfish mustache in the third row from the bottom. Grivon saw his face at this point and stopped to stare. The man sat just short of one meter. Grivon remembered the man being only a little over one meter standing.

The Chronicles of Merkadiah:
The Rise of the Gryphon

The man looked kind but stern, and he gave Grivon a weird feeling. Restarting his descent, he arrived in front of the Guild Master. Grivon noticed that he looked even uglier now up close than far away. He looked like he was about a hundred, but that didn't matter, only the title he bore. The completion of the tenth level assessment was his only goal, and he couldn't be distracted.

"Cite the rites, Sir Gryphon," spoke the Guild Master coldly.

"The first rite," Began Grivon in a loud clear voice. "I as the ninth level applicant will perform the High Thay're Form and will then be instructed by the Guild Master his wishes of my teacher the Guild Lord Sy Therah."

A man in the masses stood. He was Guild Lord Sy Therah, and he spoke in a manner just above disgust, "Please show the Guild the completed form of your choice and recite it before the Guild Master and the students of the Chaos Guild."

Grivon nodded and gripped his sword in his right hand and pulled it from its scabbard. The metal sang as it was pulled from the wood. Its blade shone brightly as Grivon lifted it above his head and angled it down. He began to twirl in a counterclockwise motion spinning the sword as he went. He extended his right arm in a way that almost broke his wrist, but he corrected at the right moment and brought the blade back down into the scabbard.

The Form was the shortest to recite but was the hardest to learn only in the sense that it required strain on the wrist. If you strained it too much it would break, and you would be in the actual classroom learning the book side of forms.

"The second rite: Will Guild Lord Sy Therah please cite to me his wishes on how to complete my assessment." Grivon asked.

"You will fight and kill twelve Wergare clones. You must kill all of them within thirty minutes and use the most complicated form you know or any compilation of forms; begin now."

The Guild Master stepped away, and twelve hulking masses walked into the arena from the left. Each of the Wergare clones looked like Grivon. All of them had shoulder-length platinum hair and pale green eyes, were holding a saber, and wearing a black robe with a green sash.

Grivon hesitated for a moment. Then took a step back before running straight into the line of clones. Each one of the clones stepped back into a circle surrounding him.

Out of the corner of his eye, Grivon saw the silent satisfaction in the faces of the Guild Master and Sy Therah, knowing that they had set him up to fail, but he had an ace up his sleeve. A form that centered around one death, the cutting of him, and the deaths of the other clones involved.

As the clones began to close in on him, Grivon thrust his sword forward stabbing one of the clones in the neck. He brought it back, ejected the dagger in the pommel, cut his left hand, and in one fluid motion, he flourished the sword and brought the blade down to where it was almost touching the ground. The blade began to glow orange and then red. Then right before the blade turned white, a shock wave came from the point eviscerating the remaining clones.

As the bodies fell to the ground Grivon bowed low and said, "The third rite: Life. Try to master it and you will be mastered. Let it master you and you shall be its master."

The arena was silent. The Guild Master, Guild Lord Sy Therah and the short bald man each shared a look that expressed both astonishment and disgust, but on the face of the short man, there was more astonishment than anything. They watched as Grivon bowed and stood straight in front of the rest of the students. Everyone was silent.

Most faces looked angry, and others were white with shock. The gory scene was a little much for some of the younger students, making them wretch and vomit.

Grivon stood silent and tall looking out over the faces of his enemies. No one said anything, and no one moved. He just killed twelve Wergare clones in a matter of seconds. No one knew what this meant, but one man in the crowd did. It was the short bald man with the long mustache.

He knew all too well what had just happened. It was a Magiah technique called The Thread of Life. He had the ability. The one that could make him very dangerous, an ability so powerful it could level cities. This boy was the first to use that technique who had not been to his planet. The planet on the edge of the system that allowed him privacy and anyone who heard of him would find him, but today he heard of Grivon.

He had teleported in that morning and was hoping to talk to the boy. It looked like he would soon get his chance.

Chapter Two
Winds of Change

"Everything changes. No one can stop the hand of time." -Pantherine Proverb

I

Phoy stood watching Grivon through a viewing wall in The Guild Master's Office. The youth was an impressive specimen to say the least.

Less than seventy-two hours ago, the boy displayed an impressively violent technique; he had eviscerated twelve clones of himself in a matter of seconds. More impressive was that he did it without any reservation. His face was still red from training, and he was vigorously tapping his foot.

He is afraid, Phoy thought. This simple tell made him smile. The stories he had heard about the young man's exploits made him seem like a god, but gods did not get nervous or feel fear for that matter. The youth had been the talk of The Senate lately, and his contacts in it had been reporting as such.

Even the Guild Master was up in arms about his abilities, but from the looks of it, he had been grossly overestimated. Smirking, Phoy spoke to the men standing behind him.

"When I designed the disciplines, I wanted there to be no distractions. That is why the students were to wear masks, and I watched as you stripped them of their anonymity." He turned to the Guild Master and Senate Liaison, and then pointed to Grivon, "He is the direct result of what happens without distraction.

You and the other Guild Masters have colluded with The Senate to damper exceptionalism and embrace mediocrity. By allowing the students access to the Quasar network you have hampered their progress. That youth there has very few distractions and excels. What do you do? You hold him back and withhold training from him." He took a step forward causing the men to step back.

"Congratulations. If he achieves half of what he has allegedly set his mind to, you will find your heads promptly removed from your bodies. He may be good, but he could be better if you cultivated his natural talents. Instead, he has resorted to subterfuge to learn what you will not teach him."

Phoy stormed out to meet the so-called prodigy.

II

Grivon sat in a large green velvet chair in front of The Guild Master's desk. His leg jerked up and down in response to an unknown feeling, fear. Wiping his sweaty palms on the side of the chair he tried his hardest to ignore the knot in his stomach.

Never had he been this nervous. In four years of training, he was never called into this office. The office always held a level of holy terror for him. The door was always closed, and no one ever went in or out.

He often wondered what the office looked like, and now that he saw it, it wasn't impressive. It was populated by a large redwood desk and two large redwood bookshelves filled with history books, training manuals, and knick-knacks.

A large tapestry, with a green field and five large black orbs in a cluster in the center, hung between them. It looked like what he always imagined a politician's office would look like. The door slid open and a short man with small coal eyes strode into the room.

If Grivon had been standing the man would have only come up to his shoulder. He had a shaved head except for a long black braided ponytail, a long thin mustache, and a thin pointed goatee. The man hopped up on the edge of the desk and stared into Grivon's eyes.

The gaze made Grivon sink into the chair making him wish he could disappear. Suddenly, the man sat up straight and smiled, "It is nice to finally meet you Master Grivon." Grivon sat stunned looking at the strange man.

"Charmed. Who are you?"

The man chuckled, "For now, you can call me Phoy. Tomorrow you will call me Master." The arrogance made Griovn's temper flare. A crackle of electricity coursed through his right arm, "I have a Guild-assigned master, thank you."

Phoy's countenance changed from one of a jovial man to thin eyed and angry, "I am your new instructor, and you will do as you are told!" Without a second thought, Grivon was on his feet and face to face with Phoy.

Phoy cackled and poked a sharp finger into Grivon's chest "That is why I am here."

The comment took him off guard, "Who are you?" Grivon demanded.

"I already told you. Why don't you sit down and prepare for a story?"

Grivon slumped down into the chair and motioned for Phoy to get on with his story.

"You thirst for knowledge, but first I must ask you a question. How did you learn of the Thread of Life?"

"The what?" Grivon asked bewildered.

Phoy clapped his hands, "As I thought. You know most people would be unable to look at a clone of themselves and kill it, let alone twelve. How did you do that?"

Grivon put a hand over his face and leaned his head back. "Ever since I was level four, I've been fighting clones of myself. I killed the first to obtain level eight."

"I see, and how has that played on your psyche?"

"Okay, I guess." Grivon replied nonchalantly.

"You hear voices or have any hallucinations?"

"No. What is this, an interrogation?"

Phoy chuckled, "No. Just me trying to learn about you."

"You said you had a story?" Grivon's voice cracked with irritation.

"That I did. One last question first. Have you ever heard of Clyde Freemont?"

"The man who created the Aurora and the Kartah."

"Yes, very good. Clyde was a good friend of mine."

Grivon shot up, "You're full of slag."

"No. I can tell you that Clyde was an avid reader of an ancient philosopher and mathematician named Rene Descartes. That is how the Kartah got their namesake. You see Rene was fascinated by a small cone-shaped gland in the back of your brain called the Pineal gland. It was often thought of as a third eye that could see into the future or give a person mystical power. In times after, they found that it was little more than a gland to produce melatonin, but Clyde believed his hero and began researching how to unlock the potential of the gland.

"He found that once properly stimulated, the gland could control the body's natural electromagnetic field and with proper training use it as a weapon. That is where I came in. I was given the first Aurora and could use it as a shield. After a while, I could do other, more extraordinary things, but that is neither here nor there."

At this point, Grivon's irritation frothed. His new teacher was a blowhard just like his current one, "What does any of that have to do with me?"

Phoy narrowed his eyes, "You are good, but you are not great! I can make you into what you want to become."

Grivon scowled back at Phoy, "What do you know of what I wish to be?"

Phoy smirked and a timeless twinkle flashed in his eye, "I know you want to rule. I know you want to make this system a better place, but before you can do that you need to learn a few things that only I can teach you and that will start tomorrow."

"Why wait?"

"A day off never hurt anyone, and your body needs rest. I suggest taking a walk if you feel restless," he said with a smile. "Now if you will excuse me, I must prepare for tomorrow."

Phoy hopped off the desk and strode out the door. Grivon sat staring blankly at the closed door. He was confused and angry. The audacity of that man was infuriating. Not only was he full of slag, but he was pretentious and arrogant.

"Wait!"

Phoy turned around, "Yes?"

"What does any of this have to do with me?"

A blank look of impatience crossed Phoy's face. "You could rule the universe," Phoy turned and walked off.

The more Grivon thought about it the more he couldn't contain himself any longer. That crackle of energy that was coursing down his arm was getting harder to control. Without a thought, he sprung forward and drew the saber on his side. The next thing he knew, the desk was in shambles. Having blacked out in fury caused the irritation to boil over into rage.

He turned and saw an offending bookcase. It was like it mocked him in its sheer existence. He took a basic attack stance and destroyed it with one downward stroke, and his saber was bathed in blue when he did it.

His tirade was interrupted when The Guild Master shouted, "Just what the hell are you doing?"

"What does it look like I'm doing?" Grivon roared.

"Destroying my office!" The Guild Master shouted.

"Then why ask stupid questions?" Grivon pushed passed him sword in hand still angry.

"Don't you dare walk away from me you little bastard! You will replace the things in my office or so help me..." The sword point stopped a hair's breadth away from his gullet.

"You'll do what?" Grivon seethed.

The Guild Master swallowed a knot in his throat. Never in the fifty years he had been in control of The Guild had a student drawn a weapon on him. He knew that with time and sitting behind a desk, he couldn't beat the angry young man in front of him. "I'll have to pick it up myself."

Grivon sheathed the sword, "Good," and walked off.

The Guild Master breathed a sigh of relief. This boy was proving to be a problem and with what Phoy had said he knew, he had to be dealt with sooner rather than later.

III

Phoy watched the scene through the viewing wall. The boy was a hothead with little to no self-control. He stroked his mustache as he contemplated the best way to handle his new student's temperamental nature.

Chuckling, he watched The Guild Master clean up Grivon's mess. He could only imagine the colorful words coming from the antiquated idiot's mouth. Sooner or later he would find himself in a situation he could not use his words to get out of. Phoy turned around to leave and came face to face with Jerimiah Jericho.

"Well if isn't the infamous Phoy Yin." He said with a grin.

"Let's see I have not seen you since..." Phoy trailed off stroking his mustache.

"Since The Purging." Jerimiah said.

"Has it been that long?"

"Longer. The last time we spoke you tried to kill me."

"I always try to kill a Xóaist when I find one." Phoy said grinning.

"The only reason you let me live was because I changed sides."

Phoy laughed, "It is good to see you. How did you get this appointment?"

Jerimiah scratched his head, "I asked myself the same question. One day I'm running errands as an aide to Lord Arik and then the next thing I know

I'm talking to The Autocrat himself. He said he was hand picking liaisons for each guild, and he wanted me here. He said that I was to report all of your new student's exploits to him. I'll have to tell him about what he did to the office."

Phoy continued to stroke his mustache considering what Jerimiah had told him. After several minutes of silence, he said, "Could you help me help him?"

"Exactly what do you mean by that?"

"If I know The Autocrat, which I do, I am sure he wants to kill him.

If you can convince The Autocrat to create a tournament amongst the guilds. Then the winner can graduate early." Phoy put his hands behind his back and locked them together. He paced in a circle as he thought for a minute on how to best sell this idea to The Autocrat.

"Tell The Autocrat that he can stack the event however he likes. He could even plant a Barrim Sister or two in the event. I am sure Grivon would be unable to defeat even one of those."

Jerimiah considered this for a moment, "You have very little faith in the boy, don't you?"

Phoy's eyes flashed. "On the contrary. I have full faith that he will rise to the occasion. Schedule the event in three months. I will have him ready to take on the most practiced assassin."

Jerimiah nodded and looked through the viewing wall. The Guild Master chucked a broken vase against the wall smashing it into a million pieces. Jerimiah looked over at Phoy and said, "I'll contact The Autocrat in the morning. In the meantime, I'll talk to The Guild Master."

Phoy laughed as The Guild Master picked up a large book and it slid apart. He patted Jerimiah on the shoulder and headed for the door.

"I do not envy the job you have been ordered to do."

Jerimiah shook his head and watched as Phoy left.

IV

Grivon stood in the door of his room. His muscles ached from his tantrum in the Guild Master's office. Never had he sliced anything thicker than a human bone. Wood proved to be denser and contained less give. The act had left his muscles sore. His stomach growled for something to eat. At this point he rather eat another piece of the fruit on his windowsill than the meal outside his room.

The Chronicles of Merkadiah:
The Rise of the Gryphon

Feeling uncomfortable in his own skin he shed his robe. He tossed his sword on the bed and ate a piece of the fruit. The sour juice ran down and his chin onto his chest. He walked to the bathroom and washed his face and chest. Walking back into his room, he disrobed and put his soiled clothes in the laundry shoot.

Seeing the laundry shoot turned his thoughts to how often he spent time in the laundry room after assessments. Usually, the punishment of folding clothes and linens was for students who failed their assessments.

It was almost like passing an assessment was a failure of some kind, at east to Sy. He shook the thought from his mind. Exhaustion was beginning to rear its head, but he wasn't interested in sleeping. There was too much on his mind to think about sleep. Grabbing his practice sword off his bed, he savored the moment he could simply practice forms. He cleared his head and began pressing the day's events into the inexhaustible furnace within.

Chapter Three
The Senate

"If power is all that you seek then power will seek and destroy you,"-Pantherine Proverb

I

Depublic Trey Satah was running late. He was to attend an emergency Senate hearing, and he was behind. The Autocrat didn't like people to run late. In his eyes, it was grounds for a treason hearing with trumped-up charges and making it look like you were in league with the Pantherines. Of course, he was owed a favor, and as long as this didn't happen again, he could keep his head.

As he walked through the glass-enclosed bridge on his way to the Senate building, he wondered what an emergency hearing was all about. They were common, but not in the middle of the night. It was almost morning. Couldn't it have waited at least three more hours? Trey yawned.

He had just gone to bed after a long drawn-out fight with his wife. The worst thing about it was, it had absolutely nothing to do with him at all. She was angry that the Autocrat had been raising taxes and wondered why he couldn't do anything about it. It still angered him that she blamed him, but could he really blame her for being concerned about the everyday peasant?

As Trey walked on into the large green building, he checked to make sure, he was wearing the correct robes; Depublics always wore green robes, Kofahs always wore red and Aridaunts always wore white. The Autocrat wore whatever color he wanted.

Trey wanted nothing more than to change this government, but in thirty years, he was promoted twice, and that was rare. Becoming Autocrat would be a far-fetched hope and even more so since the Autocrat was at least twenty years his junior. Trey was born into the class of Aridaunt and studied at the Water Guild only to be a Kartah. He chuckled at the thought of how morganatic it was.

He had fought and earned his Aridaunt status. It seemed that positions of power never came easy, especially if you were born into them.

After being on a team of Aridaunts that brought to light the dealings of a gangster named Orsin Steven Anthony III, he had been promoted to

The Chronicles of Merkadiah:
The Rise of the Gryphon

Kofah. After ten years of being a Kofah, the Pantherines began a rebellion, so he headed to the outer world of Semiramus to try to suppress the uprising of the Pantherines. He ended up being the one to defeat their champion in the third month of the siege. When he got back, he was promoted to Depublic.

Trey arrived at the weapon check. He nodded to the guard and pulled off his saber. He hated being separated from his weapon. For the last forty years, it had been an extension of his arm, but recently all weapons had been banned from the Senate chambers.

This made several of the general politicians in the lower levels of the Senate a little uncomfortable. Most of these politicians had just been recently promoted from Kartah within the fiefs of their Aridaunts. Each Aridaunt had a budget that included funds for Kartah, Governors, and miscellaneous officials. Some Aridaunts had more funds than others and of course, they had larger fiefs than most, and if Aridaunts needed to, they could raise taxes for a brief amount of time.

If a tax levied was ever more than a person's wage, then that person was exempt from that temporary tax. Of course, if the tax levied was longer than six standard months it came under review and could be vetoed. Trey groaned as he opened the door to the opulent Senate chamber.

The room was a wide rectangle and held hundreds of booths with voice amplifiers and water decanters. Each Depublic sat in a box on either side of the Autocrat and their Kofahs sat in a row farther down in the room.

The room seemed to slope downward from the high seat of the Autocrat and the seats of the two Depublics. The booths were for Aridaunts, their Governors, and aides. Each planet was represented by at least five Aridaunts unless that planet was small or a moon. If the Aridaunt did represent the fiefs on a small planet or moon, he was usually the only one, except on special occasions when the moon or planet was a little bigger than could be managed by a single Aridaunt.

Trey looked at the high seat and saw the Autocrat sitting there asleep. He laughed to himself as he went to sit beside him. His seat was on his right-hand side. It was the place where the most trusted sat. He couldn't figure out how he had gotten it. When the old Autocrat died and the new one was appointed, he chose his right and left hands. It was a seat of honor, but it was also a lonely seat. Often, he was called to bear witness to assassination orders or to put Pantherines on trial. Those were always the worst.

They would want to come to the human planets and get jobs. Female Pantherines wanted to be in the human worlds so badly, that when they were smuggled in, they became either low-class prostitutes or dancers in seedy clubs. The male Pantherines would come to human worlds to trying to find work, building houses, or getting involved with gangsters.

When Trey reached his seat, he picked up his robes and sat down in a slouch and put his right hand on his cheek. He looked around the room.

Hardly anyone was there, and he could hear snoring. After taking a quick look around, the only sleeping person was The Autocrat. Trey rolled his eyes and pulled on the sleeve of his deep purple robe. The Autocrat stirred and looked around, most everyone that could make it was there. He looked down at Trey and nodded with a smile.

"This emergency session of the Senate of Merkadiah will now come to order. The first order is a new work law for Pantherines. This will enable them to come to our planets and work for short periods. Each one will need a permit that is good for either six standard months or a standard year. This will also give us the opportunity to monitor their illegal movements and deal with them sooner rather than later. Now we can give them a small leash."

"The other business that has come to my attention from one of the many confidential informants of the Guilds is that there is a student in the Chaos Guild on Tygrano that is possibly the next great Kartah. He passed his level ten assessments at only eighteen, and to make matters worse, he did it in only twenty-five seconds. This could be very dangerous for us since he bears the name Grivon D'Gaul."

The Autocrat paused to let the last bit sink in. The silence hung thick in the air. The Autocrat shivered with anticipation before continuing.

"He could be the one that would destroy us. He is a fifth of the way to the end and could possibly skip the other forty levels. He could run the gauntlet today if he wished. I have given strict orders that he must pass the other forty levels. The reasons I tell you this is because one day he could unite the Pantherines under the guise of the Winged God.

"And to make matters worse he is the direct descendant of Darrian de Gaul."

This time the pause brought some chatter. The Autocrat smiled his evil smile that brought the most practiced Activist to their knees. Trey leaned back in his seat to garner a better look at The Autocrat. What The Autocrat said sparked some interest, "What do you suppose we do about him?" Trey asked.

"I will try and have him expelled. We had the Chaos Guild remove their masks yesterday. He didn't react to the sight of his two closest friends without their masks. Of course, neither did half of the students there, so either we have all our most promising Kartah expelled or we try to expel just three. He is teaching them something that may end up being the demise of this government. He must be stopped at any cost. Now we will take a vote on the first matter."

"I object," spoke the Aridaunt from the forested world of Rhokahl.

"We are at less than sixty percent, so how will a vote on this be kept from being vetoed?"

"I'm using my first annual decree. My vote alone will make up the other votes to get this working law passed. This law alone will make it easier to track the Pantherines' motives and movements. So, all in favor raise your hands and say aye."

The response was unanimous. Trey knew that less than half of the Senate was in favor of the Autocrat, so it was no surprise to him that it was at a time when only a handful of people would be able to respond. Those like him had to be there. Each Depublic and Kofah had to be present and their votes had to be for the new law or budget or whatever was being proposed even if none of them agreed it was always a sure vote. There were always two Depublics and eight Kofahs.

"Now to the matter of Grivon D'Gaul; he must not graduate the Chaos Guild. He must also never find Phoy Yin. If he does, he will be unstoppable. His third rite was spoken out of the Pantherine religious book. He is dangerous. He combined the four tribes' melee forms and completed a Magiah technique known only by those who have studied under Phoy or who study Pantherine melee combat. He is dangerous, does anyone have any suggestions?"

"Assassinate him." cried the Senate in a single voice.

Trey sat shocked, not making a sound. Neither did the other higher members of the Senate. It was all the small Aridaunts and politicians that had made the outlandish cry. If it came to a vote, he would have to vote.

It was a sure win for the idiotic Aridaunts. They all opposed anyone that would take their power and thus assassination was their only means of eliminating opposition. Trey shook his head; this was going to be a bloodbath, even without the assassination. If Grivon got the scent, he could lash out at them.

Trey looked up at the Autocrat and gave the signal for a private conversation. The Autocrat nodded his head yes and he, Trey Satah and Theo Lagrihd, who was the left hand, stood and walked into the office of the Autocrat.

II

The Autocrat's office was a small opulent box. The floor was blanketed with posh red carpet and framed with thick obsidian walls which helped draw attention to the large wormwood desk. Piles of paperwork, squares of wax, and various wax seals lay neatly in a row. Each seal was of unique design and none of them familiar to Trey. Along the edge of the desk water and liquor decanters sat on a silver tray surrounded by five crystal glasses. Trey wondered why they were there but pushed the thought out of his mind and focused on the moment.

The Autocrat sat down in his black leather chair and sighed. He picked up a decanter and poured himself a glass of liquor, took a deep drink, and sighed, "Would either of you like a drink?"

Trey responded, "I don't drink before the afternoon, but some water would be nice."

Theo replied, "Please, thank you." He took a sip of the blue liquor. The sharp burn helping wake him up.

"Now why did you call me in here Mr. Satah?" Asked the Autocrat with very little patience and his left eyebrow twitching.

"The Aridaunts and general politicians are willing to kill a boy who they don't even know. They are too afraid as are you to let him come to his full potential, how do you know he will destroy us?

"This boy could possibly be the one person to help the Pantherines to adjust to normal society. He could help us more than hinder if given the right opportunities. Let him finish like everyone else and it may take him the

40

standard thirty years, or he may end up being a fluke. This D'Gaul guy may just be a prodigy who got lucky."

Theo snorted and began to laugh. He was twenty years younger than Trey and therefore was more idealistic and had less common sense. He felt he was right just because he was a Depublic at forty-five. It made him arrogant, and he was so arrogant that he sometimes just ended up sounding stupid, like now.

"Hush," The Autocrat exclaimed, "he has a point." Theo's smile faded, and he looked dumbfounded. "Trey is right. He may just be a fluke, but he still could be a viable threat. What do you suggest Trey?"

"Make his assessments harder. That alone should slow him down, and if it doesn't, then assassinate him after he passes the gauntlet, if he chooses to seek out Phoy. Besides, he can't get a job until he defeats a political enemy of the Aridaunt he wants to be under."

The Autocrat thought about it for a few moments, "Fine, it is so ordered. The Senate need not vote, and today's session is canceled. I have not had any sleep in about a day. A couple of days off would be nice. Wouldn't you agree, Theo?"

A stunned Theo stuttered, "Yes sir. A couple of days off would be good."

"Good, now have a good night gentleman," the Autocrat got up and walked out a back door of the office. Trey nodded to Theo and began his walk home. He passed by the weapon check and picked up his saber and nodded to the man guarding the doors into the Senate chamber.

As he walked in the glass bride that connected the Senate building to the Senate apartments, he thought about the trenches of Semiramus and what it used to mean to be a great Kartah. His mind wandered to that horrid place where he had proven who he was. Even though he didn't want to be thinking about it, he did. The memories came over him, and his spine began to tingle. He tried hard to fight them off, but they refused to go away. Staggering from the sudden weight of flashbacks, Trey sat on a bench overlooking a garden and watched the rising sun, as the memories broke like waves on a beach.

III

He was there again, under the green skies of Semiramus. It was cold, and when the sun went down it was darker than what he was used to. The brightest of lamps couldn't even bring light to the base camp, where he stayed under lock and key. The Autocrat feared he would be killed, even at night.

The Pantherine leader had yet to be defeated, and the human champion had yet to be named. It didn't stop the Pantherines from waging guerilla warfare. They almost seemed to prefer the night for their raids. The trench warfare was effective during the day because only the Chisis, the cheetah spotted Pantherine tribe, came out. They were so fast they could almost dodge ammunition.

By nightfall, the Pantherines were already hitting the barracks in the trenches. Gas grenades were always the prelude, and somehow seemed to make everything colder, as well as create a smoke screen. The grenades were then followed by horrific screams of people being stabbed. The Pantherines didn't use firearms, opting for archaic tribal weapons.

Trey shivered as he thought about those horrific weapons. The wooden handles were less than one meter in length, and the blades were just a little longer than the handles. At the end of the handle a half meter cord was tied to a metal loop. The Pantherines then tied the cords in slipknots around their wrists, so that they could sling them at opponents from a distance.

The Leonis were scouts and always had the element of surprise on their side. Attacking in the middle of the night when it was pitch black. Semiramus was the moon of Hades and didn't get a lot of light except on certain days of the year and even then, it was minimal. It was on one such night by accident that he had seen the Pantherine's leader. He was a tall Leonis with golden fur. He was surrounded by several Leonis soldiers with shaved heads. The only one with a full mane was their commander. It shimmered in the dim light, and he heard the name spoken by the others, Sykler.

The next day a message was dispatched that Sykler and he duel to settle the uprising. Considering that it was a battle of attrition, how could it make things worse if a Kofah was killed in battle.

They stood looking at each other for over an hour. Each circling the other, until one struck. Sykler slung his blade at Trey, who ducked. In a quick sprint, he stabbed Sykler in the heart. A twisted look of pain came over the cat-man's face, and Trey sliced him almost in half, wanting to make sure the deed was finished.

IV

Trey shook as a cold chill ran up his spine. The sun was now over the horizon and painting the clouds bright purple and magenta. His heart was beating fast and large drops of sweat were beginning to create a puddle in his lap. It was going to be an exhausting day.

Chapter Four
Steven Anthony IV

"Displaying one's full strength is not always the best approach," -Steven Anthony
III

I

It just didn't make sense, Steven thought as he lay on his bed. He and Barbarah sat and watched Grivon finish his assessment in less than a minute. Steven gritted his teeth; how could he have done it? Grivon had never taught him or Barbarah anything like it before. It was as if he had been holding something back, but at the same time, he had been teaching them everything he knew.

Steven slapped his head. It had to be something. The kid only completed two levels in three years; of course, most students don't do that in ten. The Aurora had a lot to do with that.

Before it was made, people only lived to be about seventy or eighty; but now with this microchip, they had many different options. The most famous benefit was that the chip made people live a lot longer than usual It was said that one Kartah lived to be three hundred years old without any trips to the rejuvenator.

Steven sighed and shook his head as he stood up and stretched. He hadn't removed his robes, and they were bunched up around his back. With a strained grunt, he untied the black sash that held the robes together and let them drop to the floor.

Flexing his muscles, he picked his sword up from his desk. Then bent over, hit a button on his console, and tapped down on another one. A loud beat of music began to play. It was fast paced with short fast downbeats. Then in a loud scream, a deep guttural voice began bellowing violent lyrics.

Steven loosened his limbs as he thought about his written test on the history of the Aurora. He drew his sword and started to try to imitate the form that Grivon had used earlier. After several attempts, he sat down at the desk and began to read over his books on the Aurora. As he did, he remembered what his Guild Lord told him.

The Chronicles of Merkadiah:
The Rise of the Gryphon

The Aurora was created by a man named Dr. Clyde Freemont. He was a Mutiny veteran and had seen the horrors that war brought to the people of Merkadiah. After the Empire's agents had been defeated what was left was mistrust. The system's inhabitants were once broken down into three Houses. There was House Gaulia, House Glideria, and House Nguyen. The Pantherines had long ago been sent off to Hades and its moon of Semiramus.

After the houses formed, the Senate and the Aridaunts were born. Each Aridaunt oversaw several fiefs that had a garrison of soldiers from their House and a vital resource. An Aridaunt was not given any more than five fiefs. Soon disputes in the Senate began to erupt between the Aridaunts.

Small battles between Aridaunts of different Houses or the same House began to happen. More damage was done, and the economies of the Houses almost collapsed. So, to keep those things from happening again, Dr. Freemont presented his findings of nanotechnologies.

He argued in front of the newly formed Senate that it would help catch the illegal importation of Pantherines and help keep people alive longer. The thing that made it appealing to the Senators was that if they were seriously injured, and they didn't lose any of their brain or heart function. They would be teleported into a tank filled with stem cells, amino acids, and other biochemical agents. The Aurora would teleport them into one of the millions of rejuvenation tanks kept in secret locations. The best part about it was that a person could theoretically live forever.

Aurora chips were implanted into the pineal gland. It allowed a person to call upon their body's electromagnetic field to protect them from harm and gave them an invisible armor that glowed with an array of colors to let opponents know how powerful they were. Steven shivered as he thought about the next part of history, and the part that he, Barbarah and Grivon would soon make again.

It was when the Senate realized they needed leadership. They held a tournament of the new champions of Merkadiah. Each Aridaunt selected three of their best Kartah and sent them off to a planet called Ne-Le.

They fought to the death and the last one standing was the one that the other Aridaunts bowed to. His name was Zerath D'Gaul. He called himself the Autocrat and designed the igneous political system that united the three Houses. He remained the Autocrat until he died in his sleep forty years later.

As Steven read more about the history of the Aurora, a series of beeps came from his Quasar terminal. He closed his book, smiled, looked at his time display, and chuckled to himself. It was time to pull the strings of the government. Day after day, he sat here doing things in duty to his father. Then he tapped a button on his terminal stopping the music.

At first, Steven didn't like doing the things his father had to push off on him. Before his father died, he made Steven promise to take control of the family business of organized crime. His father was the head of the Orsin crime syndicate. When Steven was seven, his father was charged with the smuggling of Pantherines into the capital city of Ormah and convicted of other crimes including contract killing and illegal gambling.

Before his father was beheaded, he talked with Steven for four hours. Steven's instructions were above all else, to continue the family business and since his father's face was never shown or his trial public, "The Jackal" still lived on as an identity in the Quasar Network. From the Guild, Steven could control the Ten Dons of the organization. Each Don was loyal to him and was known to the others only as Dragoons.

They were numbered one through ten and were given the control of several territories that had paid officials and S.P.A. that were loyal to them. Steven reached into a secret drawer, pulled out an obsidian mask in the shape of a jackal's head and slipped it over his face. Steven smiled as he hit the button on his keyboard to display visual communication. The man standing before the screen smiled and gave a slight bow. Steven rolled his eyes at this ancient formality.

It was his father's mandate that anyone other than the First Don had to bow when facing the Jackal. The Quasar Networking terminal had a feature to alter one's voice; his father used it and now he used it. It allowed for successors of the Jackal to not be known. If any of the underlings found out they were being controlled by a man that was barely twenty, they would hunt him down and kill him, so it was a good thing that the voice-changing technology stayed intact over the years.

"Good morning your Excellency," declared the man standing in front of him on the screen. He wore a full, black bodysuit that showed off his toned physique. His mask was solid black except for a long red stripe that ran from the forehead to the chin. He wore some type of sword at his right side, and on his left arm was a weapon that Steven had never seen before. In the man's right hand, he held a long quarterstaff.

The Chronicles of Merkadiah:
The Rise of the Gryphon

"Good morning assassin." spoke Steven calmly.

"I have been selected by the Assassins Guild to fulfill your request for an assassination. Let me introduce myself, I am 'The Scorpion.' I have three weapons that you may want to know about, all of which are top of the line and have been developed over the course of twenty years and are not known by the government or any Kartah at that. I am skillful enough for any job you need."

"Hmmm," purred Steven. "Yes, knowledge of your weapons would be nice, but before you tell me what they are, let me tell you your assignment. You must kill the Autocrat. He killed a close business associate of mine and I want him to pay. And if you can, bring me his head. I will pay extra for the head of the man I want dead."

"I see." He replied. "For that kind of job, the price is triple the normal rate and if you want his head, well that will cost you an extra five thousand. Are you still interested in my services?"

"Yes, and if you need that much money, then I will pay you seventy thousand now and one hundred thousand after you bring me his head. Do we have a deal?"

The Scorpion gulped and began to stammer, "Yes I can work for that, considering it is eight times the normal rate. Now, do you want to know what my weapons are?"

"Yes, go on." Steven sighed.

"I have a cryogenic dart gun that can stun a person for over five hours; I have a Pantherine war saber and my own weapon that I personally built. A staff with a weapon no one has ever seen," The Scorpion tapped the Quarter Staff and a long-curved blade jutted out the left side of the staff at the top.

Steven shook his head and spoke with authority and power in his voice, "Well, all of that is quite fascinating. So if you wouldn't mind, get to it!"

Steven pressed the button that turned off the screen. Sighing, he removed his mask. People like The Scorpion made this job hard. There was one more person to talk to and then it was over until tomorrow.

That was his Senate contact, Theo Lagrihd. As an Aridaunt, The Depublic was opposed to the idea of his father being executed, so Steven had bought him after the execution. He had ended up lying about his age, but that was a minor detail since no one ever saw his face.

Steven shook out his limbs, put his jackal mask on, and pressed the call button on his terminal board. He typed in the address of Theo and waited. After several minutes, a face appeared in front of him. Normally Theo was well put together, but today his brilliant blue eyes were dull, and his brown hair disheveled. He oozed exhaustion. Of course, it was very early in the morning where he was, and it was late afternoon where Steven was.

"You have looked better in the past, Depublic Lagrihd." Steven said in an even tone.

"Yes, at the fourth hour of the night we were called into session. A young upstart at one of the guilds has the Autocrat worried. The boy has some sort of knowledge of things he shouldn't and if he ever finds the elusive Phoy Yin, the Autocrat thinks he could be more of a liability than an asset. He could take over the System and the rest of the galaxy. He is

a menace to..."

"Quit your whining." Steven barked. "I've already dealt with one idiot today; I don't need you to be the second. Now, this is going to be short, so listen up. The Autocrat will be dead soon, and I want you to take his place. I want you to pull the strings to make yourself into the new Autocrat. Do whatever it takes," Steven hit the disconnect button before Theo could speak a word.

He leaned back in his chair as he pulled off the mask and thought about something that was very irrelevant to everything. Barbarah. Whenever he, Grivon, and Barbarah would practice at night in the veldt outside the guild, he could see the wonderful curves of her body.

Watching her move, he would imagine her naked. He could feel himself getting excited just thinking about her. Sadly, her eyes were always on Grivon no matter how he felt. She didn't know, but he wanted her. No, he needed her. Making a fist, he slammed his hand on his desk in frustration. Someone needed to die, and soon.

Since the new guy showed up and changed things around, he could spar with anyone. He just had to find the right girl, and she would never forget their day together if she lived. In fact, he would even make sure she saw his face in her dreams. She was about to be honored. If he was lucky, he might find her in a tournament. Grabbing his saber off his desk, he put a clean robe on and secured his saber in the sash.

Then it dawned on him before he walked out, there was a ball coming up. He could find her there. That's when he would honor her. She would be most privileged to be with him that night.

He steeled himself, hoping to find a ranked tournament out on the sparring grounds. There he would show the weaklings what an undefeated man looked like. Maybe he could find the one he would honor. She had to be perfect; she had to possess traits like Barbarah.

Either in looks, or the way she carried herself. Now he really was excited and craved a release, and since in rank tournaments you could kill your opponents; he was about to honor many people.

II

Steven passed through the archway that led into the sparring grounds. The sparring grounds were nothing more than a large square courtyard. The only difference was that a circle in the middle of the yard almost touched all four corners of the sparring ground. There was a place for the contenders to stand, and the circle was filled with alabaster dust, which was from years of masks being destroyed after someone lost a match. Hematite rocks with pure white mortar made up the walls surrounding the small courtyard.

Steven slipped his fingers into the metal guard of his sword, gripping the hilt until his knuckles turned white. He felt a gnawing sensation in the pit of his stomach that grew with each passing moment.

Surveying the grounds, he looked for his competition. There were ten students including him there. He sighed and spotted the guild's chaperone. Steven walked with long even strides that commanded respect. He moved effortlessly past several students sparring. Soon he was right in front of the guild's chaperone. The man looked stunned to see Steven standing in front of him.

The chaperone looked Steven up and down before saying anything and when he finally spoke, it was in a low raspy voice that was hard to hear. The voice did not match the young features of the chaperone standing in front of him.

"How may I help you?" asked the chaperone.

"Is there a rank tournament today or is it just spar with whomever you wish?" Steven asked.

"Yes, we were waiting for another person for a rank tournament. In addition, if I'm not mistaken you are almost to achieving your tenth straight win, and with that new representative here you can fight people of all classes and genders. So, since you are the ranking leader here you get to compete in the first round against the student known as 'Destroyer.'"

Steven grinned. This was going to be fun, and the students with names like 'Destroyer' were usually weaklings that needed to feel important. He was going to honor 'Destroyer' and it would feel so good to feel blood between his fingers again.

Stepping into the ring, he waited for his opponent to show up. When he did, Steven realized he had grossly underestimated the name.

'Destroyer' stood a good thirty centimeters taller than Steven and weighed several kilograms more. He flexed his massive biceps as Steven stretched out his arms. Things were going to be different. Instead of honoring this opponent in a quick death, he would humble him with a painful one. A death that said no one should look more powerful than Steven.

When the chaperone threw a green flag into the middle of the circle, and all the students present were quiet, the opponents drew their sabers. Steven held the sword with the blade down and the guard out. Destroyer pointed his blade at Steven. Steven charged. As did Destroyer.

Steven thrust the metal guard toward Destroyer's face and was parried away. Twirling into a backward counterattack, Steven thrust his sword back toward Destroyer's heart but was parried once again.

Frustrated, Steven twirled around to face his opponent, and as he did, he flourished and gained a new grip on his sword. Destroyer faked left but was met on the right by Steven. Steven let a wicked smile form on his lips as he forced the blade away and in a downward stroke chopped off Destroyer's left leg. Destroyer fell to the ground screaming in agony. Steven needed to act quickly, or the student known as Destroyer would be teleported into rejuvenation. The saber clattered on the ground when Steven dropped it. Then he gripped Destroyer's head in his hands.

Licking his lips in delicious anticipation, Steven forced his thumbs into his opponent's eyes. The small balls popped like grapes, and maroon liquid flowed down the weakling's face. Relishing the feel of thick inky blood pour into his hands, he let Destroyer fall to the ground.

The Chronicles of Merkadiah:
The Rise of the Gryphon

Steven dipped to pick up the sword wondering why the man had yet to be teleported. The thought of a kill was more pressing, as was the collection of a new trophy. Steven strode over to the screaming man who was groping around trying to find his sword. Suddenly, Destroyer started screaming a horrid guttural scream. He was sure the scream would shake ordinary people to their cores and possibly shake the foundations of Hell.

He picked up the hulking man by the neck of his robe. It was surprising at how effortlessly he could lift him. When 'Destroyer's' head had been lifted high enough; Steven raised his sword and decapitated him. The big body fell to the ground with a loud thud and his audience gasped.

Steven was the winner of the tournament by default. No one else wanted to die that day and Steven went back to his quarters with the much-needed feeling of release. On his way back, he spotted a girl that looked almost identical to Barbarah. She agreed to go to the ball with him and to "spar" with him that same evening afterward. He thought about the girl's name, Jenah. What a pretty face for such a pretty name. Soon, he would honor her, and she would be grateful of his attention to her.

Chapter Five

Passions

"Passion is like a rose. It is beautiful, but is painful," -Pantherine Proverb

I

Barbarah stood in front of her mirror examining herself. Red marks scared her face where tears had streaked under her eyes. Shaking her head, she looked over her ugly body. No matter how hard she tried, she couldn't understand what made the bastards want to look her way.

Her left breast was smaller than her right and her right breast pulled over to the left. There was extra fat on her sides, and to top it all off she was just downright ugly. Who in their right mind would even like sandy blonde hair and emerald, green eyes? What difference did it make that she was only one of a hundred girls in the whole guild? It was unfair that those animals should even look at her.

The Guild Lady that she was assigned refused to teach her anything. Her whole life had been spent in a place that made the ghettos of Semiramus seem appealing. Pantherines were more respectful to their queens than these bastards were to her. At least a Pantherine knew when to stop.

Barbarah opened a drawer in her desk and pulled out a pair of scissors. She grabbed a lock of hair and put it between the blades, but she couldn't bring herself to cut it. Grivon liked her hair now that it was long and even. When she first met him, she would wear a wig, so no one would know that she cut her hair. The fact that she did that to herself made her angry. Examining the blades of the scissors she thought about how easy it would be to open her veins and end all the suffering.

But the thought of what it would do to Grivon made her put them back in the drawer. All these men cared about was what she could give them. Four times she laid there and took it. It was a wonder she wasn't with child yet. She just let herself drift into her own little world where she imagined herself enacting vengeance upon whomever she was with, but in the last few years, these things had stopped happening.

Thankfully, Grivon was there. Grivon knew what she wanted, and it wasn't carnal pleasure. All she really wanted was to be respected and taught how to fight. She wanted nothing more than to be the first female Autocrat that would serve under the first dictator of the galaxy.

However, all of that was just a dream. She knew Grivon wouldn't share power, but he would share his love with her. The one thing that made the difference was that Grivon was teaching her things that no one else knew. How he knew such things was beyond her. He just seemed to know what he was doing.

Barbara finally walked away from her mirror and with a sigh lay down on her bed. She covered herself with a blanket and shivered as she thought about how many times she had wanted to give into those carnal desires.

She was feeling that way right now but whom would she turn to? Grivon would if she really wanted to, but on the other hand, if she used the term "spar" he would think it was to fight. She was so frustrated at this point, it was making her head hurt and the more she thought about it, the more she knew what she wanted. For once, it would be nice to do it because she wanted to, but how to convince Grivon.

She got up and put on a body suit that zipped up the front. It was made of purple skin-tight material made just for the guilds. She put on the black guild robes and as she walked out the door, grabbed a practice sword. Then pretended she was walking to the practice yard. As she approached the last courtyard before turning into it, she flattened her back up against the wall on her left. She looked both ways and pressed a small depression in the cement between the rocks.

A small door about her size opened and slid to the right. Looking both ways once more, she slipped into the crevasse and down the dark passage. The passage led to a small hole in a wall. Why this passageway existed, she didn't know but for some strange reason, it led to Grivon's room.

She considered the hole in the wall and saw her love practicing forms.

II

Grivon stood shirtless. Streams of sweat cascaded off his silver hair and slid down his chest. He had a focused look on his face. She guessed he was trying hard to keep control over his fury or was trying not to think about everything wrong in his life. He was the one that would save the system and then conquer the galaxy.

This man made her feel something she had never felt before. She watched him as she often did for a few minutes, wanting so bad to feel his chest. She ached for his touch.

"Grivon," whispered Barbara. "Can we go and spar? I need to work off some steam."

"Sure," he whispered back. He continued his practice as if she weren't talking to him through a hole in his wall. "Meet me at the usual spot. Do I need to get Steven?"

"No, it'll be just us," she said breathless. She could feel heat spread from her cheeks through her body.

III

The third moon hung high in the sky; it's bright yellow accented by a crimson ring around the circumference. Grivon and Barbara stood facing each other. Each holding a practice sword and ready to fight.

"Grivon, could we just grapple tonight? I need to work on grapple techniques and, well I'm really worked up after what I saw yesterday."

"I suppose we could. We will have to remove our robes. Is that all right?"

"Yes!"

As soon as their robes hit the ground Barbara tackled Grivon, they rolled over and down a hill. When they came to a stop Barbara was sitting on Grivon's stomach. She ran her hands over his body suit, feeling his muscles tight under the material. She started to unzip her body suit, but Grivon caught her hand.

"What are you doing, I thought we were sparring?"

"You are one naive little boy, you know that?"

"I'm not a little boy. How is taking off…"

"Do you love me?" She blat.

The question was jarring. He was silent for a few minutes before speaking.

"Yes, with all my heart. I would never hurt you, and I will always protect you no matter what."

"Good," she kissed him passionately.

Grivon lay on his back looking up at the most beautiful sight he had ever seen. He felt something stir within him; something he only experienced when he was around Barbarah. She was so beautiful he felt a burning, almost animal-type desire deep within himself. For once in his life, the fury that burned was a different feeling. It was a feeling that he enjoyed. Then a horrible thought burst unbidden into his head.

This could be just a one-time thing, he realized. An event such as this could leave him with a broken heart, but he wanted this, he needed this. He knew something was missing and for the first time in his life, he felt complete, as if some forgotten puzzle piece had fallen into place. Opening his eyes, he saw a hungry look on Barbarah's face.

Barbara stared down at Grivon sighing deeply to herself. This moment was intense, a memory that she would always cherish. She moved her hand down in a gentle caress and felt his face. A sharp gasp escaped his lips. She blushed as a deep, bottomless well sprang up inside her. Not wanting to let the moment pass, she pulled him to her and gave him a lover's kiss.

IV

Barbarah lay in the tall grass looking up at the full moons and tried to catch her breath. Grivon looked over at her, sweat streaming down his body. He looked at her skin, shimmering in the moonlight and sighed. For the first time in a long time, he was happy.

"Can we do that again or was it just a onetime thing?" he said between shallow breaths. Before she could answer, "It doesn't matter, I still love you." He pulled her close to him. She laid there quiet beside him as the insects sang their nightly song.

"We can do that as often as you like," she said tracing a circle on dry spot on his chest. "I love you so much. Take me on your journeys to become the first galactic dictator. You are the salvation of this system and maybe humans."

"I'm not God or anything, I'm just me."

Barbarah sighed and let out a small chuckle before she looked at Grivon and laughed, "We need to grapple more often!"

V

Stevens' sword passed dangerously close to Grivon's face. Grivon held a saber in each hand as he fought Steven and Barbarah both. Each kept coming at him while his back was turned. This exercise was exhilarating. He was barely able to keep his defenses up. Try as he may, he never seemed to get the upper hand. They all had been practicing a lot. Barbarah had just passed her level ten assessment. Grivon was proud

and hoped that she would excel faster as time went on. He was jerked from his thoughts when he felt a sharp sting across his hand. Steven had drawn first blood. Grivon nodded with a smile, Steven was getting better.

"Well, I think that is enough for tonight," Grivon said examining the superficial wound. "Steven, I want you to take your level ten assessments the day after tomorrow."

Nodding his head, Steven spoke with all the sincerity he could muster, "How's your hand?"

"I'll live," Grivon replied with a smile. Steven and Barbarah laughed.

"I've had enough for today. If you two want to stay out all night and fight, go right ahead," Steven said with a grin on his face. He sheathed his saber and sauntered off into the warm night.

Barbarah and Grivon looked at each other and shrugged. They had only been outside for an hour. When they were sure Steven was gone, they sighed and kissed deeply. Barbarah pulled away and sighed. With a mischievous grin, Grivon asked, "You want some grapple practice?"

Barbarah let out a small growl while smiling and letting down her blonde hair. It had grown six inches and was now to her shoulders. She stopped cutting it and now was long and straight. Grivon grabbed a fistful of her luxurious hair, as they started kissing again. They slowly moved to the grassy ground not caring that it made them itch. All they had was time to be alone.

VI

Steven watched over the hill disgusted. Grivon, the little bastard; she was supposed to be his. He was her first, even though she didn't know it. In fact, all of those she sought after had been him. His mind flashed to his closet and the pyramid of masks that hung from nails in the wall.

Each having belonged to a woman he had honored or to a weakling he had destroyed. In either case there was a residual electricity that came from touching one, and it made him excited. His body tingled with pleasure from the thought of his collection. The capstone of his pyramid of masks remained empty as it was for a special mask, Grivon's.

Nothing would give him more pleasure than to kill the bastard.

He let out a soft chuckle. His thoughts slid back to the first time with Barbarah. It had been a wonderful night. He showed her what passion was, and she had been pleased. She had been begging him for it for several weeks.

The way she said excuse me when they passed each other in the halls, or how her eyes lit up when they bumped into each other. Finally, she asked him if they could "spar" before curfew. However, when it had happened, she didn't know it was him. It was before she had seen his face and he had been wearing a different mask. The mask from one of the first weaklings he killed, Faun.

After memorizing her habits, he made sure to wear a different mask to throw her off course. Sometimes it took weeks for her to ask for the sparring and others only a matter of days. Sometimes she let him have his way, others he had to find ways to motivate her. It was all inconsequential. When Grivon graduated, she would cling to him and then he would be her only lover.

VII

The next day all the students sat in the arena area listening to Mr. Jericho. The ball was now going to involve all the guilds, and it would also include a tournament. The winner would be able to run the gauntlet in two weeks after the event. Signups for the event were beginning that day and would last for two weeks. Anyone of level ten or higher could enter.

The rules would be disclosed on the day of the event. Everyone was extremely excited. They would get to meet the other students and see how they fought. Jeremiah smiled to himself. Phoy was a smart man. Grivon could progress and if he didn't, it would accomplish his mission to prevent the boy from graduating.

Anyone not ranking in the top one hundred by the semifinals of the tournament would be expelled from the guild. It was harsh, but it was effective. Too many people wanted to be Kartah and that was an overly glorified position.

In times of war, the Kartah were sent to be the "super soldiers" of the Senate. Of course, most of the wars were fought with Pantherines, and the worst atrocities committed were by the Kartah. Honor and Glory, what a load of slag, it was all violence and the Autocrat knew it.

This tournament would undoubtedly save thousands of lives just by expelling them from the guilds. It seemed harsh but was merciful and that was what Phoy hoped to accomplish by all of this.

Jeremiah smiled and walked off the stage.

Grivon, Steven, and Barbarah sat in the stands looking at each other.

Grivon spoke quietly to Steven and Barbarah, "I'm going to enter and you two need not. If you don't rank like he just said," Grivon pointed to Jeremiah, "you will be expelled, and our goals will not be realized."

Steven looked a little perturbed and Barbarah nodded that she understood. Steven whispered harshly, "You may be able to control her, and even though you are my friend, I cannot be controlled. I will enter, and you and I will fight each other and let the best man win."

Grivon nodded. He had expected this. It was Steven's way. His assessment had gone wonderfully. His was easy. All he had to do was recite from memory the various forms, then show the High form for each one. It was easy. Everyone else's assessments were easy. However, it seemed like every single one of Grivon's assessments were ten times harder than everyone else's. It was almost like it was a ploy to see him fail.

His fury started rising. He had to quiet it somehow. Hoping to find a ranked tournament, he stood up, and left the arena in a huff. Barbarah sat stunned at how fast Grivon and Steven had decided to leave. She hoped that they both weren't headed for the same place, and hoped that if that were the case, Grivon would humble Steven.

Chapter Six

Shift

"The desire to dominate is something hardwired into the mind of every human,"

-Darrian de Gaul, Political Journal Volume II

I

The Autocrat sat at his desk signing paperwork dealing with the new work law for the Pantherines. He sighed as he signed the last paper. *All this power and I'm still stuck doing paperwork*, he thought.

It was almost unbearable because everything he decided had to be voted on by the Senate. The Senate was nothing more than a bunch of idiotic squabbling politicians. That's all they did, argue. Aridaunts, Kofahs, Depublics, all of it should be dissolved and supreme power should be given to the Autocrat.

This position he was in was meaningless. He had no real power. Oh, he could propose things, send them to vote, and then sign a stack of paperwork if it passed through as a law. It was all grossly unfair. He was stuck in this place until he knew he would die; then and only then could he abdicate his power to a person of his choosing.

He sat back in his chair and put his right hand over his eyes, rubbed his forehead and sighed. It was going to be a long night. His lover would surely leave him this time. All they did was fight, he never saw the point in having a wife. His wife was the Senate. Most women couldn't understand that his first love was politics.

Looking back at his desk, he had over a hundred more papers to stamp, sign, and file. He thought about who he wanted to take over for him. Theo was a warmonger and a coward, Trey was wise and calculating, but old. The Autocrat once again began to think about how he had achieved power.

II

As the second Depublic, he heard the best rumors. The rumor was that the current Autocrat was about to ask for an end to the feudal democratic system and make a feudal dynastic government. He would be the first, and his children would be the next and so on. No one other than the Depublics ever knew an Autocrat's name.

They could only call him by title. His name was Daggot D'Gaul, and he could trace his line from Darrin de Gaul. It was no secret that most people in Merkadiah hated the D'Gaul line.

In fact, the D'Gauls once were the dynastic ruling family of Merkadiah, until Sandor Reinhardt took power as Autocrat. This was a fluke and for four hundred years the D'Gauls held no political office other than aide to an Aridaunt. That was until Daggot wormed his way to the top.

Back then he was known as Jamier Mumbala. He was Second Depublic like Theo. He had the ear of Daggot and was close to him. He even knew the name of his son, the boy who was making trouble for hi now.

Why couldn't he just follow the rules and become a Kartah at the age of fifty like everyone else was beyond comprehension? The crazy kid was at level ten and he wasn't even twenty-five. The thought made Jamier's blood boil.

The son of Daggot would end up making his life hell. Grivon they called him. In some ancient tongue, it meant Gryphon. What a load of slag that was. Before he became Autocrat, a lot of people believed that he was the one that the Pantherines would call the Winged God. It was ridiculous.

The lower politicians already began to call Daggot's family "Blue Bloods." It was stupid. Daggot would have ultimate power and soon the Senate would be dissolved and then everyone would bow to one leader. It was all a big deal, so the night it came time for the Autocrat to sign a law into action, Jamier snuck into his office. Daggot was sitting at his desk with his back to the door. Jamier silently drew his sword and put it to Daggot's throat. Daggot stiffened and Jamier spoke coldly in his ear.

"Abdicate your power to me now. You are ill-suited to be the Autocrat. The fact that dynastical rein intrigues you is disgusting. After you abdicate; I will kill you. You and your family will die at my hand once I have the power. Now kneel and I will end you swiftly."

Daggot disappeared only to reappear behind Jamier. Daggot's sword was raised to strike. Jamier could see the fury in his eyes. Thankfully, he remembered the words of his Water Guild Lord, At the moment of the strike become fluid like water.

Jamier bent backward to avoid the strike and Daggot's sword sliced at air. Jamier popped back up, flourished the blade, and drove his sword through

The Chronicles of Merkadiah:
The Rise of the Gryphon

Daggot's heart. The look on Daggot's face would forever haunt his dreams. It was a mixture of defeat, betrayal, and surprise.

His face contorted as if to speak before the life went from his eyes. The bulky body slid to the hilt of Jamier's saber; he ended up having to stain his favorite boots to pry his sword free of the corpse. Three days later Jamier was given the insignia to signify he was the Autocrat.

It was a grand ceremony. All Aridaunts, Kofahs, Depublics, lobbyists and various other politicians were there. All his favorite foods were placed in front of him. They ate, drank, and danced into the night. It was wonderful until he was hit with all the paperwork and no real power at all.

He had more power as a Depublic. They had the true power. Each Depublic carried two hundred votes, and each Kofah carried twenty votes, each Aridaunt carried five votes, each senator carried two votes, and lobbyists and courtiers carried only one vote each. In comparison to what the Autocrat could do; the lesser politicians could do more.

He could propose laws and new policies, but the Senate still had to vote on what he wanted to do. Most of the time he was shot down with his ideas, even though the Depublics and Kofah's had to side with him, and carried exceptionally large numbers of votes, most of the Senate hated him.

They all knew he had killed their joy by assassinating Daggot. Nevertheless, it was for the good of the system. Blueblood had no place here, and thankfully, now most of the Aridaunt's saw it that way. Things were almost to the way the Blue Star was before the colonization of the stars. Few people knew the true history of Merkadiah.

Merkadiah was a system in the center of the Milky Way. The Blue Star was a place called Earth and had many problems in its last days. At the end of the first century after the third millennium, a war that raged since the beginning of the millennium went from being sieges and skirmishes to a large-scale war that brought almost every country into it.

It was not long before the governing powers found out that their enemy could not be defeated through normal means. In a means to end the war once and for all, genetic soldiers were made to fight. Soldiers whose DNA was fused with that of lions, tigers, cheetahs and leopards were the units of these soldiers. Which rooted out the enemy and killed them. At the end of that century, the war was finished.

What baffled many was that after the war, things went sour. A powerful dictator took power and conquered the world. He realized that the soldiers created a few decades earlier were multiplying and wanting to be recognized as a sovereign people. However, what humans fear most is something they do not fully understand, so another war started.

Except, this time it was the genocide of the new super soldiers who didn't want to die, not misguided extremists. Once their race was rounded up, they were sent to a planet called Merk. After they were sent away a group of freedom fighters, calling themselves Xóaists arose. They claimed that their leader was immortal and would conquer the oppressive tyrant.

The Xóaists did, but at a cost that lost them three hundred years of recorded history, economy, and technology. To win against a government with a highly technological army, a bomb that emitted an electromagnetic pulse was developed. The bombs that won the coup were set off in all major cities on the planet. The bombs were composed of a depleted radioactive material that was launched and detonated over each of the cities and small surrounding towns.

After a brief time, people forgot about the super soldiers and in one hundred and fifty years they had rebuilt themselves to the point they were before the end of the Xóaist coup. They developed space travel that was faster and more effective by using Selmar technology. The technology had been well established before the rise of Xóa.

A meteorite exploded over the city of Chelyabinsk. Scientists were baffled by the amount of energy released from the explosion and upon examining a few of the smaller rocks remaining, they found a unique crystal element not found on earth. The translucent crimson rock grew at an alarming rate and a single gram held more kinetic energy than a

small nuclear reactor without the resulting waste. They called it Selmar after Doctor Gregory Selmar, the geologist who unlocked its potential.

Years later, a young astrophysicist named Allan Freemont figured out that selmar could recognize other parts of itself great distances away. After several years of research, he created the first Einstein-Rosen Gate, a teleportation device that could send large amounts of matter from one place to another. This was immediately applied to the space program and used to create a mining colony on other planets.

A new industry started, and every major manufacturing corporation that could buy the blueprints to the E.R.G.s did. Thankfully Xóa had managed to save the technology and developed it over the course of his first century as emperor of the earth. Even though Selmar grew at a rapid rate everyone still wanted more of it, and Xóa began ramping up mining colonies as well as penal colonies.

Merk was to be a hybrid of the two. When Darrian crash-landed his ships on the planets of the system, they found the Pantherines on Merk. Ever the opportunist, Darrian tricked the cats into believing he was their prophesied Winged God and subjugated them. It made him chuckle that Grivon held so many traits of his ancestor.

At that moment, a thought occurred to him that he had never realized before, and that was no one knew what had happened on Earth, or for the other colonies for that matter. Selmar had been found on Merk and was hoarded for use in the Aurora and in the teleporters. In fact, he remembered something from when he had first taken over.

Half the Selmar mined from Merk was shipped to an unknown location, and large sums of money often found its way into The Senate's

coffers every week from a supposed sale of the crystal. He was going to have to look into that later. Perhaps the other colonies were still around and thriving; perhaps the humans in this solar system weren't alone in the galaxy. It was funny that the thought to look into where it went never really occurred to him before.

Jamier shook his head to gather his thoughts. He had to finish signing the paperwork to be filed for reference by the next Autocrat, but history still filled his mind.

It was amazing the advancements that were lost once humans came this close to the edge of the galaxy. The only technology that the colonists had was swords, armor, flechette guns, some old guns called sluggers, and teleportation devices made with the technology of their ruined starships.

The only one who had anything that was advanced was Darrian De Gaul. He was equipped with a Carbonic Command Rod. It could create any stave or sword the wielder could imagine. Everyone in the colonies envied the weapon. He also had a device that could show you which planet you were on and how close the closest moon was, and which planet was the closest to the one you were on.

Darrian also had one more thing that made people envious, a suit of battle armor that could break swords and deflect ammunition. It was an inky black that seemed to suck all light into it. It was all fascinating how the previous Autocrats wanted to keep this knowledge from the people.

Why did it matter so much that these things be kept from people? Was it to prevent having another mutiny? In either case he would be putting that to a vote soon. Knowledge of history needed to be shared, not restricted.

Jamier stacked his finished paperwork and turned around in his chair to go home when he ran into a sword point. It was Theo. Jamier felt the color drain from his face and a knot form in his throat. He was to face the same end as Daggot. He was going to get what he deserved.

"Do it quickly," he squeaked.

Theo stood with a confused look on his face and finally spoke, "I'm

not going to kill you. I just want you to abdicate to me instead of Trey. That is all I want; are you willing to do that?"

All Jamier could do was nod his head.

"Good, that is what I wanted. I will be seeing you shortly in the next session," Theo turned and walked out of the Autocrat's office.

When Theo was sure he was out of hearing distance he called his boss, The Jackal on a handheld Quasar pad.

"Phase one is complete. There will be a feast in two days for the nineteen years that the Autocrat has been in power. Your man will have a clear shot then, and then I can become..." The Jackal disconnected. Theo let out a stifled snort; after all, it was somewhat late. At least everything was going according to plan.

III

The Scorpion sat in the dark room thumbing his Kadar. The weapon was of unique design. Whoever came up with it was a genius. The hilt was less than a meter long, and the blade was only a few centimeters longer than the hilt and curved at the very end. On the pommel was a small band of elastic rope tied to the wielder's wrist in a slipknot.

The Scorpion hummed with joy. This was the first kill he had ever been hired for. He had been training as an assassin for over twenty years. At the age

of twenty-five, he could outsmart most Kartah.

Upon the completion of his training, he was given the top-of-the-line battle armor. It was so advanced the security forces did not have one. This was special to him. Painted yellow and black it was a full bodysuit with a special targeting visor that gave heart rate, body temperature, and blood pressure on all humanoids within a five-meter radius. On Kartah and other developed Aurora users, it gave the exact amount of time their armor would last.

The cybernetics that controlled the rest of the suit was worth more than the yearly budget of a single fief planet. The suit itself could enhance the movements of its wearer and increased the output of his reactions, but the most important part of the suit was the tail. It sat small in the back of the suit right above the bottom. The tail was forty centimeters in diameter and could extend to a maximum of five meters.

The tail contained the cryogenic dart gun. It could only hold a hundred rounds at a time, but still, it was fun to use and was going to be used this very evening.

IV

The Autocrat held up his glass of wine and said, "A toast to my fifteen years of service to the people of Merkadiah." All the politicians in the room began clapping their hands and cheering. Each politician drank from their glass.

As the Autocrat finished his glass of wine, he smiled to himself as two Aridaunts stood up at the large table. One was blonde and the other red-headed. The redhead bowed deeply and spoke in strong words, "I, the Aridaunt of Semiramus, have been insulted by an Aridaunt from the planet of Odin. I wish for a tournament this very night for fifty percent of the taxes from your fief."

A quiet murmur spread through the politicians. The Autocrat smiled and thought it's all going as planned.

"Fine," spoke The Autocrat, "but I choose your champions. I choose Trey Sata and Theo Lagrihd in a fight to the death." The Autocrat smiled.

Trey is a battle-hardened soldier ; he can destroy Theo, who is nothing but a weasel, Jamier thought.

Trey nodded and began to prepare himself for the coming duel. Theo stood aghast. T his is a trap, he thought, t he Jackal set me up. The two Depublics walked into the center of the room. Each politician had been allowed to keep their swords. To keep the peace, each politician had brought their masks and wore their rank colors. Trey and Theo placed their masks over their faces and drew their swords. Trey drew into the High Thay're form.

Theo took a basic stance and the Autocrat clapped his hands. Unmoving the two stared at one another. Each contemplated the other's impending assault. Everyone else in the audience sat waiting for the two Depublics to move. Everyone knew that promotions would soon be given. Each politician was nothing more than an ant. Once one died, three more arose in their place.

Theo reached down to scratch his leg. As he did, he activated a timer that would let The Scorpion know when to strike. After he finished, he rushed toward Trey. Trey met his blade with a dagger in the pommel and forced Theo back. Theo stumbled and only saw Trey turn and counterattack with the longer blade of his saber. Theo was able to gain his footing and make a half-hearted attempt at a block.

After the poor block, Trey spun and smashed Theo's nose with the guard on the hilt. Theo fell to one knee as a loud hush filled the room. Trey brought his saber up to deliver the coup de grace, when a loud gasp broke the silence.

Turning around, he saw an interesting sight. The Scorpion stood with his tail raised over his left shoulder. He shot small darts at everyone but the Autocrat and the two Depublics and tapped his quarterstaff on the tile floor. The long-curved blade flung out of the staff creating a wicked looking scythe.

The Scorpion jumped and landed in front of his target. The Autocrat stood still and closed his eyes and had one last quiet thought, my time has finally come for killing D'Gaul. The Scorpion undercut the Autocrat's left arm, and in a smooth swift motion cut the Autocrats head off. He picked it up.

Trey stood stunned. With his back turned he could not see the devious grin on Theo's face. Theo sprung from his knees and drove his sword into the back of Trey's head execution style. The lesser politicians gasped as the blade jutted through Trey's gullet.

Theo stood victorious. He looked at The Scorpion and shouted, "Depublic Guards, seize him."

Four men who had been standing out of sight in each corner walked to the center of the room. One of the men had the look of a jaded soldier who enjoyed the art of killing. The guard drew his sword, and with deadly accuracy threw it at The Scorpion. The Scorpion only had one thought before he died, which one was the Jackals contact? The blade pierced his chest and killed him instantly.

As the four men cleaned up the bodies, Theo stood and addressed the crowd, "Before this horrid assassination, the Autocrat had abdicated his position to me. In three weeks, the Ceremony of Abdication will take place. At that time, new Depublics and Kofahs will be selected. I now have the power to control certain things; I make this declaration:

Each Aridaunt is to mobilize their security forces and Kartah as of now. All Pantherine work permits are revoked, and all Pantherines working with a permit or without are to be arrested and sent back to Hades or Semiramus. I have reports on activities within several key cities, and they are responsible. Be expecting to see a bolster in the Special Protection Agency. I urge each Aridaunt to let their citizens know that if anything suspicious happens then, to let the S.P.A. know.

This is the first of my yearly decrees. It is my desire to complete the work that was begun before the Blue Bloods took control. Today is the beginning of a new era! An era free of the Pantherines!"

V

Karen Sata was livid. She crushed the paper in her hands into a tiny wad. It was an official letter stating the reason her husband had been violently murdered. He had been killed in a duel with the Second Depublic. The letter had given the Autocrats deepest condolences for her loss.

She was eight months pregnant and Trey was dead. He had died in defense of the Autocrat, even though the old one had died. However, she did not believe it for a minute. He had been murdered for his position by Theo. Theo was a ladder-climbing weasel. He bribed and killed to earn his way to the top. Certain rumors even said he was in league with the Orsin crime family, that he let them infiltrate the Senate as lobbyists and activists.

Trey used to say the whole realm of politics was a giant spider, Web. The Aridaunts were the outer rings of the web, then the smaller inner rings were the Kofahs, then the Depublics as the last rings and the Autocrat was the spider. However, what held it all together were the finical contributions of lobbyists and activists. Their special interests were what fueled the government and its citizens.

Karen felt a gush of warm fluid flow from her. Her stomach began to cramp as labored breaths seared her lungs. The baby's head was starting to push against her. She stumbled over to the Quasar terminal and quickly keyed the address for her midwife. As she finished the message, she doubled over in pain.

VI

The Autocrat walked through a raised arbor of swords. The purple carpet squished under his boots. His sword smacked his left leg as he strode to the dais. Theo smirked at how easy it was to achieve his power. Moreover, the announcement he was going to make was going to change the way everything worked right down to the way lobbyists worked the minds of their puppets.

Theo walked up onto the dais and sat in the Autocrats chair. His two Depublics sat on either side of him. A courtier brought to him the insignia of power. He grasped it in his hand and looked over the whole of the Senate chamber, smiling with intoxicated pleasure at the thought of all the power. He thought about his first policy, the one that would bring war to the Pantherines.

In the last several days he had seen reports of an uprising on Semiramus. Soon the cat-people would no longer exist. K'datra Dater was the name of their leader. He had inspired the Tigris and Lepridis to take over the armory and was now waging a guerrilla war on Hades.

Lord Arik was beside himself with paranoia. Not so much for his own life, but for the profits gained from exploiting the cat-people. Why was all this happening now ? Theo thought. It was like someone, or something was playing it all against him.

Here he was about to lose control before he even had it. Nevertheless, the policy he was about to enact, was going to ensure that he would have his seat of power for a very long time.

"Today is a momentous day for Merkadiah. Today I am implementing the second of my two-yearly decrees. This is a policy that I think everyone will be pleased to hear. As of today, open war is going

to be a way to solve our disputes. It will keep the population of certain fiefs in check and will help us keep the Pantherines in line." Before he could finish his speech, the Senate began to grumble and talk amongst themselves. Certain phrases could be heard throughout the chamber.

The Chronicles of Merkadiah:
The Rise of the Gryphon

"Has he gone mad?" one Aridaunt whispered.

"This is unbelievable," whispered a Kofah Theo shouted as loudly as he could in the acoustically amplified chamber. "Be silent, or you will all be silenced!"

The rabble died. Theo shook his head at the control he had over these people. It was worth every life he had taken. It was worth all the money paid to assassins. It was worth getting into bed with the Orsin crime family. He licked his lips as a sea of faces stared back at him.

"This idea of open war will replace the current system of tournaments, because it does not work with Pantherine barbarians. These creatures need to be dealt with on their own terms. Fight fire with fire, as the old saying goes. If it is an open war they seek, we shall give it back to them."

"But sir, what about peasant uprisings in several of the fiefs?" asked an Aridaunt with olive skin and slanted eyes. "There are uprisings on Niriah, Nithia, and Tūhl."

"Are those not your fiefs, Count Ing?" asked Theo.

"Well yes. But…"

"Then why can't your Kartah deal with a bunch of disorganized peasants?"

"Well you see sir, they, well the peasants have organized themselves. All the groups on each of these fiefs are fighting under a single banner known only as The Barrim Clan. They are well organized, and their women are odd."

"Why is that?" Theo inquired.

"They are mistresses of seduction. It has been reported that they have metal balls embedded in their tongues and they take out my Kartah before they can finish copulating. All of my Kartah are dead, sir!" Ing shouted. sure, Jaymes will give you adequate Kartah that can keep their pants on."

"That is all very well sir, but my petitions have been denied six times. In addition, the words of my lobbyists are ignored. Am I then to go and subvert these uprisings personally?"

Theo grinned and cackled. Once he had composed himself, he looked at Chin Moa Ing and said devilishly, "You have just proved my point."

"But sir I don't understand?"

"There are uprisings all over this damned system. Your fiefs are not the only ones being besieged by terrorists. The Autocrats in the past have always kept reserve soldiers in training and on the payroll for such times as these. You see after the Purging, when everyone was hoping for peace and prosperity, this senate was formed. Clyde Freemont, the last of his kind of man, developed the system we use today to resolve conflicts between others of our class.

However, in case of an uprising, we would always have at least fifteen battalions of elite soldiers at our command. This was instituted so that in a few months, each Aridaunt could have an army of their own. You see, there is really nothing to worry about.

The Barrim Clan will soon be crushed and so shall the Pantherines, and it will be business as usual."

The chambers were silent. Each person in the room let the words of their new leader sink in. They all knew open war between them was dangerous, but uprisings of peasants were worse. This was because if one started to think for himself, then his neighbors would soon follow.

Then their neighbors would follow them, and so on until an unstoppable army was about to stage a coup and the Aridaunt was facing execution for failure by the Senate. It was all a house of cards.

For once, the weak minded raised their fists, then the frail fists of the Senate would send Kartah. Then when those Kartah were expended, it was up to the Aridaunt to bring things under control. So, when that did not work, The Autocrat stepped in and all were destroyed in his fury.

Theo looked at the faces in the Senate chambers. They finally realized that what he had done was the right thing. What he didn't tell them was that these uprisings were due to financing from the Orsins. The Jackal had been very clear that a war needed to be started so that a new order could come into being an order that excited Theo.

The Jackal didn't like politics. He enjoyed controlling them, and if Theo were willing to be his puppet, he could rule the system and then maybe the galaxy. It was so exciting. Everything was going according to plan. The Orsins would be financing both sides of the conflict to make sure that in thirty years, there would no longer be any need for a Senate.

Chapter Seven

Preparations

"Only through intense physical, emotional, and psychological training can one become the warrior he wishes to be."-Fire Guild Training Axiom

I

Grivon sat on the stone table in his favorite courtyard reflecting, the same place he sat the first time Barbarah had approached him. Sitting cross-legged, he was thinking about the up-and-coming ball and tournament. He sighed as he sensed a presence in front of him. Squinting open an eye and there stood Phoy.

Huffing he opened his eyes. The man was so short he didn't have to look down. His inky black eyes stared at Grivon with an intensity that could only be made by a person who had mastered his emotions.

Phoy gave him a sly smile and a wink. Grivon looked confused as he began to stand up. Stepping away, Phoy spoke in a manner that surprised Grivon.

"I am sorry for the things I said, and the way I said them." Phoy apologized. "I was upset at the Guild Master for his attitude toward you. It is wrong for students of any Guild to have to wait until they are fifty to even be considered to run the gauntlet. Now, I believe we have your training to address."

Grivon grunted and shrugged and started to walk off. Phoy grabbed his left shoulder and spun him around. He looked down into Phoy's eyes. Phoy shook his head, "You are so much like your father it isn't even funny. He was moody and had a hard way about him. But you, my young friend, also have your mothers charming charismatic personality."

Grivon smiled a little when hearing about his parents, the people who had left him in the hellhole he lived in now. It was true that he found love and acceptance from Barbarah, but it was lonely not having any family anywhere near him.

He never knew anyone who had known his parents. Strangling back tears, his voice began to crack and quiver as he asked the question that he had been longing to ask someone since he could remember, "Can you tell me about my parents."

Phoy looked blankly at Grivon and nodded. It brought back painful memories of the day that Daggot was killed by his first Depublic. Phoy had a slight look of pain and sadness as he tried to find the words to explain everything to Grivon.

"You are descended from a line of great leaders and conquerors. Your father was Daggot D'Gaul, the last Autocrat. He was a terrific swordsman and passed some of the best policies this system has ever seen.

He was on the brink of making a dynasty, until he was killed by his left-hand man, his Second Depublic. Just before she was assassinated, your mother and an aide were able to bring you here from the Senate planet. She was killed by 'Pantherine terrorists.'"

"Why would the Pantherines kill my mother?"

"Actually, they didn't. She was killed by the S.P.A. Then the blame was put on the Pantherines to further the oppression of an elegant race who just want freedom. It was all because you were born. I'm not saying it is your fault. In fact, the reason your father was murdered was that he wanted a guarantee that you would someday rule in his stead.

He was called a Blue Blood and so were you. So, a group of lobbyists paid off the current Autocrat, and he killed your father and had your mother killed. It was a sad day in Gaul.

"I'm sorry if this troubles you, but you could use it to take your rightful place as the ruler of Merkadiah and possibly even the universe. However, there are still ists in this galaxy and God knows what in the rest of the universe. Even in the last five hundred years, I've seen my share of strange, just being on my planet." Grivon couldn't contain his excitement.

"You have a planet? What is it called? Where is it?"

"One question at a time," laughed Phoy. "Yes, it was a virgin planet as they used to call them. When I awoke from rejuvenation, I developed the training that is taught at each of the five Guilds. I developed the forms of them as well as the training in certain knowledge. It was my idea to switch from military battles to battles between Kartah. I also helped in our political structure. As an award, I was given the planet I live on now."

"Okay, but what is it called?"

The Chronicles of Merkadiah:
The Rise of the Gryphon

"That is my most closely guarded secret. I am sought out by Guild graduates every year to receive special training."

"Special training?"

"Yes, but I will tell you more about that later."

"But how do they find your planet?"

"Oh, from this clue that I can give you now. It is said that on my planet the dead walk and the living never sleep, that daemons slip into our world and that the very planet itself never ceases in devouring people seeking power." Phoy said, lowering his voice. Grivon stared blankly at Phoy. A long moment of silence passed before Grivon spoke with a tone that was unsettled and worried, "That has to be the most outlandish and morbid riddle I've ever heard!"

Phoy cocked his head back and let a loud laugh roll from the depths of his lungs. He laughed like that for several minutes before gaining his composure. Grivon looked blankly at the old man and cocked his head in an uncharacteristic manner with a confused look on his face.

When Phoy stopped laughing he spoke in a winded voice, "You are the first person to call it what it is. I must admit, you are very astute. have to ask you a very important question before the tournament begins, do you know how to charge up your Aurora?"

"What do you mean?" Grivon asked confused.

"When I came up with the training, it was designed to teach a person from the age of four to the age of eighteen to either be a soldier, politician, Kartah, or all the above. Then, they were to come to me for more advanced training that could lead to the mastery of their Aurora, which you have achieved some of those things out of order, but over the years the ones who pull the strings realized too many people were graduating, so they extended the training to the age of fifty and if you weren't able to run the gauntlet, you were put out into the system to try and forge your way in this life. I, for one, did not agree with their decision at the very least.

"Then one day about a hundred Guild graduates came to me to learn how the more advanced training worked, I had named Magiah. A Magiah is a Kartah who can take the power of a person that has a lower armor level than them. Their bodies absorb the level of armor that is provided by that person's electromagnetic field.

However, the effect is like a drug and can become addictive. Some of these Magiah become devoted to gathering more and more power until they become echoes of who they were. Their bodies begin to rot from the inside out and as they rot, the more and more frequent their killings become until their bodies are so corrupted that they solidify into a half-desiccated corpse that only wishes to feed its addiction to power.

They cannot be controlled, and worse, it is extremely hard to kill them. If you manage to kill one, don't take its power. It will corrupt you."

"What do you call these creatures they turn into?"

"I call them Revenants. They are so far gone from who they used to be, that they might as well have died and been brought back to life by some sort of evil machination."

"But what does any of that have to do with the Aurora?"

Phoy looked at Grivon blankly for a moment and then shook his head, "Sorry, it was something that needed to be told and I got ahead of myself. The Aurora is what protects you from things that would normally kill you. Do you want to know how to charge your chip?"

"Sure, what do I have to do?"

"Close your eyes and envision your brain."

Grivon closed his eyes and thought about a chart he had once seen with a picture of the brain on it. He could hear Phoy's voice giving him instructions on visualizing a full-body energy field. He did and chose its color, silver. Then as Phoy's voice droned on he saw a long hallway full of doors.

He could no longer hear Phoy's voice, only a knocking coming from a door at the end of the hall. Where there should have been a dead end, there was a large ornate door. It looked like it was carved out of redwood and had no handle, but where the handle should have been there was a single golden keyhole.

The knocking grew louder. He touched the door and was amazed at how cold it was. The knocking intensified. When he touched the keyhole, the door swung open. A blinding white light shot from the door. When it had gone, Grivon could see into an endless, dimly lit cavern.

The bottom of the cavern was filled with water, and he could hear drops of water echoing off the walls. A boat came across the water. He stood paralyzed as it approached. In the boat stood a man who looked a lot like himself. As the boat came to rest on the rocky shore, anxiety unlike any he had ever felt washed over him.

The man hopped off the boat and began to walk toward him. Grivon turned to run, but the door he had come through was gone. He was in the cave alone with the man from the boat. There was nowhere to run. The man walked up to him and opened his mouth to speak. A blinding light erased the scene and Grivon sat staring at Phoy. The side of his head hurt, and the sun was gone.

"What happened?"

"I hit you," Phoy said flatly.

"Why did you do that?"

"I'm guessing you saw the Akashic Hallway. The room with the doors? Some people see it when they first try to activate their Aurora. I suggest you do not open the doors."

Grivon scratched his head, "Why?"

"They lead to places and things better left unknown. I once heard of a man who had opened a door and became possessed by an Owb."

"What's an Owb?"

"A foul creature that likes to create havoc wherever it goes, but that is another lesson for another time. Anyway, did you see your Aurora Level?"

"Not sure. All I saw was the hallway with the doors."

"We still have some time left. I want you to try again. This time close your eyes and focus on the darkness behind them. Now I want you to concentrate and focus on the image of a pinecone."

Grivon closed his eyes and began concentrating on seeing a pinecone. After what felt like an eternity, he saw a purple outline of one. He focused, and it took a more definite shape, "I see the cone."

Phoy's voice seemed far away when he spoke, "Good. Now relax and you should see a three-digit number. That is the amount of time you can maintain a prolonged Aurora Field. What do you see?"

Grivon squinted and then relaxed. Three red numbers appeared, and he said, "Looks like three hundred."

Phoy's heart sank. His was only two hundred sixty. The boy was already much stronger and had a lot less training. Everyone had a different number; no two were alike. As far as he knew no one else had ever surpassed two hundred fifty, except for those that craved power and became consumed by it.

"I'm going to guess that is a weak number."

Phoy chuckled, "Far from it. You can sustain an Aurora Field for five hours. Now, that is if you do not expend energy like you have been or participate in a duel. Dueling will cause the field to only last for a few seconds equal to the number. The field will weaken further if your opponent lands a blow. Your field will have a color that signals how strong you are. Your field is unique, so be prepared for some harassment.

"As time runs down or you take hits your field will begin to change color. Everybody's field does this. First it will turn a dull yellow and then crimson. As it is about to dissipate completely, it will blink with a pale pink. Once it is gone you are vulnerable. Take care to protect your heart and your neck. If your heart stops or your head leaves your neck you can never get rejuvenation."

Grivon huffed, "I know that last bit about losing my head."

"Good, at least they taught you that much. Today's training is over. I want you to get some rest and tell your friends what I told you." Grivon nodded his head and walked back to his quarters.

II

"Did you know that Magiah forms use the shield provided by the body's electromagnetic field as a weapon?" asked Phoy as he and Grivon stood to face each other with their swords in hand, the next morning.

"No," replied Grivon with a hint of questioning in his voice.

"Well that little form you did the other day was one of many techniques in the element of Chaos known as The Thread of Life. That particular one can destroy an entire planet if done correctly."

Grivon felt as if his jaw would hit the soft sand of the training yards fourth training circle.

"I see that you truly don't know much about such things. You must have stumbled upon that technique by accident in some of your self-teaching." Phoy restated.

Grivon blushed and nodded at what Phoy just said. He had been reading a book of Pantherine proverbs and stumbled upon the one he had quoted as the third rite of his assessment.

The Chronicles of Merkadiah:
The Rise of the Gryphon

"In order to survive to the top one hundred in the upcoming tournament, you must know the main teaching of forms for the other four Guilds. The Water Guild is flow and defense. They will dodge your attacks as a river dodges rocks and flows over them. Then in the last moment of weakness, they strike you down like a weak tree on the side of the river.

"The Matter Guild is solidarity and defense. They will absorb and deflect every single attack and counterattack you can throw at them, until you pass out and they have won by the simple fact that you wore yourself down.

"The Wind Guild assaults you with quick attacks and speed and will try and force you out of bounds. Remember that three times out of bounds is a win for your opponent.

"The Fire Guild uses their rage to win. They will use attacks that force you to defend yourself or die."

Grivon swallowed hard. It was three days from the Tournament and that evening was the night that the contenders would be arriving and the students from every guild across the system to try to win a chance for an early out. It was going to be a hard week as the tournament would devour untold hundreds of students, so that only a few elites would be the ones to become future leaders.

Grivon had a thought and broke the silence with a question that brought a smile to Phoy's lips.

"What are the Chaos Guilds main form teachings?"

"Balance, to use all of the other Guilds main teachings against everyone and anyone, and even against the ones who think they know them the best. Now down to business. We will see you activate your armor. I will be able to see it emanating from you like an aura. Now, before we begin let me give you a few warnings.

"First off. this effect of The Aurora will severally weaken you. You will tire easily as your body's electromagnetic field is being used to act as armor to keep you safe. That means less of that electricity is being used to help with muscle control and other nervous system functions, so as you fight the more you will weaken as the field will get less protective and if you absorb any hits from a weapon, it will weaken further.

Once your enemy sees that you no longer have an Aurora, they will strike and kill you. Does that make sense?" Grivon only nodded as he tried to take it all in.

"Subsequently, don't panic. You'll do fine. Panic will also cause you to weaken faster. As you feel fear, your body will start to release adrenaline, and that combined with a lack of electricity, will cause your muscles to seize up and you will die. Not from the cramps, but from the fact that no self-respecting swordsman would not exploit his enemy's weakness."

Grivon felt a tight lump forming in his throat. For the first time in his life, he was afraid, afraid he would be killed by the agents of the Autocrat. Nevertheless, he began to feel a small satisfaction from the fact that the Autocrat was afraid of him. It meant that he was a threat for some untold reason other than he was a D'Gaul.

"And finally, think of an emotion that runs strong in your soul, and use it to call out your Aurora. Focus hard and long on that emotion, and you will call out a strong Aurora. You see, emotion will stimulate the chip with chemicals, and you will show your strongest Aurora."

Grivon stood and began to focus on his rage and anger. He called his fury but found no anger there. Looking down at his arm he didn't see anything. Then he looked over at Phoy, and Phoy shook his head no. For the first time, he thought about what made him happy, and he saw Barbarah's face in his mind's eye.

He thought about making love to her out under the stars and about the first time they kissed. Suddenly, a quiet hum filled his ears, and he felt a strange tingly feeling throughout his body. He looked at his arm and didn't see anything. He looked at Phoy through a silver fog.

Euphoria swept over him making him smile, as Phoy stood astonished.

"What? What did I do? Did I do it right?" asked Grivon. He thought his voice sounded somewhat fuzzy.

"I have never seen an armor field quite like yours. Mine is green and I have the highest armor of anyone. However, yours is silver. It is a color that I have never seen before. Indeed, you are destined for greatness.

Now let us spar and see who the better swordsman is."

The two men stood about a meter apart with swords drawn and spaced to where they were barely touching and positioned in an acute x. Their armor fields arched and clashed with a hum as they stood to face each other.

Grivon stood at least half a foot taller than Phoy. Nevertheless, Grivon knew that Phoy was extremely powerful. The two swordsmen stood looking at each other, waiting for the other to move. Grivon slightly flexed his right bicep with the strain of his arm being extended.

The Chronicles of Merkadiah:
The Rise of the Gryphon

Phoy's arm twitched with the strain as well. The arching fields echoed through the practice yard. In a small twitch, Grivon moved right and swung his sword in a downward motion toward Phoy's head. Phoy sidestepped and met Grivon's blade in the downstroke. The edge of Phoy's blade rested on the top of Grivon's. Grivon forced his sword from underneath Phoy's.

He brought the short blade toward Phoy's neck. Phoy blocked with the guard. He forced Grivon away. Grivon stumbled a few steps and Phoy kicked him on the inside of his left thigh. Grivon fell for a moment and recovered by tucking into a roll, but Phoy had succeeded in dropping Grivon's armor field.

Grivon sprung up behind Phoy and struck Phoy square in the nose. Phoy's armor field dropped two colors and he fell to the ground. Grivon pointed his blade at Phoy and spat the words he had been hoping to say since he had first met the bastard, "You're beaten old man."

"Not until I say so," responded Phoy with a smirk on his face. Phoy extended his left arm and several lightning bolts shot from his hand. The white-hot pain forced Grivon back several steps and he landed on his bottom, his hair slightly burned and the smell of ozone all around.

Phoy stood over him with his sword pointed at Grivon. His chest heaved, as he said, "No, you are beaten."

Grivon rocked back and said, "Only because you cheated."

Phoy felt his temper spark and ignite, "You are such a child! You are telling me that just because I used a technique you did not know was coming does not mean I 'cheated.' You have a very childish outlook on the world.

"All you do is whine about how everyone says that you are supposed to be great and that you do not see why. There are those out there who would kill you just for the name you bear. The D'Gaul line is not the most loved in this system. Now stop your whining and fight me you little freak!"

All the color drained from Grivon's face and he jumped up and ran toward Phoy screaming and struck Phoy hard in the stomach with the guard of his saber. Phoy doubled over, not expecting such a violent attack. Grivon jarred Phoy's leg with his knee and caught his braid in his left hand, and in fluid motion brought the metal guard of his sword into a final blow in the solar plexus.

Phoy vomited a mixture of blood, bile, and water. He coughed and fell to the ground. He gasped for breath as his lungs ached for breath. Warm spittle splattered his face and before he passed out, he heard Grivon say with malice in his voice, "Be glad that I have learned to control my temper."

Phoy was amazed at how calm the boy's voice had been. As he slipped into oblivion, he thought to himself, *so am I.*

III

The students of the Chaos Guild were lined up in two rows in the teleportation chamber. The room was the only way in or out of the Guild whether you were to leave with the Guild Masters graces, or you were being expelled. This was where the students from the other guilds were about to enter. The room was a long hallway with one door in and out and the stones were made of solid obsidian with a crushed ruby grout.

Banners of the symbol of Chaos were spaced every two meters on both sides of the room. Each of the students stood in straight attention. They were arranged from the lowest rank on the right side of the hall starting from the Guild Master and ending with a highest-ranking student on the left at the opening of the teleportation gate.

Each student wore their black guild robes and their alabaster masks. The Guild Master shouted at the top of his voice, "Prepare the path of esteem."

A long royal purple rug was rolled from the foot of the Guild Master down the hall to the teleportation gate. In precision, all the students drew their swords and held the top edge almost touching their noses. Then they extended their blades high and touched the tips gently causing a slight ring to resonate throughout the obsidian hall.

The teleportation gate glowed orange and a line of single file Fire Guild students with their swords drawn and raised with the blades extended outward. Each student marched with their swords raised, barely touching the raised arbor above them. The Fire Guild students all wore crimson red robes.

The leader stopped in front of the Guild Master and shouted, "We are all the level forty students from the Fire Guild on Dumas. We salute you Chaos Guild Master, may our actions bring honor to your Guild."

The Guild Master nodded and motioned for the students to march on through the door behind him. After they left, four more Fire Guild

troops came into the obsidian hall. Each was at least over level thirty. Grivon could feel his throat tighten as he realized it was all stacked against him. That the Senate and the Autocrat wanted him to fail, but he had a small thought in the back of his head. What if the Fire Guild was the only Guild sending their best? Not all the students that came through were of level forty, but one thing prevailed, each one was over level thirty.

Grivon was snapped out of his musings when the Matter Guild marched through. Their robes looked as if they had been spun from

silver dust. They too marched with their swords barely touching the arbor. When the leader of the troop spoke to the Guild Master Grivon's lump got bigger.

The leader of the Matter Guild troop spoke in a loud voice, "We are all tenth level or higher from the Matter Guild."

The Guild Master motioned for the troop to leave. The lump in Grivon's throat lessened a bit when he heard there were going to be some level ten opponents. Then he remembered the tactics and styles of the Matter Guild, solidarity. The absorption of punishment until you were weak, and they pushed you out of the way.

His lump got bigger and soon the Water Guild came through the gate. Their robes were long and flowing. Their blue robes shimmered like sapphires as they walked through the arbor. They kept their blades sheathed to show their passive-aggressive nature.

They announced their levels ranging from twenty-five to forty-nine. Grivon was almost in tears. These students were serious. Grivon's lump tightened even more.

Grivon realized that his time in the Guild was short. If he lost, he would be a wandering swordsman, but if he won, he would be looking for Phoy's planet. His musings were interrupted when the Wind Guild marched in. Their robes shimmered as if made of pearls.

They too kept their swords sheathed. Then they drew them in front of the Guild Master. They all were level thirty-five. By this time Grivon could feel sweat staining his body suit. He knew that he was going to be expelled. Then he remembered that he was "destined for greatness." He always had a way of pulling impossible feats from nowhere.

Then finally, he heard the Guild Master announce that Chaos Guild was on the planet Tygrano. Then he turned and walked out the door. In a rush of movement, all the students sheathed their swords. It was time for the ball. A night of debauchery for certain.

Grivon was happy he would get to be next to Barbarah for the evening. He would get to wear informal attire for a change. His thoughts turned to the evenings attire, black pants and a navy-blue tunic with crimson lace sewn around the wrists. It had been a birthday present from his Guild Lord.

All the students went to their private quarters, and Grivon walked into his room. He looked at his desk. His terminal was blinking. Sitting down, he typed in his password on the keyboard. The screen blinked alive and the hub's processor began to roar. Grivon pressed the process key and the message came up.

The cryptic message read:

You cannot win this tournament. You will fail, and then your woman will be mine! -The Jackal.

Grivon sat down in his chair. Who was The Jackal? No one in the whole guild was named The Jackal. This must be some sort of agitation from one of the other competitors. He shrugged it off. Standing, he stretched his aching muscles and began undressing.

Who would want to agitate him? It was a way to agitate him, but who would know that he and Barbarah were being intimate? Not even Steven knew their feelings for one another, so who could it be?

Grivon just finished putting on his belt and tying up his boots when a soft knock came from his door. He let out an exhausted sigh. It was going to be a long night. Then the day after tomorrow was the big tournament. It was almost as if the Guild were trying to make certain people lose.

When he opened the door, Barbarah stood in front of him. His jaw went slack. She was wearing a short-pleated dress that was lightly ruffled at the bottom and a bodice that made her breasts plump out in a way that took his breath away. She had her arms on the sides of her breasts and her hands intertwined at her stomach. She tilted her head to the side and said in a shy voice, "How do I look?"

Grivon struggled to find his voice. When he was finally able to talk, he said, "Beautiful."

Barbarah giggled and grabbed his left hand and said as she started to run, "Come on, we're going to miss The Plague."

"Why would I want to willingly get sick?"

She giggled some more and then said, "You're so silly. It's a band. They had them and, a band called The Hague come; oh, and they also were able to get Vindicated."

"What are you talking about? These names have no meaning to me."

Barbarah stopped running and let go of Grivon's hand and said, "Do you listen to music?"

"What's music?" He asked confused.

Barbarah rolled her eyes. She grabbed Grivon's hand and started running again. They ran down the crowded halls toward the mess hall where the ball was going to be. Grivon felt a pop in his shoulder and tried hard to keep from yelling in pain. She was so excited to be going to see the people who sang that he did not want her to know she had hurt him.

He would have to take a painkiller and lay in bed that night. When they finally arrived at the Guild Lord's mess hall, Grivon covered his ears. Suddenly, he forgot about the pain in his shoulder. The noise coming from the mess hall hurt his ears. He turned to leave. *Why be here when I could be resting for the tournament,* he thought.

Barbarah noticed how Grivon looked like he was in pain. Her smile dropped, and she shouted over the din, "What's wrong?"

"What is that horrible noise?"

"It's music silly."

"I hate music!" He yelled out over the clamor.

"Well at least stay so I can see you. You've been spending a lot of time with Phoy lately. At least stay and listen to music and eat some food. Is that all right?" Barbarah pleaded batting her lashes. Grivon let out an exasperated sigh, "All right, I'll stay awhile."

Barbarah jumped and let out a little squeak. She clapped her hands lightly and then held out her right arm in a loop. Grivon smiled and looped his left hand through hers. The couple walked into the hall and looked around. It looked like it always did, except the lamps had colored film over their glass. A small stage was raised at the end of the hall.

Upon the stage stood five men, each was playing some sort of instrument. Grivon couldn't begin to identify them. He tilted his face next to Barbarah's ear and said in a semi-loud voice, "Who is on the stage?"

"The Plague, aren't they talented."

"I guess, hey, why are you acting so giddy and silly?"

She shrugged her shoulders and said, "I don't know. Last week I missed my cycle, and I have been having strange moods. I've been sick in the mornings and been a bear to my Guild Lady. She asked me what was wrong, and I said that I was tired. But I think that I'm pregnant."

The world started spinning. Grivon felt dizzy. He was going to be a father. He drank some of the blue drink that Barbarah had gotten him. It burned on the way down. It did not matter it was all falling apart, what would a little alcohol do to him? It was all going to be okay.

He would win the tournament and become the first Merkadian dictator, but how would she take care of the baby without any money?

"Barbarah, if you are pregnant, please stay here and have the baby. Let Steven take care of you. When I am done finding Phoy, I will find you and Steven and be the father I need to be. Once that is done, we will continue until I am Autocrat. I promise. Never lose hope.

"When I get back, we will get married. If the guild wants the child let them have him or her. Only good can come of it. When he passes the gauntlet and proves to me that he can take my place I will tell him his destiny and he will embrace me for the father he always wanted."

Grivon's voice was cracking with emotion, and he could feel hot tears running down his face. Barbarah leaned over, hugged him and said barely above a whisper, "Okay, I love you and trust you. Are you sure that you want me to leave our baby here?"

"Not unless they tell you that you must. I want to be with my wife and child if possible. Even though I don't really trust Steven, he is my friend and I think that he will take good care of you until I get back after I graduate."

All Barbarah could do was nod. Then the music stopped. The Plague left the stage. Then Vindicated got up and started their set off with a soft song that sounded as if it had been written for him and Barbarah:

Tonight, let's get away.
Go to the fields.
To watch the stars come out,
And bask in the moonlight.

To stay close,
And keep each other warm.
Will you come with me?
I want to hold you.

I want you near and dear.

You have brought me joy.
You have made me better.
Your beauty is beyond words.

So please come with me.
Watch the stars with me.
Because you are everything I ever wanted.

Grivon looked at Barbarah and said, "Are all of their songs like this?"

"Yes and no. They sing ballads and they sing, well, I'm not sure what you call it. I know that Steven likes them. Certain songs you can barely understand them. Others are soft just like the one they started with."

She had barely finished speaking when Grivon heard a heavy downbeat and then the vocals became distorted and growling. Grivon rolled his eyes. Beautiful talent wasted on noise. He looked at Barbarah and said, "I'm tired let's go."

Barbarah nodded and they left. On their way to Grivon's quarters, Barbarah led them to the secret passageway that went outside onto the veldt. Making sure no one was watching; they pushed the secret stone that led outside.

The sun was just setting, and they walked on for a while not saying anything. When they came to a spot where the Guild looked like a toy castle on a faraway hill, they lay down beside each other.

Barbarah laid her head on Grivon's chest and placed her left hand on his stomach. For a while, they just lay there in the grass enjoying each other's company. Grivon was a sea of emotion. Not only was he going to be a father, but Barbarah was going to be his wife. He was happy that he would get to spend the rest of his life with her.

Euphoria filled his veins, giving him a sense of security he had never felt. With her head on Grivon's chest, Barbarah felt as if she were going mad. She was happy, sad, scared, excited, and angry all at once. Would she be a good mother if the Guild let her keep the child? It was all confusing. Then she thought about names.

"What do you want the name to be?" asked Barbarah.

"I like the name Terry for a boy and Jade for a girl."

Barbarah giggled a little bit and said, "Those are nice. What about a last name? I don't like mine. Can we use yours?"

Grivon thought for a moment and said, "No. My name is hated across the system. How about if we just name him after the Guild Lord that will end up caring for him or her?

"Why?"

"I don't know. It's just that I don't want him or her to have any obstructions on their own quest for greatness."

Barbarah hugged up to him and started kissing him passionately.

Grivon closed his eyes and melted into it. Barbarah stopped and unlaced her bodice. Then she looked deep into Grivon's eyes and said in a sultry voice, "I'm not wearing any under clothes."

IV

Steven sat in the crowded mess hall, bouncing his leg in anticipation of his favorite band, Vindicated, playing. While it appeared to anyone looking his way, he was nervous, in reality he was calm. Jenah had snubbed him for a Level Forty-nine Fire Guild Student, but that didn't matter; a patient predator always got his meal, and he would soon get his.

He would honor the woman he chose. After he had given her his special attentions, she would feel extraordinary in the freedom of death.

Fantasies of her blood running between his fingers filled his mind. It was enough to get him excited to the point of aching. Licking his lips, he scanned the floor drinking in the tight revealing clothes all the women were wearing. So many choices, and yet the one he wanted had to be perfect.

As he was looking around when he saw Barbarah and Grivon walk in. When he saw her skirt and bodice, he started painfully aching for just a moment with her. He had to calm himself and go on looking for his chosen beauty.

He had to find someone who was vulnerable and thought low of herself. She had to have the right figure, and she had to have a reflection of Barbarah at least in some way. As he was scanning the room a third time, he saw Grivon and Barbarah leave.

The Chronicles of Merkadiah:
The Rise of the Gryphon

Steven figured they were on their way to fornicate in the moonlight Stupid bastard ! Grivon was going to screw her, while he had to find an unfamiliar place to plant his seeds. He was going to need an heir, and when Grivon was gone Barbarah would be his. He wanted desperately to face Grivon in the tournament and kill him as The Jackal.

He was not going as Pegasus, if he could help it. This tournament would be the defining moment of history in Merkadiah. He leaned back and started thinking about the forms and mental tactics that he would use for the tournament.

Then he saw her. She walked in wearing the blue robes of the Water Guild. She had straight shoulder length sandy blonde hair, and a sad shy look on her face. Steven grinned and stood up. Pushing his way through the throng of people, he approached her.

She was barely standing at the entrance and looked nervous. He cleared his throat making her jump and put a hand to her chest.

"I beg your pardon; I didn't mean to frighten you. My name is Steven. I'm a level ten student. Can I offer you my company this evening?" He said trying to ooze as much charm as he could.

"Oh, well you see I'm looking for a certain member of this Guild. He is very talented, and I would like to spar with him if you catch my meaning?" She replied in a silky voice.

"Well then let me help you. Who are you looking for?"

"I'm looking for The Gryphon."

Steven sputtered and fumbled over words trying to get control of his temper.

That stinking bastard! How is it he is known all over and I'm not. Surely, my brutality with a blade precedes me? A sudden and delicious realization came to him, she wouldn't know the difference even if they were both standing right in front of her.

"Well then, fate has brought us together my fine young lady."

"You mean you're him?" She said with wonder.

"Why yes. I am Grivon D'Gaul himself." Steven lied. "My middle name is Steven and I didn't want any undue attention from someone seeking to kill me."

"Well then, my name is Heather Barrim. My family is so happy that I was accepted into this event."

87

"So, do you know of true love my beautiful Heather?"

Heather giggled. She drew her hands behind her back and nodded.

"You are my first love Master Gryphon," her eyes danced with delight, as she drank in his form. "Seeing as you are so strong and devilishly handsome."

Steven nodded and thought to himself, if she is saying what I think she is, I can have some fun before sunrise tomorrow.

"Well, I know the perfect spot to go and teach you, my young friend."

They departed the mess hall into the starry night. Steven was happy with the lie he had told. After all, she was willing to believe he was Grivon. Steven smiled to himself. She would be a fun toy.

They walked arm in arm to his quarters. No one was monitoring the corridors tonight since they were all worried about more lustful things happening at the ball. What did they expect would happen? That all the students would conduct an orgy in the mess hall? The real problem was outside the ball in the courtyards. Steven sighed heavily as he opened the door to his quarters. Heather automatically flopped down on his bed and started to undo her dress.

"No. We are picking up two Sabers. If we are going to spar, we have to fool anyone who sees us."

Heather nodded and stood up. Steven and Heather left his room and began to walk up the corridor and into the practice yard. He needed privacy, so he was going to take her to his private place. The place he always took girls when he was in his moods.

They came to a high stone wall. Steven looked both ways and pressed the stone that opened the secret passageway. He looped his arm in hers and they ran toward the woods. Once they were in the thicket they kept running and laughing until they came to a meadow that was bathed in pure light from the full moons. Heather gasped at the beautiful scene before her.

They walked hand in hand into the center and embraced with a passionate kiss. In the quiet night, they could hear insects and the roar of a nearby river. Steven was home. This was his place, his private secret haven where he could meditate and escape the life of the Guild and his duties as the Jackal.

He brought her here for two reasons. No one could see them rut and no one would hear her blood-curdling screams of pain. When they stopped kissing, Heather removed her Water Guild robe to reveal a sight Steven beheld as wonderful. It was slightly toned, and it appeared that she practiced for hours every day.

She smiled at him wonderfully. He too was only wearing his Guild robes. He shrugged them off in a fluid motion. He watched her eyes rove over his body. After several minutes, she walked over to him and kissed him again. He melted into her and lost himself in her kiss.

She squeezed his pectoral muscles running her hands over his stiff nipples. Steven felt her tongue in his mouth. He began massaging her tongue with his. Suddenly, an alarm went off in his mind when his tongue flipped across a metal ball embedded in her tongue.

He shoved her away from himself and shouted, "Are you trying to poison me? What faction do you work for?" Scared she looked at him and said, "What are you talking about? I don't work for anybody! If you don't like me, that's fine but don't scream at me! If you don't like what I'm doing, just ask me to stop, you jerk."

"Then what's that metal ball on your tongue?"

She giggled and said, "Oh it's a tongue stud. The women on my home planet get one at birth. It's for added pleasure for their mates, if you want to feel it or look at it that's fine." Heather stuck out her tongue to show him the piercing.

Steven got close enough to see the little metal ball embedded in the fleshy muscle. He reached out and felt it between his thumb and forefinger. The smooth metal of the bar was wet with her saliva.

He stepped back and looked her over. He licked his lips with anticipation of her, but he had to know about that piercing.

"So how does it work?"

Heather giggled a little and said, "I'll show you if you lay still."

V

When Steven awoke, it was late in the night, he was raw and his pelvis sore from the night's activities. He stretched and relieved himself in the woods. After having the longest piss, he could remember; he grabbed one of the Sabers and walked over to where Heather lay sleeping. What a waste, he thought.

He drove the sword into her breasts, and she awoke, screaming like a banshee. Her screams gave him power. Cackling, he stabbed her in her pelvis. She rolled over and tried to crawl away, he stabbed the small of her back paralyzing her. Stopping long enough to roll her over so he could see her face; he faintly heard her beg him to stop. But he was so caught up in the revelry that he couldn't hear her, and he began to sing his favorite song. Vile, grotesque, lyrics spilled from his mouth as he stabbed her continually.

He kept on driving the sword into various parts of her body singing the song with glee. He was happy that he had a teleportation jammer in the hilt of his saber. It only prevented a person from being teleported from bodily injury, but not by their own will.

Extreme excitement filled him with an ecstasy he hadn't felt in a long time. Pulling her face to his, he said, "My name is Orsin Steven Anthony, it was nice to rut with you Heather Barrim. May you always remember the honor I gave you before you died!"

He ended it by driving the sword through her neck. Only a small trickle of blood ran out of the wound. The lack of blood left him feeling hollow and craving more.

Chapter Eight

The Tournament

"Violence can solve many problems." -Fire Guild Training Axiom

I

The day of the tournament finally dawned. The students gathered around a large earthen circle outside the walls of the Guild. Each student wore their Guild robes and their alabaster masks. Today they would be called by their Guild names. It was going to be a fine day to see the students compete for the chance of an early gauntlet running.

There was nervous talk all through the guild of rumors, of certain combatant's strange styles and abilities. However, there was one thing that Grivon had gotten wind of that made his blood run cold.

A girl from one of the Water Guilds was missing. She had been seen leaving the mess hall with a boy from the Chaos Guild, but no one could remember what he looked like. The general thought was she ran away because of the pressure of the tournament.

Grivon had his own thoughts on that subject. There was a killer in the Guild. For as long as he could remember there were always a large number of female students. Then when he turned about fourteen, girls started to go missing. No one had ever seen or heard from them since; they simply vanished. Most of the students shrugged it off to losing matches in the practice yards.

However, Grivon always thought that it was because someone was killing them. Nevertheless, he didn't know who or even why. It was a mystery.

Grivon was snapped out of his thoughts when he felt a familiar hand on his shoulder. He turned around to see Barbarah. She was smiling, but she was different than she was last night. Last night she was in a highly sexual mood, now she was back to herself. He found it weird why she was so different from last night to now. Maybe it had something to do with the baby, but then again, their lovemaking was always as reckless as it was last night.

Barbarah looked at Grivon looking back at her. She noticed the familiar sadness that she had seen a few other times in his eyes. She wished that she

91

could cup his cheek and kiss him, but that would not be an appropriate thing to do at this moment.

Not that Grivon would mind, but that it might be seen by the wrong person and that would lead to expulsion. Then their personal house of cards would collapse. A loud trumpet brought the lovers out of their musings of each other.

Phoy and Jeremiah stood looking over the students. Each one's face was placid. Grivon couldn't read anything from Phoy's stone visage. Jeremiah spoke loudly so that everyone could hear him, "Today is the day that you all have been anticipating. There will be three parts to this tournament.

"In the first four rounds, it will be with practice swords. After these rounds, the remaining students will then use their sabers. You cannot kill your opponent! Anyone of the contenders that kills an opponent will be immediately expelled and then arrested. All other rules of engagement as far as the Senates rules on tournaments go will be followed."

Grivon listened carefully. This was a crucial time. He would be the youngest graduate from the Chaos Guild in history. Today was historic and soon everything after would be too. Now, he could rise and take his place in antiquity without complaint. It was his time to rise above all others and take his place in the seat of power.

He was deep in thought and didn't hear who he was paired against. The only thing he heard was he was the first match. His heart jumped into his throat and began to beat in a heavy staccato. Walking over to the sandy circle, Phoy handed him a practice sword. Grivon gripped the smooth handle tightly.

Shedding his robes, he revealed his black body suit. Catcalls erupted from some of the girls from other guilds, making his face flush. Grivon centered his thoughts and looked across the circle to see his opponent.

He was a good head taller than him with shaggy red hair and lifeless green eyes. He looked possessed. The man staring at him grinned. Grivon could tell without seeing his robes that he was a Fire Guild student.

The man licked his lips the grin widening into a sneer. Grivon closed his eyes and exhaled all his breath and then took a deep breath. This was it. He then heard a whisper in his mind. It was the echo of the students at his sixth level assessment, Freak.

It was his mantra. He felt the anger and rage build within him. He saw Jeremiah motion toward him and then the other person. He walked to his marker in the center of the circle. Jeremiah reminded them both of the rules. Each nodded without looking. They each wanted the other's head. They were ready. Jeremiah gave the signal to start the first match.

It was over before it began. Grivon rushed the man and ran past him. Before the man could move, Grivon pivoted and hit him solidly in the base of his back. A sickening crack followed by an inhuman scream echoed all around the spectators. His attack had broken the man's back reducing him to a screaming lump in the sand.

The man would be paralyzed unless he voluntarily went into a rejuvenation tank.

Phoy's face was still stone. Jeremiah looked on, mouth hanging open in awe. The Guild Master rolled his eyes. His old guild lord, Syah, shook his head and the crowd was silent. Grivon walked to his personal tent without saying a word. He sat down on the stool and sighed heavily.

One down, he thought. Then a strange thought entered his mind. Was that supposed to be challenging ? Before he could finish his morbid musing, Steven and Barbarah walked into the tent. Barbarah had a ten-foot grin on her face. Steven looked livid.

"What?" Grivon asked.

"What do you mean, what?" spat Steven. "You know good and well that you never taught me or your girlfriend here what you just did!"

Grivon scratched an itch on the back of his head and looked blankly at Steven. "Huh?" was all he could muster. He had no idea what Steven was talking about.

"I really don't think he knows what he just did." Said Barbarah to Steven.

"Perhaps you're right, but still that was a very impressive attack," Steven's voice was still thick with malice.

"All I did was break his back. That isn't all that impressive, at least I don't think so anyway." He honestly didn't know why they were awestruck.

"What's impressive about it is that no one saw you move," said a familiar voice. The trio looked and saw Phoy walking in through the folds of the tent. Grivon looked at Phoy blankly.

Steven looked down at Phoy and sneered, "Who's the dwarf?"

Steven's words no sooner left his mouth, then he was on his hands and knees yelling in pain. Phoy had hit him in the stomach with the back of his hand. Barbarah stifled a giggle, and Grivon smiled for the first time in weeks. Steven was cursing Phoy and kept on calling him a stupid dwarf.

Phoy leaned down and whispered something in Steven's ear. Steven stopped his moaning and went ash white.

"May I have a word alone with your friend please?" Phoy asked politely.

Barbarah made a face and said, "We may not get to talk to him for much longer; he will have another round shortly."

Phoy smiled and said, "No, each person will only fight in one round each day until some of the numbers thin down a bit. So, give me a few moments with your friend and then you can have him back. Agreed?"

"Yes." Spoke Steven and Barbarah at the same time. Barbarah gave Grivon a wave and walked out the tent's entrance behind Steven. After the two left, Phoy closed the tent entrance. Then he smacked Grivon as hard as he could across the face.

"What the hell was that for?" Grivon exclaimed, holding his cheek.

"Showing off!" Phoy yelled poking a finger into his sternum.

"I wasn't!"

"How long ago did you teach yourself to teleport?" Phoy's eyes squinted with accusing accuracy.

"Err..." Grivon started with a blank expression across his face.

Phoy looked at him and then his face relaxed, "I suppose you don't know what I'm talking about, do you?"

"Not really, no."

"Well you see," Phoy started. "You did what is called a short jump.

You began in one place and ended up in another place only a few steps away. In essence, you phased."

"I what?" Grivon's eyes widened as he searched his brain for anything remotely related to what his master was saying.

"You passed through a small window in reality and then as you came out of it you hit the man so hard it broke his back. I think it was just a fluke, but when this is all said and done, I will teach you how to control it. But I will say this though. That sure was one hell of a performance."

Phoy grinned and chuckled.

"You took out a level forty-nine Fire Guild student. You are a very talented young man Grivon, but don't let it go to your head. You have not won yet." Phoy turned to walk away, then stopped and turned back around, "All the contenders are to keep quarter here in their tents for the duration of the tournament. A cot will be provided for you. You may also select one person to be an attendant for you during that time.

Who would you choose, you have first pick?"

Grivon thought about it and then grinned, "I would like my friend Barbarah to be my attendant."

Phoy was taken aback and then shook his head, "Very well a cot will be put in here for her as well, but just don't be doing anything that would put her honor to test."

Grivon didn't tell him about the child so Phoy was still thinking it was an innocent thing. Grivon's cheeks flushed a little and then nodded his head. It was going to be good practice for when they got married.

II

The days of the tournament went by quickly. Grivon won every single round he was in and afterward, Barbarah would rub his back and make him something to eat in his tent. He did not watch Steven's battles, but he knew that eventually, he would have to fight him. Grivon sighed;

Steven would be a tough opponent. One of his only friends and yet they were so distant from each other. Grivon thought about how he and Steven became friends.

Grivon entered one of the Guild's ranked tournaments. It was where students could go to fight in live tournaments to weed out the weaker students. You could kill your opponent, or you could send them to rejuvenation. It was a lot better than fighting with wooden swords.

It had been a sweltering day, and it was down to Steven and Grivon. Steven stood with no form in mind, and Grivon gripped his sword loosely in its scabbard. They stood watching each other intently.

Then at the slightest twitch, Grivon drew his saber in one swift motion and ran at Steven. Steven was quick and blocked the attack with the guard of his sword.

Grivon grinned and jumped back. Then he turned in a counterattack to which Steven met his blow. They attacked and parried each other for several minutes. Each one never tiring until, Steven made a mistake.

He overextended his wrist in one of the High forms. The cracking sound echoed off the stone walls of the practice yard. He screamed with pain and cowered to the ground. Grivon walked over and kicked him in the stomach. Steven sailed backward and landed on his back with a great thud. Grivon stood over him with the point of his sword only a breath away from Steven's jugular.

"You are beaten!" cried Grivon victoriously.

"Yes, now kill me!" shouted Steven with pain in his voice.

Grivon shook his head and walked away. He could hear Steven screaming at the top of his voice.

"Coward! Don't you dare turn your back on me! You little freak, the next time I see you, you are dead meat. You hear me?"

Grivon kept on walking smiling to himself. For once it didn't bother him that someone called him a freak. He had beaten someone due to their own stupidity. Laughing to himself, he walked out of the practice yard.

It was a few weeks before he ever saw Steven again. He wore his alabaster mask and was trying to wield a left-handed sword. Grivon approached him and offered to teach him how not to overstrain his wrist while fighting. Steven agreed and from then on, they, and Barbarah, would sneak out at night and practice things that only Grivon was willing to show them.

Grivon was brought from his musings as Barbarah walked in. She had a very concerned look on her face. Grivon studied the look and realized what was wrong.

"I'm fighting Steven next, aren't I?" he asked in a faint voice.

"I am afraid so. It would seem this is the beginning of the top one hundred. It's going to be real swords. Do you think you can beat him without hurting him too badly?"

"Sure," responded Grivon with a grin on his face.

"What are you smiling about?" asked Barbarah, her own smile spread across her face.

"That the last time we were in a situation like this I beat him because of his inability to fight. He broke his wrist, then I kicked him in the stomach. He wanted me to kill him, but I let him live, just for the simple fact that it would humble him."

Barbarah nodded, "You have ten minutes before the start of your rounds. Each person is fighting two in a row today; that is, the ones that win."

Grivon nodded and began the process of fueling the furnace. It was time to turn it back onto those who caused it. His anger was like a mudslide, once it started rolling downhill, it didn't stop for anybody. If he were to let it stop because of friendship, it would never be the same again.

The Chronicles of Merkadiah:
The Rise of the Gryphon

He told Steven not to enter for this very reason. But being headstrong and stupid, Steven would do whatever he wanted. Grivon made his way through the crowd and to the circle. He took his place and dropped his robes and began to warm up. Not thinking about anything but forms and his memories, he could feel his mind going numb.

It's just another battle, he told himself. Once again, Grivon was brought back to reality by the judge's voice. He gripped the leather handle of his sword so tightly that the metal guard was cutting into the flesh of his fingers. He heard the judge give the signal to begin.

III

Steven's heart pounded in his chest making his whole body vibrate. These sensations invigorated him. Each thump gave him focus like he never felt before. He felt holy. That in this moment the great truth about Grivon was about to be revealed.

Fantasies about the coming bout and how Grivon would die filled his mind, refining the focus to euphoric proportions. Visions of a broken and subdued Barbarah in his bed gave him power and confidence. He had been waiting for this moment for a very long time. In this moment he was king, he was a god, and he would kill the bastard.

IV

At first, they both stood watching each other. Then in an instant, they engaged. When their swords met sparks flew from the blades. They attacked and parried each other for hours, neither of them tiring. The crowd watched with intent eyes as these two evenly matched warriors from the same Guild fought.

It ended as suddenly as it had begun. Grivon saw the open spot and smashed Steven's nose with the guard. Steven closed his eyes and dropped his sword. He put both hands over his face and cried out in agony. Grivon walked over and kicked Steven firmly in the chin. A loud cracking noise echoed off the acacia trees. Grivon noticed that the sun was setting. He casually walked over to the kneeling Steven who was whimpering about his broken nose and jaw.

Grivon looked down at him and asked coldly, "Do you submit to me as the winner?"

"Never!" shouted Steven as best he could with a broken jaw.

Grivon nodded, grabbed Steven by the hair and lifted him off the ground. Steven hung limply as Grivon punched him in the face a second time. Steven let go an unearthly scream as Grivon held him above the ground.

"Do you submit to me as the winner?"

All Steven could do was spit blood at Grivon. Nodding, he punched Steven in the stomach three times and threw him out of the ring. The match was over. Once again, the crowd stood stunned. The match they had just witnessed lasted four hours. It was almost like seeing the titans of old clash and compete. Steven would be sent to the sick bay seeing as how the wounds he sustained were not bad enough to warrant teleportation.

Grivon walked back to his tent where Barbarah was sleeping. His eyes roved over her every centimeter of her making a memory. Her back rose and fall with the deep sleep, and he wondered what she was dreaming about. Never in his life did he think he would be standing here admiring someone as wonderful as Barbarah. This was a perfect moment and he never wanted it to end.

V

The next few days of the tournament were slow and uneventful. Each opponent that Grivon came up against fell within moments. He began to hear the now-familiar chant when he did something that he was not supposed to be able to do.

"Freak," the crowd chanted.

Grivon sat on his cot with only a pair of shorts on. He flexed his fists as he cooled off from the day's events. His match for the day had been very easy and left him feeling empty. No one had ever been able to give him a proper fight. He looked over at Barbarah who was cooking dinner.

He smiled at her halfheartedly. She stirred the stew in the pot and walked over to him. She began to rub her hands through his hair. Grivon closed his eyes as the rage began to fade. Reaching behind his head, she tickled his ears.

Opening his eyes, tears welled up and his lower lip began to quiver. The sudden sound of giggling turned Barbarah's attention outside his tent. She turned and looked outside the tent flap. Three Water Guild women were looking in. They witnessed everything.

Barbarah resisted the urge to shout obscenities at the three women. Instead, she grabbed one of the spare practice swords and walked outside into the cool sunset. The smiles dropped from the other women's faces.

Barbarah pointed the wooden sword a breath away from the woman in the middle's neck. A sudden worried look came across her face.

"Breathe, and I'll show you what he has taught me," said Barbarah with a voice barely above a whisper. "If you wish, the circle is available for sparring. I'll show you what a freak can do." Barbarah spat.

The woman in the middle began to chuckle, "Fine," she spoke with a silky voice. "But with live weapons to the death. I'm a level forty-nine student. I'll keep your head as a trophy, you overprotective b…" The girl fell to the ground. Barbarah hit her in the neck with the practice sword.

"Now who's the bitch!" screamed Barbarah.

At that time, Phoy and Jeremiah were walking toward Grivon's tent. They were coming to tell him of some last-minute changes in the final round but were stopped short by the fiasco before them. Phoy looked up at Jeremiah and Jeremiah cocked an eyebrow.

The girl that Barbarah had just struck got up and popped her neck, and in an icy tone said, "Instead of keeping your head as a trophy, after I kill you, I'll come here and enslave your boyfriend. Then when he's exhausted, I'll mutilate him. But after I bear his daughter. And just for the hell of it, I will mount both your heads above my bed, so I can show my daughter who her father was. A washed-up little boy who couldn't last in passion."

By this time, Barbarah was shaking with anger. She raised the practice sword and said, "Why don't you spend some time in Hell, you WHORE!" Barbarah was about to strike, when a strong hand caught her wrist.

"Stay your blade love," said Grivon in her ear.

Barbarah turned around to see him standing behind her. She was at a loss for words. All the rage melted like ice on the veldt. Confused, she wondered, *Why was he here? Right I'm his attendant and was cooking for him.*

"Stews almost finished, why don't you go and finish dinner while I take out the trash?"

Barbarah nodded, then paused for a second, as if to ask a question, before scampering into the tent closing the flap behind her. Grivon stood looking at the woman. He smiled slightly as a warm breeze blew on his bare back. Phoy and Jeremiah stood off to the side watching the exchange.

He knew who she was. The only other competitor to go undefeated throughout the tournament. She was the second to last test before he could become a Kartah and achieve his goal.

"I would offer to fight in her stead but seeing as how we will be facing each other in combat tomorrow it seems kind of pointless. Besides, she has been a little on edge, while I've been fighting in the tournament. Now move along, or Phoy and Jeremiah will make me the technical winner."

Grivon pointed behind the trio to where Phoy and Jeremiah stood with arms crossed and scowls on their faces.

"So, what do you say? Is she really worth it?"

After a long pause, the girl spoke softly, "No." Then the small troupe turned and walked away from Grivon, Phoy, and Jeremiah. When the women were out of sight, the two men approached.

"That could have been worse than it really needed to be. Barbarah would have killed her," said Phoy with a slight chuckle in his voice.

Grivon and Jeremiah both lifted an eyebrow at what Phoy said. Phoy grinned, winked at Grivon and said, "I'll tell you when you're older."

Jeremiah shook his head smiling. Then his face became serious. Grivon stopped grinning and looked at the two men with concern on his face. Jeremiah gave Phoy a sideways look. Phoy nodded and motioned for Grivon to follow them. Grivon nodded. It was important not to talk until the three of them were alone.

Grivon walked back into his tent and set the practice sword down. Barbarah looked at him funny and began to ask what was wrong, but before she could form the words, Grivon put his index finger to his lips.

She nodded and pointed at the pot of stew. Grivon nodded and mouthed, "I'll eat later."

Barbarah mouthed back, "Okay," and hugged him tight as he moved the flap and walked outside the tent. The sun had finished setting and Jeremiah and Phoy were holding lamps to light their way.

The night air was cool as Grivon walked towards them. He cursed himself for not dressing before they left for the walk. The seasons were about to change, and the Blue Star would be out of sight for a while.

Grivon sighed and looked at the planets that surrounded Tygrano. Each looked like a dull star, but he could name some of them. He saw Nomah, Tūhl, and a few others. He grinned as he noticed where they were. They were at the spot where he and Barbarah had first sparred and later had first made love under the stars.

Phoy and Jeremiah stopped and turned around facing Grivon. Each of them had a grave expression on their faces. Grivon looked at them with confusion on his face. Phoy looked up at Jeremiah and nodded. Jeremiah stepped a little toward Grivon and spoke with fear in his voice.

"Your situation has become much graver. You're to fight Ubiroe.

That was the girl Barbarah was going to kill earlier. Barbarah would have beaten her. You will not," before Jeremiah could finish Grivon cut in forcefully.

"I can beat anyone. I'll kill the bitch. She had no right..." Jeremiah held up a hand to quiet him down.

"She fights naked. At least close to it," said Phoy nonchalantly.

"Huh? That's wholly impractical," Grivon said rubbing his chin.

"Yes," said Phoy with a slight grin on his face. "She is uh, well adept at fighting male opponents."

"Dirty old man," said Jeremiah with disgust. "This is no laughing matter. She will use whatever seductive trick she can against you. Unless you and Barbarah have...well...you know."

Grivon's face flushed as he bellowed, "That's none of your damn business!"

Jerimiah laughed, "Well then you can beat her. Your disregard for the rules is apparent in everything you do. Honestly, I'm not surprised. Anyway, a change of rules that I'm supposed to let you and her know.

We've already talked with Ubiroe and that's why she came by your tent. Anyway, you are to fight to the death. The teleportation stations have been deactivated so that if you suffer a loss of limb or the like, it will not result in teleportation and rejuvenation, but you should still be able to make short jumps. This fight is to prove once and for all who is the best.

This is life or death. You could die, and she will not let Barbarah's insults go unpunished. If you fail, who will protect her?"

"Steven Anthony, my best friend."

Phoy had to hold his tongue to keep from blurting out what he knew about Steven. Steven was Orsin Steven Anthony IV, the leader of the Orsin Crime Family. Would he really entrust him with Barbarah's life?

Jeremiah looked at Phoy and asked, "You all right?"

Phoy nodded, faking coughing. He forced himself to spit and then said, "Insect," and began to cough again. Jeremiah shook his head and muttered something under his breath and then turned back to Grivon and speaking harshly, "You will do well to use every tactic at your disposal, whatever they may be. Do whatever you can to win. If she wins, she will face her gauntlet and then she will go into service of her mother, and then when her mother dies, she will make a bid to be Nomah's Aridaunt.

If she gets it, she will start making bids for advancement. She will try to become a Kofah. Her mother has already been granted several of Chin Mao Ing's fiefs to help settle the Barrim Clan."

"What are you talking about?"

Jeremiah winced, "Oh, that's right, you don't listen to the nightly broadcasts from around the system. Chin took a cut in fiefs and let Ubiroe's mother take control over his fiefs so that a group of peasants calling themselves the Barrim Clan can have their own territory and voice within the senate. It was reported that at least two of them infiltrated this Guild under the guise of Water Guild students.

"One was seeking you, but someone else got to her first. The report I read determined her companion for the ball had sex with her and killed her. When her body was found she had been mutilated by shallow stab wounds covering most of her body. Her attacker eventually stabbed her in the throat. Most of the wounds were shallow and not life-threatening but were still painful."

Grivon felt like he was about to be sick. The thought that someone could do that to another human was not only disturbing but just downright cruel. Then he had a thought.

"Why would this Barrim Clan want me dead?"

"On the contrary," said Phoy. "The Autocrat most likely sent them here as plants to kill you cheap. Their current leader, the one who took over Chin's fiefs, was once your father's torture master. She held no loyalty. I can promise you that and is anticipating a new Kartah, provided you lose to Ubiroe. You can worry about this type of thing later. It's getting late and I'm sure you are hungry?"

Grivon's stomach growled and he realized that he hadn't eaten since before his last round, so he bade each man good evening and ran off leaving Phoy and Jeremiah in silence.

VI

"Do you think he knows about his friend?" asked Jeremiah

"No," said Phoy. "He really trusts him. You know I followed him with that girl back during the ball."

"And?"

"He is one demented person. She was asleep, and he just mutilated her. She screamed for him to stop but he just kept on stabbing, all while singing some vile song. Then after numerous stabs, he cut her throat and let her bleed out. I filed the report."

"How could you stomach that?" Jerimiah said with disgust.

"During my travels, I encountered a young Kartah named Arik Small.

He, how to put this without you retching, has a thing for cats if you catch my meaning?"

Jeremiah shuddered, "Why didn't you kill him?"

"He teleported away before I could get at him. Now he's an Aridaunt on Semiramus."

"...I was referring more toward Steven."

"Ah yes my mistake," Phoy started. "If I killed Steven, Grivon would be less amusing than he currently is and would never learn another thing I have to teach him. If he is not taught properly and becomes what everyone fears, it will be a reign of darkness and tyranny we have not seen since the time of Xóa.

"Back to Arik. He currently has one of the Pantherine Ghettos. It is a nice little set up to earn money. He has created a pleasure house that has nothing but Pantherine queens in it. He charges four hundred credits per every quarter of an hour."

"What! That's ten times more than some of the best harlots on Niriah!"

"Exactly, there are more people who share his compulsion, and they are willing to pay for it. He doesn't charge himself but, still, he kills them and skins them and puts their pelts up in his grand hall, but rumor has it there was a coup in both ghettos recently."

"And?" Jerimiah asked, his voice thick with anticipation at the destruction of such a reprobate.

"I hope he's dead."

Jeremiah just shook his head. Phoy became quiet and started playing with a strand of the veldt grass. Jeremiah let him be. He hated it when his old teacher talked about the things he had seen in his life, but he hated not telling him of the plan that he and The Guild Lord had concocted using ten Barrim Sisters.

Only one remained, the rest either killed in the tournament, with the exception of the one found murdered. Hopefully, Ubiroe would put an end to all this nonsense and fuss about Grivon D'Gaul.

VII

A warm breeze blew across the tournament grounds. It brought with it the heat from the veldt and the scents of grass and acacia trees. The students who remained after the second round stood shoulder to shoulder looking on to what should be the best event of the tournament.

Grivon stood on his side of the dirt dueling circle facing Ubiroe, and as Jeremiah said, she was completely naked. Tilting his head, Grivon looked her over a couple of times. No, she wasn't completely naked. She wore a tight fitting unitard made from a skin colored fabric that clung to her lithe frame like a second skin.

The bodysuit left little to the imagination as every curve of her body was sharply defined. He could make out the shape of her small breasts, but from where he stood it was almost impossible to tell if the light was making the fabric see through or he was just imagining things.

There was no doubt as to why her Guild name was 'The Man Slayer.' Her thighs were well toned, as were her arms and abdomen. Finally, he looked at her face one last time. She had short platinum spiked hair, staggering gray eyes set in large almond shaped sockets, and elfin facial features. She was beautiful.

It was easy to see why anyone, male or female, could be distracted by her. Ubiroe took a High Pressure stance with her saber in the left hand.

Grivon grunted under his breath and took the same form except in his right hand. Another breeze blew across the Tournament Grounds. This time it blew on Grivon's back, sending chills up his spin and making goose flesh run across his bare skin.

Grivon studied his opponent's eyes as best he could trying to see into her soul. However, she was good at blocking people's attempts at getting in. He sighed. This isn't going to be easy, he thought. After what seemed like hours, Grivon's arm begin to tire, but he knew the second that he dropped it she would attack. He had to remain vigilant.

The Chronicles of Merkadiah:
The Rise of the Gryphon

She was going to try her best to kill him. As the sun set the two stood still looking at each other. Jeremiah walked into the center of the circle and spoke loudly, "Since the sun is setting, let us and the contenders get some rest." Upset, the crowd shuffled back to their tents to eat and talk.

Grivon walked back to his tent to find Barbarah had already fixed his supper. It was his favorite, venison, local roots and a leafy green vegetable that resembled spinach. Grivon began to shovel the food in and Barbarah sat across from him with her head in her hands watching him eat.

He looked up and saw her looking at him, "Do you want some?" he paused to finish his bite. "I didn't even think that you might not have eaten."

Barbarah smiled and her green eyes lit up, and in a soft sultry voice said, "I'm fine. Did you win?"

"We didn't even fight. She is one well-trained woman. I think she might have cross trained," said Grivon, as he placed a large forkful of food in his mouth.

"Is that so. Does she have as nice of a body as they say she does?"

Grivon almost choked as he took a sip of tonic. "Err," was all that came to his lips. He was fearful of what she said. If he said yes, she would likely kill him. If he said no, well that could be disastrous in and of itself, so he thought as he sputtered to keep himself from strangling.

Then he said when his throat was clear, "Not nearly as beautiful as you."

Barbarah grinned and giggled a little bit, "Good answer," she purred.

"Now what does she look like?"

Grivon described her to Barbarah and she listened intently. When he finished, she stood up and closed the flap to the tent. Then she bent over and took the plate that Grivon was still eating from. He opened his mouth in protest, but she put her finger to her lips to make him be quiet.

Grivon tilted his head in confusion and looked at her with wonder in his eyes. In the past few weeks, there hadn't been much time for intimacy. Ever since that night on the veldt, she had awakened something primal in him. It was hard to focus without thinking of her soft skin pressed against him.

Too afraid to overtly ask, he always let her set the pace to make certain not to trigger any bad memories. Then she asked another question, and this time Grivon almost fell over.

"So, whose body is better; mine or hers?" She dropped the cloak that she was wearing to exposing herself to him. Grivon looked her over for the first time in artificial light. Words could not describe the way the sun lamps accented her curves.

Barbarah stood with her arms at her sides. Grivon let out a shocked gasp, wanting to touch her. His voice caught in his throat as he moved his eyes to her face. She was staring at him. Their gazes locked. Blushing, she looked away.

"Why so shy?" he asked.

"No one has ever seen me like this, other than myself and my Guild Lady," she spoke barely above a whisper.

"Why would your Guild Lady want to look at you like this?"

"She, well she was," her voice trailed off and she blushed some more.

"She was teaching me how to make myself feel good in case I got 'urges' as she put it."

"I see. Well, I have an answer to your question."

"What is that?" a little bit of dread resounding in her voice.

"Yours is much better. I love your creamy skin. I've wanted to make love too you for a while now. Will you tonight? Will you help me to relax?

She's going to be a tough opponent?"

Barbarah laughed and put out the lamp. Grivon yelped with a twinge of fear, as she pushed him back against the chair and ravenously attacked his robes.

IX

The next day Grivon once again faced Ubiroe. This time she wore no top and only a thin loin cloth looking bottom. She took an odd stance he didn't recognize. She drove her sword into the soft dirt behind her and

rested her hands on her hips and spread her legs. The men in the crowd hollered at the disgraceful show. She acted as if she were in another world as obscene things were called out to her. Taking it in stride, she looked at him with a cocky smirk on her face.

Sheathing his sword, he stood across from her with his arms crossed. Taking a moment to look her up and down, he took in her exposed flesh to see if she had, any scars whatsoever. He couldn't find a single blemish.

She was flawless. They stood watching each other most of the day, neither one moving an inch. At one point, she got an itch and scratched herself.

The Chronicles of Merkadiah:
The Rise of the Gryphon

The women in the crowd turned and left, and the men whooped and hollered for an obscene show. She ignored it all. She was as completely focused on Grivon as he was on her.

As noon came, she spoke for the first time, "Well I guess you are smarter than I thought. I would usually kill the poor bastard that dare stand against me, but you, there is something different about you."

She stretched out her arm and pointed to Grivon. "You are not fazed by my stage of undress, are you?"

Ubiroe casually waltzed over to Grivon making sure to show off for the all-male audience. She put on a flamboyantly grotesque show for the men in the crowd. This drove them to a frenzy as they hollered vile things to her about what they would do or what she should do.

When Ubiroe was but a few inches from Grivon, she looked deep into his pale green eyes. Suddenly, she grabbed a pressure point on his left collar bone. Trying to fight the sudden pain, he was unaware that she was kissing him. It was a prolonged sloppy kiss, causing an unfamiliar wave of nausea to wash over him. The men in the crowd called out to Grivon.

Some whistled, others booed. When she was finished, he wiped mouth, spit, and simply said, "My girlfriend's better."

Ubiroe didn't even speak and slapped him across the face. Grivon had the blade of his sword at her throat before she could breathe. Her eyes went to a joyful pleading gaze and her lower lip puckered out as she spoke "Oh, I'm scared. The big bad level ten is going to kill me.

When this is over your bitch of a girlfriend will die, after I stuff your head, and turn it into a trophy!" By this time Ubiroe and the male crowd were laughing.

Grivon fed his fury faster than he ever had before and after a smooth downstroke of the small blade, she screamed curses at him. Ubiroe was holding the left side of her head. Blood oozed between her fingers, and her ear lay baking in the sun. Grivon bent down picked it up and stuffed it in a small pocket on the back of his shorts.

The men in the crowd gasped as he quickly flourished the sword and had the tip of the blade at Ubiroe's throat.

"How many men have you castrated or killed just for your own pleasure, you twisted little bitch!"

Ubiroe spit in his face and screamed, "Go to Hell, you bastard!"

Grivon smirked and said, "Wrong answer," and in another smooth stroke he cut off her other ear. Ubiroe screamed as she brought her other hand over the bloody stump. Grivon smiled. Ubiroe found the strength to speak, "Over a hundred, but what are you going to do to me?

You think having your way is new to me?" she screamed at him. By this time, the crowd was silent.

"No, not really, but then again I'm not going to force you to do something like that. I'm beyond such brutalities. I've taken what you treasure most. Your looks give you, your power. I hope that before I take your ugly, head you know the pain that you caused just because some little boy who thought he was a man decided he wanted you as a toy."

Ubiroe looked at Grivon and smirked, "This isn't over."

She removed her hands from her head, and she was healed. Grivon looked at her puzzled and said, "How did you do that?"

"These," she showed him the palms of her hands where there were implanted portable rejuvenators. "All's fair in this round," she spat. Ubiroe backflipped back to where her sword was. Grivon took a guarded position expecting an attack, but Ubiroe stayed where she was staring daggers at him.

Grivon knew by the look on her face that he had taken what little power she still possessed away from her. He would have to be very careful in the future, as he was almost another victim of this psychotic woman. Keeping his stance, the rest of the day proved to be harder than he thought.

The sword that normally only weighed a few kilograms now felt as if it weighed a hundred and when the sun set, he picked up Ubiroe's other severed ear and wiped it off.

When Grivon arrived at his tent, he was surprised to see Ubiroe waiting for him. Barbarah sat on the cot crying. Ubiroe was clad in her powder blue Water Guild robe. She still had that self-absorbed look on her face. Grivon stopped three meters from the tent and asked in a terse tone, "What the hell do you want!"

Barbarah looked up and mouthed, 'Me?' Grivon shook his head and pointed to Ubiroe. Ubiroe smiled and got up from the chair she was sitting in and began to walk toward Grivon. When she was but a breath away from him, she stopped and whispered in his ear, "I told her all about our little kiss.

Oh, and you were right, your girlfriend is better. She was great," Ubiroe made a mock kiss, turned around and left cackling. Grivon's blood boiled for a minute but calmed down as he walked over to his tent and closed the flap.

Barbarah was a little worse for wear but otherwise, she was fine. She asked Grivon why Ubiroe had done that to him and he told her exactly what had happened. Barbarah nodded and leaned up and kissed Grivon passionately.

He melted into it and then broke away. He asked her what Ubiroe had done to her. She shuddered and told him that she kissed her. Then Ubiroe had put her sword against her neck and told her to massage her until she reached climax. She had done it in front of all the people she could.

Ubiroe had even gone so far as to say things like, 'That's how you do it lover,' and 'Oh, you are good at this.'"

Grivon was enraged, "Tomorrow I'm killing that bitch if I have to die trying," by this time he was screaming at the top of his voice. Barbarah looked up at him, her tear stained cheeks red. Grivon saw a flash of fear in her eyes and in response brought her closer.

Remembering his trophies, Grivon reached into his pocket and brought out the ears from earlier. Barbarah gazed at them and then opened her mouth to speak, but Grivon put a finger to her lip for her to be quiet.

"Trophies for you to cherish or toss to the slag pile," he said smiling.

Barbarah's eyes lit up and she stretched out her hand to take them. They were cold and felt like leathery rocks. She threw them into the refuse receptacle that composted their trash from the days of living on the veldt. Reaching up she cupped Grivon's cheek and gave him a toothy smile, "A wonderful gift, but unnecessary. Just kill her for me and I'll be most appreciative."

Grivon put his hand over his abdomen and bowed, "I will fulfill your request my lady."

Barbarah giggled, "Kiss me, my silly little boy."

Grivon approached the Tournament Grounds. There stood Ubiroe in all her glory. She was strutting extra hard today. He shook the thoughts from his mind and shed his robes. He had decided to change things up.

Instead of wearing his approved combatant clothing, he chose to wear a simple pair of tight-fitting exercise shorts. A cool breeze flowed through his legs making him twitch. The women in the crowd had gathered to watch with the men today.

They catcalled him. Ubiroe stopped strutting and gawked at what was standing across from her. She stared at him as if she had never seen a man before. She struggled to speak as she continued to gawk at him. Then Grivon smirked and said,

"How 'bout one last round?"

Ubiroe couldn't reply. She sputtered and just gawked at Grivon's near perfect body. Smirking, he seized the opportunity. Drawing his sword, he exhaled. He dematerialized only to reappear behind her. Before she could react, he had his left arm around her neck, and she was making gurgling sounds.

He ejected the hidden blade of his sword into the small of her back paralyzing her. He laughed as her limp body flopped to the ground. She tried to crawl

away but Grivon was too quick. He grabbed her hair and stood her on her feet only to let her fall again. She landed on her face. The force of the fall breaking her nose.

With blood oozing from her nostrils, she pleaded, "Please I surrender! I'll take expulsion!"

Grivon shook his head and put a finger over her lips. She tried to bite it, but he grabbed her hair just in time to yank her neck away so she only bit at the air, "No expulsion, only death!"

Grivon spat in her face. Pulling her close he whispered in her ear, "I'll take your power again and this time you cannot heal yourself!"

Spitting in her face once more, he cut off her ears in two swift strokes. He knelt back next to her and whispered, "If I were less than a man, I'd toss you into that mob of men you created and watch them ravage your body before I cut off your head, but you are little more than human slag and you shall die for what you did to the mother of my child."

Ubiroe's eyes got wide and shook her head, "I didn't know. I didn't.."

Grivon held her in place as he used the dagger to cut out her tongue. With a flick of his thumb the dagger retracted back into the pommel of his saber. Brandishing the saber, he drove the blade through her chest, and in a fluid motion, pulled it free. A rage filled roar escaped his lips, and her head leapt from her shoulders landing on the ground with a wet thud.

He threw what remained of her body into the raving crowd. Just as he began to walk away, three figures in front of him motioned for him to stop.

The Chronicles of Merkadiah:
The Rise of the Gryphon

In the middle was the Guild Master. On the right, stood Jeremiah Jericho, and on the left, stood Phoy.

Phoy had a ten-meter grin on his face. The other two were not so happy. Grivon smirked and looked at

the Guild Master, mockingly bowed and said, "I will run the Gauntlet in one week's time."

The Guild Master spoke with a smirk on his face, "A last minute rule change states that any student of your level will not be able to run the Gauntlet but will progress thirty levels and will be able to run the Gauntlet in ten years," the Guild Master's eyes shifted to Jeremiah.

"I'm afraid that he is right my young friend; rules are rules," said Jeremiah.

Then the Guild Master and Jeremiah both turned to leave when Phoy exhaled sharply.

"When I designed this program, students were to excel at their own pace. Not this slag about how since we are living longer, we cannot have too many Kartah running around. Open your eyes! This boy just defeated a member of the Barrim clan that you put here in place of the real Ubiroe!"

The Guild Master turned around sharply and spoke with a terse edge to his voice, "How dare you suggest that one of those barbarians was able to infiltrate the Chaos Guild!"

Phoy looked at Grivon and motioned for the tongue of Ubiroe. He walked over and with the limp muscle in his hand. Looking down, Grivon immediately noticed a round silver ball near the tip of the tongue.

Shrugging at the strange piercing, he wondered what it was for before handing it over to his mentor. Phoy looked at the detached muscle and shook his head before screaming at the Guild Master and Jeremiah.

"Do you two take me for a fool? This whole thing was one big run around trying to kill a person who The Autocrat thinks is dangerous."

Phoy shook his head, "You both make me sick."

"What can you do about it, old friend?" Jerimiah boomed.

"This!" Phoy yelled as he thrust his hands out and grabbed both men's necks and, in a few moments, they turned to dust with just their skulls lying in a pile of ashes.

Grivon looked down at the ground and then looked back at Phoy with a confused look on his face. Phoy shook his head and turned to the gawking crowd and shouted, "All non-Chaos Guild Students have twenty-four standard hours to pack their belongings and leave or be executed. This is by order of Phoy Yen, interim Guild Master."

Chapter Nine

The Gauntlet

"In the testing of students, psychotropic drugs are often employed to make sure that the acolyte can handle the emotional duress of combat." -Guild Training Report

I

Grivon sat on the edge of his bed exhausted. He had been sparring and training with Phoy every day since the Tournament. Phoy was sure he was ready for the Gauntlet, but he kept pushing Grivon harder. His muscles ached and screamed, and he had not been able to see Barbarah or Steven.

That last bit was frustrating and made him want to lash out at Phoy. His idea that his friends were distractions was a pot of slag. Pushing past the exhaustion, he gripped his sword and started practicing his forms. Each strike and movement brought new dimensions of pain and protest from his bones and back.

After only a few minutes of the rigorous exercise his body gave one final protest and his saber clattered to the stone floor of his room. An acute cramp surged through his right arm making him cry out in pain.

Leaving the weapon on the floor, he flopped onto his bed. Sweat rifled off his face and stained the white blanket covering his place of respite. I should just lay here until tomorrow, he thought. After several minutes of the surging pain, he stood and walked to his shower.

Shedding the stinking clothes, he turned on the water and got in. It never ceased to amaze him how some hot water could refocus your thoughts and ease the pain of your muscles. His mind was tired too, and just standing under the steaming water brought solace to his overall being.

Soon, he thought. Soon I will have the title of Kartah, and soon I will be the next Autocrat. When he was finished, he dried off and flopped onto his bed once more. Staring at the wooden ceiling, he tried to make sense of the wood grain.

Some of it looked like mythical creatures, others looked like demons spawned from his deepest nightmares. Black edges creeped in on the periphery of his vison, and soon deep sleep enveloped him in its velvet arms.

II

The sound of a woman's voice woke him up. She was standing over him naked. His wrists and ankles had long spikes driven through them pinning him to the stone floor of his room. Ubiroe put her hands on her hips, bent over, looked down at him and said in an almost playful voice, "Let's see, what shall we make this pathetic little thing do?"

Five other girls who looked the same walked over and surrounded him. Grivon winced at the pain in his legs. Two of the evil women were drilling holes through his shins, all the while two more severed the tendons in his legs. He screamed and Ubiroe smirked a little.

She squatted down and painfully grabbed his testicles and put a knife to his penis. He tried to turn his head but one of the others grabbed his face and made him look, so he closed his eyes tight as Ubiroe began to cut into him.

Grivon awoke screaming holding his legs. He was drenched in a cold sweat and he had a foul taste in his mouth. *Where am I ? Was it a dream ?*

He had no memory of having fallen asleep. Searching the room his eyes found his desk console and saw that the time was around twenty hundred or so. It was dark outside, so he knew it was nighttime.

Cradling his head in his hands, he sat up and shook his head. He had been having dreams like this a lot after the tournament. It had been the first time he had killed a real person. In the time since then, he often wanted to tell Phoy about his dreams, but worried the mentor would think him ill.

He wanted to tell Barbarah, but she was getting so emotional that he could hardly stand to be around her. Sighing, he stood up and stretched his stiff arms and legs. His lights came on and from the pattern of sweat on the sheets, he had been asleep for several hours in a fetal position.

Bending down, he touched his toes and exhaled. Then he bent back as far as his back would let him and exhaled. A tendril of electricity shot through him, and he collapsed to the floor with tears in his eyes. He was so close to fulfilling his desire to be gone from the hellhole he had been stuck in.

His mind wandered onto different topics, and his eyes wandered to the ceiling high above him. All the events of the last few weeks had left him emotionally drained and near defeat. It felt as if the world were careening out of control and that he was going to hit a wall full force at any moment.

114

Barbarah was pregnant. He had killed a human being. It was all heading toward a fire so hot that he would have to go into the voids of Hell just to cool off. He had two options. One, he could let the fire consume him and then prove to all around him that he was nothing more than an arrogant child.

The second option was to set his resolve and push through that fire. He sat up and put his head in his hands wondering if anyone cared enough about him to see his suffering.

Somewhere in it he could sense that no matter what Phoy would be there to push him along.

Grivon wiped the tears from his eyes. He was going to be a father, and he could not sit around moping about the past. It was going to be a long hard road, but in the end, he would be the creator of a new empire that could cause a storm so great that not even the mighty Autocrat could stop.

His body surging with new strength he stood up and put on a fresh set of clothes and grabbed his sword. He had to practice his forms. In less than two days, he was going to face the horrors of the gauntlet.

Sleep would be a welcome pleasure after he was through that trial.

III

The morning of Grivon's final assessment was upon him before he knew it. He had been forbidden to sleep in the last twelve hours before the gauntlet and was also forbidden to eat.

Phoy locked him in a small stone room for the twelve hours without any type of weapon to practice forms with, so he spent the time going over forms in his mind and practicing grappling and unarmed forms.

His stomach rolled and spun, from having been denied food. Then taste of bile kept making him heave every few moments. The lack of food made him feel as if he were stepping in and out of his body. Like he was two people trapped in a single space.

When the time came for him to begin the rites of The Gauntlet, he was led to the main courtyard, by a Guild Lord, where the fountain sat. The foul waters that flowed from it were a purple color in the early morning darkness. As he and his escort approached the courtyard the only person outside was Phoy.

He had his back turned toward Grivon with both hands behind his back and the tip of his long braid almost
touching his palms.

When Grivon was but a meter away from Phoy, the escort left the two men alone. He stood in silence until Phoy turned around. The waiting killed him. Each second felt like an hour and each minute felt like a day.

Once Phoy had turned around Grivon waited for him to speak. Still his mentor said nothing. Time elapsed slowly making him anxious, and the sun began to peak in the east painting the sky a dark gray purple to bright magenta.

As the two men stood looking at each other the sun rose even more and as it did, the sky lit up with a deep crimson. When Phoy saw the sunrise, he looked over at Grivon and spoke in a soft stern voice.

"The sky tells me that today will be a day of great passion, sorrow and victory. Tell me of what you wish for today to mean for you?" Grivon was stunned by the question. He mulled them over in his mind like a precious gem, examining the facets and implications.

"Today is the day that I truly learn what it means to be a Kartah.

Whether I fail or succeed I will know for sure that a Kartah's duties lie on a path far deeper than my future Aridaunt's whims. I will know that it is my duty to protect those weaker than myself and to bring to justice those who prey on those weaker than me."

Phoy was silent for a moment and answered, "I see. Then prepare yourself for a spectrum of emotion that few people experience. And even fewer people live through. Most people of your level who have tried this have been driven mad or have been killed in the process.

This is the last time as your Guild Master that I will ask you, are you sure you want to do this?"

There is no turning back, he thought.

"Yes," he answered without hesitation.

"Very well then, before you begin, you must learn some history. This Guild is built in a maze pattern. Today all students are waiting in the assembly chamber for you to emerge. Now, take this goblet and drink from the Fountain of Passage."

Phoy handed Grivon a golden goblet that had been sitting on the brown bricks of the fountain. Grivon walked over to the fountain and held it under a stream of the foul-smelling liquid. When he brought the goblet to his face the liquid was no longer purple but a spectrum of colors.

Grivon frowned and looked at Phoy and bowed his head and asked, "What is this?"

"What you make it. No more questions. Either drink it all in one swallow or be gone in shame!" he hissed.

Grivon nodded and put the goblet to his lips. He closed his eyes in anticipation for the worst taste of his life. When the cool liquid poured into his mouth, he was surprised at how sweet it was. The flavor was beyond words.

It burned his throat as it made its way down into his stomach. An uncomfortable warmth spread throughout his body. His first thought was that it was some sort of alcohol, but when he pulled the goblet away from his lips, his stomach shattered into glass.

He fell to the ground in a fetal position and clutched his bowels, knowing that in a moment the contents of his stomach would be spewed upon the cobble stone ground. Then the feeling subsided and he opened his eyes, but when he did, white-hot pain speared through his skull.

It felt as if a long-jagged nail had been driven into the back of his head. Grivon grabbed his head and screamed in pain. He lay on the ground and convulsed for what felt like hours until he passed out.

IV

When Grivon awoke, his head had stopped hurting, as had his stomach and bowels. He stood up and looked around the courtyard. Everything shimmered in crystalline rainbows. The ground beneath him spun under his feet and Phoy was nowhere in sight.

Grivon cursed foully at Phoy for his trickery and disregard for his wellbeing. Closing his eyes, he focused on the task at hand. Using a technique learned from one of the files he had stolen, he took seven deep breaths.

Upon opening his eyes, the world still looked as if it were sculpted from prismatic glass, but the ground was no longer spinning. He needed to find a weapon. Mustering the will to focus, he studied his surrounds.

The courtyard was not the same courtyard he had been in. In fact, he was sure he had never been to this one. He cursed a few fouler oaths and looked up into the sky. The sun had not yet reached its full height.

Sighing, he scanned the area around him as best as he could. Best he could tell there were three ways out. One way was clearly blocked by a large stonewall. The other two were clear. One went into a tunnel and went on straight forever. The other one went into a tunnel and made a sharp right angle.

Grivon noticed that the one that went on straight ran with the cardinal direction of west. It was better the sun be at his back in case it opened, because it seemed that if he looked anywhere near the sun his head would explode into a thousand tiny splinters.

He turned and began to walk when something long and shiny stuck in the ground to his left caught his eye.

With guarded steps, he walked over to the object. It was a saber. He pulled it free from the sand and gripped it tightly in his hand. A new confidence surged in him. I can do this ! I will not be led away in shame.

With his newfound confidence, he began trotting to the west where the long straight corridor was located. As he passed into the tunnel, he saw something shimmer ahead. It was too far away to make out. Then when he was almost upon it, he realized what it was. It was Ubiroe.

Grivon's heart leapt into his throat. She ran toward him with her sword raised. Panic took hold. Electricity surged through his skull making him take a hasty stance. Ubiroe charged faster, and as she closed in, he sliced her in half. The image disappeared. Suddenly, the sound of rain filled the tunnel, and the spray of her blood on his skin burned like acid.

Hot electric pain shot across his skin making him scream in agony. Looking down, his skin boiled and melted away exposing bone through dozens of marble sized holes. All he could do was move forward in hopes of escaping this hellish landscape.

Instead it got worse. Each time he saw a door of light at the end of a hallway, it opened into another crossroad. In each entrance he ran into, there Ubiroe stood. Fear began to take control of his mind. His heart pounded hard in his chest making his stomach tighten. Hot sticky sweat poured from every pore, and every turn he made, only increased the terror of the coming ambush, so he ran.

The more he ran the harder his heart pumped, and a gray blur began to encompass his sight. Then it all went black. He was falling.

He tumbled through darkness and into space and into the void again. His skin began to burn as he glimpsed the maw of Hell. Suddenly, he was sucked into a mirror and his skin ripped as the shining glass shattered and flayed him. Blood poured through the cuts, but it didn't matter.

He was still falling. Time morphed and stretched, and a hundred voices all yelled and called to him. The chant of his peers screeching, "Freak!" echoed through the tunnel of time and space.

A small light the size of a needle head appeared before him. It grew bigger, and brighter by the second, and he tumbled into plane of red sky and desolate sand, he was surrounded by a circle of a hundred Ubiroes, each one holding a sword point to his throat. All of them unabashedly naked and each one asked if he was finished.

Without hesitation, he stabbed one of the women in the throat and then cut his wrist with the small end of the sword, but the sky melted and changed. They were all on a planet with no sky just stars shimmering in darkness.

Grivon paused to look around and that's when the Ubiroe's started getting closer. They each had a gleeful sneer on their face and swords raised.

Grivon cursed. In his confusion, he lost the form, so he had to repeat it. This time instead of stopping a centimeter above the ground, he buried the sword into the sandy footing. The planet erupted in an explosion of lava and magma.

And in an instant, he was hovering above the planet to watch it cleave in half in a fiery eruption. He looked down and saw that he still held his sword and fell backwards through another mirror.

When he landed, he was faced with the most terrifying sight he had seen that day. Barbarah was standing before him in nothing but a small loincloth holding a sword. He lowered his sword and walked over to her, smiling, and went to embrace her.

Instead of embracing him back, she swung the sword at him. Confused Grivon jumped back and took a guarded stance and asked in a worried tone, "What's wrong my love?"

"You!" she shouted. "All you care about is yourself and your stupid conquest of this solar system. You left me to raise your child while you went off to conquer worlds. She died. I was left with Steven to take comfort.

"He defiled me!" She shrieked. "Why weren't you there to stop him?" Tears were streaming from her face and he started sobbing. He fell to his knees in front of Barbarah. She walked over to him and bent down close to his ear and whispered, "And even though I was forced to his will, he is still a better lover than you ever were. I even had his child. This one lived, and we named him Terry."

Grivon sobbed harder as Barbarah withdrew from his ear. He looked up with a plea in his eyes, and when he did, Ubiroe stood where Barbarah once had, but it was her head on Barbarh's body.

Grivon gripped the hilt of the sword so hard he felt his knuckles split against the metal guard. He punched Ubiroe in the face with the guard of his saber. She screamed holding her broken nose. When she went to attack him, he severed her arm and leg.

As she fell to one knee, she no longer had Barbarah's body, but her own unattractive shell. Grivon gritted his teeth with the effort as he rammed the long end of his sword threw Ubiroe's forehead.

She blew into a thousand bloody pieces. Her devious demented laughter echoed through his brain until it subsided like thunder after a storm. The world turned upside down, and he fell once more into the fear that came with the knowledge he had failed.

Closing his eyes, he fell backwards through another mirror, the pain was stopped by a bottomless void that felt oddly like sleep. For the first time in months he felt peace. He heard a loud roar and then his head exploded into a million white-hot splinters of agony.

Once the pain subsided, he felt the peace again. He embraced it and prepared himself for death.

V

Grivon awoke with a jolt. Eyes fluttering, he took in his surroundings. Barbarah, Steven and Phoy were standing over him. Looking past them, he saw the ceiling of the infirmary. He sat up in the bed he was laying on and saw the myriad cuts and scrapes on his arms and legs.

There were others elsewhere, but he couldn't see them. Focusing on Barbarah to the exclusion of everyone else; he looked deep into her eyes. She was a sea of emotions. He gave a weak smile that was returned with a large toothy smile. Then shook his head. The last time he had seen her she was distraught and was about to kill him.

Unable to hold it in any longer, he blurted out, "Please tell me, do you still love me even though I failed the gauntlet?"

Barbarah's smile disappeared, "Why do you ask such hurtful questions when it is such a wonderful day to celebrate?"

The Chronicles of Merkadiah:
The Rise of the Gryphon

Grivon sat stunned. *Was it a dream* ? He shook his head to try and get the fuzzy feelings out of his head. After he cleared his head, he looked to Steven and Phoy and asked in a highly irritated voice, "What is she talking about?"

Phoy began to chuckle, "You passed the gauntlet in record time. You flew through it in a matter of one hundred fifty minutes."

"What?" was all Grivon could mutter.

This time Phoy cackled like a mad man. Then spoke in a hoarse voice with a slightly childish edge to it, "Aw, what is the matter? Do you not remember?"

Grivon shook his head no.

"The liquid in the fountain is a slight neuro-poison. When taken it begins to work almost immediately. Under normal circumstances, the poison would have killed you, but since you have the Aurora, it draws the poison straight to the brain and then the chip filters out the harmful parts and then it is pumped through out your body causing an intoxicating effect at first.

Then as it soaks into the body, various neurological centers and cardiovascular system it causes an effect that can only be described as madness. It is known as Ayahuasca.

"Overcoming this physical as well as psychological assault is what the gauntlet is all about. Not to mention that fact that throughout the maze several hundred Wergare clones were scattered with the express programing to try their best to kill you.

"You my young friend ran through the maze like a demon. You screamed unintelligible words throughout the whole thing. You would slice through several clones only to fall and be surrounded by a sizable number and then in a swift dancing like motion cut through them.

Then at the end, there was one last one and you began to cry and plead for it not to be angry with you and to always love you. Then after a few minutes of the groveling, you snarled like a rabid animal and killed the clone in a brutal combination of the Thread of Life form and the Thay're form. It was quite gory."

Grivon sat stunned that's not how I remember it happening.

"So, you poisoned me and pit me against myself and at least five hundred single-minded clones? So, that was it?"

Phoy's smile turned to a frown, "Well if it was so easy, then why the hell did it take you a week to wake up?"

121

Grivon was taken aback. *A week, had it already been that long?* He felt as if he had just laid down to sleep five minutes earlier. *Amazing.*

"Sorry Phoy. It's just that it's finally over and now I can be trained by you. Correct?"

"Well," Phoy began. "Not exactly. You will have to find your way to my planet and then I will train you. Don't worry I will be there before you get there. In fact, it will probably end up being at least a year before you figure out where I am."

Grivon nodded and then Phoy and Steven turned around and left. He was slightly annoyed that Steven didn't talk and that Phoy would just turn around and walk off like he did, but the one who loved him was still there.

Lying back, he looked deep into her eyes, and let his mind sink

into her. Barbarah put a hand on his forehead, and he closed his eyes. Sinking into her touch, he let her soft hand stroke his cares away. She rubbed his hair and face for a long time before she spoke, "It was bad, wasn't it?"

Grivon nodded and before he even knew what he was doing the words and emotions poured out of his mouth like a broken bottle. He told her about the dreams and about the visions he had while facing the Wergare. Barbarah sat and listened to him for over an hour as he told her about his torment after the Tournament.

When he was finished, she smiled and said, "I can tell that she really got to you. It's okay. As long as you love me and care for me in the years to come then everything will be fine. I just wish I could go with you, but then I would have to face the gauntlet and fail.

Even then, I know that I am nowhere near ready to face the horrors that lie within my own shattered mind," her voice trailed off, and he noticed her eyes went hollow.

Regarding her for a moment, he reached up to caress her face. The light came back in her eyes and she slowly made her way back to the present. Sleep started pulling at his eyes and he looked at her lovely gaze and yawned.

"Stay with me until I'm better," he nuzzled his check against her warm arm. Barbarah answered him by kissing him lightly on the forehead.

Political Interludes

K'datra

The sky was dark with everlasting snow clouds. It was always cold on Hades. At least it wasn't dark like on Semiramus, where it snowed and was dark most of the time. K'datra Dater hated living on the moon. He missed living on Tygrano. There the sun would warm his mane and fur. The beautiful moonlight would illuminate the veldts.

Home was not the ghetto where he and half the Pantherine race lived. The Leonis and the Tigris lived in horrid conditions. The moon was nothing more than a dirty city that stretched half the landscape.

The other half was owned by an Aridaunt named Lord Arik Small. Arik was a corrupt, sadistic bastard. He came into the camps and took the most beautiful of the young queens. The title of Lord was reserved for honorable men like Trey Satah, not evil sadists.

At least Trey had shown remorse for killing K'datra's father. Now war was upon them and Lord Arik was about to deliver the final blow to the Pantherines. They were considered nothing but vermin to most people, but the last Autocrat had given them the chance to better themselves.

Visas for work, and other subsidies were given out but only for a few short weeks. The engineers were busy digging trenches for the upcoming battle. The fields before had once been where the humans farmed for roots.

However, he had ordered that all the serfs be captured and killed. From where he stood, K'datra could see the outline of the palace of Lord Arik.

The Leonis' units would lie down in the trenches with weapons that were stolen from the armory a few months earlier. They would use suppressive fire to keep the human soldiers out of the way so that the Tigris units could get in close and force them into the crossfire.

Tactical analysis was a key part of any battle. He wasn't sure what the Lepridis and the Chisis had done on Semiramus, but it wasn't pretty. Thankfully, some Leonis units had been deported from other worlds to Semiramus for violation of work visas, so now the Great War would begin.

Three days prior K'datra received a visual call from someone in a mask. She had a beautiful feminine voice and called herself Sekhet. She had told them that the Winged God was about to reveal himself and that they should mobilize.

The Chronicles of Merkadiah:
The Rise of the Gryphon

At first, he had been weary, but as they talked, he realized their goddess could take whatever form she wanted. K'datra had sent visuals to other tribal leaders that Sekhet had come at last and that The Gryphon was coming. Everyone had wept, and now they were ready to die to see freedom once and for all.

That was all they wanted. Pantherine males were so willing to be free that they sold themselves to the Orsin crime family, and the females sold themselves as prostitutes to human men who wanted something exotic. That thought spiked a deep anger in him.

Lord Arik had a taste for the exotic; he would violate the queens, kill them, and eat them. He would then take their hides and hang them in his chambers as trophies. Arik was sick beyond words, one of the most depraved humans in Merkadiah.

Arik would be in the nice section of city he constructed. There he had pleasure dens where the females were sold to other depraved humans. Suddenly, an idea began forming in his mind.

He could destroy Arik on his way home from the pleasure dens. He often stayed there until late in the night. K'datra signaled for a squad of Tigris scouts. They walked over and knelt before him. K'datra took a moment to look them over.

The leader was at least two and a half meters tall with thick obsidian and ginger stripes. At that moment, he decided the terrifying Tigris would be good for a future mission. If he survived the one K'datra was about to give him.

"I want you to go into the city and watch for Lord Arik. Plant the explosives we stole from the armory about six strides up the street. When he walks by, destroy him. Are these instructions clear?" said K'datra.

The squad nodded as one and saluted. They ran off to see the command finished. K'datra smiled to himself, no one would have thought that in almost five hundred years the Pantherine tribes would unite once more and stand together against their oppressors.

Arik

Lord Arik was washing his hands. He always washed his hands after skinning a queen. Licking his lips, he thought about what had just happened. She had been a lithe and gorgeous Tigris queen. Hours before, he watched her dance in his brothel.

Now he looked at her broken body lying on the bed of the booth of his brothel. He loved Pantherines. They were so much like humans but so different. Queens had one pair of breasts like those on a human, but also had four smaller nipples that stretched all the way down their bodies to only a few centimeters over their bellies. Sensual and majestic, they oozed strength and charisma.

Arik licked his lips with ecstasy. He was getting excited again. Euphoria washed over him, bathing him pleasures he only felt after loving a queen. Desiring another queen, he pinched his wrist to calm down.

Having been with the one on the bed for over three hours was enough. Continuing to clean his hands, he considered the mirror in front of him and studied the handsome features of his face. His piercing green eyes studied the high cheek bones, and well-oiled jet-black hair.

Truly, his features were chiseled by the hand of God Himself. Running a wet hand through his hair, he shuddered. More than the feel of a Pantherine pelt, he loved the slick feel of his hair. Moreover, he liked the glossy feeling of blood between his fingers when he skinned a queen.

It was a powerful feeling knowing that he was the last person she would see for the rest of eternity. It was all so invigorating that he was given such free reign over his fief that he felt invincible.

Arik walked out through the main entrance of the pleasure house. On his way out, he saw a few Chisis queens he wanted. However, he needed to control himself. If he didn't, he would have more pelts than cats and lose money.

He looked around at the orgy of humans and Pantherines. Charging four hundred credits for a quarter of a standard hour, he made money hand over fist. It was good to profit from a fief with no natural resources, or peasants to exploit.

He didn't have to pay taxes and could keep his security force well feed and housed in warm barracks. A slight chill in the air made him shiver, as he stepped out on to the street. The sun was setting and Semiramus was sinking behind the horizon at the same time, painting the perfect ending to a wonderful day.

Beginning his walk down the main street of the small city of Herdaron to his opulent palace; he passed by a dark storefront. For a moment several pairs of bright shining eyes shimmered in the window.

His spine tingled and he stepped back. All his senses on alert, he looked around again but saw nothing. Shrugging, he walked on down the street and started whistling his favorite song.

As he rounded a corner that led to barracks, his mind turned to the new pelt he had acquired. She had been a fantastic choice, and the time they had shared was wonderful. The way her face contorted in pain when he drove his dagger through her heart, would be forever burned into his mind.

Just like the faces of countless other queens. He was about three meters from the door when he saw two pairs of

shining yellow eyes. He looked hard at them, drawing his saber. An overwhelming feeling of dread washed over him. Only one other time had he felt this way; was when he lost her. He took the Pressure stance and prepared himself for combat.

Before he could yell a challenge, the eyes blinked out and the sidewalk on which he stood erupted into a sea of blue and yellow waves of heat. His legs disintegrated, and sharp sudden pain exploded in the back of his head, followed by a paralyzing pain that filled his spine.

A cocoon engulfed his body and he slipped from this world. The last thing he remembered was splashing into a large tank of stinking thick liquid. Then it all went black. The Tigris unit ran as fast as they could all while laughing and cackling in a din of roars. Lord Arik may not have been dead, but he would be out of their fur for about a century.

The Great War was beginning, and they had just struck a blow into the heart of the Senate. An Aridaunt would need replacing and hopefully, it would be one less depraved than the one that was just sent to Hell.

Martxapahn

The only sound in the deserted hall was the heavy footfalls echoing off marble floors. The footsteps were made by a man in a magenta robe, ruby mask, and a walking cane with a large Alexandrite head.

He kept a slow measured pace as he approached the Senate chambers. His high heeled boots tapping out the cadence by which he walked. He had been able to keep the cane as he walked into the Senate building.

The Depublic Guard had checked it repeatedly trying to make sure it wasn't a weapon. To their credit, they didn't realize it was a weapon.

As he reached the door, he could hear shouting coming from within the chambers. The man opened the ornately carved oak doors. When he walked into the chamber, the shouting stopped, and all heads turned to look at the unusual character that had just walked in.

His gray eyes surveyed the room like a hawk scanning for prey. After he had taken in the group of Aridaunts, Kofahs, Depublics, Lobbyists, Governors and lesser Aides, he turned his raptor gaze toward the Autocrat.

He grinned when he saw the Autocrat swallow hard. The man began to walk once again in his slow measured pace as he approached the raised seats of the Autocrat and his two Depublics. The Depublics gave each other nervous looks as the man approached the three men.

The Autocrat stood and pointed to the strange man and spoke in an angry voice, "Who let you in here!" The Autocrat demanded.

The man's lips went thin as he smiled. He chuckled a little bit to himself and then spoke in a voice that showed of colloquial training and practice, "Well it didn't take too much persuasion with the Depublic Guard.

They saw my outfit and let me in. If you didn't want visitors, then perhaps you shouldn't have doors."

The Autocrat opened his mouth to speak but he stopped when the man in the magenta robes removed his mask. He looked human for the most part, but he had distinct features on his face that were almost feline.

The man's eyes had the pupils of a cat. His ears were slightly pointed in an elfin fashion. His nose was almost like that of a tiger's and he was extremely hairy. The hair on his head was the brightest auburn and had what looked like solid black stripes in it. The hair around his face and neck was also like this.

128

The Chronicles of Merkadiah:
The Rise of the Gryphon

"What are you?" asked The Autocrat with a tremble in his voice.

"I'm what you in this filth hole call anathema, a second-generation Therian."

Whispers echoed throughout the chambers. After the sudden burst of whispers stopped The Autocrat asked, "What the hell is a Therian?"

The man laughed, "A human-Pantherine hybrid. We sometimes come out of the unnatural union of a human and a Pantherine. I just happen to be two generations removed from my origins. But as you can see, I still bare the curse that haunts my genetics."

"What brings you here?" asked the Depublic to the left of The Autocrat.

"I thought you would never ask," said the man with a smirk and a twinkle in his eyes, "Allow me to introduce myself. I am Martxapahn Maximillia Xóa II."

This time instead of whispers, it was shouts. The members of the Senate began to hiss and shout at him. He bore the name of the enemy that took over sixty years to purge from the system.

"How does an abomination like you even exist?" cried a Kofah from the far left of the chamber. Martxapahn smirked again, "Before Lord Xóa was killed by that dwarf, he mated with a Tigris queen, and my father was born, Martxapahn Maximillia Xóa.

When he was born, my grandmother was forced from the tribe. She tried to seek sanctuary here with Xóa. Nevertheless, by then the Purging was in full bloom. So, after several years of running and hiding she and my father were accepted by a large family of peasants.

There he was accepted and married my mother who had me. She gave me the name of my father as he was killed in a Kartesian raid on our village on Tūhl.

"So not wanting me to lack a proper place in this world she gave me over to the Chaos guild. There I graduated in fifty years only to be shunned by every piece of slag in this chamber, so I went back to Tūhl to see my family.

When I arrived, I found my mother's house burned and left in an empty city. When I was finally able to find my family, they had almost been destroyed by the Kartah whelps that each of you use to further your positions, so I united them with other peasants.

"They all came together easily under the banner of The Barrim clan."

A single shocked shout echoed through the chamber. Martxapahn turned to see an Aridaunt clamoring toward him. He was wearing all white and his face was exposed. He stomped straight up to Martxapahn and stopped.

He put his hands on his hips and leaned forward his brow furrowed, and his eyes narrowed. Martxapahn stood several inches over the short bald man giving him the satisfaction of knowing he could end him at any point.

"Count Moa-Ing, stand down. This man has not asked to challenge you to a duel," shouted The Autocrat.

"This worthless abomination has been killing my Kartah!" Chin screamed.

"That may be so, but he has not requested that the forms be met."

Growling slightly Chin spit at the feet of Martxapahn and stormed away, but before he was five feet away from the abomination, he heard him growl. It echoed around the chamber like a thunderclap.

All the color drained from Chin's face as he turned around to face the Therian. He stood face to face with a mouth full of razor-sharp fangs.

"Do you wish to declare the forms for a duel?" asked The Autocrat with a slight air of mockery in his voice.

"Yes!" hissed Martxapahn.

The Autocrat clapped his hands and two guards brought a weapon for each man. Martxapahn declined as he held out his cane. He twirled it over his head, and it turned into a katana. He gripped it in both hands and took a stance holding it over his head. No sooner had he taken the stance than he thrust at Chin.

The Autocrat looked on in shock that the Depublic Guard would let a weapon into the chamber, but it was moot now. The duel was under way and it was time to watch with interest.

Chin wasted no time in deflecting the blow and counter attacked. Martxapahn quickly dodged the strike. Chin huffed, regained his footing, and struck out again. Martxapahn blocked the halfhearted attack, flourished, and struck home severing Chin's arm.

The severed arm fell to the ground and Chin screamed loudly. Then Martxapahn cut Chin in half before the teleportation could take effect. Chin's body fell to the ground and his upper torso was teleported away leaving a severed set of legs and an arm.

The Autocrat clapped his hands and stood up, "Bravo, dear friend. What would you like in exchange for your victory?"

Martxapahn looked at him and smirked, "His fiefdoms."

"Done, but you will need Kartah."

"Already done," Martxapahn clapped his hands and the doors of the chamber burst open and five stunning women walked in. Each one had short platinum spiked hair and piercing green eyes.

Each wore sky blue robes with a katana stuffed into the sash and what appeared to be a long baton on the opposite side.

"Who are these women?" demanded The Autocrat

"Five of my strongest sisters, we will take over Chin's fiefs and holdings and then when he gets out of rejuvenation, I will do it all over again for what he did to my mother."

The Autocrat nodded, "I would ask that you and your sisters begin to wear the proper attire for Aridaunts and Kartah. I do not object to your cane, but the robes and mask must be changed. Also, in the future see to it that if you wish to challenge someone in a duel you submit the forms a week in advance."

Martxapahn nodded wordlessly and walked over to where Chin once sat and sat down in his black leather chair. He slid up to the round table and looked over the paperwork lying before him. His sisters went and stood at the wall where the other Kartah stood waiting for orders.

The other Kartah eyed them uneasily. The girl in the middle looked at one and showed him her studded tongue, flicked it up and down, then winked. The Kartah's eyes went wide and he snapped back to looking forward without emotion.

Theo

Damn it!" shouted Theo slamming his fist down onto his desk. Papers scattered everywhere. He had just received a report that Grivon D'Gaul had passed the gauntlet and set a record. It took most normal people several hours to complete their respective gauntlets.

It wasn't fair. This time instead of pounding his thrice-sore fist on the desk, he picked up a penholder and chucked it across his office. It hit the wall and shattered, sending pieces of ceramic flying across the room.

Cursing foul oaths, he stood up knocking over his chair. Enraged at his lack of self-control, he turned around and kicked the chair across the room. The chair clattered into a pile of tangled wood.

Seeing white, Theo growled like a caged animal and began jumping up and down on the broken chair, breaking even more of the damaged wood. As he jumped up and down on his chair, he called out several curses that he made up off the top of his head, along with a steady stream of "Damn Its."

It had been a very stressful day. The incident involving Martxapahn was stressful enough due to him filling several requests for tournaments and duels. Theo kicked the remains of his chair and let out one last stream of vile profanity. He had to see what the Jackal's thoughts on Grivon were.

Theo walked to his Network terminal and typed in the call codes for the Jackal. The Jackal answered in a terse tone, "What do you want?"

"Grivon D'Gaul has now become a Kartah."

"Not yet. He is still healing. His ceremony hasn't happened yet."

"Then, can he be taken care of beforehand?"

The Jackal chuckled, "No. He is still under Guild protection, but once he leaves the Guild to find Phoy Yin he will be extremely vulnerable. I will send the best assassin in the Assassin Guild, and this one I intend on keeping."

Theo knew what his employer was talking about. When he had taken power, the Scorpion was supposed to be captured and then released in three days, but he was killed by overeager loyalists to the previous Autocrat. Those troublesome ants had been stamped from existence.

Theo was aware of someone screaming at him. He shook himself, as he was jolted back to reality.

"Is that all!" the Jackal screamed.

"Yes sir," stammered Theo.

"Good," purred the Jackal, and the screen went blue.

Forgetting about his tantrum earlier, Theo went to sit back in his chair and fell on the floor.

Xiao Zhang

It had been three months since Karen had passed away during childbirth. She had been such a lovely caring woman, mused Lady Zhang. She and her husband had always wanted a child but could never have one.

Having been close friends of the Satah's Lady Zhang and her husband, Count Lin Zhang had adopted little Sio Satah. Lady Zhang was feeding him in his nursery when a beep for a visual message on her Network console went off.

Frowning slightly, she, laid Sio down in his crib and walked across the large room. Lady Zhang and Lin had decorated it for everything a little boy would need growing up, from toys all the way to books and puzzles.

Lady Zhang and Lin had such high hopes for him that they even thought about sending him to the water guild to try and follow in his father's footsteps.

When Lady Zhang reached the console, she sighed and straightened her hair a little bit before hitting the receive button. When she did, all color drained from her face. It was the new Aridaunt, Martxapahn.

He wore his magenta mask, but she knew what he looked like underneath, ugly.

"What a pleasant surprise Lord Martxapahn," began Lady Zhang with a hint of disdain in her voice. "How can I help you today?"

"I was wondering if Count Zhang were about today? He has left Ormah for a while, so I was hoping to catch him at home."

"I am afraid that he is not here. He does have several fiefdoms to look after and quite a few Kartah to manage, so he could be anywhere. I can try and find him if you like."

"Oh, it's no bother. I wanted to invite him to a party in honor of my latest achievement."

"Oh, and what is that?"

"The acquisition of three new fiefdoms, it puts me up to one third of the fiefs in the system. I was hoping to have you and your husband come to Nomah for the most opulent masquerade in over a century.

Even the Autocrat himself is coming. I hope that you and your husband would honor me with your presence?"

The Chronicles of Merkadiah:
The Rise of the Gryphon

Bowing slightly as the custom of her and her husband's families over the course of several millennia Lady Zhang answered, "We would be honored to be there," Lady Zhang turned off the console and swore a violent oath.

Having heard her uncharacteristic behavior Lin walked into the nursery. Lady Zhang turned and looked at her husband. He opened his mouth to speak but before he could she did, "We have been invited to a masquerade on Nomah."

"Well that's wonderful news, so why the heavy swearing?" asked Lin with a light chuckle in his voice.

"Lord Martxapahn was the one to invite us."

All color drained from Lin's face. He started to speak but was cut off once more by his wife.

"He is celebrating having conquered a third of the system. If he keeps it up, we will not be able to hold on to our fiefdoms and then we will have no income and wind up on the streets, or worse."

Sighing heavily Lin said, "Xiao, we need not worry. Remember I am a Kofah now and everything will be fine. I will still have some control over things if we lose our current Aridaunts, he cannot challenge a Kofah even if he did control all of the system, he cannot progress any further than an Aridaunt until a Depublic dies and one of us gets promoted."

Xiao and Lin embraced lovingly. It was a scary time, but all would be made right in the fullness of time. As they were enjoying their moment of intimacy, a high-pitched wail echoed through the room. Sio was still hungry.

K'datra

K'datra Dater sat in Lord Arik's throne room. The former Aridaunt had overseen a single special fief. He was not limited to Senate duties. He was free to do as he wished and was given a small grant of money to run the ghettos, and that had led to Arik opening the Pantherine Pleasure House.

Now K'datra was sitting on Arik's throne and was about to host The Feast of Sekhet. The throne room was a large cavernous hall with large ruby red tiles contrasted by obsidian tiles forming a checkerboard pattern all through the room.

The pelts of countless queens lined the walls giving this room an eerie macabre feel. Once the feast was over, he would have his newly acquired human servants take them down.

The Feast of Sekhet was a sacred rite that dated back to when the Pantherine civilization started. Once a year the Leonis would have a great hunt, and all the Leonis cubs that had proven themselves during the hunt would be granted permission to grow a mane.

Growing a mane was only allowed by the fiercest hunters or warriors if the clans of the Leonis had gone to war, but this feast was to be different. The cubs that had proven themselves in the battle for Hades were to be given manes, but first there was a small amount of business to take care of.

K'datra was going to send a message to the Aridaunts in the Senate. If he could cause enough damage, then the Senate would realize that it had been wrong to force them into a corner. Once a Pantherine was forced into a corner, he came out with the blood of the other on his fur.

It was time to begin Operation Shadow Kat. The operation's commander was named Kossahk D'Alred, or Kossahk Aridaunt's Bane. He was now held in high regard with his tribe.

K'datra looked over the tall beast of a Pantherine. He was taller than most and his girth exceeded that of most normal Pantherines, but he was all muscle. Each of his black and red stripes was one paw wide and his rare green eyes held an unrequited fury that came from a spurned heart.

Kossahk's queen had left him to go work in Arik's pleasure house. She had said that mating with humans sounded exciting and that she hoped to have a Therian. She never completed her goal. Arik had singled her out and had killed her after she had been there only a couple of days.

The Chronicles of Merkadiah:
The Rise of the Gryphon

The way Kossahk had found out was he had gone to drag her back but saw Arik with her pelt. Overcome with grief and rage, Kossahk tried to kill Arik, but Arik was trained as one of those damnable Kartah.

Arik wrestled Kossahk to the ground and pinned him. Arik told him that if he ever stepped foot in the pleasure house again that he would not live to see another sunrise, so when K'datra needed a commander to lead Operation Shadow Kat he immediately thought of Kossahk.

Kossahk was cold and calculating. He had learned all he could about explosives when the Tigris scouts had raided Arik's armory. After the battle of Hades, Kossahk had immersed himself in the construction of improvised explosives, making him one of the deadliest warriors K'datra had ever known.

If the politicians and Aridaunts didn't wake up and notice the destructive power of the cornered "animal," no one would.

"Kossahk, the time has come that you and your handpicked team commence Operation Shadow Kat," K'datra boomed.

"I was hoping that you could tell me which planets we are supposed to target." Kossahk said kneeling and bowing low before the Leonis.

"The planets you are to target should be ones with a large population and preferably ones that have at least an Aridaunts palace. The object is to inflict fear in our enemies. I hope that you will succeed.

If you come across Martxapahn's palace, don't destroy it. He is still considered one of us. Even though he is part human, he is still a Pantherine in heart and is fighting for us." At least that is what I would like to believe, K'datra said to himself.

Kossahk nodded his head and said, "I would like to requisition a few more scouts. I have an idea for some of the missions. Who would want to die for you? Who do you know would be willing to die for our cause?"

K'datra thought and then smiled a large tooth filled smile, and said, "Use the prisoners. Tell them that if they help you and your unit get into the human worlds, they can be absolved and then they and their families can find someplace else to live."

Kossahk smiled, "Release the prisoners only to have them die. I like that; it's poetic."

"Good, I'm glad that you can be happy, if only for a moment."

Kossahk

Baktüth was a planet whose topography was nothing but water. It had taken the better part of three hundred years to build the single vast city that covered less than a quarter of the planet. The rest of the planet was littered with large mining platforms and hydroponic farms.

Baktüth, unlike most planets with vast seas, was entirely fresh water. People could drink the water straight from the ocean, but in the areas around Buthak and the platforms most people were afraid of pollution in the water, so large aqueducts were built on the other side of the planet to bring fresh water to the main city and the surrounding platforms.

Baktüth's entire economy was based on its banking, hydroponic farms, sea food, and undersea titanium mines. Additionally, this was the only planet controlled by the Baron Simon D'Shovah. He had limited Senate duties, but mostly just managed commerce of his fiefdom.

Seven barely dressed humans carrying a large amount of luggage and seven tall hooded men stepped through the teleportation gate into the transportation hall. The large room was filled with Transportation Agents and bustling travelers.

There were several gates letting people transport onto the planet as well as several letting others leave. Some of the travelers were farmers or fishermen off to visit family or take a short vacation.

Others were bankers and businessmen. Still others were Aridaunts or political aides conducting personal business. Buthak was the largest center of commerce for the entire system.

The travelers were an imposing bunch, making everyone in the transportation hall pause for a moment before returning to their business. Not swayed by the gawking, the intrepid travelers continued on their course.

The motley group approached the security area. It had six gates and each gate had a booth with a uniformed person checking weapons and bags. This was to make sure no firearms were to be brought into the city.

The only people that could carry firearms or swords were the Baktüth Guards. They were specially trained security personal specializing in urban combat. The Baktüth Guard would often conduct mock battles within the city to perfect their response time.

The Chronicles of Merkadiah:
The Rise of the Gryphon

These drills usually took place during a busy day so that the Guard could work around people trying to flee the city. The group stuck together and got in a line filled with bankers. The seven human travelers were dressed in sackcloth robes and were carrying several bags each.

Kossahk and his unit were garbed in long brown hooded robes. The hoods were long enough to cover their faces. They waited for several minutes as people before them walked through the turnstile and into the city.

"Welcome to Buthak, the only city of Baktüth. Do you have anything to declare?" asked the female guard. She looked like she had seen lots of strange things come through the gate which helped calm Kossahk's nerves.

"We are members of the old Scion religion. We have our belongings to declare and invoke our right of religious exclusion."

"I have never heard of such a group. What planet do you hail from?"

"We jumped from Ne-Le to Hades to here. Would you like to trace our jumps?" said the human in the front.

"That won't be necessary. Please state your business here."

"We are here to bring the word of Enlightenment to Baron D'Shovah."

"You have four days. You probably won't be able to get an audience, so best of luck. Remember to be here in four days to return to your original destination, otherwise you could be arrested."

"Thank you, where can we stay?"

"I will give you a list of inns and pleasure hotels that you can stay at with, the one nearest the Baron's Palace circled."

"Thank you miss. Have an enlightened day."

The group walked through the turnstile and out onto the streets of Buthak. Most of the humans had never seen buildings so tall and none of the Pantherines ever had. The smallest building was at least forty floors.

Most of the buildings were housing apartments, inns or pleasure hotels. The others were a mixture of bureaucratic suites or some sort of government building. Other buildings were dedicated to the Senate run banking industry. There were only six banks for the system to choose from.

There was Anthony Security Investments, a newer bank that had just opened with in the last few weeks. There was the D'Shovah co-op banking group. Another of the banks was Satah Limited.

Other lesser banks were also in the buildings, but the group could care less about banks or the size of the buildings; they were there to find the Baron's palace.

After wandering the streets for several hours, they found the inn circled on the paper. It was right across the street from the Baron's Palace. The palace was surrounded by a large black iron fence.

It had a large green yard and bushes cut into shapes of animals. The palace itself was a large white mansion that had seven pillars which held up a balcony which ran the length of the house with a single double door as the only way onto it. Kossahk swore a vile oath.

"It's too well guarded," he said. "He probably has two or three battalions of The Baktüth Guard in there. There has to be some way to get the explosives in under that palace."

Kossahk then began to survey the surrounding area. There were two extremely tall buildings on both sides that if they fell the right way they could fall onto the palace. Then as Kossahk was turning to look at the rest of the group, he saw a service-hole cover in the street.

If the underside of the streets were like the ones on Hades, then he could plant explosives on the underside of the palace. In addition, he would set up a row of smoke cylinders for when the guards came running. Hopefully he could also still bring down those two buildings.

Considering they were both banks, and it would seem more horrible if he could get three buildings instead of one.

The sewer tunnels were easy to navigate and even easier to walk. There was a path on either side of the foul river large enough for three Pantherines to walk side by side, and the damned river was too far to jump.

This forced him to try and find some sort of bridge or crossing. Kossahk noticed that every few meters a large pipe dumped a thick, inky liquid into streams that joined the river of filth. He walked over to one and touched it. It smelled familiar and felt sticky.

He wracked his brain trying to figure out how he knew the substance, but he couldn't light a candle to recall. Shrugging, he led his team through the well-lit maze of paths and tunnels.

After a long time, he heard the sound of crashing water. They had found a bridge to cross the river and walk back to where a group of several large pipes dumped a combination of the strange inky substance and sewage.

The Chronicles of Merkadiah:
The Rise of the Gryphon

As the group crossed, they looked over the bridge at the filthy waterfall. The foul-smelling river ran over a spillway into a large gaping pipe. He looked over as far as he could and noticed several smaller pipes splitting off the larger one and being monitored by machines.

One pipe read, "Reclamation." Another read, "Solid Waste," and another read, "Reclaimed Water." At least they were trying to keep pollution to a minimum, Kossahk thought as he walked to his waiting unit.

It took four hours but Kossahk had finished setting the explosives. He had put several pounds of selmar crystal under the drains of each building and the palace, but something still did not feel right. The grates he had placed the explosives inside were trickling that thick black liquid.

Kossahk was putting the last kilogram pouch of selmar up around the drains of the building on the left of the palace. He had just set the timer for two hours and twenty minutes and was getting ready to meet back up with the rest of the unit when he heard voices.

They were distant but coming his way. He drew his Kadar from under the brown robes. He put his right hand into the slip loop connected at the pommel of the weapon.

He waited as the two men approached. When they were within range, he slung the Kadar at the man on the right. The blade pierced the heart of the man and stuck into his chest. Kossahk jumped and pulled the blade from the dying man's heart. As soon as the blade was free, Kossahk decapitated the other man.

They threw the bodies into the foul river. Kossahk laughed as he ran. As he was running through the tunnels, he realized what that black inky liquid was. It was a fuel used in buildings to keep them warm in the cooler parts of the year. It was dumped after the cold season and reclaimed to use the next year.

Kossahk laughed as he said to himself, I think I over did it. It took Kossahk nearly the entire time he had set on the timers for him and his unit to reach the surface of the city. He confirmed that the smoke screen was in place.

Then each human was given a firearm from a pack kept by one of the scouts in the unit. Each Pantherine drew his Kadar and gave a shout. Suddenly Kossahk started running.

Then one of the scouts asked, "Why is Kossahk running so fast?"

Kossahk looked back as he was running, "This just happens to be the end of the cold session, so when I packed the selmar, the explosion will cause the fuel to combust. Let's just say this whole city is going to be a greasy smear in less than three minutes."

The rest of the group was just standing there when Kossahk shouted back, "If you don't run now you and the city will blow up!"

They all started running. As they began running, the first of the explosives began to go off. They all ran to the nearest teleportation station they could find. As they entered frightened people who had felt the first explosion began to run.

The people became even more frightened when the Pantherines and humans with them started to kill the guards and prepare to teleport wherever. Kossahk looked up to watch a news terminal as the two buildings on either side of the blown-out palace collapsed and fell in the opposite direction of the palace and crashed into the buildings on their sides.

It was a domino effect as tops of buildings fell to the streets at the same time, they became engulfed in flames like giant metal and glass trees.

Kossahk let out a roar of pleasure as he hopped into the teleportation gate.

Martxapahn

Martxapahn's ball went off without incident. Everyone was dressed beautifully. The Kartah, Aridaunts, Kofahs and Republic's all wore their robes. Their wives or dates each wore large Victorian dresses that matched the colors of the robes.

Everyone danced to a stringed quartet made up of two violinists, a violist and a cellist. They played the old minuets and gavottes brought with them from the Blue Star. They also played more contemporary music written by composers who understood the minds of the ancients from the Blue Star.

Despite his horrid looks and abrasive personality, Martxapahn had a deep appreciation for ancient history. He loved what the Scions called the Victorian era. He really liked that era due to the massive wars that raged for years.

He loved the ancient histories and cultures that had survived the wars. Little was known of the Blue Star culture but what had been recovered and sent out with the original settlers. He loved their archaic weapons and battle tactics.

The Blue Star's wars were brutal and killed millions, and that was what he wanted to do with Merkadiah. Purge those that had betrayed his grandfather and reestablish the reign of a Xóa.

Martxapahn sighed as he watched the ball. The palace that Martxapahn now owned once belonged to Moa-Ing Chin. The Gothic architecture was breathtaking, to say the least.

The palace that Chin had commissioned looked a lot like a cathedral. It had a high ceiling that was supported by flying buttresses and was three stories tall. The area where Martxapahn was holding the ball was what the cleaning staff and servants had referred to as The Grand Audience Chamber. The room was over three hundred thousand square feet. The walls were made of a black stone that Martxapahn had never seen before. At the back of the room was a raised platform that had three small steps leading up to it.

At the very back of the platform sat a large armed swivel chair that had a Network console on the right arm and a visual screen on the left. The chair was mounted on a section of the floor that could rise into what looked like a giant pipe organ pipe.

This led to the second-floor balcony that overlooked the Grand Audience Chamber. From there he could continue to ride the chair up to the third floor where his private quarters and housing for his Kartah and house staff were located.

Martxapahn watched with pleasure as his guests waltzed to a Minuet. It was amazing at what the guilds taught. Some were finishing schools and others a place to learn tactical warfare, but they all taught ancient dance.

It was required learning to run the gauntlet, or so he was told. Martxapahn frowned in distress. The Autocrat was not there. He had invited the man. Of course, he had to send a message instead of a face to face conversation.

If he were a Depublic, he could have access to the Autocrat. That was when he decided that the plan to slowly kill off everyone ahead of him was futile. He could simply say that the First Depublic had wronged him in some way and challenge him to a duel.

This would give him access to half of Merkadiah and all the money he wanted. Not to mention he could influence the Autocrat and have the best access to kill him.

A servant brought a tray with a tall fluted champagne glass filled with a bubbling blue drink. Martxapahn took the glass and nodded to the servant. He stood up as more servants baring trays of the same drink came walking into the room from a door on the back-right side of the Grand Audience Chamber.

Once everyone had a glass, Martxapahn stood and walked to the edge of the top stair. He held the glass up and said, "A toast to the accomplishment of society for which some of us have lost loved ones.

Others have sacrificed their time and others, like me, have suffered the degradation of hatred. I know there aren't too many Therians running around, but my family has been spat upon by this government for the last four hundred years.

From the Mutiny, to Purging, to the overzealous taxation of my Barrim relatives, all the way to the oppression of the Pantherines, an ancient people who we forced from their home planets and packed into ghettos on cold, unlivable planets."

At this point, most of the people in the crowd had lowered their drinks and had disgruntled looks on their faces.

The Chronicles of Merkadiah:
The Rise of the Gryphon

"Many of you are wondering why I say these things. I say these things so that you will know that this ball which melds Victorian culture and Gothic architecture was designed by me to show you that I am not a lesser 'evolved' monster, but a civilized person who has earned his place in this society.

Please drink with me in this celebration of accomplishment," Martxapahn tilted the glass back and gulped the drink. When he was finished drinking everyone down in the ball dropped their glasses creating an echoing cacophony that threatened to deafen anyone still in the room. They filed out of the audience chamber to gather their effects and teleport home.

Martxapahn broke the empty glass in his hand and smiled. He was glad they were so honest with him. Especially since they would soon be his subjects under the rule of a new Xóa emperor, so he let them run like the vermin they were.

He decided to see what was on the Network. When he saw the media reports, he grinned wildly. His Pantherine relatives were finally lashing out.

They knew what was happening to them was wrong, but leveling an entire city was a little excessive considering it was the only city on that planet. Attacking them in the middle of the warm season purge was a touch on the side of overkill.

Though the Pantherines most likely didn't know that the city purged its heating fuel at that time, it was most likely an accident that the entire city was leveled.

Martxapahn smiled. The Senate would be convening soon. He could almost count on it. It was better to be early than late. Martxapahn pressed the button that would take him up to his quarters. He glided up into his personal quarters laughing.

It was time for him to exert himself as the rightful heir of Xóa and disband this corrupt system of government that now poisoned the people of Merkadiah.

In his confidence Martxapahn donned his magenta robes and mask. It was time to challenge the First Depublic and kill him. Then in a few days' time kill The Autocrat. It was all so intriguing, even to him.

He would soon control the whole of Merkadiah. Then that slimy killer of plans snuck into his head: Doubt. His mind's voice began to sow the seeds of doubt in his plans and he pondered, what if I fail? If the Autocrat did not allow the duel, then what he was going to do to show the members of the Senate that he was a lion with teeth?

In a flash of brilliance Martxapahn realized just how to do it. He and his fiefs would secede from the Senate and then he would do something that had been taboo for over two centuries. Declare open war.

Martxapahn ended up being slightly later than everyone else. Additionally, all the guests at his ball were there as well. It was as if they had left his palace and came right here. They had convened a session of voting without him, so he went and took his seat and pressed a purple button on the side of his Senate box.

This button lit up a red light with a number. It showed the Autocrat that an Aridaunt wished to take the floor and in what order he was to take it.

At this point, anyone who had wished to say something had already spoken. Martxapahn looked around at the Senate and noticed that all eyes were on him. That was when he realized dueling against the First Depublic would be out of the question. He was going to have to go ahead with his backup plan of open war.

"The Autocrat recognizes Lord Martxapahn," said the First Depublic flatly.

"Thank you," he began. "I will try and be as brief as possible. I can tell by the looks on your faces that you all have no doubt heard of the tragedy on Baktüth, and no doubt that is why you are here, but I have this feeling that you all are here about me as well. Am I correct?"

The Autocrat nodded and then said, "It has come to my attention that you are trying to position yourself into my seat. It has come to vote that due to the brash way you attend to your duties and that you have

had more Tournaments in your short reign than most Aridaunts have in a lifetime tells me that you think that once you control so much of Merkadiah that you can waltz up to my seat and take over.

Because of your brazen and unorthodox approach to our governmental system, an emergency session of this Senate was convened due to the terrorist attack on Baktüth. Once we decided on how to deal with the terrorist's; we voted for you to be stripped of your fiefdoms and executed for being the last remaining heir of Xóa.

Do you have anything to say for yourself?"

Martxapahn stood in stunned silence, thinking about what was just spoke. His body ached from the sudden verbal assault, leaving him stunned. A sudden primal rage frothed inside him making his right hand grip the alexandrite on the top of his cane until his fingers turned blue and blood started to pour from underneath his fingernails.

He clenched his teeth together so hard they began to grind and then somewhere deep within him he felt a scream. To him it was a silent scream of animalistic rage, but the members of the Senate covered their ears as a deafening roar escaped his throat and echoed through the cavernous chamber.

"Bastards all of you!" he roared. "You have awoken in me the beast that has slept for over a decade. I was going to be polite about this but as of now, my fiefs are under my direct rule. If you want them back either face me in open war or face me in combat!"

Martxapahn pointed to The Autocrat with fire burning in his eyes. Then he turned around and stormed out of the Senate chambers, forever vowing to destroy all that oppose him.

Jaymes Wenda

Recently promoted First Depublic Jaymes Wenda looked up to The Autocrat and whispered, "You just let him walk out with half of Merkadiah under his direct control. Why?"

Theo smirked and lowered his voice, "Because, I wish for war. It will give us a viable excuse for finally killing those damnable Pantherines once and for all. We can take back Hades and Semiramus in one fell swoop."

"Semiramus, I wasn't aware it fell."

The Autocrat smiled and said, "It fell this morning and this time all the humans were executed. Chisis lancers are nothing to underestimate.

Our under trained and useless security forces fell. Anyway, I have something important for you to do."

"Yes, my liege?" answered The First Depublic

"Raise taxes by four percent and conscript all useful men and women for training as soldiers. Also, give half the budget to the Department of Military Research. Doctor Nguyen has been whining about funding for several years now. Tell her that we need something that will go toe to toe with a Pantherine."

"You mean reopen the Chimera project?"

The Autocrat leaned forward smiling and said, "Exactly."

Jaymes sat looking up at Theo with a mental conflict raging inside his head. The use of "disposable" manpower to create the ultimate Pantherine killer was not just unethical, it was immoral. Cloning a human to use as a soulless slave was unethical but using the cloning process to add in the DNA of different animals, insects, and such was immoral.

Through several hundred years of research, it was found that all animals and the like were found to have very slight differences genetically between humans. So, it was said by Doctor Susan Nguyen who was the most respected authority in genetic research. Jaymes set aside his thoughts on the Chimera project to think about a battle on his home world Tūhl.

To save him from being mutilated as a young boy his mother had sent him off to the Water Guild. There he was safe from the matriarchal rule of the Barrim Clan. It was time to show those women that a man can help them. Not to mention he might be able to get close enough to Martxapahn to kill him, but he was going to have to sacrifice his position.

Even if he could stave off a whole army of Wergare soldiers on his own, The Autocrat would execute him for treason. It was an act of patriotism toward his home world. Even though none of the planets had any autonomy, people from them still had a deep sense of patriotism toward their home planets.

Jaymes was brought out of his thoughts when The Autocrat said, "Jaymes are you all right?"

"Yes sir," said Jaymes. "I wish to formally resign my position and return to Tūhl to fight for my home world."

"As you very well know, I can give you a command to fight against the forces of Martxapahn."

"Sir with all due respect, I don't think you understand. I am going to fight for Martxapahn."

If Jaymes could have seen The Autocrat's face, he would have rethought what he had just said, "Fine, don't ever come back here again.

You are now a civilian and therefore have no place in this house of law and justice. Furthermore, you are now a traitor. You better teleport away before I kill you."

Jaymes disappeared before The Autocrat's eyes.

Theo

Theo looked at the empty seat and smiled. For the first, time in four centuries, a civil war between Xóa and the people of Merkadiah was upon them. Open war was going to tear the system apart, but it was going to boost the economy of Merkadiah as one lucky weapons company was about to score a big contract.

He just needed the go ahead from The Jackal. He would know from which company to buy his weapons.

Part II

Prisoners

Chapter One

Shackles: Grivon

"We all are prisoners of our own making," -Pantherine Proverb

I

Grivon sat in a chair in the Guild Master's office waiting for Phoy. He was released from the infirmary earlier that day, and when he returned to his room, he found a letter waiting for him on his bed. It contained a simple letter of instruction sending him to The Guild Master's office. Now he sat staring at the plain beige wall impatiently waiting for his instructor.

The events of the past week had been trying. He had killed the woman called Ubiroe, won the tournament and made it through the gauntlet. It was turning out to be a long week and it seemed like it was getting longer. Barbarah was beginning to show and her mood swings were getting worse. She was hiding in her room to keep her pregnancy a secret.

Grivon sighed as he reflected on these things. His life was changing. He was changing. Perhaps it was anticipation of leaving what had been his home for the last fourteen years or perhaps it was the anxiety that once he left, it was a whole new world and that things were not so cut and dry.

His right leg began to shake as he realized that anxiety was taking over. It was the fear of the unknown that began to grip his mind. Not to mention the fact that his dreams were still plagued by Ubiroe and her flamboyant displays. She was his bane. He thought about her night and day and at the same time loathed her. He was glad she was dead, but at the same time wondered what exactly would have happened if she had won.

Would she had been merciful and killed him or would she have gone ahead and humiliated him even more. Those two questions would always remain unanswered.

The more he thought about telling Phoy what was happening, the faster he decided that he could not tell Phoy his physiological failings. Phoy would think that he was not suitable to be a Kartah or his student, so Grivon did his best to center his thoughts and bring composure to his mind.

The Chronicles of Merkadiah:
The Rise of the Gryphon

The longer he thought about his failings, the sooner it would consume him. Suddenly he heard a faint whisper in his ear, "Surrender. Surrender to me."

Grivon's eyes widened as he looked around to see who was behind him. He was alone. Then he thought he heard a chuckle. His heart began to pound as he wondered where the voice had come from. Perhaps it was just his imagination, but at the same time it had been so real.

Cradling his head in his hands he began to rock back forth wondering what was happening to him. The door opening made Grivon jump as Phoy walked in. He stood and bowed respectfully to his teacher.

Phoy returned the gesture and motioned for him to sit. Locking his thoughts out, he concentrated only on Phoy, and looked deep into his obsidian eyes.

"Grivon," Phoy said softly, "I have called you here because it is time for you to tell me what you want to do with your life. Do you want to tr and find an Aridaunt who will employ you and from there try and succeed with your goal or do you want to try and find my planet where I can teach you things beyond your wildest dreams?"

Grivon thought about it for a moment. He knew exactly what he wanted, and it was going to happen.

"I wish to find your planet and seek your training," said Grivon confidently.

"I see. So where do you want to go and start your search?" Grivon smiled devilishly, "Tūhl."

"What!"

"Did I hit it too close to where you are?"

Phoy ignored the baiting and spoke harshly to Grivon, "Tūhl is the planet where the Barrim clan is the strongest. Especially since their patriarch oversees that planet now. Martxapahn sent Chin to rejuvenation and took his fiefdom.

Those people are dangerous, and they kill Kartah. Even you are not immune to attack from these people. You could die there. So, is there anywhere else you want to start?"

"Nope, the closer I am to danger the better. Besides, I can then try and eliminate them from the system. Perhaps if Martxapahn takes most of the other fiefdoms then I can kill him and have already taken control of a vast amount of territory.

"Then I can take my seat in the Senate and when the time is right strike out at the Autocrat."

Phoy only nodded and sat stroking his catfish mustache coming from his top lip. Then he finally spoke, "Fine. Follow all leads you get there but, Martxapahn is the grandson of Xóa."

"How is that possible? I thought all his children were purged as were his operatives." Grivon exclaimed.

"They were, but when a large group of people oppose all established forms of government, they tend to hide operatives or in this case a child of Xóa. It makes sense that the Barrim clan would hide his only surviving heir.

"Then they could groom him to become their first and only patriarch. Since the Barrim's see women as superior to men, that should tell you where their loyalties lie. They want nothing more than to usurp the current government and find a way to dominate all people with their tyrannical beliefs about men and women.

"Did you know that these women believe that it is man's duty to women to have their tongues cut out so that they cannot talk back? This is only what some of them do, but others are more depraved. They even castrate baby boys if they feel that he will grow up to be a weakling.

"Then when he is about fifteen, he is given a test of endurance that if he fails, he is beheaded."

Grivon let it all sink in. Seemed more like Phoy was blowing smoke than anything else. He shrugged and said, "So."

Phoy turned three shades of red before speaking a low tone through gritted teeth, "Fine. Kill yourself for all I care. Why you want to go there to look for my planet is beyond me but go right ahead.

"Now, for the next matter of business, I will need to take a DNA sample as well as your fingerprints. This is so that if you get detained by the S.P.A. for being a rogue Kartah, they can release you in a few days, and you can be on your way.

Now here is your Kartah patch. Stitch it over the left breast of a tunic or some other garment that you want to wear on a constant basis."

Grivon nodded, taking the patch and then asked, "Am I going to get a ceremony?"

154

"I'm sorry but you're not. Your success apparently has always been a point of contention with the other students. So, to keep you safe I decided that you don't need one."

Grivon gave a knowing nod and went to get up. Phoy motioned for him to sit. Grivon nodded and held out his hands to be printed and blood to be drawn.

II

After Phoy had taken the blood sample and fingerprint, Barbarah and Steven walked in the door. Phoy stood up and winked at Grivon and let Barbarah have his seat. Grivon looked up at his friends and smiled superficially.

His leg quivered and shook, all the while his stomach flipped making bile bubble in the back of his throat. Steven looked bored and aloof as usual. Barbarah, beginning to show, looked extremely tired.

Grivon let out a stressed sigh. It was time that Phoy knew about him and Barbarah and the baby she carried. Again, he smiled superficially. He hated to leave the only woman he had ever loved, not to mention the only other person who had ever loved him.

Barbarah knew something was bothering Grivon. She wished that she could hold him close and stroke his hair. Then she could get at what was bothering him, but that was out of the question. Especially since Steven was here and they were in Phoy's office.

It was so frustrating that Grivon seemed to be spiraling into despair, and she was powerless to stop it. Steven gave out a loud sigh and with a brazen and loud voice screamed, "Just what the hell is bothering you!"

Barbarah flinched at the outburst. Grivon just blinked. Never had he seen Steven so angry outside of a sparring match or Guild Tournament. Maybe he was upset that Grivon was leaving.

Grivon exhaled sharply and turned his face to Barbarah. Then he spoke directly toward her with a sober tone to his voice, "It's time Barbarah."

"Time for what?" she asked confused.

Frustrated Grivon snapped, "You know exactly what I mean." Barbarah gasped and leaned back in her chair, but before she could speak Steven burst out, "So what in the name of God is going on between the two of you?

Grivon's face turned beat red. He was beginning to get more than a little annoyed with Steven's outbursts. Before he could think about it, he screamed, "Shut up Steven, you self-absorbed blowhard!"

Steven's jaw fell open and then snapped shut. Barbarah looked wide-eyed at him, wondering what had brought the sudden outburst of rage.

"Barbarah's pregnant and I'm the father." The words seemed to flow from his mouth without thought or desire.

"No slag!" Steven bellowed.

Then before either Barbarah or Grivon could say a word, he flew out the door and slammed it so hard it came open again. Grivon put his forehead in between his thumb and index fingers and rubbed hard. Barbarah was on the verge of tears and looked to Grivon for strength, but all she saw was a scarred young man who was under a lot of stress.

Phoy stood looking at the two for several minutes. Then he sighed and sat down on the edge of his desk. Grivon looked up and Barbarah turned her head to look at Phoy. For the first time Grivon really looked at Phoy and noticed how old he really was.

The age wasn't in his skin. It wasn't even in his physical being at all. His age was in his eyes. A man who had lived longer than most and would probably outlive Grivon's grandchildren. It was amazing what the Aurora could do to a person.

"I wonder what his problem is?" Phoy pondered, stroking his mustache.

"I guess because Barbarah's pregnant." Grivon said.

It was all he could do to muster those words out of his mouth. They seemed like poison or a different language. It felt like an eternity before anyone spoke and, in that eternity, he felt himself under the cold scrutiny of a mentor that he could possibly never be able to locate, let alone see again.

For the first time in years, he felt so powerless and futile.

Barbarah's lungs tightened as if she had dived into an ice-covered river. She tried to regulate her breathing, but it was like she was drowning on dry land. It was almost impossible to believe she would soon be a mother, and Grivon would be the baby's father. When Barbarah finally caught her breath, Phoy was speaking.

"I knew that it might happen, but not so soon," he started, "sadly, it happens a lot ever since any sort of contact was banned between young men and women.

The Chronicles of Merkadiah:
The Rise of the Gryphon

"As far as I know, Barbarah can stay at the Guild for the duration of the pregnancy, but she must name the male student that she slept with and after that baby is born, he or she will be raised by the Guild and the parents expelled, but this is an extremely different case.

"In this case, you have one student about to graduate and another several assessments away from graduation. We must follow these rules or else I will get into trouble. Even a person with as much political clout as I have cannot disobey the Senate about this one. So Barbarah, can you tell me who the father is?"

Barbarah was at a loss for words. To follow procedure and make sure that Grivon could continue his journey for greatness, she would be played to look like a slut. *But isn't that what those bastards already thought*?

Especially after what happened at the Tournament. That bitch Ubiroe or whatever her name was had her posse hold her arms and legs while Ubiroe kissed and touched her. And in front of all those people. It was humiliating. Her face flushed with shame just thinking about it.

"Steven, Steven Anthony is the father of my child," Barbarah said, as hot tears ran down her checks. This was worse than all those times she had been violated. Her heart hardened and she gave a strike to both Phoy and Grivon.

*If either of them ever made her feel this way again…*The thought cut itself short. What was she going to do? Kill the best swordsmen in Merkadiah? Defeat fell heavy on her shoulders and she slumped back into the large swivel chair.

Phoy nodded his head. It was not going to be a good thing to get Orsin Steven Anthony to agree to this. Phoy stood and walked out of the room and left Barbarah and Grivon alone. But before he shut the door he turned around and said, "You two can use my private quarters to be alone for the next three days and no one will know about it.

Then you must leave Grivon. It's best if you don't stay too long."

When the door shut, Barbarah ran over to Grivon and threw her arms around him. She began sobbing and wailing at what was happening. All Grivon could do was rub her back and tell her that it would be okay.

That he would send her messages over the Network. Barbarah nodded with a smile on her face. At least he still cared, for now. Grivon hated what Phoy wanted him to do, but it was the only way things could continue as planned.

Tears welled up in his eyes as he thought about the child he may never know. He gripped Barbarah tighter and then she stopped crying and said, "We do have three days all to ourselves. We can still spend lots of time together and talk this out.

It may not be as bad as it seems. At least the two of us will be together."

Grivon rubbed his eyes clear on his robe and nodded his head. It was going to be three days he was sure to remember for the rest of his life.

III

Grivon materialized in Tūhlead, the capital of Tūhl. The teleportation gate stood in the center of town and was a single pillar in the middle of an earthen dusty street. It was early morning just a little after sunrise.

Tūhl's moon, Nomah, hung low on the horizon. All around the skyline was filled with three story buildings with boardwalks and false fronts connecting them. In other places larger buildings were being erected, and all around the town was a thick forest. This place was vastly different than Tygrano.

He sighed. It was hard leaving Barbarah behind while she sobbed hysterically. She knew he was leaving, but it was still hard to watch the only man in your life leave and still be stuck in the Guild.

Grivon rubbed the patch he had sewn over the heart of his black robes, trying not to think about her. He would have to keep his head clear if he wanted to find Phoy's planet, but it was proving difficult. His body already ached for her touch and he felt as if he were constantly suffering from indigestion.

He sighed at his apathy for her feelings. It was not that he wanted to forget her or their baby; it was that he had a goal to achieve, and to do that he couldn't have mixed feelings of duty and love roaming about his head.

He would have to think about those things when time presented itself, not when he was hunting for Phoy. Trying to take his mind off of things, he looked more closely at the city that he teleported into.

The Chronicles of Merkadiah:
The Rise of the Gryphon

Since he had never been there, he could not teleport by using his chip, so he had to take the Path of Esteem out of the Guild and from there he wound up here. The moon looked like any normal place as far as he could tell.

The city was bigger than anything he had ever seen, but that was to be expected, seeing as how he had never seen a city before.

The buildings were bunched together on both sides of a dirt walkway. People were busy going up and down that dirt walkway, entering and exiting various buildings. It was all fascinating. Grivon had his head upturned looking at gargoyles on the top of a rather tall gray-bricked building when something hit him hard in his chest.

He walked right into a young woman running down the walkway. She lay sprawled out on the ground in front of him. Her eyes were closed, and she appeared to be breathing. Grivon knelt, grabbed her shoulders, and shook her.

She moaned, and her eyes fluttered open. When she opened her eyes, Grivon looked her over. She had long platinum blonde hair, gray eyes, and her face looked a lot like Barbarah.

"I'm sorry Miss. This is my first time to your lovely city, and I was gazing at that building over there," Grivon pointed to the one with the gargoyles on top.

Standing up the young woman dusted herself off. She smiled at Grivon and then said in a sultry voice, "Oh, its fine. I was in a hurry. My name is Bebe Barrim, what's yours?"

Anxiety gripped his chest. If he told his real name, he could be killed for winning the tournament and killing Ubiroe. He paused as he formulated an alias. The name of Steven's Guild Lord was the first to come to mind, "I'm Gray Sander. I just got here, and I was hoping someone could tell me where I could find some lodging and food?"

"I would show you myself, but I have a meeting I have attend. But if you go down this street about five or so buildings there is a boarding house. I think she charges fifty credits a week or something like that.

Anyway, she is my mother and if you take lodging there then I can show you around in a day or so."

Grivon nodded his head and said, "What's the name of the boarding house and does it have Network access?"

"Um, well the name is Barrim Boarding, and as far as Network access goes, I don't think that she has any, but you can ask. I really do have to go."

Bebe pushed aside Grivon and ran off down the street. The anxiety he was feeling let go, but a new tightening in his stomach took over. If anyone found out his real name, he was a dead man. As soon as he found lodging and food, he would begin asking around about Phoy. The sooner he was gone from this place the better.

IV

The Demon Hunter watched as the girl purposefully ran into Grivon. She laughed slightly and watched as they had a short conversation before the girl ran away. The Demon Hunter laughed harder. She would have to watch her target for a few more days.

Her real name was Angela Simone. She was a member of the Assassin Guild and specialized in killing Kartah. The Assassin Guild had taken her in after she had failed at the Fire Guild.

They had trained her to kill indiscriminately, and she could kill a child if that was her target. She would even kill a pregnant woman if the price was right. Being cold blooded had made her rich and she was never picky with her assignments, especially if they came from politicians.

She watched Grivon, wondering if he would be like every other Kartah she ever killed. They all seemed to want to get into a fight or trouble. This one seemed different. Then she saw him go into the Barrim Boarding House. Maybe he was more predicable than she thought. Renting a room from the leader of the Barrim Clan was definitely trouble.

V

Grivon began walking down the street. After five buildings, he came across a house that looked like it belonged in a fairy tale. It was made of large stones stacked like brick. The building was four floors high and looked like a small fortress. The whole thing was imposing, but he might as well swallow his pride and face his fear.

If the women of the city didn't find out anything about him, he would be fine. Now he wished he hadn't been so brazen and listened to Phoy.

He walked up to the covered terrace and looked at the imposing door. It was made of wood and painted onyx. He tried to swallow the growing lump in his throat. With an unquenchable fear burning in his chest, he rapped on the door. The woman who opened it looked just like Ubiroe.

This gave Grivon pause, forcing him to summon as much control as he could to keep from wetting himself. The woman in front of him looked a little older than Ubiroe, but still she had the same hair, eyes and facial structure; but it was the eyes that made Grivon want to panic.

The same piercing gray eyes with that psychotic look about them.

"Uh…I was told I could find lodging here," said Grivon.

"Yes, you can, but can you pay for lodging here?" asked the woman sharply.

"I just graduated from the Chaos Guild on Tygrano. I have a year's worth of Guild funds at my disposal," Grivon lied. He knew he had more, but that was his money to do with what he wanted. He had no problems using the Guild's funds for his personal expenses. "Do you have a room?"

A little shocked the woman said, "Why yes, I just require two weeks rent in advance."

Grivon fished out a small card with an account number on it. "I expect this back. Can I pay a year in advance?"

The woman began to stammer, "Well yes, will you still have enough to do other things with, I mean I give you room and board, but you will

have to pay for your own linens and such."

Grivon smirked slightly, "Oh yes, the Guilds take care of emerging Kartah."

The woman opened the door wider and, Grivon stepped inside. The inside of the house was less imposing. She had decorated it with decorative plates and paintings. He could see part of the kitchen from where he was standing. The way the house sat it caught the morning sun.

The dining room was adjoined to the kitchen. Though something about the dining room reminded him of the Guild Lord's mess hall at the Guild.

It had one long table and a bench on each side. The woman motioned for Grivon to follow and led him to a primitive lift. The lift was little more than piece of sturdy wood big enough for three people to stand on. On the right side were two ropes and a lever.

The woman pushed the lever causing the plank to jerk and Grivon's heart to jump and kickstart the fear of falling. Then she began to pull down on one of the ropes and they slowly went up.

At each floor, Grivon noticed several women outside of doors. Some were simply standing in their underwear with a foot against the wall, and others were either going into their room or leaving.

Grivon began to wonder if it was a house just for women. Then as if she were reading his mind the woman said, "This house is also home to me, my daughters and their families. I still charge them, but at a reduced rate."

"I met a woman earlier who said she was your daughter," said Grivon "What was her name?" "Bebe."

"Yes, she is my daughter, and she still lives here, but she is a wild one and has yet to have a daughter of her own."

"Why, she is very beautiful," said Grivon thinking about how much she looked like Barbarah.

"Do you want her for yourself?" she was spitting the words now.

"No, I am promised to someone else after I finish looking for someone."

"Who are you looking for? For fifty credits, I could tell you just about anything you want to know."

"Maybe, I'll make you a deal, I will give you twenty-five and ask you about the person and if you can give me some information, I will give you an extra twenty-five, but if you can't then you have still made twenty- five."

The woman thought it over. Then she answered, "Deal, what's your question?"

"Do you know of a place called, 'The Planet Where the Dead Walk?'"

The woman thought about it. Very slowly she said, "Yes, but I don't know where it is. I'm sorry I can't tell you more."

"Okay since you have heard of the planet, I'll honor the deal. I've been meaning to ask, what is your name?"

"Dahra Barrim. My husband was the Governor here, but he died a few months back. He was beheaded by S.P.A. for his loyalties. When he died, he left me this house and I use it for income. My husband was appointed by Chin Moa Ing.

When Chin lost his fiefdom to the Therian Martxapahn, Martxapahn had S.P.A. arrest anyone loyal to the old Aridaunt and had them killed. Here we are."

Grivon got the impression that story was practiced and only partially true. He would have to do some snooping to be sure.

Dahra stopped the lift and pulled the lever to stabilize the lift. She motioned for Grivon to follow her. When they were off the lift, the entire fourth floor was a room. It had a bed, a desk and a set of double doors going out to a large balcony that overlooked a large garden in the back.

Grivon looked it over and nodded his head.

"Will this do?" asked Dahra.

"Yes, but do you happen to have Network access?"

"Yes, I do. This floor was my husband's office. On the desk is a red button. If you press it, you will have access to the only Network console in Tuhlead. I gave you this floor, because my husband was a Chaos graduate.

I know how much he valued his privacy. Around the corner past the bed is a full water closet. It has a shower, toilet, and a sink. However, as I mentioned earlier, you will still have to provide your own linens.

"Also, if you want to come down for food or want to leave there are stairs or you can pull the string by the lift shaft four times. I or one of my girls will come and get you, when she returns, do you want Bebe to come and see you?"

Grivon sighed thinking of Barbarah, "Yes, I could use the company. She reminds me of my promised."

Dahra nodded and smiled a sad smile, "Don't let her get to attached to you. She will try and keep you here when it is your time to leave."

Grivon nodded and walked over to the double doors and walked out onto his balcony. He leaned over the railing to look at the garden. It had a large pond with a fountain in the middle. There were small shadows that looked like fish in it.

To the left of the pond was a statue of a person holding a pot with water pouring out into the pond, and to the right of the pond was what looked to be a large shrub maze.

He chuckled thinking it would be good training every morning, running through the maze and seeing how long it would take to get to the center and then back again to the start. Living here was going to be nice. As he leaned and strained to see the maze and how big it was, he felt something prick his arm. He turned to see what it was.

It was his Saber. He had forgotten it was on. Walking back into the room he stretched, unbuckled the baldric, and laid it down on his bed. He stripped out of his robe and stretched some more. It was time to write a letter to Barbarah.

She would want to hear from him and since he had Network access, he could send it to her without Guild interference. Grivon walked over to the mahogany desk and pressed the red button Dahra mentioned.

A screen popped up from the top of the desk and a keyboard slid out from underneath the desk. He slid the rolling chair over to the Network console, punched in his personal credentials, typed in the command that let him send messages without visual recording or sound, and started composing his letter to Barbarah.

She would be thrilled to hear from him. He hadn't been gone a day, but it already felt like an eternity.

Dear Barbarah,

I already miss seeing your lovely face. You mean the world to me and I love you. Your green eyes hold so much life that not getting to see them any longer pains my heart. I feel as if a piece of me is missing. I am so lost without you. You complete me and when my journey is over, I will return to you and marry you. Is Steven taking care of you? I hope for his sake he is.

He is a good man. At least, in my opinion. He and Phoy will guide you through the next five months. I hope that everything will be made right in the end. I promise after Phoy finishes training me, I will do my best to find you and help you carry on your hopes and dreams.

Love Always,
Grivon

He closed the screen, once again making the wood in the desktop seamless, and leaned back putting his hands behind his head, and sighing.

The now familiar feeling of indigestion was back, but he knew it was more heartbreak than heartburn. It was breaking his heart to be away from Barbarah. In all his life he never felt as he did now. All his muscles and joints ached.

He closed his eyes and rubbed his temples. It was all so confusing. How come he couldn't just quiet his feelings? Why did she affect him so much? This made him feel weak and powerless. Unbidden his fury started rising.

He needed a fight. He needed anything that would take his mind off her. Grabbing his robe, he dressed, and walked to the stairs to see how big that maze was.

VI

Grivon was asleep. For the first time in a long time, he wasn't dreaming of Ubiroe and her four "sisters." He was awakened by footfalls and then silence. He was tired but not so tired that he could not hear the strained footfalls.

Figuring it was Dahra coming up the stairs, he rolled over. Then he remembered she said she would send Bebe up when she got home. Forcing his eyes open, he looked around the room. He had lain down after running to the center of the maze and back.

The whole ordeal lasted four hours leaving him exhausted. When he lay down it was early afternoon. Now it was almost sunset and a woman in her underwear was standing over him. Panic went through Grivon as he turned on a light.

It was Bebe, and she looked ready for a wild night. What he thought was underwear was a nearly see-through one-piece nightdress. He turned his head as not to look at her.

"Can I help you?" he asked.

"Mother said that I looked like your promised and that you could use some company." Her voice husky and seductive.

"I meant conversation." Grivon said flatly.

"Oh, I guess I took it to mean that you wanted something else," her voice trailed off with disappointment.

"No, I reserve that for my promised."

"Ah, then let me change, and we can talk after dinner. It will be ready in about half an hour."

She turned around and walked out. Grivon sighed. This was going to be hard. He missed Barbarah, but Bebe was a lot different than anything he had ever encountered. It was frightening how free she was with herself.

Grivon walked down the spiral staircase that let out in the kitchen and took a seat. Every eye at the table was on him. He nodded politely to each of the women. He turned his head straight ahead.

When the plate was set down in front of him, he smiled. It looked like roasted fowl covered in gravy with a side of steamed greens and whole grains. Grivon thanked Dahra and began eating. No sooner did he eat three bites, than the world went black.

VII

A single drop of water splashing into a larger pool of water echoed somewhere in the dark, and Grivon awoke to searing pain in his wrists and ankles. His eyes fluttered revealing a dimly lit room made of stone.

His wrists were bound in titanium cuffs attached to ropes tied to an anchor in the ceiling. While each ankle was tied to a single rope anchored to the floor. There he hung naked and afraid. A wooden door in front of him was the only way in best he could tell.

Another drop of water splashed into an unseen pool and echoed off the stones. Suddenly the wooden door creaked open, and Dahra walked in carrying a thick baton with metal prongs on the end. She also carried a long, thick piece of cane cut into several strips at the top.

Another drop of water echoed through the room. Dahra wore a tight orange bodysuit, what appeared to be studded leather gloves the same color, and a flagrum hanging loose on her left hip. A twisted smirk formed on her lips as she approached him.

Still another drop of water bounced off the rocks in the walls and floor. When she was only a few centimeters from his face, she backhanded him across the face splitting his lip and making him spit blood. She

grinned and back handed him again with the other hand. Laughing, she grabbed his jaw forcing him to look at her, then she spit in his face. The room echoed with the sound of a single drop of water.

His mind reeled from the sudden and violent pain. She squeezed his cheeks hard and pursed her lips before saying, "Welcome to my hell. This is the place where you will be broken.

No one leaves here without my permission or dying, whichever comes first. From now on you must answer me and my daughters only as Herrin. Do I make myself clear?"

166

The Chronicles of Merkadiah:
The Rise of the Gryphon

A drop of crashed off the walls in the tiny room. Grivon's fury ignited and before he could know what he was saying he yelled, "Eat slag, bitch." A drop of water splashed into a puddle, creating a deafening din.

The joy fled from Dahra's face as she jabbed the prongs of the baton into his stomach sending white hot pain surging through his body. His heart raced, and the smell of burnt flesh and hair filled the room. She sneered as she let him catch his breath, and then jabbed him with it again making his bladder drain onto the floor. The single drop of water reverberated through the room.

"This lovely little device is called a picana. It's one of the only surviving pieces of technology from the Blue Star. It sends a low current of electricity through the body, so you won't die, but it will just hurt like a bitch. Now do you understand the severity of this situation you so willingly waltzed into?" The cacophonic crash of single drop of water resonated from the walls.

Grivon sneered and spat in her face, "Let me free or so help me..." This time the drop of water sounded like cymbals ringing. She smirked, "You'll what? I think you're in the wrong position to threaten me. Since you seem so bent on fighting perhaps this will take some of that from you." The drop of water threatened to drive him into insanity.

Dahra placed the cane and picana on the floor and unhooked the flagrum from her underwear. She moved it about Grivon's face making the ceramic beads sewn into the nine leather cords click and rattle.

With a cackle she walked behind him. Suddenly, sharp stabbing pain exploded through his body as the maddening drop of water echoed off the walls yet again.

Time and space faded from him as the cackling witch tore chunks out of his back. His mind raced trying to deal with the pain, but all he could do was focus on the mind-altering agony, and the infernal drops of water.

Each blow was kept in time with the dripping water. In the eternal void of time between blow and drip a voice whispered soothing words to his ear. The voice was subtle and slowly pulled him away from what was happening.

He found himself standing in the cavern where he had seen the man that looked like him when Phoy taught him how to energize his Aurora.

Again, he stood before the doppelganger and this time he smiled. His mouth formed words, but Grivon couldn't understand what was being said.

Darkness enveloped his vision as the ever-present sound of dripping water echoed through his consciousness and into oblivion.

VIII

Grivon was awoken by the smell of something succulent wafting through the stone room. There was a plate of hot food sitting on a small table in the corner of the room near the door. His wrists and ankles ached worse, and there was something warm on his back.

Looking down, he saw bandages around his torso and stomach. Dahra must have wrapped him in bandages after what had happened the night before. The sound of dripping water no longer echoed through the room. He wondered how long he had been there.

The door opened, and Bebe walked in. She wore a blue latex body suit and a cane stuffed through a loose black belt. Closing the door behind her, she strode over to the plate of food and picked it up.

Grivon greedily licked his lips as the smell coming from the plate tempted his nostrils. Bebe pulled the plate away and put a finger over her lip.

"I can help you," she whispered.

"How?" Grivon groaned.

"I'll keep your wounds dressed, keep you fed, and meet any other needs you have," she said fluttering her eyes.

"I don't think I need any of your help."

Bebe's countenance changed, and suddenly the cane at her waist slapped against his face. Flesh tore from bone as the skin was pinched between small slits in the cane. Blood streamed down his face like crimson tears.

"Oh, I think you do." Bebe seethed.

With a titanic strength that it didn't seem she could possess, Bebe chucked the plate of food against a stone wall sending pieces of ceramic and food flying through the air.

When she turned back around her eyes looked black and all the color was gone from her cheeks. Then, with the same level of strength proceeded to beat Grivon anywhere her mother had left unscathed.

A great scream formed in the back of Griovn's already raw throat and echoed through the room, bouncing off the walls and floor, mixing with the psychotic laughter coming from his tormenter. A blow to the face, another to his stomach, neck, and arms.

The Chronicles of Merkadiah:
The Rise of the Gryphon

She danced around him like a practice mannequin and beat him about his legs and anywhere else that wasn't bandaged.

"I brought you food!" She screamed as she landed a hit square on the top of his head. "I would have given you my body!" Another blow to his left side. This one struck a wounded piece of flesh and tore healing tissue from clean tissue, making him scream louder.

Suddenly, he was standing in the now familiar cave looking at himself through a hole in the crags of rock. He watched as the woman worked his body over head to toe with the thick cane. The look on his face was one of indifferent complacency.

It almost seemed like he was enjoying it. Then the man spoke behind him, "This is your place. Your home away from what exists in the present. I and this room exist to help you.

You can come here at any point you need to."

Before he could ask any questions, the hole in the crag Grivon was looking through suddenly sucked him back into it, and he was now lying on the cold stone floor with Dahra and Bebe standing over him.

"Is he supposed to look like that?" Bebe asked.

"That glazed-over look in his eyes?" Dahra replied.

"Yes mother." Bebe said with a tinge of worry in her voice.

Dahra shook her head, "Tsk, tsk. It's a damn shame. I've seen this happen before. Usually means we hit him too hard. Feed him well and dress his wounds for a few days. Then we shall suspend him between heaven and hell."

All Grivon could do was moan. It felt like someone had clubbed him to death and somehow brought him back. He was pretty sure there were some broken bones and dislocated joints.

He looked all around the room trying to find some way to escape, but instead he saw the tear in reality that was the door back to the cave. Reaching forward he pulled himself into it and embraced the new home he had found.

Edgar Lewis

Chapter Two
Shackles: Barbarah

"Facing your demons is the only way to break the shackles of your own making,"
-Pantherine Proverb

I

Barbarah awoke with sharp pains in her abdomen and pelvis. The baby was coming! As she felt around to activate the light, she felt something wet on the bed. Her water had broken. She began to hyperventilate. This was it. Once she had the baby, she and Steven would be out on their own.

She finally found the light and dialed up Phoy on her Network console. He nodded and said for her to lie down on her bed and wait for the medical team, and just relax.

She lay on her bed and began to think about how much her life was going to change. Her biggest hope was that Steven would take care of her.

He was upset that he was going to be forced out with her. When Phoy told him, what was going to happen, he screamed and ranted for over an hour. After his tirade a bizarre look came across his face, and with a heavy sigh, he said that he would see to it she was looked after.

The door sliding open made her jump. Phoy, followed by the medical team, flooded into her room. Thankfully, she had been wearing a nightdress, and they didn't need to rip off her clothes.

Unbelievable pain shot through her. It was a contraction. She heard herself screaming. It didn't sound like her. Another contraction. The pain was getting worse. She could feel the baby's head crowning.

Another contraction, another scream. She wished Grivon were there. That bastard had skipped out before he should have. It should have been him getting denied his dreams, not Steven. Steven had no responsibility in this. She screamed for Grivon.

Suddenly, someone grabbed her hand. She looked and saw it was Steven. For the first time ever, he wore a look of compassion on his face. Clamping his hand, she screamed again.

The Chronicles of Merkadiah:
The Rise of the Gryphon

It hurt! Oh, it hurt! A sharp, manly scream pierced the room. She glanced over and saw that Steven's hand was turning purple. Letting it go, she screamed again as the baby's shoulders came out. It was happening so fast.

When it was over the baby was taken to a special wing in the Guild and given to a wet nurse before Barbarah could bond with the child, but it was too late. She loved the baby even before she gave birth.

Tears streamed down her face as the reality that she would never be able to hold her child set in. Steven put a reassuring hand on her shoulder, "You gave birth to a boy," Steven said as he pecked the top of her head. "Phoy wants to know what you wanted to name him."

"Grivon said his name should be Terry. His last name is not to be given until he gets a Guild Lord."

Steven cocked an eyebrow, "What?"

Barbarah shrugged, "He said that if something should happen that his son should have a chance at a normal life. That his family's namesake would create the same type of social exile that he dealt with."

Steven nodded and said, "You know, I love you. I will watch after you when we have to leave in the next five weeks."

Barbarah felt her cheeks flush. That was the first good thing she had heard in weeks.

"Where are you going to take me?" asked Barbarah.

Steven smiled, "Nomah, the capital city. I am kind of taking over the family business."

II

The lights in the room lit up as Steven walked in. He looked around at the sheet-covered furniture and Network terminals. It smelled of dust and mildew. Barbarah sneezed as she walked into the room. Needless to say, no one had been in place for a long time.

Steven began to uncover the terminals and the furniture. Dust and mold plumed into the air as sheet after sheet was removed from various objects. When it was all uncovered what lay before Steven and Barbarah was a large room broken down into ten cubicles with a large enclosed office facing out toward them.

Each cubicle had a Network terminal and a rolling swivel chair.

"Well what do you think?" asked Steven with a swell of pride in his voice.

"Um, it seems a little dusty, but other than that I can see some potential," said Barbarah with little more than disdain in her voice. She was still feeling bad after leaving her baby and not knowing where Grivon was.

It was frightening to know that she may not see him ever again, and the pain in her heart was enough to want to die. But she couldn't, not when Grivon could still be alive. If that hope were still within her, she could keep going.

Not to mention she needed to keep tabs on the assignment Grivon had given her almost a year ago.

The assignment was that she should encourage the Pantherines tom riot and try a coup. From news reports that she had seen on the Network, they were doing just that. It was only a matter of time before the Pantherines would cry out for their own house with Aridaunts, Kartah, and Governors.

Once this happened, it would create a huge disturbance, and Grivon hoped to capitalize on it.

"Hey, you awake?" asked Steven, snapping his fingers, his voice quaking with rage.

"Sorry, just daydreaming. What are you going to call this place, and what are you going to do with it?"

"The name of our business is Anthony Security Investments Limited.

We will invest the money of Politicians and anyone else who wants to grow their holdings. We will invest it into the economy of the hotels and apartment buildings I own, and we will take a ten percent cut. Not to mention, my father left me a very lucrative ice cream business, and to top it all off I know some of his friends who can help me run all this.

I will create an economic empire that will make the hydroponics farms of Baktüth look like a peasant's vegetable stand. I still have access to my father's off world accounts on Nithia and Felonius. I am currently considering buying out several casinos and pleasure houses, and you can manage anything your heart desires," he said gripping her chin a little harder than she would have liked.

Barbarah moved his hand and gave Steven a blank stare. He spoke with such eloquence that she believed that he could do almost anything he wanted. She did not know who his father was, but he must have been a very good executive to amass such copious amounts of money and property.

One thing that confused her was how Steven's father made so much money just by selling ice cream.

The Chronicles of Merkadiah:
The Rise of the Gryphon

Without thinking she said, "How did your father make so much money selling ice cream?"

She wished she could have seen his hand moving. The white-hot pain stunned her as she saw the back of his hand leaving her peripheral vision. She felt blood run down her lower lip.

"How dare you insult my father!" screamed Steven. "He was publicly executed because of a stupid Aridaunt when I was only four years old.

My mother hung herself in the kitchen while I watched the next day. My father had terrific recipes for all sorts of ice cream. Thankfully, his best friend has been running it since he died."

Through chokes and sobs Barbarah labored to catch her breath. Once she caught her breath, she looked up at Steven with hate and anger in her eyes and screamed, "You Bastard! How could you hit a woman?

You coward, you're angry at the government for killing your daddy and now you take it out on me? You're little more than an animal," then she spat in his face. Enraged, Steven wiped the spit from his face and reached down and grabbed Barbarah by the throat making her gurgle.

He pulled her to his face, her legs dangled, and she gurgled as eternal night encroached on her. Suddenly, a hot viscous fluid splashed her face. Vomit built in the small space that was currently her pinched throat. She forced it down.

"Stupid cow, I am the only man in your life now. From now on, you are to call me sir, and you are to keep your mouth shut about what goes on here. I am going to put taka in the ice cream. 'Hook 'em while their young,' my father used to say.

Don't worry, it's not enough to kill anyone, but it will ensure I have a steady income for the rest of my days. Now, as far as my hitting you, I will do with you as I please when I please. And when the time comes, you will bare me a son.

One who will take over for me when I am gone. Now tell me do you understand?" He growled through clenched teeth.

That bizarre and unsettling look was back, and all Barbarah could do was nod and mutter a weak "Yes sir." Who was this person? Never had she seen him like this. Her heart was beating so fast that it felt like it was going to burst from her chest.

He let go, and she fell to the ground in a heap. Now she was too afraid to move without his permission. When he finally gave the go ahead to follow him, she obeyed, and then walked five feet behind him to give him a wide berth.

This was mostly because she was afraid he would hit her, just for the fact that she was there. She kept her head down and her thoughts to herself. This level of fear and shame was something she hadn't felt in a long time.

She felt weak and exposed, like someone was looking inside her where she did not want anyone to see. It was a feeling with which she was all too familiar with. It was the feeling she used to have before she met Grivon, back when she would be beaten and violated.

Suddenly the words Steven said set in. He was going to force her! That was all there was to it. All to give him an heir to the 'empire' he was going to build. For the first time in a long time, she felt alone and ugly. She wanted to die. Flashbacks flooded her mind.

It was too much. Everything that had happened was happening over again. Invisible hands crawled over her body, her head began to hurt, and with a painful scream, the entire world went black.

III

Barbarah Watts was dreaming. She dreamed of Grivon. She dreamed of blue skies and fields of flowers. She dreamed of life and freedom. She dreamed about forgotten birds and plants. She dreamed a fanciful dream of broken promises made true and an eternity where she and Grivon could be together without consequence.

She dreamed a universe of soft creatures bathed in light. She was finally happy. No more horrid dreams or memories. No more Steven. Just her and Grivon and the beautiful

world she had invented for her and her lover. It was so beautiful and so real. She called it the land of Verdance. Then she heard a soft worried, voice come to her. The voice bounced and rolled in her head making her world disappear.

The hold she held on her special world slipped, and she cried. Barbarah's eyes fluttered and she was looking into Steven's eyes. She flinched and screamed, trying to back away from his relieved looking face, but she did not get far.

The Chronicles of Merkadiah:
The Rise of the Gryphon

The headboard of the large bed she lay in kept her from moving any farther. She was trapped between a grinning demon and a piece of wood.

Steven smoothed her hair sending cold goosebumps and chills all over her body. Here it comes she thought to herself as she began to put up barriers in her mind to keep from feeling anything, he would do to her.

The horizon of the world she had created filled her mind's eye when he said something out of character.

"Barbarah, I am really sorry about my actions at the office. Here Grivon left you in my care and I go and do this. You must know that I would never hurt you, but you should also realize that you provoked me to it.

I know you think of me as a horrible monster. Can you find it in your heart of gold to forgive me?" The look on his face was one of genuine regret. Forgive him she thought. How dare he ask for such a thing?

Forgiveness was something given when someone said something that they didn't mean. But the way he was acting, it probably wasn't wise to smart off at him. Too afraid not to, Barbarah swallowed the knot in her throat and said, "I will forgive you, sir." She tried to say it with as much venom as possible.

Elated Steven said, "Oh, thank you so very much. Now, you get some rest, I have some errands to take care of in town." He leaned down and kissed Barbarah on the forehead and failed to see her wince as his dry lips touched her skin.

As he left the room, Barbarah let out a sigh of relief as her thoughts drifted toward Grivon. She wished she knew where he was. He hadn't sent her any letters or any Quasar feeds.

It was strange that since Steven had begun to "look after" her Grivon stopped talking to her, but then again, maybe something terrible had happened to him. Tūhl was a harsh place considering some of the things she had been told by Phoy.

She rolled over and fell asleep finding the world she had dreamt of again.

IV

Steven was livid. He had been back to the office that his father had used to run "The Business." None of the Dons were there. The First Don should have been there at the very least. This was incompetence at its finest.

All he wanted were the current files on who owed debt and what businesses had paid their tithes and which ones needed to be given a slight nudge.

Steven punched in some keys on his Network terminal. He looked for an address roster of lieutenants that his father trusted and of assassins that his father had on retainer. The list was short just as Steven expected.

Two lieutenants and three assassins. Of the three assassins one was listed as missing, one was listed as dead and the last one had just taken a Sabbatical. Of the two lieutenants, one was missing, and the other had been injured in a pleasure house raid six months ago.

She was listed as active and her Network Address was listed. A few keystrokes later, a horribly burned face was looking at Steven. It would have been better if her face had been burnt on both sides.

Instead, she was burnt on patches over her left eye and in patches under her right eye. She was bald except for a single scarlet ponytail pluming from the center of her head. A look of murder filled her ice blue eyes.

Steven let her look him over then she spoke rather tersely, "If you're looking for Netsex this is the wrong number."

Steven chuckled. Then he said in the smoothest most charming voice he could muster, "I'm afraid you don't realize who I am. I usually address my employees in my full regalia. I am The Jackal, the son of the last Orsin Steven Anthony."

The woman on the other side of the screen began to laugh then said, "If a kid like you is the new boss, then I really will have Netsex with you." Steven's eyes narrowed and then said harshly, "If I were you then streetwalking would be a better profession, Miss Nichole Rendale Cie."

The little color that was left on her burnt face drained. Stammering she said, "Sorry, you don't look like the son of our last boss, but of course, if you knew my full real name, then either you have hacked the boss's mainframe or you're the real deal."

"Be glad I am the real deal and that I do give second chances."

"So, what do I owe this call from the obviously underdressed godfather of all fiendish pleasures this side of The Blue Star?"

"Where are the others?"

"You mean the Dons."

176

The Chronicles of Merkadiah:
The Rise of the Gryphon

"Yes, the Dons. Are they dead? Or have they just figured since there wasn't a boss around, they didn't have to listen to orders and keep the offices tidy for my inevitable arrival?"

"Well, some of them were found by the Special Protection Agency for racketeering. The rest set up shop in a pleasure house called Fox's Den. It's run by a rouge bartender named Daniel Fox. He doesn't pay us to operate or the S.P.A. to keep the dregs from really trashing the place.

Your Dons set up shop there and have been living well on your father's money. They've probably only spent a small margin, but then again, I don't get paid since this." She pointed to the burn scars on her face.

"Interesting. First, I want to know why you didn't get teleported or one of the Dons didn't give you a rejuvenation implant beforehand."

"Well, I was given a pleasure house to supervise. It was paid for with the money of the S.P.A. and most of the local governors used it, as did some of the Aridaunts and Kartah. Anyway, some little punk comes into the place and runs up a huge tab. Then he tries to skip it, so I have my bouncers bring him to my office.

"I asked him why he wanted to skip the bill. He said his girl wasn't good enough. But when I asked him about the other items on his bill, like the five glasses of Van Gough he had, or the three hundred credit gambling debt he racked up he said someone else must have done it

because he was trying to be pleased by the horrible girl he had bought for two hours. So I went and got the girl. He had spent an extra hour with the girl.

"I ran his ID and sure enough, he had been charged an extra hour.

Then noticed that he had swiped his ID, not orally given it to the bartender or the gambling madam. I had to hold him to it. Then he says that he refuses to pay and that his uncle is the Chief of Criminal affairs.

I say, yeah right, and have my bouncers hold him upside down until his wallet falls out. There I find three four thousand-credit cards. I kept all three and told him he was lucky he left with his life.

"Then about three hours later, right around the time I am getting ready to go home and my morning manager is coming in, I see him and four other punks coming towards me. They're all drunk. They force me and my manager into the back room. Once they are in the light, I notice that none of the guys are S.P.A.

The little scumbag from earlier tells me he is going to get his twelve thousand back from me either from free gambling and drinks, or he was going to beat me until I give it back. So I do what I know he doesn't expect. I pulled a knife from my pants and stab him in the inner thigh. He fell over bleeding.

"I wipe my knife off, get up, and start kicking him. As I am singlehandedly fighting these drunken goons one pulls out a vial of Pantherines' bane and hits the ground with it.

Instantly, I am surrounded by flames and my face feels like the flesh is being peeled off. Then to make matters worse, the punk who I stabbed was wearing a teleportation jammer, and his stupid friends leave him there bleeding out.

My face is melting off the bone, and that is what happened. Needless to say, the house was repaired, and I got the boot because I am no longer a pretty face to draw in customers. So Derik Fythur, the third Don, put me out to pasture."

Steven took it all in. She was smart, tough and resourceful and seemed to be able to make on-the-spot decisions. Nichole was going to be his special pet. The others were going to pay, with their lives.

"How would you like to be the new First Don?" asked Steven.

"Okay, but only if I can have my way with Derik and the rest of those idiots."

Steven smirked, "Then we'll do it tonight, and tomorrow we can start looking for new recruits for our "management" program. You might want to put something on to hide the scars. Just so they don't know it's you at first." Nichole nodded.

"What do you want your new name to be? It used to be Nicky Two Swords, but I think since you might want to change your image, you might want to change your Orsin name."

"Venice!" she shouted with vengeance in her voice.

Steven grinned and said, "Meet me at the office in thirty minutes."

V

It was a pain looking for the full Jackal attire his father had left him. Once he found it, he understood the mask. It went with a solid black bodysuit with a black cape covered in fine fur like a dog. It also came with a black cane with a large orb of obsidian on the top and a silver ring on the bottom.

178

The Chronicles of Merkadiah:
The Rise of the Gryphon

Hidden within it was a sword that could be summoned with the slightest movement from his thumb. It acted like a large stiletto. On the end with the sliver ring, a half-meter blade would pop out, and the pole of the cane could be used as the hilt of the sword.

A rather impractical looking weapon but a deadly one still. Steven waited in the cool misty air until he heard footsteps on the cobblestones behind him. This made him turn to see who it might be. At first, no one was there, then a lithe form began to form in the mist until he saw that it was Venice.

She wore a single piece black body suit that showed off all her curves. Her face was hidden by a mask that looked like a sword blade that had been stretched around her face all the way to her ears where poly-cotton joined to the steel very carefully and wrapped around her entire head except for a long-braided ponytail that flew backward like a scarlet banner.

The face of her mask was black and had two large holes where the deepest violet eyes peered at Steven. Then at the bottom was more poly-cotton that met at the jaw and neck area. At the bottom of the mask where her mouth should be there were a dozen small holes barely visible that allowed her to breathe.

Steven noticed the hilts of two short swords barely cresting her shoulders, but what he could not see was two crossed Orsin Service Pistols hidden up underneath the baldric where the short swords were. She was ready for revenge.

As Steven and his new protégé walked up to The Foxes Den, Steven surveyed the layout of it. An old colony house had been converted into a pleasure house. Exactly what pleasures Steven could only guess.

It could be any type of vice. It could be drugs, liquor, women, men, gambling or any combination of the list. His attentions turned once more to the house on the hill. It was located on a secluded hill surrounded by what could be the last forest on Niriah.

The cobblestone path looped up and around the back of the house forming two paths that joined at the bottom. One went right and was not so steep and the other was a steep climb.

Steven smirked, the man who owned this place was either going to surrender ownership over to him or die. This place could easily be a gold mine.

They began up the right path and saw to their right an empty dirt lot littered with debris. Once upon a time, it could have been a garden for the colonists that owned the property, but now it was just a graveyard of liquor bottles, stumps, and statues that once populated it.

When they got to the back of the house, they were staring at a wonderful sight. To the right of them, was a path that looked like a romantic walk waiting to happen. On the left of it was a large rock fountain embedded in a hill, and at the beginning of the path was a small wooden gate painted white with a large off-white lattice arbor full of periwinkle behind it.

The path went on into the forested hill and disappeared from view. They continued their walk until they came to a gated porch. They went through the gate and into the back door of the house. When they walked in, what they saw was shocking. It was clean. The bar was to their immediate right and was just over a meter long but was a good meter wide.

Behind the bar was a full kitchen and, on the left, were several small tables that were empty. Directly in front of them was a large room with a cathedral ceiling and several gambling tables.

There was a hall to the right with four doors at the end, and on the left were three closed doors that could be seen before a wall blocked their view. Steven nodded at Venice and at the man behind the bar.

He was a tall skinny man with tan skin that had seen a lot of sun. He had shaggy black hair, brown eyes, a mustache with goatee, and a tattoo of a black Pantherine on his left bicep.

Steven looked at him and said, "I am the Jackal, the godfather of the Orsin Crime Family. As of right now you don't pay bribes to The S.P.A, and you don't pay me a tithe to operate. So, if you value your health, you will start giving me a forty percent cut of your weekly profits, or my friend here will gladly educate you on the need to give it to me." Steven pointed behind him at Venice.

Daniel nodded his head and wiped the sweat from his face. Steven smiled. He liked threatening people. It turned him on and gave him power. Now it was time to take care of the problem he came to eradicate.

VI

Mori Sullivan was the First Don. He had decided to move the operation to this pleasure house. It was remote and didn't have any S.P.A. affiliations and was the only place on the planet that was clean and did not care if you ran up a tab or not. Foxe's also offered an exclusive gambling game called "Fast Hands."

Mori just rolled his second "Fast Hands" in thirty minutes when the chaos started. He heard the back door of the building slam shut. Never really paying much attention to who came and went, he was too busy counting his money.

Neither did he hear the threat to Mr. Foxe, and he never saw the two figures clad in black walk into the small gambling room. He was too busy winking at Derik Fythur and the other eight Dons.

They were all getting good rolls. Tonight, was a good night to gamble it seemed. The last thing that went through Derik Fyther's mind, was the blade of a short sword.

Venice had thrown the first one faster than the eye could see. Then, she threw the other one at the Fourth Don. The blade sank into his chest like a hot knife in butter. Steven had ejected the blade in his cane and began to slice through the remaining Dons like weeds.

Just when he had cut down the tenth Don, he saw The First Don surrounded by five bodyguards. Steven glanced at Venice who was wielding two Orsin Service Pistols.

"Where did the guns come from?" shouted Steven with wonder in his voice. Venice chuckled and winked. All Steven could do was raise an eyebrow and shake his head.

Before Steven could act, Venice pulled the triggers and shot all the bodyguards in the head and put two slugs in each of Mori's knees. He screamed in pain as he fell to the floor with the rest of his gang. Steven walked over to him and picked him up by his hair. He brought Mori up to his face, and with his free hand removed the obsidian mask.

For the first time Mori saw the face of the new Jackal. Mori swallowed the knot that was forming in his throat. He knew that his power had come to an end. The rumors of the Jackal still in power were true, and now he was going to die for betrayal.

Steven spat in Mori's face. Venice watched with a burning hate in her eyes. She loved watching the violence and started getting excited watching the brutality. She hadn't been with a man since the fire. Steven was a handsome man and ruthless; plus, he had power, but would he sleep with someone that looked like her? That was the question.

Venice watched with wonder as Steven cut off Mori's head. She licked her lips as the arterial spray splattered her mask. She had to have Steven, or she was going to go insane.

Steven and Venice dumped the bodies of the fallen gangsters in the surrounding forest. When they were finished, they began to walk back to their homes: Steven to his ancestral home and Venice to her hovel.

As they walked through the empty streets, Venice felt giddy like she was a teen-age girl with the boy she had a crush on. The two of them were covered in blood, and she was wondering if Steven was having the same thoughts and feelings.

She knew that she was disfigured now and that a lot of her beauty was gone, but she still had a good figure. Steven was excited to the point of aggression. He loved being brutal.

It was his favorite pleasure to kill and then have sex. He loved the feel of sticky blood on his body. He loved the feel of thrusting a knife into someone. He loved disfiguring, maiming, violating and killing.

He wondered if Venice would be willing to sleep with him. She may have been slightly disfigured, but as far as he knew, she was still whole everywhere else. Since she was going to be his new plaything, he should ask all the questions he wanted.

"In the fire did anything other than your face get burnt?"

Venice was silent for a moment and then said, "No, why?"

"As a condition of being my new First Don since you are female, I have to inspect your body."

A wave of excitement fell over Venice. She would try and seduce him when she showed him her body. Since Steven had needed to see Venice's body, they went back to his house. Venice was not surprised at how big or opulent his house was.

As they walked through the large house, Venice noticed large portraits of Steven's ancestors and large tapestries that held family crests and symbols. She also noticed the coat of arms of several prominent Aridaunts.

As she saw this priceless treasure trove of history, she realized just how imbedded the Orsin's were in the government. When they reached Steven's room, she was somewhat impressed.

It was the size of her hovel alone. It had a large king-sized canopy bed, and a bathroom off the side that looked like it belonged in some sort of stadium.

The Chronicles of Merkadiah:
The Rise of the Gryphon

In the left corner of the room sat a large Network set up. It filled the whole corner of the room and had at least a dozen visual screens some of them were split into sixteen different views showing rooms of the house, including a view of a beautiful young woman sleeping in a room just like the one she was in.

Except this room looked like it was made to keep someone in. Venice shrugged. If Steven was keeping someone captive, it was his business.

Steven walked out of his walk-in closet only wearing a pair of thin cotton shorts. Venice blushed at seeing how well developed he was. He had large pectoral muscles, and his stomach could pass for a washboard.

His arms were not extremely large, but still impressive. She let her eyes roam to the bulge in his shorts. Venice was almost panting when he walked over to her holding a small knife. She wasn't shy about the blade.

In fact, she hoped that he might cut her just a little bit. She loved pain during sex. It was the greatest feeling she could experience. Steven put the knife to her throat and said, "Take off all your clothes and finish with the mask."

Venice acted like she was shocked, but she was getting more excited all the time.

"Turn around and put your hands on the bed. I am going to show you who your boss is and if you don't like it, I'll kill you."

Venice nodded and did what he told her. She went to the bed and put her hands on the side and acted as if she was bracing herself. It was over quickly, but the aftermath was something she could have only hoped for.

He was cruel in all the right ways and loved every painful second of the beating he gave her. Steven was happy. As it turned out Venice was just like him, except in the reverse. She enjoyed being slapped, punched and cut.

He looked down and surveyed her body, as she slept peacefully on his bed. He relished the knowledge of her scars, and the details she gave about how they were acquired. She had scars on her breasts, arms, legs, back, buttocks and, Steven had been happy to add to them a black eye, a split lip and two cuts on both her thighs. She was going to be a fun toy to keep around.

VII

183

Barbarah awoke in a cold sweat that made her night gown cling to her body. The sounds of a woman screaming had forced her from her slumber. It bothered her that Steven seemed to have a different woman every night, but she was glad it wasn't her.

An overwhelming dread permeated her every thought of the day that he would come and tell her it was time to bear him an heir. A cold chill ran up her spine at the mere thought of the violence she would soon endure, regardless of how far into the future it was.

She walked over to a full-length mirror on her large double doors. She looked at the green silk gown that Steven had bought her a few months ago. It seemed funny. He would come in once a week and do nothing but berate her and sometimes even hit her.

Then in a couple of days he would bring her a present of some sort. It was as if Steven were trying somehow to buy her affections, or perhaps it was some sort of twisted courtship.

Either way, it was draining and degrading. Barbarah sighed. She needed a bath. A good soaking would help alleviate some of her worries. Now, she had several things on her mind.

One thing was that she still had heard nothing from Grivon. Of course, even if he were all right how would he know where she was, and her other worry was Steven. How he refused to let her leave her room and how all her food was brought in through a slit in the door.

It was delicious food, but the way it was delivered made her feel like she was in some sort of high-class prison. To top it off, the only conversation she got aside from Stevens random visits, was when the maid came in to change her linens and clean her bathroom.

Even the maid brushed her off and told her to be happy the master cared so much about her. The way the maids talked about Steven gave her the idea they were slaves instead of hired help.

Barbarah sighed and went to her dresser to retrieve a towel and a new gown. She sighed once more and hoped that things would change soon. When she walked into the bathroom, there was a sink and toilet on the right of the room.

hen to the left was a set of three stairs that led down to a large basin with ten water faucets. The floor was made of tiny brown tiles. From the top of the basin to the bottom was a meter. It was like bathing in a small swimming pool. Barbarah disrobed at the toilet and walked down into the basin.

184

The Chronicles of Merkadiah:
The Rise of the Gryphon

She only needed one of the faucets to bathe but she wanted to soak away her troubles. She started all the faucets and let the warm water flow into the basin. Barbarah sat down on the warming tile floor and let out a contented sigh as the water flowed over her silky legs.

She put her head back against the wall of the basin and closed her eyes. She didn't have to worry about cutting off the water as it would stop once the basin was full. As she laid there, the water flowed over her, and she began to think of Grivon.

She wondered where he was and what he was doing. Was he with Phoy yet, or had he been killed by the Autocrat, or worse had he been imprisoned? Wherever he was, she wished that she were with him.

Her heart ached with the thought of him not being near her. It was all so frustrating. Here she was a prisoner with Steven. He gave her food and everything she needed, but she wasn't allowed to leave her room.

She needed Grivon. Tears welled up in her eyes and splashed into the water. She was dead, and this was Hell.

Chapter Three
Angela Simone

"Sometimes angels come in all shapes and sizes," -The Musings of Phoy Yen

Ten Months Later

I

The splash of freezing water shook him awake violently. It made his heart race and he felt like puking. He was in a dark featureless room that was made of stone. He couldn't remember where he was or why he was there. In fact, what day was it? How long had he been here? All he knew was that the last thing he could remember was being beaten.

He couldn't remember what his name was. He couldn't remember anything. Had he always been there? His thoughts were all jumbled. It were as if his mind was broken into tiny shards of glass. He tried grasping at them to remember who he was, but all he saw in front of him was a naked woman.

He cocked his head, looking at her, bewildered by her presence. He was on all fours and naked himself. He only knew that she was there to take care of him. In fact, he was thirsty. He got up on his knees and begged like a dog.

"Thirsty, boy?" the woman spat.

All Grivon could do was nod with a goofy grin on his face.

"I thought so, now lick the water off the floor, and then we will begin."

Grivon lapped at the water greedily. The water felt cool on his throat and as it hit his stomach, the sudden cold spread through his body. When he was finished, he looked up at the woman.

"Now it is time to play your favorite game, Heaven and Hell." said the woman as she began to rub her right breast with her hand, "Today I feel like more Heaven than Hell, but only if you do as I tell you."

Grivon smiled and nodded his head with the same goofy grin on his face. He had forgotten that he had been there for over a year. He had forgotten who he was. He had forgotten why he was even there. In less than two months, he had been broken. The game that she always wanted to play, fifteen minutes of Heaven and Hell, was the tool.

"First, we are going to start off with you pleasing me," she said as she walked over to Grivon.

"Yes," Grivon said.

She grabbed his hair and spat in his face, "Yes, who?"

Grunting he muttered, "Yes, Herrin."

Smiling she cupped his cheek in her hand and said, "That's a good boy."

II

When they finished Bebe wrapped a loincloth around Grivon's waist. She then secured an iron collar around his neck. The collar had a chain that attached to a pair of manacles clamped around his wrists. It felt strange with all the extra weight from the iron. She then chained him to a wall and left the room for a long time.

Time passed slowly and the all too familiar dripping water started. Anytime that maddening drip echoed through the room, he would be left alone for what seemed to be days. When she returned, she was wearing a tight purple dress that barely covered her thighs. Grivon shied his face away.

He wasn't allowed to look at her while she was clothed. Bebe grabbed the chain, unhooked him from the wall, and pulled it hard. She took him up a spiral staircase that came out in the kitchen of the boarding house. Grivon heard a strange sound. As he listened harder, it became apparent that there was a baby in the common area of the house.

He shook his head at the sound. It sounded so foreign to him. Of course, seeing daylight was a foreign concept as well. In fact, it was sensory overload. It was starting to give him a headache. The headache was made worse when Bebe pulled him outside.

Grivon could barely walk as he was yanked through the street. The sunlight beat down on his face. He had to close his eyes to keep it from blinding him. It was all so overwhelming. He couldn't help but fall to the dusty street. Bebe yanked the chain hard, and he began making a gurgling noise.

"Get up! Lazy, stubborn, son of a bitch!" She screamed.

"Herrin, the sun. It hurts my eyes. Can you make it stop?" asked Grivon meekly.

"Oh, my poor little thrall, I can blindfold you and lead you around so you can fall more! Of course, I won't make it stop! You are nothing more than a piece of meat, you stupid little man. You have served your purpose and have given me a child. Now I am going to sell you, and then you will be somebody else's problem."

Jerking hard on the chain Bebe forced Grivon to his feet. She began to walk down the street toward the teleportation station, but before they reached it, they turned down a side street that led to a large warehouse.

Inside the warehouse were hundreds more women, each holding a man in chains like the ones Grivon was in. If the men weren't wearing a loincloth, then they were wearing nothing at all. Most of the men seemed to be used to what was happening. Then a woman clothed in a white suit walked onto a stage and stood behind a podium.

There she called out a name, and a woman with a naked man on a chain walked on stage. In an unintelligible voice, the woman in the white suit began to cry out numbers extremely quick. Grivon noticed that only a small majority of the men being sold were wearing loincloths.

"Herrin how come only me, and a few others are wearing loin cloths?" asked Grivon with childlike wonder.

"Because I and some of the others don't want you to be bought solely on your assets," she said as she grabbed him, making him groan in pain.

The auction went on for several hours. Then it was Bebe's turn. As she led Grivon onto the stage he asked, "Herrin, why did you do this to me? I can't remember anything about myself, why?"

"You killed my sister."

Grivon began to think hard. It made his head hurt. Trying to remember what your brain had forgotten was horrible. Finally, as the headache got worse a name formed on his lips, "Ubiroe?" Bebe turned to look at him. Then the world went white as Bebe slapped him hard across the face.

"How dare you say that name in my presence!" she said in a hushed yell. "That was the name of my best friend! You killed her too!"

"Only her, Herrin," said Grivon weakly.

"Damn you! Now with this display you may only sale for a few hundred."

"Miss Bebe, what would you like to start the bid off at?" asked the auctioneer

"Four hundred?" asked Bebe with a touch of hope in her voice.

"Prove to me why I should, considering he can still ask questions."

The Chronicles of Merkadiah:
The Rise of the Gryphon

Bebe yanked the loincloth from around his waist, exposing him. A deep shame washed over him as hundreds of hungry eyes took in his exposed skin. Goosebumps formed on his arms and legs.

Trying to find a way to end the shamefulness of the situation he was drawn to a woman that stood out of place in the back. She was dressed all in black and had long raven hair. It was as if she knew him, and as if she read his mind she smirked.

"We will start the bidding for this stud at six hundred," the auctioneer said smiling. She turned back to the crowd and said, "Here we have a nineteen-year-old stud. Standing here in all his glory, he is good for making daughters. So, a starting bid at six hundred marks. I see six, do I hear six fifty?"

"Ten Thousand!" shouted a woman in the back of the room.

A quiet hush came over the group for a few minutes. Then the auctioneer composed herself and said, "Do I hear ten thousand five hundred?"

The room was silent once again. Several minutes later after no one said anything else, the auctioneer struck her gavel against the podium.

"Sold, to the woman wearing black!"

A solid lump formed in the back of his throat.

III

The house that Angela had bought shortly after she had arrived on Tūhl was small in comparison to the boarding house. It had only two stories instead of four and sat on the outskirts of town away from the psychotic women of the Barrim Clan. It had a high rock wall that ran the perimeter of the property, which provided some privacy.

Inside. Grivon shared a room with Angela. He had been at her house for a little over a week. This new woman who owned him was nice. She didn't beat him or humiliate him, and she fed him more than once a day.

Not to mention, she fed him more than bread and water when she did. Then every night, she gave him a hot drink that tasted a lot like mocha. Then she would ask him questions about his past, and the funny thing was little by little he began to remember things.

However, what he remembered most was the first night Angela had brought him there. He was tired and nervous. She had fed him, then bathed him. Scrubbing ever so gentle around his raw wounds.

Then she took him into her bedroom and lay next to him. He found comfort in her small almond-shaped eyes. The soft brown of her irises gave him a feeling of security. Her raven tresses captivated him.

When she rolled over to go to sleep, he was surprised that she had not tried to have her way with him. The next morning, he asked her why.

She simply said that it would not have been right and that she had other motives for buying him. Then she said that she was an assassin and that she had been hired to kill him, but that she wanted to make sure he remembered who he was before she tried to kill him.

That way he could at least fight back. For some strange reason, he found comfort in this knowledge.

IV

Grivon had taken to chopping wood for the furnace that helped keep hot water and power going. It felt good to do physical work. It felt as if his body was made for this sort of thing. He could chop a little over two piles a day.

After having gotten used to the strenuous activity, he started to do pushups and other exercises. One day Angela came outside and tossed Grivon a wooden sword. It was familiar in shape, but he couldn't place it.

He looked at the sword and felt the weight of the wood in his hand. Angela stood across from him stretching and flexing.

"It's called a bokken. It was the practice sword I was trained on. I'm hoping that once you get a sword in your hand you will start to remember more," said Angela with concern in her voice. Then she added, "The bitch really did a number on you, didn't she?"

Grivon just stared. He wasn't sure what to do. As far as he knew, he had never used a sword before. All he could remember was the dank stone room that Bebe kept him in. It seemed to him that he had always been there. Then again, he saw a face in his dreams that looked like Bebe's but kinder.

He often saw her kissing him in his dreams. He could tell she loved him, but who was she?

Grivon was brought back from his musings when white-hot pain flashed through his head. Angela had hit him in the head with her bokken. Reeling Grivon looked at her. Then as if it were second nature, he flourished the sword and struck at Angela. She blocked him effortlessly.

Then she drove the wood into his stomach. Grivon's lungs became fire as the breath was driven from him. It took several minutes for him to stop coughing and regain his breath. When he stood to his feet, Angela saw a quiet fire burning in his eyes.

She knew that he still didn't know who he was, but she had awoken something deep inside of him that made him want to fight. Something that made her wish that she had not awoken it.

Then she watched as he straightened himself and put the sword out in front of him in a basic stance. She took a basic stance as well. They stood looking at each other for several minutes.

Then Grivon broke his stance and charged Angela. She tried to sidestep and was hit on the back of her head. She shook it off and tumbled away to center her stance.

Grivon did not let her. He charged faster than a bull. Then he raised the bokken above his head and delivered three quick strikes. Angela blocked two. On the second her bokken broke. Grivon used this to his advantage and hit her arm and put the cold wood against her neck.

"Very good," she said.

Grivon dropped the bokken and fell to his knees. His whole body was shaking, and he began sobbing. All Angela could do was rub his back as he sobbed and pounded the dirt. That woman really had worked him over.

She had stolen who he was. Even if he were a lousy Kartah, he still didn't deserve what she had done to him. No one deserved to be brutalized for ten months, then sold to someone else who would do the same thing.

It was inhuman, but what could you expect from a bunch of backwater sluts. When Grivon had finished crying, Angela helped him stand up and walked him back into the house. She led him to the bathroom and ran him a hot bath.

She added lavender soap to the bath to help relax him. Grivon slid into the tub, and the hot water rushed over his aching body. Why did it hurt? He was still shaking, and he reached forward and gripped his knees. He began to sob as his mind began to whorl like a drain.

All his thoughts and memories swirling together made him shake all the harder. Until a primal scream came from his throat. Angela covered her ears. When he finished, he was still clutching his knees and sobbing.

Angela put her hand on his back to try and comfort him. When she did, she felt the long jagged scars running down his back. Then she looked at them. They were superficial wounds, but they still ran deep.

Only a Kartah had access to a teleportation jammer. This was getting worse. The more that was revealed about what happened to him, the more she did not want to kill him. She was starting to understand that Grivon had suffered enough and that killing him would only add insult to injury.

Then she remembered. His black guild robe, the only patch on his lapel was the graduation patch. He wasn't even employed yet! How could she kill him? He wasn't even legally a Kartah. He was looking for something, or someone.

The fact that the Chimera had chosen her personally for this assignment was clear. He had just graduated. That meant he was a Kartah but wasn't at the same time. He still had to find an Aridaunt that would take him.

Then he had to prove his worth to that Aridaunt. The poor bastard was just looking for employment when those psychotic sluts captured him.

"Nine weeks of hell. Nine weeks of heaven," spoke Grivon softly.

"What's that?" asked Angela brought out of her thoughts.

"When I woke up, I was chained to a beam in the dark room. I was completely naked, and my ankles were tied, and my legs spread. I don't know how long I had been hanging there. I know something terrible had been happening, but I couldn't for the life of me remember," He began his voice strangely childlike.

"Some things I can remember, but other parts are really fuzzy." He said scratching at several lattice-like scars on his left arm. With tear-filled eyes he looked up at Angela and started talking. Memories began spilling from his mouth like a broken bottle.

"When she came into the dark room, light flooded in. I had to close my eyes to keep my head from exploding. Then she shut the door and lit a candle. It hurt my eyes, but not as badly. When my eyes adjusted, I looked at her," he started.

"She was completely naked and was holding a strange looking whip. It had ceramic studs woven into it. It looked like it had nine long cords spewing from its handle, and in the dim light it looked like some evil device from the pits of Hell. She came close and pranced around in front of me.

She asked me, 'Don't you like my body?' I said, 'No.' She swung that demonic weapon of hers and struck my stomach. I even felt some of the strands hitting my back. I coughed up blood. Then she twisted me until the chain began to wrap around my fingers. She did not stop until my fingers were smashed and bleeding.

Then she said, 'From now on my name is Herrin.' Then she proceeded to beat my back with that thing until eventually I passed out.

"The next day her mother came into my room and gave me a bite of bread and a small gulp of water. They barely quenched my thirst and hunger. Then she put warm, wet cloths and poultices on my stomach and back. It felt good at first, and then it began to burn.

Then Bebe's mother left the room, closing the door behind her. I don't know how long I was there until the sound began, the sound of a single drop of water hitting stone and echoing. At first, I didn't mind it.

Then after a while, it slowly began to eat at my mind. I began to scream for it to stop. I began to beg for it to stop. Then Herrin entered the room.

"Once again, she lit a candle. This time she was holding a long cane.

It was made of a long thick piece of bamboo that had been split into thin strips and then retied again at the base. The rest of the strips were loose. This time she didn't say anything. She removed the healing cloths and once again wound the chain until my fingers bled.

Then she began to hit me with the cane pole. On the first hit, I thought I was going to die. It ripped skin and tissue from my back. Cackling, she began to do it harder and faster until I once again passed out.

"Then sometime later her mother came back and did what she did before. Again, the dripping sound started, and once more until my brain couldn't handle it. Herrin entered the room as always with a candle.

This time she was pulling a basin behind her with hot coals in it. When it got closer and my eyes had adjusted, I noticed small sharp pieces of metal in the basin. She left for a moment only to return with large iron tongs.

Then without speaking, she picked out one of the pieces of metal. She forced it hard against my sternum. It sizzled, and I could smell my skin burn off. I heard someone screaming. Then I realized it was me. I was screaming. I could do nothing but scream. I passed out.

"When I awoke this time, I was in a bigger room, and my wounds were healed. I also had been given a larger cell. I also was free. However, I was several feet underground, not to mention I was in a room made of stone with a big metal door in front of me.

I could walk around and stretch my legs. At least I was somewhat free. Then Herrin opened the door. The hinges creaked, and shivers ran up my spine. I looked at her. She was holding a device she called a picana. Without speaking or blinking, she began to hit me. With more space, it was worse.

The more I ran, the more she laughed, and the harder she swung. When I was finally tired, I just lay there as she beat me until the shocks from the electrodes made me unconscious.

"When I woke up, I was lying on a wooden bench. My arms and legs tied together underneath the bench. Above me was a small bag. In it was some sort of fluid. Every two or three seconds a drop of water would hit me on the forehead.

All I could think about was the water dropping on my forehead. Soon I began to lose myself in the dripping and before I knew it, I had no name.

"The next thing I knew, she wanted me almost every hour, and I liked it. Whether it was painful or not I didn't care. I was a mindless beast used for her pleasure. Soon she stopped, and I saw less and less of her and more of her mother.

Her mother fed me more often until one day Herrin came in extremely angry. She took the bamboo cane and started hitting my face and then the rest of my body. She kept screeching 'Bastard!' and that was all she said as she tore strip after strip of flesh from my body.

"Once my wounds were healed, she had her way with me one more time and took me to that building where you bought me."

Angela smoothed his hair and kissed him on the forehead. She pulled his head to her chest as he broke out in tears once more. A sudden thought of them hot with sweat lying beside each other in the warm night air after a round of passion.

She blushed and banished the inappropriate thought from her head. It was one thing to not want him dead; it was something totally different to want to sleep with him.

After he had washed, she took him to their room and lay down beside him. She cuddled up to him to keep him warm and comfort him. She rubbed his back as his breathing settled and he drifted to sleep.

When she was sure he was asleep, she got up and walked to her Network terminal. She keyed in the address for reaching the Chimera.

When the familiar masked face finally appeared, Angela realized that she had taken off her clothes to keep Grivon warm. She blushed when she realized her employer's eyes were fixed on her breasts.

"Don't get used to this," said Angela turning her back.

194

"Don't worry about it; no one will know you were naked. What can I do for you? Have you finally found Grivon? And, if so, have you killed him"

"Yes, I have found him, but what I wish to ask is if I can repay the advance fee and take a sabbatical. I just found out that there is something I need to do. A debt I have to repay no matter the cost."

The Chimera just sat looking off into space. After several long moments, the Chimera turned his head back to the screen. He sighed heavily before finally saying, "Keep the advance fee. It was an internal operation after all."

"What do you mean, an internal operation?"

"That is not your concern. Take your sabbatical and contact me when you wish to return to active duty. Chimera out," the screen went blue.

Angela sighed as she turned off the screen. She began to walk silently to her own bed when suddenly she heard an intense scream coming from Grivon's room.

She ran as fast as she could to find him arching his back and screaming in pain. He kept turning his head and shouting, "No! Stop it!"

Angela went and held his arms to keep him from flailing. Then she lay on top of him and let go of his flailing arms. His arms locked around her back, and she kissed him hard on the lips. His eyes opened and then he relaxed his breathing becoming placid.

"Just hold me please," he whispered.

Angela rolled off Grivon and snuggled up to his back and placed a hand on his scarred torso. Feeling his scars made her mind return to a place and time she would rather forget, but no matter how much she wanted to she would never be able to.

V

She had been born and raised on the forest world of Rhokahl. The sparsely populated world hung between Merk and Felion. The planet had such a beauty that no one appreciated but her. The Aridaunt of that planet had been killed in a duel between him and another Aridaunt.

The new Aridaunt was Viscount Lyle Green. He began to harvest the ancient trees of Rhokahl, so he could sell them for large profits.

Angela and her father lived on a quiet farm fourteen kilometers outside of the main city of Rohcal. Her father made several trips each year to Rohcal to sell their fruits, vegetables, furs, meat and other wares.

The profits from these sales gave them money for seeds, more cattle, and clothes. Angela's mother had died due to complications during childbirth, so it was just the two of them. On the tenth standard month of her tenth year, Angela's father left for his last trip into Rohcal.

Tears welled in her eyes at this memory. Her father had been gone for a week when she left her home for the last time. She had traveled for about seven kilometers when she saw her father's wagon.

The fruits and vegetables were rotting, and the meat was spoiled. The furs had been stolen, and there she found her father's severed head.

His hands were still holding the reigns of the oxen, which were now gone, and his head covered in maggots and flies. She had vomited several times before she was able to compose herself.

It had to be the work of Kartah. Sometimes when she went into town to get supplies with her father, she heard the other townsmen talk about how Llye's Kartah were evil. They would sit watching on the main roads.

When anyone they considered worthless would come by, they would teleport behind them and test their speed by cutting off the heads of people.

Angela traveled for days without food and water until she made it to Rohcal. She was found lying in a ditch, hungry and in severe need of a bath. A merchant found her and nursed her back to health.

When she was strong enough, she told the kind merchant and his wife what had

happened to her father. She cried for the first time that day. Her father was dead, and now she was an orphan. She was alone, so she begged the merchant and his wife to let her leave and join the Fire Guild.

Her initial assessment was strange. She had stood naked in front of several men and women. Each had taken turns insulting her till the point that she became aware of her surroundings. She noticed a wooden sword lying on the floor nearby.

Between being humiliated and her father's death, she ran and grabbed the sword, swung and broke it over the head of the one who had called her, "A flat-breasted bitch."

That display of rage had gotten her into the fire guild and in fifteen years had gotten her kicked out. It had taken fifteen years, but her abusive Guild Lord had finally crossed the line, so she killed him.

He held her down and attempted to force himself on her. She was close to her Saber, so she gripped it and stabbed him through his neck. The Guild

The Chronicles of Merkadiah:
The Rise of the Gryphon

Master, wishing to cover up such a scandal, had expelled her and said that she had killed her Guild Lord in a training session.

That was the story that was given to the Autocrat and the Senate in the report. At this point she was twenty-five, and she had nowhere to go. She couldn't do anything but fight. All she would be good for was a whore in a brothel. That was when she met the Chimera.

He was the leader of the Assassin's Guild. He took her in and for the next ten years taught her how to kill. He taught her how not to let her emotions get in the way.

He taught her metallurgy. As one of her final tests she had to make a weapon, she fashioned a katana. An elegant weapon of an elegant culture of the Blue Star. The test she was given after her training was finished was to kill the governor of Rhokahl. She had relished killing all fifty of his Kartah.

The boys tried to fight her, but had ended up without their heads, just like her father. When she got to the governor, he was a fat, sniveling man. When she put the sword to his throat to make him beg he offered her money, power, and even his position.

He even soiled himself when she said she was going to kill him. She forced him down on his fat little knees and drove the sword through the back of his head.

Angela snickered. She named herself that day, The Demon Hunter. She vowed to rid the system of the scourge known as Kartah. They were demons disguised as humans, and she was going to rid all planets and moons of them. Any job that needed a Kartah removed she took no matter how little it paid, even if it was for free.

Angela was brought out of her memories by Grivon's soft breathing. She smiled and rested her head on an unscathed place on his chest. The sound of his strong heartbeat lured her to sleep.

Chapter Four
The Mind's Battlefield

"Seek not the path of vengeance, for it will consume you from within."
-Pantherine Proverb

I

The blade of the katana passed way too close to Grivon's face, and the blade barely grazed him. The capillaries in his face opened, and warm blood trickled down his cheek. Grunting, he rolled away from the down stroke of Angela's sword.

As soon as he was away, he sprang to his feet and jumped toward Angela sword raised above his head. She dodged, and his attack missed. Angela counter attacked at Grivon's back. He brought the sword back behind him and blocked the strike.

Then in flawless motion turned back around with the katana whirling above his head and brought the blade to rest a hair's breadth away from Angela's neck. Angela regarded Grivon for a moment. His progress with a blade was astonishing considering he had forgotten most of his training.

Though if the training he was given were worth a damn he would recover it all soon enough. Even more impressive was the progress made in learning to cope with being tortured for a year.

She thought back to the first day she had seen him, and that was over a year ago. It took months of talking to the local women to figure out where he was. She just had to wait for the right auction. Ever since Dahra took power things in this remote part of the system took a turn for the worse.

Before the women of the clan had just mutilated their son's, that was bad enough. Now they captured unsuspecting travelers to torture and pass around as slaves for work or childbearing. The fact that a woman could be so desperate to have a child as to abduct and torture an innocent person was mind boggling.

If she could, Angela would kill all of them. They all had seen and committed enough degradation and human evil to fill a lifetime. They were just as bad, if not worse, than Kartah.

The Chronicles of Merkadiah:
The Rise of the Gryphon

If she could, she would take Grivon's baby from Bebe and make sure that she would never have any more, but it was a moot point. The best she could do would be to start killing The Barrim bitches the way she killed Kartah.

Grivon watched as Angela heaved after their sparring match. It had taken a few weeks to get used to crossing blades, but it felt good to have a sword in his hands fighting again, but his mind was wandering to darker places.

He was still trying to overcome his battle with Ubiroe on a psychological level. His dreams reflected this. They were about Ubiroe doing what she pleased to Barbarah and then killing her. To top it all off, he was still trying to understand what he went through with the torture and violence he experienced with Bebe.

It felt as if a piece of him had been taken away and lost forever, and a void had formed where that piece of him used to be. His dreams and thoughts were completely dominated by everything that happened, and that was giving way to plots for revenge.

Looking over at Angela, he smiled, trying to hide his anguish. She smiled a wide and toothy smile that lit up her whole face. Suddenly, she grabbed his hand and led him into the house.

They walked into the coo foyer, and Angela regarded Grivon's sweat-covered chest and then quickly glanced away.

"You should go wash up. I'll make some lunch and you can tell me what is on your mind today." Angela said giving him a mischievous smile. Grivon nodded and walked into his room. He took off his shorts and grabbed a washrag and a towel and headed for the bath basin.

He pressed the button to run himself a hot bath. Once the water cut off, he lowered himself into the steaming water. As he settled down into the basin, goose bumps formed all over his body and he went numb.

It felt good to soak in hot water. He took his washrag and some homemade soap and began washing himself; wishing he could wash away the taint left on him by Ubiroe and Bebe.

While he could wash himself until he bled what good would it do? He would still feel dirty and alone. Unable to hold it in any longer, he began to sob as he wondered why he was so helpless when it had come to what Bebe had done.

He wondered why he failed to fight her off, and he wondered why it affected him so much. Then a stabbing thought of regret wormed its way into his thoughts, he could have activated his Aurora.

Although that may not have saved him in the long run, at least he would have tried to keep it from happening. He must have wanted this to happen on some level.

After several minutes of staring at the green tiles in the basin, his sorrow turned to anger. None of this was his fault! Dahra and Bebe were the ones to blame. They were the ones who poisoned him and tormented him.

Then another thought burrowed its way in. Had he listened to Phoy he never would have gotten into this predicament. Now his anger was frothing, more at himself than anyone else. He punched the water making it splash over the sides of the basin. Someone had to pay for what happened.

Smiling he began to fantasize about making that bitch pay for what she did. She would pay for every scar she gave him. When he finished drying himself off and dressed, he went into the dining room to see what Angela made for lunch.

He walked into the sunlit room and looked at the table. Two plates were set, and each had a sandwich and some fried roots. The sandwich was made with thin slices of meat, cheese and some leafy greens.

Grivon looked around for Angela, then sat down to wait for her. He was unsure where she was, but he would wait until she got back. For the first time in a year he thought about Barbarah. He missed her a lot, and he ached for her presence at night.

Now more than ever, he wished he could have taken her with him. If she would have been with him, she could have stopped Bebe. At least that was what he hoped.

He wished he could lie next to her and run his hands through her soft hair and look deep into eyes. He ached to caress her smooth skin and see her angelic smile. Her smile alone made him weak and could bring a smile to his own face. Grivon was pulled back to reality when he heard a voice ask, "Are you awake?"

Grivon blinked and looked up from his plate. He had yet to touch his food and Angela was sitting across from him. She had bathed and changed into a smooth purple dress, and raven locks were pulled back into a ponytail.

Grivon looked at her soft brown eyes. She was stunning. Grivon felt a catch in his stomach. For some reason he had a bad feeling.

"Yes, I was thinking about Barbarah. My lover," he said without emotion.

"You have a lover? I didn't know," Angela said, her voice thick.

"It's all right. I guess we really haven't talked about my personal life before I came here. I hope that what I want to tell you today doesn't make you not wish to be around me any longer."

"I am glad that you finally recovered most of your memory. I promise you that if I can, I will always be around. No matter what happens as long as you don't try to take advantage of me," said Angela with a wink.

"Well where do you want me to begin?" Asked Grivon taking a bite of his sandwich.

Angela swallowed a bite of her sandwich and said, "Tell me about Barbarah."

"If an angel lived here with us, it would be her. She has golden blonde hair and large emerald eyes. She is kind, sensitive, and loving. She is the mother of my child, and I miss seeing her and spending time with her under a sea of stars. Just to hold her again would be enough for me."

Angela ate a couple of the now cold fried roots before saying, "Do you not want to make love to her anymore?"

Grivon blushed and said, "Of course I do, but she was repeatedly assaulted by male members of the Chaos Guild. She has a thirst for knowledge of forms, and she could have become a great Aridaunt, but when she would ask an older or stronger member of the Guild to teach her new things she would instead be brutalized. When it comes to making love to her it is when she wants to. Why?"

"Well to be quite honest I find you very attractive and I wanted to know how important sex was to you."

Grivon's face flushed even more and said, "It is not what drives me. Yes, I like it, but it is not the most important thing in my life. It seems that most people value sex above most things and then others are consumed by it completely. Still others confuse it with love. Why, is it that important to you?"

"Well I can tell you this. When I was at the Fire Guild, my Guild Lord would touch me, as well as look at me naked. Then one day when I was twenty-five, he raped me. I killed him during the attack and was expelled, so when you say sex is her choice I can understand, but as far as I am concerned, I like it and its very important."

Grivon's face flushed and continued talking, trying to get away from the topic of sex, "I guess you would like to know what brought me to Tūhl. I am looking for a person. He lives on the planet, 'where the dead walk,' do you know where that is?"

"I can find out for you," Angela said, batting her long eyelashes. "Is there anything else you would like to talk about?"

Grivon sighed, "Sure, could you tell me why I want to torture and kill Bebe?"

Angela dropped the fried root she was holding, pushed away her plate, and turned white. She looked at Grivon with a mixture of disgust and pity.

Grivon smirked a little bit. She was disgusted at his fantasies of revenge, and for some strange reason he liked it. This was a new feeling; he was becoming the thing he hated the most.

He once hated being called a freak but now he was happy he was. At least if he was a freak, he could keep Angela's advances at bay, and then she said something that shattered the fact that he was now comfortable about being a freak.

"Because what she did to you has caused you to view things in a way that may or may not be right, but it's okay as long as you don't act on your fantasies. Remember that rape and murder are wrong, but everyone has thoughts about one of those at least once. Be careful that it doesn't consume you.

Sometimes as a part of healing on an emotional and psychological level, fantasies can help more than anything else. When you say that you would like to 'torture and kill Bebe,' it bothers me on one level, but it makes me happy to know that you are angry and can feel emotion. Until now you really haven't shown any emotion toward anything."

Grivon felt the joy he had at realizing he was changing shatter. Now he began to get angry with her. For the first time, he realized that although she was trying to help him, she was also trying to seduce him, and he refused to sleep with anyone but Barbarah.

Then he looked at her and tersely said, "So if you could, would you want to do it right here?"

With a gleam in her eyes Angela shouted, "Yes!"

Grivon stood up so quickly and that he turned over his chair and the table fell over. Their lunch crashing to the floor. Angela stood quickly and scurried toward the far wall.

The Chronicles of Merkadiah:
The Rise of the Gryphon

Grivon stalked over to her with what she thought was the scariest face she had ever seen on someone. She screamed when she found herself against the wall.

Grivon was right in front of her and then he was leaning over in her face with one hand against the wall. He glared at her and with an evil grin and ripped off her dress straps.

He stood back and looked at the fear in her face and then said, "I will not have sex with anyone other than Barbarah and that is final. So, go ahead and do what you need to do to me so that you can make yourself feel better.

If you sleep with me, it makes you no better than Bebe or your Guild Lord! Here you go, Herrin!" he shouted, as he stripped before her.

Angela looked at him with greedy anticipation. A shadow of lust passed across her face for a moment and then she must have realized what he said. That unless he absolutely wanted to have sex with her, she should stop talking about it and stop trying to get him to sleep with her.

She pulled up her top and hid her breasts from view and then lowered her head.

Grivon pulled up his pants and looked at her, "I'm going out. Don't follow me, and if I don't come back, then look for me after a week. I am in a bad mood, and I will not hesitate to make sure you cannot find me." Angela nodded with her eyes closed and began to sob.

II

Grivon walked into his room and put on his Guild robe and strapped his sword onto his lower back for easy reach. He walked out of the house and as he did, he saw Angela wearing something different and cleaning up what remained of their lunch.

He hoped she would forgive him later, but for now, he needed to get away from her. He felt himself slipping into some sort of lust-driven frenzy, and if he didn't get away from her as soon as he could, he would give in, and that would be wrong.

He felt himself tear up for a second as he walked out on a friend. He stalked away from the house toward town. By the time he reached the gate to in the wall, he was starting to cool down, but he didn't want her to know that.

He probably overdid his theatrics, but it made his point.

He would have to apologize to her when he returned, but for now let her think about it. Why was sex so important to everyone? Why couldn't they just be happy without obsessing over it? He sighed and shook his head.

As he walked into the town shaking his head and trying to wrap his head around all the insanity, he heard music. Grivon looked up from the dirt road and out into the middle of the town.

It looked as if all the women in the town were dancing and singing about something. The music being played was a lot different than the music he had heard at the ball. It was faster and had a softer bass beat, but the other beats were synthesized.

The woman standing on the stage was spouting out unintelligible words about some leader. As Grivon got closer to the din, he realized what it was. It was a celebration.

All the citizens of Tuhlead were out. Of course, the men were either wearing loincloths or nothing at all. The women were grinding into the men in animalistic fury; they all seemed elated about something.

What exactly they were so happy about was beyond knowing, but Grivon was going to find out. As Grivon got nearer to the center of Tuhlead, he looked down a dark alley to see a man and woman copulating.

She was pressed up against the wall with her legs wrapped around the man's waist and was moaning loudly. A feeling of overwhelming disgust came over him, and he was about to walk on when he recognized the woman. It was Bebe. A sinister grin came across his face.

As he waited, he tried not to listen. After half an hour, the man left. He wasn't one of the mutilated ones because he still had a tongue, eyes, and other body parts. The man had the look of satisfaction on his face.

Lucky bastard! Got to escape unscathed! He waited another few minutes to make sure she was decent. When he was sure she was clothed, he turned into the alley. Bebe just finished pulling her dress up, when he stalked into the alley.

"Oh, sorry, I'm not a prostitute. My boyfriend and I cannot control ourselves very well and with all the excitement we just had to…" her voice trailed off when she realized it was Grivon.

"It's no bother," Grivon hissed. "I think a brothel would be a better fit for a psychotic whore like yourself anyway."

"Why is that? What do you want from me? I sold you months ago. I have nothing to say to you, now if you will excuse me."

The Chronicles of Merkadiah:
The Rise of the Gryphon

Before she could move, the blade of his sword was at her throat. Startled, she walked backward with a look of fear on her face. She began walking faster as Grivon began stalking forward. A deep maniacal laugh bellowed out from his lips.

Then Bebe's back hit the wall of a building. She was cornered and in her present position, no one would come to her

Aid. Grivon's laugh started to become louder and more frantic. Bebe looked up at him with frightened, watery eyes. She was almost to tears.

His grin widened even further and then he said, "I can't believe how stupid you are. I'm a graduate of the Chaos Guild, and one of the best swordsmen in the system. Do you really think you could get by me? That you could get away with torturing me and not pay for it?"

All Bebe could do was cry. She trembled and shook, fear wracking her body. In her entire life, no man had ever tried to overpower her. It had always been the other way around, and now she was scared out of her mind. She realized what she had been doing, and so she decided to do to what any other person in her position on any other planet would do, beg.

"Please, I have a baby boy that you gave me. I am so sorry for what I did," she whimpered. "I wish I hadn't. Please don't hurt me. I don't know if I can live with those kinds of scars on my mind.

I will do whatever you wish of me. Just don't force me or beat me. I promise you will like it you'll see I can make you feel good. Please, please don't hurt me."

"So now I have two children. Both of which I will never know or touch. I know that your family won't let me near you or my son. So, go ahead beg all you want. Your pleas will fall on deaf ears, just as mine did."

Bebe fell to her knees whimpering. Crocodile tears streamed from her eyes. She was afraid, and now it seemed that he was going to hurt her in some way. She couldn't figure out how. Was he going to rape her?

Was he just going to kill her, or was it both? She let out a strangled sob. Grivon's arch laughter had stopped. Now he was focused on his target. She was a cowardly cow. She didn't beg because she wanted to take care of their child.

She wanted to live because she thought that she deserved to. It was all about her no matter what.

"So, what are you going to do?" She asked, her sobs turning to wails.

"I should take this sword and shove it between your whoring legs and cut you from there up through your brains. Then with what is left with your body, burn it, and piss on the ashes. You are nothing more

than a worthless whore who takes advantage of people just for your own pleasure and gain. Now you are going to die, Herrin. "

Grivon watched himself from that hole in the crags of his special place. How he had gotten there he didn't know. He watched himself laugh with glee as he rammed his sword threw the middle of her head.

He spat on her face and walked out of the ally covered in blood. He was going to have to go home earlier than he wanted, but at least she was dead.

III

Grivon ran all the way home laughing. He was happy with what had just happened. That horrible woman was dead and now his shattered mind was at peace. Provided of course that the local Kartah didn't try and arrest him for murder, but then those arrogant Kartah would meet their end.

Even though the act of revenge was gratifying, it was going to be hard living with the fact he could be put to death. He burst into the house panting. Angela was finished cleaning up and had changed her clothes into her black bodysuit.

Her eyes and cheeks were red from crying. Grivon regarded her with a small amount of disdain. She had driven him to a level of anger and rage that he had never felt before.

"You look like you've been in a battle, is everything okay?" asked Angela with concern.

"Yes," Grivon said giddily.

"So, what happened?" Angela asked cocking her eyebrow.

"I killed the little whore. The slut was screwing some man in an alley toward the middle of town. When she was done, I went into the alley.

She begged for her life like the coward she is. Now she rests in the streets with a hole in her head along with the rest of the garbage. I killed her. And I enjoyed it!" by this time he was cackling.

Angela regarded him with fear for a moment. Suddenly, she realized what she had driven him to. She had been trying so hard to help him that she had forgotten that by trying to seduce someone who had been traumatized might cause that person to have a psychotic break.

The Chronicles of Merkadiah:
The Rise of the Gryphon

It looked as if that happened. She felt dirty and horrible. Had she not been so self- centered, she might have realized what she was doing. He was becoming a monster.

"Grivon lets get you some clean clothes and wash the blood off you."

"Okay, but can you bathe with me? I think I am ready to be with you."

This came as a shock. Half an hour ago, he never wanted to sleep with her then suddenly, he did. This was not a good thing, so she asked, "Um, Grivon, why do you want me suddenly? Not even an hour ago you were telling me that if I ever slept with you, I was no better than Bebe, but now you want me. I just don't get it. Can you tell me what it is that has you so excited?"

Grivon was silent for several minutes before answering, "I guess it's that she is dead now, and that makes me happy. It's been a while since I have slept with anyone, I have had feelings for. I do have the right to change my mind, don't I?"

"Well yes, but I just don't think right now it will be appropriate. What if by the time we turn out the lights if you still feel the need to be with me then we will. Can you live with that?"

Grivon just nodded his head. Then he said, "Can you still bathe with me?"

"Sure."

Later that evening after they had taken their bath, they ate dinner. The bath helped relax Grivon down from his manic state, but for whatever reason he was still feeling excited. He missed Barbarah, he wanted to hold her, but if he had to, he would project her onto Angela to ease his conscience.

He knew that Angela wanted him, but he was not so sure if he really wanted her. Yes, she was pretty. Yes, he liked the way she looked and the way she helped him, but deep down he loved Barbarah.

He was so lonely and confused. At this moment, he just wanted to go numb.

"Hey, Angela?" Grivon asked looking at Angela across the table.

"Yes, Grivon?" She answered looking up from her plate.

"I thought maybe we could go down to the hot spring on the edge of the forest. Maybe watch the stars come out."

"That would be nice. It doesn't have to do with what happened earlier does it?" she said smiling.

"I figured that we could go there and soak in the water, look at the stars and see where things went."

"Okay. You know we see each other naked all the time, but now we get to touch each other too." Grivon blushed as he stood up and took the plates to the sink.

After he had put them away, they left. They took a trail that led to the west of the house. The trail led down a hill and through a grove of trees. The sun was just beginning to set as they approached the edge of the forest. The large hot spring was fed by a brook at the north side of the pool.

Angela said that it was unusual for a hot spring to be fed by a brook or at least have one run into it. When they got to the edge of the spring, they disrobes. Angela snuck a peak at Grivon's body.

She had seen it so many times while she bathed him, or when they went swimming; but she never studied the curvature of his muscles so intently. Nor noticed how the setting sun made his platinum hair shimmer.

She blushed as she imagined running her hands over his defined chest. The simple thought of touching his muscles was getting her excited. Even if they didn't make love, she would be happy. Just knowing that she was awakening something primal in him was enough to know that somehow, she had helped him.

Perhaps it was more corruption than help? She wasn't sure, but she was sure about one thing; it had been a long time since she had been with a man.

As Grivon undressed, he looked over at Angela. He always looked away from her body as best he could. Now he was drinking in her frame as if his eyes thirsted forever. Her body was extremely toned. It was lithe and hid the muscles well.

He noticed her looking at him and blushed. She quickly turned her head, her face red as the sunset. As he finished pulling off his pants, he realized that they were probably going to be here all evening.

This was a way for him and her to release their frustrations without sparring. It had been a long time since he and Barbarah last made love, and he refused to count what Bebe did.

This was something he needed more than anything after killing Bebe. Grivon hopped into the hot spring. Immediately his body tingled in the hot water. Water plumed into the air as Angela glided into the pool.

The Chronicles of Merkadiah:
The Rise of the Gryphon

He grinned as she swam over to him and began to float on her back. She arched her back forcing her breasts further out of the water. He looked down at her body with a hungry look in his eyes. She saw it and stood up. She smiled at him and bobbed over to one of the farther ends of the spring. It was a little deeper, but underneath the water at that point was a slant in the bank that you could lay back on and look at the sky.

Grivon followed her. He was glad that her back was turned. The water didn't hide him as well as he would have liked. When they reached the bank and lay back on the slope, each one noticed that the other wasn't as covered as they thought.

They looked at each other and laughed. Then Grivon rolled in the water to get closer to Angela. She pulled him on top of her, ready for him. She pulled his head down and kissed him passionately. Her head began to spin as they kissed. He was intoxicating.

After the kiss, Grivon was more than ready. Suddenly, Barbarah's sad smile thrust its way into his mind's eye, causing him to lose focus for a moment. He forced her face from his mind. For whatever reason, he needed this and if he thought of her, he wouldn't be able to do it.

Nothing could have prepared them for the other, they were a tangle of arms and legs in the growing twilight. Grivon lay beside her for several minutes panting before saying,

"Let's do that again."

With a giggle she caressed his face. Her brown eyes searching his, trying had to read to his thoughts. Shaking her head, she pulled him into a passionate kiss.

IV

Later that night after another bath, to wash away sweat and dirt, Angela and Grivon snuggled in her bed. Grivon lay on his side with his back toward her reflecting on the events of the day.

Angela lay with her hands draped over his shoulders, hands caressing his chest. She enjoyed the simple pleasure of listening to him breathe. It had been a very long day, and after five hours of passionate love making, she was glad it was over. She felt deflated and numb but satisfied.

Grivon felt the hot sting of tears begin to fall from his eyes and stream down his face. He was trying so hard not to spoil the special night he had shared with Angela, but the tears erupted unbidden from his eyes.

There was a sharp stabbing feeling in his heart, almost like bad indigestion. He had just violated the love and trust of Barbarah. The only person who he ever loved and who loved him back.

Angela knew at once Grivon's mind had reset itself from the primal acts of the day. He enacted vengeance on Bebe and had a wild afternoon, but now he was coming back to his senses.

He had a minor psychotic break, and it warped his conscience and caused him to do things that were against his nature. Angela knew that deep down he was a good man, and she loved him for it. She knew he would never love anyone more than he loved Barbarah, and that was okay with her. As long as she could be near him and try to help him as much as possible.

He felt the pressure of Angela's body weight change. She was rubbing his back. Then the sobbing began. At that point, he was alone in the dark, and he knew without the shadow of a doubt, that Angela loved him.

He wasn't sure how, but after the hours of bliss they just shared, it was apparent it was more than as a friend. He knew he couldn't love her the way she deserved, but no matter what, if he ever left this God forsaken planet, she would come with him and hold a special rank in his new government.

He was pulled from his thoughts when Angela said, "I know the name of the planet that you are looking for."

Shifting his weight, he rolled over. He looked at her and sighed before saying, "When did you find out?"

"While you were out, I called my boss, 'The Chimera.' He just so happens to be an old student of Phoy Yin. He said the man has a penchant for riddles. He also said that you should be careful, Phoy is one mean son of a bitch."

Grivon chuckled, "Yeah, I know. He is demanding and half the time I think he wants you to read his mind."

Angela smiled and said, "You're going to leave tomorrow, aren't you?"

Grivon was silent for a while then said, "Yes, is there anything you want to tell me?"

Now Angela was silent for a long while. She desperately wanted to tell him how she felt. Taking a deep breath, she held it for several seconds. Enough time to mull the idea over in her mind. It was a heavy feeling; one she had never felt for anyone before. Let out her breath, she took his cheek in her hand, and said, "I love you."

"I know."

"You do?" Angela blurted. "I mean, how did you know?"

"The way you touched me as I started to cry. The fervor you had in the thralls of passion. I have known since the night you "bought" me, and I love you as well, but not the way you love me. I will be honest and tell you that what happened this evening wasn't me using you and that I enjoyed every moment of it.

Who knows in the future I might be willing to do that again, but…"

"You don't love me the way I love you. I get it. I had already resigned myself to that. Remember, I held you that first night you were here. You wouldn't stop calling for Barbarah, and you wanted someone named Ubiroe not to hurt her. I never thought to ask who she was.

Anyway, as I was saying, I knew you would never love me with the passion and respect that you have for her, but I hoped that you could have some form of love for me."

"I do love you, and in a way, it is a lot like the way I love Barbarah. Since I'm going to leave tomorrow, I wanted to know if you would come with me. When I conquer Merkadiah, you will have a place in a position of power. Will you join me?"

Angela felt like she was going to cry. He did love her on a level deeper than she first thought. She was happy that he trusted her to come with him and would give her a position of power in his empire.

She also held these things with the highest regard and honor.

"Yes, I will. So, when do you want to leave?"

"As soon as possible. I need to leave before those stupid bitches realize I killed one of their own."

They both began dressing. Since it was possible to see Angela's house from the town, they dressed in the pale moon light that poured into room like a silver river.

Grivon put on his black robes and strapped his sword horizontally on the small of his back. Angela put on her full regalia. She put on the full black poly-cotton body suit. Then she strapped on her katana in the same fashion as Grivon.

211

Then she put on a black mask that covered half her face. It peaked in between her eyes. Then she pulled on a pair of knee-high stiletto boots. Grivon looked her over and whistled.

"What?" Angela asked, with a smile in her voice.

"You look gruesome."

"Not all the ways of the colonists have been lost."

Grivon nodded, and they left the house. Nothing happened until they reached the teleportation station. Since neither Grivon nor Angela had been to Phoy's planet, Ne-le, they would need to use the open teleportation device.

When they arrived at the end of the main street of Tuhlead, they were blocked by five Kartah. Each one bore an uncanny resemblance to Ubiroe.

The woman in the center looked at Grivon and Angela. Then she said in a shrewish tone of voice, "I am Shanna St. Emmaline. You, Grivon D'Gaul, are under arrest for the rape and murder of Bebe Barrim."

Grivon began to laugh, "You think I raped that whore? I care more about the health of The Autocrat than I do about that slut."

This obviously angered the women. The one that was doing all the talking said, "If you don't come quietly, then we will have no choice but to use force."

Grivon smiled, and quickly fed the cold fire of his fury. All the anger, rage and hate that had built up within him over the last several months flooded into his mind. He was going to have to kill five women.

He saw Angela shift to draw her sword. He put his hand to the left where she stood to keep her back. Angela let out a quiet growl.

He focused on the number in the darkness behind his eyes and called it to the front of his consciousness. This summoned the armor field from the Aurora in the back of his brain. A good portion of strength left his body, and he knew the silver aura had surrounded him.

Shanna looked at the color of the armor that surrounded her opponent. The last thing Shanna did was blink. Angela smiled as Shanna's head flew off her shoulders. She didn't see Grivon move. He was short jumping to each woman and cutting off her head.

In less than a minute, five headless bodies lay on the ground all around him. He hadn't broken a sweat. Angela was impressed. When he was ready, she typed in the quadrants of Ne-le into the teleportation device. As they waited for a link up of travel paths via the Network, a large group of soldiers and Kartah came running toward Grivon and Angela.

They saw the world go hazy as they teleported to Ne-le. They arrived at first light on a desolate world. The planet looked like any other terrestrial planet they ever saw.

The topography was mountainous with a small amount of green vegetation, but that wasn't what bothered Grivon and Angela. It was the thirty, angry humanoids standing in front of them with swords drawn.

Chapter Five
Unhealthy

"Do not seek your own demise through blind obedience,"-Pantherine Proverb

I

Barbarah hated being locked away in Steven's mansion. Not only did the time pass slowly, but she was never allowed to leave. Not to mention she was afraid to use the Network to keep up with the Pantherine's coup.

Looking back on the task Grivon gave her made her smile. They were cuddled together under the star-scattered sky talking about how Grivon could achieve his goals.

He wanted her to use her knowledge of the Network to contact the Pantherines as Sekhet. By doing this, he hoped they would revolt, and then he could unite them under his banner to overthrow The Autocrat and Senate.

From what she was able to find out, the leader of the coup, K'datra, was successful in taking over the ghettos. Sadly, she was too afraid that Steven might be monitoring what she was doing.

Barbarah let out a frustrated sigh, if only she could leave. Then she realized that if she gave Steven what he wanted from her he might let her. Her skin rippled in goose flesh, and a crawling sensation slithered up her spine.

If that's what she had to do, then she would do it. She only hoped Grivon would forgive her for it. The thought of sleeping with Steven was revolting, but if it gave her the ability to leave the mansion, then she would. She sat down at her terminal and began to type.

Once she finished the message, she went and took a bath. Then she put on a see-through gown that left nothing to the imagination. Barbarah sat on her bed and waited. She fell asleep after a couple of hours. She dreamed of her and Grivon holding hands as guards led them to the chopping block.

They were about to be executed by Steven. She awoke with a start as the door opened. Steven walked in and saw Barbarah sleeping on the bed. The gown she wore made him twitch with excitement.

214

The Chronicles of Merkadiah:
The Rise of the Gryphon

This is what he had been waiting for. The extra aphrodisiac in her food and drink everyday finally paid off. She was willing to have sex for her freedom. Sadly, this was not the right time. He still had Venice to play with.

"You wanted to see me?" Steven asked flatly.

"Yes, I want to get out. I need to breathe fresh air. I want to be free."

Steven faked being hurt. Sharply, he said, "If you don't want my hospitality anymore, then you have the door."

"That's not what I am saying." Barbarah pleaded. "I just want to be able to leave and come back as I please. I promise I won't leave you or find a job or anything. I just need to get some fresh air. Grivon told you to take care of me and give me what I needed. I need this Steven."

Steven crossed his arms and sighed, "What do you want to do with your free time?"

"I reserve the right to keep that to myself."

Steven curled his nose and huffed, "Fine, do as you will."

Steven turned and walked out the door, leaving it ajar. Barbara was surprised that her clothes didn't entice him. Maybe he had changed a little, or maybe it was because of that woman she had heard him with.

Now Barbarah was free to come and go. She hoped that Steven would stay the same. She hoped that his madness would stay quenched long enough for her to get enough money to move away from him.

She knew that Grivon charged Steven with her care, but if Grivon knew what Steven was really like, he never would have left her under his care.

II

Barbarah enjoyed the cool night air of the capital. There were so many large buildings and flashing lights. People walked into and out of monolithic hotels to gamble, fornicate, or drink away sorrows.

Couples sat at tables outside of busy restaurants eating gourmet meals at extreme prices. And everywhere thousands of people hustled and bustled by.

Barbarah sighed and wished that Grivon could be walking with her under the large flashy buildings. It had been almost two years since she last laid eyes on him. It broke her heart to think about him.

How they shared such a wonderful connection and how he had thrown it all away. Had he failed in his mission to find Phoy? Or perhaps he simply forgot about her?

Maybe he was hurt, in rejuvenation or worse, an assassin had found him and killed him at the biding of the Senate. Barbarah let out a sigh of exasperation. If she could only find out if, he was okay. Then she might feel better, but right now just being able to go outside for the first time in months was a treat in and of itself.

To her surprise Steven had given her, a personal expense account when he let her leave his mansion. It was tied to an unlimited line of credit from his shell corporation, Anthony Security Investments Limited.

He was making money hand over fist in his somewhat legitimate company, Anthony's Homemade Ice Cream. What made it semi- legitimate was that he was putting small doses of addictive drugs and herbs into the various flavors of ice cream.

She hated that children were being hooked on such horrible things as taka root painkillers. After walking around the city for several hours and was starting to get hungry.

She found a quant sidewalk stand with four barstools. Behind the counter was a short, petite woman with platinum hair, in a bob. Barbarah instantly froze. It was as if she were looking face to face with Ubiroe.

The second night after the round with Ubiroe flashed into her mind. How the depraved bitch had waltzed into her and Grivon's tent and had two of her friends hold her back, all while she was violated, until she agreed to kiss and touch Ubiroe. Barbarah was brought from the flash back when the woman began talking.

"May I help you ma'am?" the woman asked smiling.

"Sorry, I spaced for a minute." Barbarah said taking a seat. "So, what's good here?"

"Well today's steamed freshwater mussels from Baktüth on noodles with a chamomile wine sauce."

"That sounds good, how much?"

"Twenty-five credits a plate or fifty for all you can eat."

"I am starved. I'll have the all I can eat, and if I could have a glass o ginger tea, that would be wonderful."

"That's two credits a glass." The woman replied.

Barbarah waved her hand "Okay with me."

When the dish was placed before her, the aroma of it tickled her nose and her mouth watered. In half an hour, she ate five plates and drank seven glasses of tea. She ate in contemplative silence, thinking about how life had been altered by her giving birth to Terry.

She thought of how Steven had changed a little and that this was the first time she had been able to breath fresh air in a long time. After she finished the last plate, she sighed and began to stand up.

"Are you ready to settle?" Asked the matron.

"How much do I owe you?"

"Sixty-four credits or eighty-eight marks."

Barbarah pulled out a black velvet purse and found a credit card with over three thousand credits. She felt the cool metal numbers between her index finger and thumb before handing it over to the matron.

The woman took the card and went to run it for change, but when she turned around to give it back, Barbarah was gone. The woman shook her head and pocketed the card.

Barbarah walked away from the eatery. When she first went out, she withdrew five thousand credits not knowing what to do with them. An idea came to light, if she could spend all the money, she might be able to bring down Steven and his organization, but as that thought finished, she had a sounder one. Given seven lifetimes and buying everything, she saw she would never be able to spend everything he owned. He gave her an unlimited expense account, but who was to say that he didn't have other accounts elsewhere that he could draw from even if one ran out.

Even worse, he could monitor what she was spending the money on. The hopes of having her own home and getting away from the bastard shattered. She walked aimlessly around until she was in a rundown looking part of the city. Her heart started thudding hard against her chest.

All manner of vile fantasies about her fate filled her head. After a while her imagination calmed down and she decided to try and find her way back home. Letting out a heavy sigh, she turned down a dark alley to take a short cut she thought would get her back to the better part of the city.

The tight channel smelled of vomit and other unsavory smells. This was a mistake ! Just as she was about to turn back, she heard a voice call after her.

"Hey sweet thang, wanna party with some real men?"

Rolling her eyes, she turned around to see five men looking at her. They all wore black pants with silver chains connecting the pockets together. Each wore a sleeveless black fishnet shirt. They all were carrying a single carbon fiber tonfa tethered to their arm.

Barbarah looked them all over a second time and laughed to herself. If she learned one thing in the time she spent in Steven's company, it was to always carry a weapon, no matter how small.

She reached under her robe and felt the handle of the retractable energy baton she kept tucked in a fold of leather attached to her body suit. She chuckled as she thought about how powerful its charge was.

"Look fella's, she's getten' ready for our special treatment," one of the men shouted.

Barbarah palmed the baton and brought her hand out from under her robes and let her arms hang loose at her sides. In the ambient light of the buildings, she saw their lecherous grins. Smirking, she pursed her lips and slowly blinked her eyes.

The man in the middle let go of his tonfa letting it swing loose at his side. He walked over to her and put a hand on her left breast and started to rub it hard. She squeaked at the roughness of it.

Then with a flick of the wrist, the club extended, and she bashed the man on the back of his neck. He screamed in alarm at the blow and even louder at the delayed electric shock.

The other four men looked on with wide eyes as the woman they were about to assault took down their leader. Barbarah looked at the other four and winked. They all turned and ran away. Barbarah laughed and walked on home.

III

The thought to kill him entered her mind like a storm on the plains, sudden and unbidden. Nicky had been living with Steven for several months and all he seemed capable of doing was having sex every chance he got.

To make matters worse, each time they slept together he would be more violent. Last night he beat her so badly that she had bruises on her face, arms, legs and stomach. He was so rough that she started bleeding.

When she woke up, she made up her mind to kill him. Once he was dead, she would take over for him and the little psycho would burn in Hell. Nicky laughed to herself. Steven would die a most humiliating death, and she would then take over the entire operation as the Jackal.

The Chronicles of Merkadiah:
The Rise of the Gryphon

It may not be tomorrow or next week, but it would be very soon. Nicky got up out of bed and stretched her aching arms. She looked at herself in the mirror and sighed as she looked at the large shiner Steven had given her.

It was a painful addition to her already marred and scarred face. Bitter tears welled in her eyes as she examined herself as best she could. There were large bruises around her neck, on her breasts, and a deep bite on her left bicep.

Violence mixed with sex was nice, but this was ridiculous. All Steven seemed able to do was keep her locked here in their room, beating on her when he felt like it. Half the time it was just a beating, no pleasure involved.

She hoped that he would have made good on his promise to make her First Don, but that seemed like a forgotten dream now. Last night she realized that she was nothing more than a plaything.

That he gave the job to some stupid old man from outside the organization and she was locked away in here. It was a nice sham. She helped him pick out the Dons the first couple of weeks and helped him start smuggling weapons to the Pantherines and the Barrims.

Then suddenly, he had locked her away inside his room never again to see the light of day. Nicky walked to the bed and put on her gown. It didn't matter if she wore her clothes or a gown.

Steven always came in and threw her onto the bed, ripped off her clothes and then proceeded to have rough sex with her. It was as if that was all that dominated his mind, sex and violence.

If he wasn't bragging about how he had had a politician killed or how the wars were making him rich, he was making her feel like less than a human.

Nicky shook her head. Why? Was it because she was ugly and burnt or was it simply that he loved the fact that she was as ugly on the outside as he was on the inside? It was frustrating. Then she had an idea.

She could hollow out part of the mattress and store a knife there, and then in a few weeks when he was asleep, she would kill him.

IV

Steven sat in his office talking with an imbecile. He was an older man who designed the RA and DT line of firearms given to security forces and bodyguards.

He was now the controlling executive of Freemont Firearms. Steven had been inundated with these morons ever since Venice tried to find people to replace the other nine Dons.

It was infuriating to say the least. None of the idiots she had brought in here knew anything about being discrete or circumspect. Each one had been a tempting choice but when it got right down to it, they were just plain stupid. Where did she find these people?

"Tell me how you can benefit me?" Steven asked the man

The man stuttered and stammered and then said, "I can supply you with weapons at little to no cost and not to mention I can tell you of some good people who might be good for your operation"

Steven thought for a minute and then chuckled, "Fine I will give you a chance. But if you fail me, I will have your head mounted for my bedroom." The man swallowed hard and nodded.

"By the way, what is your name?"

"My name is Traviat Burnes."

"Your Orsin name will be, Mr. Burnes."

"Thank you, sir, when do I begin?"

"Tomorrow, and you will relocate your office here to an assigned cubical and you will begin to find a way to sell the weapons you make to people on planets with firearm laws and to the Pantherines."

Mr. Burnes just nodded. He seemed scared and excited at the same time. Steven motioned for him to leave. Traviat left in an excited hurry. Steven put his head in his hands and rubbed his temples.

That was the last of them. He finally had his ten Dons. Each one overseeing a crucial part of the organization and all of them were just as incompetent and stupid as the man that just left, but at least they would be easy to control.

The only person that wouldn't be easy to control was Venice. Steven was pulled out of his thoughts when he heard the special chime on his Network Terminal for Theo. Steven rolled his eyes.

The man was annoying. Even though he was "in charge" of everything, he couldn't think for himself, but at least he was loyal enough to ask permission before he did anything he thought might be considered disloyal. In some ways it was nice to have a useful, insecure lapdog.

"Make it quick," said Steven, without even turning to look at the monitor.

The Chronicles of Merkadiah:
The Rise of the Gryphon

"Ah, yes I'll try," stammered Theo. "The Senate has just declared open war on Martxapahn and his Barrim peasants."

"Wait, isn't Marzipan a candy?"

"Well, um, yes."

"So, you declared war on a candy?" said Steven suppressing a laugh.

Theo turned red and said, "No! Martxapahn is the grandson of Xóa.

He appeared almost a year ago and started taking planets. Our Aridaunts have been cut in half and then yesterday he seceded. We are also going to try to kill off the rest of the Pantherines with an army of Experiments."

Two things made Steven's ears peak up. The first was the war against the 'candy man' and the possibility of loaning money to the Senate for the research of Experiments. This made Steven ask, "Who is financing the war and the research?"

"Well that was why I was bothering you. Who do you want to get the weapons contract and which bank do I need to get a loan from?"

"The weapons will come from Freemont Firearms and the money will come from Anthony Security Investments Limited. Both are legitimate companies controlled by me. In turn, the invested revenues of my ice cream company in those companies will increase.

Remember I control twelve different companies and each one pays into the larger pool of my very own large shadow company that is full of legitimate monies, but the money has a criminal twist."

"What criminal twist?"

Steven, who was now looking in the monitor, smiled, "The fact that taka is in the ice cream and the fact that it is illegal to own more than one company.

I owe that one to our last Autocrat. Also, that I gross more than a million credits a day without paying taxes. I also arm the Barrim clan. My corporations give Pantherines weapons and supplies. I supply the entire system with both legal and illegal pleasures.

Not to mention I own the Assassins Guild, and as you well know I ordered the death of the last Autocrat."

All the color drained from Theo's face, "Sorry to bother you I will begin the proceedings. Theo out." The screen went blue and Steven started laughing. This was wonderful.

He was going to make a fortune on the war and the scourge against the Pantherines. He felt like dancing he was so happy. He was giddy to the point of silliness, and couldn't ask for anything better, except Grivon's head on a platter.

V

Nicky lay awake next to Steven. They just finished several hours of routine rough sex. He was more furious and violent than usual. He almost broke her jaw and demanded things she deemed unnatural. She had never been violated like that by anyone and her sphincter had finally stopped bleeding.

In the past week, he had split her lip, made her nose bleed and blacked both her eyes. Steven had ended up being a real monster. She hated herself for even getting involved with him.

He initially gave her the rank of First Don, but now she was little more than a toy. She got up and went into his bathroom. Starting herself a bath, she sat down in the large basin and wept.

Since the second week she was in his company, Steven made her feel uglier than she already was. Large tears erupted from her face and splashed into the basin as the water stopped.

It was like it was with her ex-boyfriend. Only Steven was much worse. At least her former boyfriend asked for sex. Steven didn't. It was expected, all the time.

After she washed herself, she put on her black bodysuit, and crept back to the bed to the spot where she hid her favorite dagger. She loved the feel of the ivory handle and the little sugilite orb on the pommel.

Her father had given it to her before she had left home for the big city. Being from a small farming village on Odin, her father worried about her being assaulted or killed, so with what little money he had he bought her this dagger.

It was a shame that shortly after she left home, he was killed by a Kartah on his way into town to sell honey that his bees made. Nicky took a deep breath as she positioned the dagger over Steven's black heart.

Steven's eyes popped open right before she brought the dagger down. He caught her hand and overpowered her. Grabbing the dagger, he threw it against the far wall, where she couldn't reach it.

He pushed his thumb into the pressure point in her wrist, making her scream. He kept applying pressure until she fell to her knees. He grabbed the pressure points at the left of her neck and left shoulder at the same time.

She screamed louder and finally fell prostrate to the floor. Then he ground his knee between her shoulders.

"Now what in the hell were you trying to do?" he seethed through clenched teeth. Nicky groaned from the sharp pain of rug burns and Steven's knee in her shoulders.

"No matter I know what you were going to do. You were going to kill me and take control over the organization. That can't happen. You're stupid and slow. I will show you what happens to those that cross me.

I am the great Orsin Steven Anthony and I will punish you in the cruelest, demeaning, and degrading way I know how. You will not live out the night. I will make sure you do not like what I am about to do."

Nicky trembled with fear as Steven's mouth parted into a sadistic grin, and he licked her right cheek.

VI

When the deed was finished, Steven was covered in blood and Nicky's mutilated body lie on the floor beneath him. He cut off the plume of crimson hair from her head and ran the silky trophy under his nose.

It smelled of lilac and berries. He missed the thrill of killing. It was an extremely long time since he last killed, and it felt good to exert control over a woman, especially an extremely stupid one.

Steven laughed to himself and realized that now he had no one to give him his heir. He sighed. It was time to pay Barbarah a visit and fulfill his promise to her.

He rang a bell and a servant appeared. Steven pointed to Nicky's corpse. The servant nodded and walked out. Steven went into his bathroom and ran himself a bath. He washed the blood from his hair and the bloodstains off his hands, arms and legs.

Nicky had been an excellent source of practice and a pleasing distraction for several months, but now it was time to ensure his family's future within the system.

When he was finished bathing, Steven put on a long purple robe. He walked out of his room and down the hall to Barbarah's. He thought back to the night he had first taken her outside The Guild. She was still a virgin then, and he was the one that took that from her. She enjoyed herself that night and she was going to again.

VII

For the first time in a long time, Barbarah was happy. She decided that ending a wonderful evening with a long soak would be divine. Peeling off her clothes, she walked into her bathroom and began running her bath.

As she descended the steps into her basin, her body quivered from the heat. Once she was fully submerged, she let out a contented sigh and melted into the quiet escape of her bath.

Afterward, she sat in front of her mirror combing her waist length hair. She hummed a song that she once knew but could no longer remember its name. As she sat her comb down on the vanity, she heard the handle of her door click.

The door creaked open, and Steven walked in. He was clothed only in a pair of black shorts. His demeanor was haughty as he swaggered into the room. With each step, a door in the back of Barbarah's mind cracked open.

Images of the night she asked a student called The Jackal to spar with her came back. He walked with the same swanky gait that Steven was. She remembered him taking off his mask.

The door in her mind flew open with a torrent of tormented memories and images she once labored to forget. Her skin crawled with the feeling of unseen hands. She screamed and yelled at Steven to stay away.

This only made his smirk larger and his pace quicker. Rolling off her stool, she ran to the other side of the room. Steven's smirk twisted into a sadistic smile.

Suddenly, Barbarah realized that she had been cornered. She put both hands against the wall as if hoping to somehow sink into it. Steven forced his face into hers and let out a steamy exhale that smelled of putrid garlic.

He grabbed her through her silk gown and sneered. She squeaked at the sharpness of the pain. All she could do was scream in horror as his other hand forced up her night skirt.

Between the flash backs and what was happening to her in the present she had a moment of clarity. With all her might she hammered both hands against Steven's ears. Dazed Steven stopped his assault and staggered backward.

The Chronicles of Merkadiah:
The Rise of the Gryphon

As he was trying to regain his footing; Barbarah kicked him hard in the stomach, then spun around to kick him again in the face. With a look of stunned horror Steven fell to the ground.

Barbarah smiled with glee as she stepped on his sternum and ground her heel into his chest. She was about to stomp on his groin when he looked up at her and said, "Did you learn nothing all those nights training with your idiot of a lover? Lesson number one is always press your advantage."

Steven grabbed a pressure point in her ankle and speared his foot into the small of her back. She flew off him and landed in a heap a meter away. Through blurry eyes, she watched as Steven pulled himself off the ground and hobbled over to her.

She tried to make herself move, but for some reason her body was frozen. In silent horror, she watched as Steven took off his shorts. She forced her mind to a different place and time as she often did in these situations.

She tried her best to think about Grivon and their time together, but that kept her too close to reality. With each passing moment, she realized there was no escaping what was happening, and in that moment, she began to build a mental shelter safe from all the pain of the past, present, and future.

Chapter Six
Phoy's Tasks

"Somewhere between awake and asleep is the world in which we live. We strive to sleep but we stay awake and weary. Sleep makes us safe." -Pantherine Funeral Dirge

I

Grivon and Angela surveyed the people in front of them. They had dark sullen eye sockets and pale-yellow skin. The irises of their eyes were crimson red. Their fingernails thick, yellow, and they breathed heavily.

One had its mouth open in a gruesome grin, and Grivon could see nothing but long needle teeth and a pale blue light where the tongue once was. The creature looked like it used to be human, if you could call it human at all.

The thing grinned as it stepped up to Grivon. It breathed a toxic smelling breath in Grivon's face, and stood looking at Grivon in the eyes, studying him.

"Your Aurora is full of power," the thing said in a preternatural voice.

"You don't say?" Grivon said with a smirk.

"Yes, and I want it. Then when I take it, they will fight me for it," the thing said pointing a finger at the other creatures.

"How about I fight you all for it?"

The thing regarded Grivon for a moment. Then it motioned the others to form a circle around him Angela was forced aside and left outside the ring of creatures. She couldn't see him anymore.

She looked on in horror, wondering if he would live. She hoped he was as good a fighter as she thought he was, or else he was going to die a horrible death.

As fast as he could he fed his fury and activated his Aurora. It was do or die. The temptation to use the Thread of Life form was strong, but it was risky.

He could end up killing Angela, since he didn't know where she was, so he began recalling various forms for fighting against multiple opponents.

Then he remembered a form he once read about but never practiced, because he didn't know how to activate his Aurora yet. Before the group of creatures could move, he summoned the furnace of emotion to his right hand.

The familiar crackle of energy ran down his arm. Channeling the crackle to his hand, he twirled his sword above his head three times, and thrust his saber as high in the air as he could.

An arch of blue lightning shot from the end of the sword and to the head of each creature in the circle. Angela shielded her eyes from the bright blue electricity. Suddenly, thirty heads exploded into blood, bone and brains.

She stood horrified as the bodies dropped to the ground. Grivon stood in the center of the macabre scene, breathing hard. His silver Aurora shimmered like a distant star in the morning light.

He knew that if he didn't retract his Aurora soon, he would collapse. The amount of energy the attack required, was more than he had ever used before. While he may know how to use these Magiah techniques, he had no idea how to properly prepare his body for their use and hoped Phoy could guide him towards their proper use.

It was amazing that how he had channeled so much of his body's natural electricity into the attack that his arms and legs didn't want to work. At that point, he knew that it was too late to retract.

His arms and legs twisted in positions he didn't think they could bend before falling face first into the sand. Blackness enveloped his sight as his lip split and the taste of blood filled his mouth.

Angela watched as Grivon struggled to remain conscious. She raced over to catch him before he fell, but it was too late. Gently, she picked him up off the ground and held his head in her lap.

She moved his hair out of his face and began to gently message his temples. After a while, she heard him begin to breathe more normally and realized he was asleep.

She wondered where exactly they were, and why the teleportation device stood in the middle of nowhere on such a desolate world. The darkness was fading faster as the sun started to peak over the tall mountains in the distance.

Her eyes were suddenly flooded with a picturesque view of a kaleidoscopic mountain range. In the distance on a green-rocked mountain a waterfall billowed down between two smaller peaks and large river ran from the bottom and to the south west.

Sitting beside the river stood a large house surrounded by smaller huts. A low wooden fence encircled the compound and a torii marked the entrance. A wave of relief washed over her.

Looking around to make sure there were no more of the crazed inhuman creatures Grivon killed, she shouldered her lover's body and began walking toward the house.

As she trudged along the rocks and lichen toward the house a realization came to her. The house may not belong to Phoy, and if it did would he even know what to do with the man she now piggybacked.

Then as if someone changed a channel on the Network in her head it suddenly made sense why there was a teleportation station sitting in the middle of nowhere. Whoever was responsible for building the little compound she was walking towards wanted it to serve as some sort of beacon of hope. At least that's what she hoped.

After several hours of trudging Grivon's lifeless body, Angela arrived at the compound. Oddly, there were guards of any kind. The only activity she saw was several people in white robes bustling about with trays of food.

Each person delivered the food to one of the many huts. Angela continued trudging toward the porch of the large oriental house. As she laid Grivon on the ground, a sliding door opened, and a short olive-skinned man, wearing a brown and gold kimono with a black circle and two thick white stripes over the heart, stepped out of the house.

With dramatic flair, he put a hand behind his back and stroked his long catfish mustache and goatee.

"Two questions. What the hell happened to him, and who the hell are you?" the man demanded.

Angela pulled a loose strand of hair back over her shoulder and said, "For now you can call me Angela, and as to your other question. A Barrim bitch named Bebe."

His eyes narrowed, and he swore a vile, vulgar oath, "I told that bastard not to go there. How did he come to be in your company?"

Angela crossed her arms growing weary of his questions and attitude, "I bought him. You're welcome." Phoy cocked his head back and laughed, "I am sure you did."

He clapped his hands and two men in pale green kimonos came out of the house behind him, picked up Grivon's lifeless body, and took him into the house.

The Chronicles of Merkadiah:
The Rise of the Gryphon

"Now, what do I owe the owner of this slave?" Phoy asked walking down the steps his hands now tucked into his kimono. Angela watched as the short man walked up to her.

When he was a half meter away, she looked down at him and said, "All I ask for him is room, board, and training."

Phoy pulled out a hand from his kimono, and stroked his mustache for a moment, "What kind of training?" Angela smirked, "I heard you can make me immortal."

Phoy smirked, "Not in the way you may think, but it can be taught. Please come inside."

II

Grivon awoke with a start. He was in a strange room laying on the world's hardest mattress. His eyes darted around the foreign room. It had three wooden walls and a paper and wooden wall on his left.

The room was not decorated and when he looked, he wasn't even on a bed. He was on a thin bamboo mat. Standing up, he stretched his aching muscles. He put on his body suit and walked out the shoji. As he walked into the hallway, directly in front of him was a large garden filled with dwarfed junipers and maples.

A small stream came from under a wall on the other side of the room and ran under the floor next to a small set of stairs. Looking to the right, he saw another door like the one he walked through.

He looked down the hall to his left and saw a hallway leading outside. When he reached, the edge of the porch outside, he saw a large rock garden.

There were three large boulders in a large sandy area. The area was raked in straight horizontal lines with circular ones around the three boulders. Grivon looked around the garden for Phoy or Angela.

All he saw were people beyond the garden sparring. Then he heard a familiar voice behind him.

"Good you're up. Are you ready for your first task?"

Grivon turned and saw Phoy standing behind him stroking his thin imperial mustache. "Good morning Master," he said.

Phoy smiled slightly then said, "I see you have already adopted the proper formalities, but when you greet me, I ask that you bow after your greeting."

"Sir?" asked Grivon confused.

"I come from an extensive line of ancient families. Our country was a great one before Xóa took power in the west. When his empire spread across The Blue Star, my family being one of great power and wealth for many generations in our country, sold its loyalty to Xóa.

We had to change our family name since my family became regents over the entire country. I don't think the citizens could have handled knowing that the descendants of a ruler who plunged the country into a one-hundred-year civil war had become a regent under the new Emperor."

"I see. Do you know the name of the country?"

"Nippon." said Phoy.

Grivon looked confused again as Phoy began stroking his goatee.

"We can talk about ancient history later. What is the first task that you were talking about?" Grivon asked annoyed

"Walk to the center of the rock garden. The first lesson to learn is sometimes the simplest solution is the best. Oh, by the way, your use of the Steal of Thunder Magiah technique was executed perfectly.

I thank you for killing those worthless monsters."

Grivon nodded, already thinking on what the hidden meaning in the lesson could be. They walked on into the center of the garden and found a large pit with a metal interior.

The pit looked a lot like a grave in its dimensions except it had a sloping ramp at one end. Grivon walked around it a few times before looking back at Phoy and shouting, "Now what?"

"Walk into it and wait at the far end. Do not let your back touch the rear of the pit, keep still and keep your arms at your sides."

Grivon walked down into the pit and did as Phoy said. That was when he noticed several holes in the bottom of the pit as well as on the sides. He was wondering what they were for when the pit suddenly began filling with sand.

Panic of being buried alive washed over him, but Phoy told him not to move, so he didn't. When the pit finished filling with sand, Grivon was buried up to his neck. He tried to move his legs, but they were not moving.

He could wiggle his arms but only a little. Phoy's face made a shadow on the sand in front of him.

"Now get out. You have until sunset or else you do this again tomorrow. While you are there, I want you to think of the main reason that you are so hellbent on your coup."

"What do you mean coup? Where is Angela?" Grivon demanded.

Phoy smirked, "She is doing some of her own training. Her skills are a little more refined than yours, so she has a different set of tasks that she must overcome. You will see her soon enough. Good luck."

Phoy walked away and Grivon was left alone with only his thoughts. A sudden feeling of hopelessness came over him. He journeyed all this way, suffered through ten months of torture and, then was nursed back to health just to be buried in a pit with cryptic instructions.

Hopelessness gave way to anger, and his fury boiled. If he ever passed this test, he was going to punch Phoy in his smug face. He stood there postulating how he was going to get out.

After what seemed like an eternity, he started trying to move his arms. He found he could lift them up and out of the sand with relative ease.

When he tried his legs, he found that he could move forward. Gritting his teeth, he started wading through the sand to the other side. After only moving a few centimeters and with the exertion of wading through neck deep sand, combined with the sweltering heat, he was exhausted.

After resting for several minutes, Grivon began to dig at his legs. He was to his knees when the sand began to fill back in the hole he had just dug. In frustration, he swore an obscene curse about Phoy, and struck the sand so hard his right hand began to trickle blood.

He cursed again and then threw himself as hard as he could against the sand and began to sob. His life was over. He failed. Nothing the Guild had ever used as training compared to this. He wished Barbarah were with him.

He longed to see her face and stroke her hair. He wished she were here to encourage him like she did at The Guild. Grivon eventually fell asleep with the hot sun beating down on him.

"Sleeping is a sign of weakness Grivon," said a voice.

Grivon looked up at the voice and grinned. It was Angela. She was wearing a tight white body suit that accentuated all of her curves.

"How goes it?" she asked smiling.

"Badly." Grivon growled.

"I can tell. I already finished my first task. Of course, I am older and more refined," Angela said with a smile and swish of her hair. "You look distracted, what's wrong?"

"I miss Barbarah. Not to mention, I feel like I have failed in my goal. I can't figure out this stupid task, and I just don't get what he is trying to teach me."

"I know what he is trying to teach you. I can't tell you or else you will never learn on your own. I know I can't replace her in your mind, but I will be here to encourage you through the tasks and training.

Do yourself a favor. Stop being such a whinny bitch. It's unbecoming of a future ruler." she said winking.

"I am not a whinny bitch!"

"Then prove it! I finished very quickly, and you still haven't figured yours out yet. Let's make a wager, shall we? How important to you is it that we sleep together?"

"I don't know, why?"

"If in three weeks you haven't improved to the next task, I get to have my way with you. If you have progressed, I will give you a night off. So, do we have a deal?"

Grivon thought about it for a while, wondering why sex was so important to her. Knowing that he still longed for Barbarah and knowing that Angela loved him made him realize that she was only trying to express her love for him in a way that she thought he could understand. At least that was what he hopped.

"Fine, we have a wager then."

"Good, now Phoy will get you out of there in a few hours. Keep thinking on what he told you to do, and I will see you at dinner." He watched her sway her hips in dramatic fashion, as she walked away.

Grivon stood in the sand thinking for the rest of the afternoon. He thought about how fine the sand was and how it stuck together. How it seemed to cling to everything. He thought about how much sand was like water. How it could flow and be soft but also be hard as rocks.

Sand could be used to destroy just like water. Just like water. That was it. He had been waiting for that answer. Just like water, sand followed the path of least resistance. Grivon remembered how his legs could pop up a little.

He wondered that if he could lay flat out and pull his legs out, he could be free. Using the furnace to fuel his strength, he laid himself across the sand pit, and began to pull his legs free. As he gained ground, he slowly pulled his legs out of the pit.

The Chronicles of Merkadiah:
The Rise of the Gryphon

As his toes reached the surface Phoy's shadow blotted out the setting sun. Phoy looked down and regarded Grivon with respect and awe.

He figured out the test. He hoped his new student would figure out the lesson as to why. If he had not, he would have to keep doing this task until he figured out what the lesson was. However, Phoy was sure that Grivon had learned the lesson.

"Get cleaned up. Dinner is in an hour," said Phoy.

Exhausted, all Grivon could do was nod.

III

The dinner was elaborate for only three people. They sat a low table sitting on thick pillows. The meal consisted of dried fish strips, broiled giant freshwater eel from Baktüth, fried roots, raw greens, pickled radishes from Tygrano, and a plum flavored tonic and brandy to drink.

The three ate silently. Each one stuck in their own thoughts. Grivon thought about how the next task would go. He wondered why it was necessary to learn what he learned in such an extreme way.

Of course, Phoy was an extreme person. He was over six hundred years old and very cantankerous. The thought came to Grivon that coming to Phoy was a bad idea. Then again, if he could survive the training and make himself more than he already was, he could be unstoppable.

Angela chewed the broiled eel slowly trying to get a handle on the flavor. It was as if the meat was getting bigger and bigger in her mouth.

She never ate anything related to a snake before. Of course, then again, she never had pickled Tygrano plums, or plum brandy either. The meal was good if you liked these sorts of foods. It was hard to eat things that you weren't familiar with, but it was food that was provided without cost.

She hoped that all the meals wouldn't be like this one. Otherwise she might get sick. Her thoughts turned to her first task, which wasn't overly arduous.

She was given a bokken and was told to take on a hundred people at once, but she had to do it in less than four standard hours. She did it in two. It was extremely easy for her. She once killed more than that in less time as an assassin.

Having to do that in the hot sun left her drained, and though she was wanting to reward her talented lover, she was simply too tired. Phoy sat eating his food, quietly watching the facial expressions of his guests.

He saw that Grivon could eat foods that are more exotic without flinching, but Angela was not sure if she liked it or not. Phoy could see the chemistry between them. Angela seemed to have deep feelings for Grivon, and Grivon seemed to have some sort of feeling for her.

But whatever that feeling was it wasn't the same way he felt for Barbarah. It was something different. It was like he was enthralled with how she had saved him and returned him to some sense of sanity.

Phoy wasn't sure, but it seemed as if Grivon had become unstable and distracted in the last eighteen months. It was time for him to ask the big question.

"How was your stay on Tūhl?" asked Phoy.

"It was less than excellent," Grivon replied.

"You haven't told me how you got here yet. I am dying to hear how."

Grivon swallowed hard and looked at Angela.

"Angela knew someone who had been here, so she told me."

"Networking is a powerful thing, but it will not help you here.

Angela's encouragement today was fine, but I do not want her giving you any help from now on. For some reason, you have become distracted. If you want to talk, do it when we have dinner.

If you want to have sex, go ahead, I won't stop you. Just make sure it does not interfere with either of your training, and that it happens after the day is finished.

Also, Grivon, I have a new task before the second one I was going to give you.

"I have noticed how unfocused you are since your stay on Tūhl. You will be given the Ayahuasca again. Then once it clears your system, I want to talk to you about what you saw.

I know that you saw Ubiroe the last time. I am curious to know what you see this time."

Grivon felt his heart begin to beat hard against his diaphragm. His stomach began to ache, and he felt faint. He knew that he would not do well in the test if he had to digest the poison again. This time the things he would see would drive him to the point of insanity.

The Chronicles of Merkadiah:
The Rise of the Gryphon

A sharp pain stabbed behind his left eye, and the room shrank as a dark tunnel edged out all but a tiny pinprick of his vision. The ache in his stomach turned to nausea, and his leg began to shake. The dank, familiar smell of the stone room in Dahra's house filled his nostrils, and the taste of fetid water coated his mouth and tongue.

He grabbed his cup of tonic and drank it in one gulp. Gripping his left eye with his left hand he slammed the glass down with the other causing it to crack, and he could hear the distant sound of laughter, followed by someone saying his name.

"Stop!" Grivon screamed. "Make it stop!" He grabbed his head, covered his face with his hands, and cradled it sobbing.

"Grivon go ahead and lie down for the night." Phoy said glancing at Angela. "Tomorrow is another day."

All Grivon could do was nod before walking out of the dining room.

"Angela, I need you to do me a favor."

"What is it?" she asked.

"I need you to give Grivon the Ayahuasca tonight. It will take about ten to twelve hours to take effect. If he takes it now it will knock him out. If you want to comfort him before he becomes incoherent, I understand."

Angela sat looking at Phoy with a little bit of disgust. Grivon was obviously sick within his mind, and all Phoy wanted to do was make it worse.

By giving him such a powerful psychoactive, it could cause him to become more withdrawn than he already was. But Phoy did know what he was doing; at least she hoped he did.

IV

Grivon was lying on his tatami mat thinking of the time he spent in Bebe's capture. He painfully remembered the beatings and sexual abuse he had suffered. He wondered what he had done to ever deserve such treatment.

On some days, he was afraid to close his eyes in fear of seeing her face. He hated that face, and how much she looked like Barbarah. The grimace she made when she hit him with the whips and rods.

The elation in her eyes as she chained him to the wall. He began to cry softly. Bebe was forever ingrained in his head. Her face and her actions splintered into his dreams.

It was a toxin that seeped into his personality and had changed him. He was scared he was becoming a monster, some sort of creature that preyed on the weakness of others.

Sleep was almost upon him when there was a quiet knock on the door. He rolled his eyes and spoke for whoever it was to enter. Angela came sweeping in through the door.

She was wearing a plain white satin robe that tied at the waist like his guild robe and carried a tray with a small ceramic cup on it. Angela smiled at him as she slid the door shut.

Grivon sat up and forced a smile back at her. She winked and sat down across from him. She flashed a smile as she handed him the small cup. Grivon took it and put it to his lips.

That was when he smelled that familiar sour smell. It was the drug from the fountain. He knew he was to drink it. He would pass out soon and so Angela was here to make sure he would be okay. Finding comfort in that, he chugged the sweet liquid. This time it was different.

The stomach shattering pain wasn't there. He looked at Angela with confusion.

"What's the matter?" she asked.

"It's different this time. Last time I drank this stuff it made me nauseous, and I passed out. This time nothing is happening."

"Phoy told me that since you have eaten and slept in the last twelve hours that the effects will be delayed and could come while you're asleep.

How about that wild night I promised you?"

Grivon just blinked a moment and realized that he was feeling very lonely and needed comforting. He needed Bebe's face and voice out of his mind. If he found his relief in Angela, then so be it.

He did care for her, but in a way that made sense only in his mind. It was not a deep love that came from the soul. It was different. He couldn't explain how or why but it was. He nodded.

A mischievous grin came to Angela's face. She untied the knot that kept her robe and exposed her toned flesh. He grinned as she knelt in front of him. Reaching out, he pulled her closer to him relishing the smell of her soft skin.

The two warriors wrestled in passion for what seemed like hours until they were tired. Grivon was ready to embrace the release of sleep when the drug took its hold.

236

His stomach shattered, and his head felt like it was going to cleave in half. He rolled over thinking he was going to vomit, but ended up passing out instead.

Angela looked on in horror as Grivon writhed around on the floor. He was moaning softly and rocking his head back and forth. Angela cradled Grivon's head in her lap and kissed his forehead.

V

Grivon's dreams were assaulted by horrible visions of Bebe. When he awoke, he was hanging in the basement of her house again. He looked around at the dimly stone room. Thankfully, Bebe wasn't there. He began to wonder if he had been beaten until the point that he passed out and dreamed a horrible yet wonderful dream.

The woman wasn't Barbarah, but she was still beautiful. His arms hurt from hanging suspended over the stone floor, and his wrists were chaffed and scabbed. The taste of blood permeated his mouth from the constant punches and slaps.

Gooseflesh crawled all across his naked body. The room was cold, damp, and musty. All in all, he was surprised that in the months that he had been in her capture that the only illness he had suffered from was a cough.

He was just about to go to sleep when Bebe entered the room. She was holding the torture device he hated the most, the picana. Holding it out toward his face, she shook it at him.

He cringed at the sight of blue electricity crackling inches from his face. Bebe looked him over and grabbed his raw member. She gripped it hard until it started bleeding. Grivon screamed in pain and Bebe cackled, her eyes dancing with delight.

"A little sensitive, are we?" Bebe asked.

Grivon began to speak but was silenced when she hit him with the rod. He screamed as flesh burnt and burst open like a roasted pig. Bebe moaned as the smell of burning flesh filled the room.

"I didn't tell you to speak, did I?"

"No," he answered tearfully.

She hit him again.

"No what!"

"No, Herrin," he whimpered.

"Now are you going to give me what I want?"

Grivon spit as much and as hard as he could at her. The hot viscous fluid landed in her eyes making her squeal. He smiled at the thought of having humiliated her. Then the dim room went white hot. Bebe backhanded him hard.

"Insolent little bitch!" she screamed. "So help me, I will break your neck! I will cut off that stinky little whore rod and shove it down your throat!" She paused for a minute to catch her breath and wipe her mouth.

"But before I do that, you will eat your balls! To save you from my wrath apologize!"

"Go to Hell you, psychotic whore!" screamed Grivon. Instantly he wondered where that little outburst had come from. It was as if someone else had taken root inside his head.

Then out of nowhere, a blow from the picana to his stomach. It made a crackling sound as it hit the soft flesh. When she pulled back on the backswing strips of flesh smoked. Grivon screamed as if someone had stabbed him in the gut.

He was bracing himself for another blow, when she spun him quickly, and the chain smashed his fingers. He yelled out in pain as she hit his neck with the rod. Then she stopped for a few minutes.

This time Grivon didn't see what was coming until he felt the ceramic spheres tear the tender tissues on his back. Bebe scourged him until she was entirely covered in his blood. She laughed and cackled the whole time.

All the while she screamed obscenities that Grivon had never heard before. Then the combined force of the last blow and the shock from loss of blood knocked him out.

When Grivon awoke, he was lying on a rock slab. His arms and legs were bound and stretched out in opposing directions. The tension pulled open the wounds on his back. The healing lacerations begin to ooze blood, or at least he hoped it was blood and that it wasn't infected.

He had been lying by himself for a while when he heard a noise. At first, it was very faint. He couldn't make out the sound at first. Then as it got louder, he heard it. It was a drop of water echoing in a cave.

He ignored it for a long time until the noise began to get louder in his head The only thing he could concentrate on was the drop of water. He closed his eyes to try and shut it out. However, it didn't help. After a while, it felt as if his brain was being forced down a swirling drain.

238

Then he saw a face in the dark. At first it was Angela's face. Then it was Ubiroe's face. Then everything went black.

VI

Angela and Phoy were standing over a comatose Grivon. Phoy pulled back Grivon's eyelids. His eyes were rolled in the back of his head. His breathing was shallow, and his heart rate was high.

Phoy and Angela shared a worried look. They stayed knelt beside him for a long time. As they watched him, Grivon flailed around on the wooden floor. He was shouting and screaming.

Phoy looked puzzled and then looked at Angela and shouted, "Tell me again what the hell happened on Tūhl?"

"He was captured by Bebe Barrim. She held him captive for almost a year. In which time, she repeatedly brutalized and tortured him, both physically and psychologically. Just so, he would give her a daughter.

He was sold at a slave auction to me. I thought I nursed him back to health. But of course, he rarely opens up about his feelings and emotions."

Phoy stroked his catfish mustache for several minutes. He did not know what to do. He could wipe Grivon's memory, but the memories could come back and torment him worse than before.

Phoy decided that Grivon had to confront his own mind. That until he did, he would continue to be a tortured soul, and it could take years to fully get him back to a semblance of sanity.

VII

Grivon awoke three days later with a headache that could have passed for an axe being driven into his skull. The visions he saw were beginning to break like a storm on the horizon. He lay looking up at the featureless ceiling.

No one was around, and he was lonely and scared. While he was unconscious, he believed that he was back with Bebe. The pain was real. As were the emotions he felt were real. He was thankful that it was all just a vision of things that had once happened.

Grivon tried to sit up and found that the entire world was spinning. The room reeled like an out-of-control merry-go-whirl. His stomach began churning, and he dry heaved. He was hungry, and his tongue was stuck to the roof of his mouth.

After a while the pain in his head subsided. He was able to stand up and dress after a while after that. His stomach still churned, but he was able to will it away and open the door.

Once he was out in the hall, he could smell food being prepared. He walked toward the dining room that he, Angela, and Phoy had eaten in. When he entered the dining room, he saw a buffet of foods before him.

There was rice porridge, boiled eggs, and an assortment of fruits and pastries. Grivon flopped down on a cushion and began to eat in a ravenous fury. He grabbed three boiled eggs and stuffed them into his mouth at once. After he had finished his eggs, he grabbed the porridge and started engulfing it.

Grivon didn't notice that Phoy was standing in the doorway watching him eat. Phoy sighed thinking about how Grivon lay in a trance, as if dead, for three days without eating.

He had been through an ordeal and a half. He had tried to warn him about Tūhl and the Barrim Clan. Phoy shook his head and sighed once more before he began his speech that he had prepared.

"You know she loves you," began Phoy.

Grivon looked up at Phoy, smiling and with a mouth full of food said, "Yoth 'ean Angewa?"

"Yes. She's the one that prepared this breakfast for you. Anyway, I warned you not to go to Tūhl, but you didn't listen. I had a feeling something like this would happen. It is all moot now," Phoy said waving his hand.

"Look, I know you need a memory wipe in a bad way, but that will only remove the events from your conscious mind. It will not, however, remove memories from your subconscious mind. You will continue to dream about it and relieve it in flashbacks unless you get a hold of yourself.

"I know that if you throw yourself into something and work hard, eventually you will get past the events that happened on Tūhl. If you want, I can either wipe your mind or you can throw yourself into the training. I know how to help you deal with this. What do you say?"

Grivon thought for several minutes before saying, "Let's do it." Phoy smiled and nodded. He whirled around and left to let Grivon eat.

VIII

The freezing water poured over Grivon's shoulders. He was sitting naked under a waterfall with his legs folded in the lotus potion. Large goosebumps covered every millimeter of his body. All he could think about was how cold and heavy the water was.

At first the water felt good after the arduous run up the mountain, but now he wondered if he would freeze to death. The falls were on the side of the emerald colored mountain behind the compound.

On the way up, he had to run up the winding trails with seven-kilogram weights around his wrists and ankles and fourteen- kilogram weights around his torso. Phoy told him that from the house to the pool of the waterfall was over ten kilometers.

Running that distance wouldn't usually be a problem except for the extra weight, and it was all up hill. Phoy and Angela stood on the rocky bank of the river watching him.

They had been watching him sit under the waterfall in quiet meditation for over five hours. Phoy glanced at Angela and smiled a knowing smile. Angela smiled back and nodded. Phoy looked down at the shivering Grivon and yelled, "Get dry and prepare for more running. Angela and I will meet you at the bottom."

Grivon rolled his eyes and stood up out from under the falls and grabbed the towel that Angela had brought for him. Once he was dry, he put on his bodysuit and strapped on the weights. The run back seemed worse than the one up.

The extra weight made it hard to stay upright, and he often tripped over rocks and fell several meters before rolling to a stop. When he finally reached the compound, he collapsed in front of Angela and Phoy.

"I guess we killed him." Angela said with a smile on her face.

"It looks that way. We will just have to bury him under the rock garden." Phoy said also smiling.

"I'm still here," said Grivon groaning.

"It lives!" cried Angela laughing.

Grivon sat up and looked at his mentor. He shook his head and rubbed the back of neck. It had been a long day. He was so tired that he wasn't even hungry. All he wanted to do was rest his burning limbs and sleep for a week, but he knew he had to eat, even if it was just some fruit.

Picking himself up off the ground, he dusted off took, and off the weights letting them fall to the dusty ground. He gave Phoy a dirty look and walked into the house to clean up. As he closed the shoji behind him, Angela's laugh permeated the hallway sounding louder than it was.

His dinner that night was large and flavorful. He barely remembered eating the food, let alone what it was. Phoy and Angela tried to engage in small talk, but he was too exhausted to give them any good conversation.

Now he lay on his mat looking at the featureless ceiling again. Angela walked in wearing her robe and began to untie it. Grivon looked her over and said, "Not tonight. I'm not in the mood."

"Oh, stop thinking with the other head."

"Huh?"

"In other words, I'm not in the mood either. Anyway, I wanted to know if I could give you a massage, so that your legs and arms don't cramp during the night."

"Oh, okay. Could you sleep in here tonight, and cuddle with me?"
He said smiling.

"Sure, now roll over."

Angela worked the tension out of his biceps first. Then she rubbed his sore wrists and ankles. Once she was finished with his ankles she moved to his calves. After working his calves, she rubbed his thighs, and finished with his hands and feet. His body felt like a limp rag.

"That was wonderful. How did you learn how to do that?" Grivon asked when she was finished. Angela winked, "I used to be the foremost assassin in this system.

I needed to be able to get close to targets, so I was trained in massage and tantric pleasures. I have killed during the throes of passion and in the relaxation of massage."

Grivon nodded as he lay back with his hands behind his head. Thankful she decided against killing him, Angela cuddled up next to him laying her head on his chest. She sighed and closed her eyes, as she smelled his skin.

Her fingers traced circles on his sternum. Grivon grabbed her hand and stopped her. She sighed and hugged up to him and said, "Are you okay?"

"Yeah, I'm fine. I'm tired and just want to be close to you tonight.
Besides, I thought you weren't wanting to do that."

Angela gave a half-hearted laugh and shook her head, "Just wanted to touch you. I guess that was the wrong thing to do."

The Chronicles of Merkadiah:
The Rise of the Gryphon

Grivon sighed, "No. I don't like mixed signals." He kissed her on her forehead and drifted off to sleep. Angela laid beside him listening to his breathing. She wished that she had met him under different circumstances.

Had they met under the ideal conditions then perhaps she could have been loved by him the way he loved Barbarah. The sounds of his breath made her long for a second chance at life, and she wondered what the future would bring for her and him.

Chapter Seven

Broken

"This life is cruel and an unforgiving place. Often the scars we are given are reminders of just how unforgiving and cruel this life is." -Phoy Yin, Journal of Philosophy

Three Months Later

I

Barbarah lay in bed, sore and bruised. Afternoon sunlight streamed in through large arched windows and warmed her, but it didn't heal her. She tried hard to remember how she got into her bed this time.

For months, she had been waking up in her bed bruised, beaten and sore. She knew what was happening, but she could not remember any of the details.

She wondered what she did wrong this time. Had she not been willing to let him have her? Or was it because it was like he said so many times in the past; she was nothing but a stupid, worthless cow. She tried so hard to make him happy, but it never seemed enough.

In the past month, she lost a whole week. She wondered how many days she lost this time, and it was always the same. Once she was awake Steven would bring her a gift and apologize and explain to her how it was her fault and that if she would just behave and do as he told her, it would stop.

She wanted so bad to believe if she just slept with him it would make things better. But a nagging voice deep inside her screamed for her to get away from him. The only reason she stayed was because of Grivon.

He trusted Steven so much. How could she betray Grivon by running away from his friend? Besides, she was broke, and Steven paid for everything.

She wished she had the forethought to stash away some of the money he gave her when he was letting her out of the mansion. Now she only got to walk on the inside of the fence that ran the perimeter of the grounds.

The Chronicles of Merkadiah:
The Rise of the Gryphon

While beautiful, it wasn't the same as being able to eat delicious food and gaze at the lights of the city up close. Barbarah sighed as the door opened and Steven walked in with a small white box and his typical pouty face.

He walked up to her and kissed her on her cheek. She fought the urge to vomit on him. She looked up into his eyes and smiled as best she could.

"I bought you a special gift," Steven said

Feigning excitement, Barbarah sat up and said, "Did you now?"

"Yes, it's in this box."

Steven opened the box and pulled out a syringe full of a clear liquid.

Barbarah gave him a wary look.

"Don't worry. It'll help you feel better. Soon all your worries will be gone. I just want you to remember that the reason all of this is happening is because I love you."

Barbarah squeaked as he injected her with the substance. Soon everything went fuzzy and the most wonderful ecstasy enveloped her.

II

When Barbarah awoke, she was in her bed and Steven was propped up on his right elbow and was looking down at her with a soft expression on his face. She looked in his eyes and saw something that had never been there before.

A deep caring for her. She couldn't remember what happened or what had transpired. All she knew was the feeling of recent passion between her thighs.

"What happened?" Barbarah asked Steven fluttering her eyes to get the sleep out.

"We've been making love for several hours. You passed out and have been asleep about two hours now. I've been watching you sleep," Steven lied. After he had his way with her, he had administered the memory wipe drug.

It removed anywhere from the last several hours to the last several years of your life, depending on dosage. The amount Steven administered Barbarah was enough for her to forget the violence of the last several months.

"Oh, wow, I must have been drained. Of course, it has been over three years now since I was with Grivon."

"I know, and I know you miss him. I hope you don't feel bad about what has happened between us?"

"I do, and I don't. I know it's wrong, but he hasn't so much as sent me a letter since before Terry was born. When he comes back to us, I just want you to know I will want to be with him, but it's like my old Guild Lady said once, 'If you can't be with who you love, love the one you're with."

"That is an odd saying for a Guild Lady. Do you know how she came by it?"

"She said it to me right before we left the Guild."

"That makes more sense. You know I love you, right?"

"I know that you love me in your own way."

Steven nodded, leaned down, and kissed her. He was going to have to be kind for a while, at least to her anyway. If he wasn't careful, he would have to continue doing what he had done earlier, and long-term usage of the memory wipe drug could have serious long-term effects.

Steven moved the blankets down to expose Barbarah and for the first time in his life, he made love with a woman without any violence.

Chapter Eight
Balance

"Order is the balance to Chaos. Water is the balance of Fire. Death is the balance of Life. In all things seek moderation, not extremes." - Pantherine Proverb

I

It had been several months since the new training had begun. Everyday Grivon would run to the waterfall and meditate for one hour then run back down. This whole exercise took a little over four hours.

Upon returning, he got a quick lunch of pickled plum rice balls and some water. Then back to training. With weights strapped to him, he would do a hundred push-ups and sit-ups.

Followed by two hours of sparing with Angela or another student, all the while wearing the weights. He even slept with the weights on.

The training was exhausting, but I slowly he was beginning to realize something; he could use the incident on Tūhl to fuel his furnace. After three months of the rigorous training, Phoy came to talk to Grivon at breakfast.

He sat down in front of Grivon and ate quietly. After several minutes of silence, Grivon became agitated.

"What do you want?" he growled.

"To give you your second task," said Phoy with a smile.

"Oh?"

"Yes, I think you are ready for the next task that will put you at a level worthy of my special training."

Grivon raised an eyebrow. Phoy reclined and bit into a large fleshy plum. This made Grivon laugh. He always thought that Phoy was melodramatic and in this moment, he was right.

II

When Grivon shed the extra twenty-seven kilograms he had been carrying around he felt a lot lighter. He felt as if he could run the whole of Ne-Le. He was happy that he could feel cool air on his weight-laden limbs.

Stretching his arms and legs, he bent backward putting both hands flat on the sandy ground. For some reason, he felt like a new person and he cartwheeled around the sandy training ground laughing like a child.

He was stopped when he heard Phoy begin to speak.

"For your next task, I want you to fight the best student I am currently training," said Phoy smiling.

Grivon grinned and replied, "No sweat."

Phoy nodded and motioned to a girl who looked no more than sixteen who was sitting cross legged on the porch. Grivon watched as she walked down to stand in front of him.

She was shorter than him, with fiery red hair, and striking blue eyes. She was wearing a purple bodysuit like the one Barbarah used to wear. Grivon could tell she was well trained due to her lithe muscle tone. He wondered why he was fighting a child.

"She is a lot older than you are," Phoy said, as if to read his mind,

"and she has been here since she was four. Her mother and I were friends and when she died, I took over as her guardian."

"How old is she then?"

It looked to Grivon as if Phoy's eyes twinkled when he answered, "Three hundred years old."

Grivon stood with his jaw hanging open gawking at Phoy and the girl. Angela put a hand over her mouth to hide her smile. Grivon looked the girl over again and then looked at Phoy, "How come she hasn't aged?"

Phoy laughed, "That's for me to know and for you to never find out."

"Why?" Grivon demanded.

Once again, Phoy chuckled before saying, "I know your wants and goals. The key to immortality does not belong to those who would overly benefit from it. Your desire to rule discounts you from any claim to immortality.

As you well know, I found out how to extend my life beyond what the Aurora normally does, and I have now lived over six hundred years. I was alive and well during 'The Purging' and survived to see the son of my closest friend begin his journey to adulthood and greatness.

"Now if we are through chatting, I want to give you your second task. I want you to spar with bokkens. It is the training weapon of my ancestors. If you can beat my goddaughter, I will give you your third task, but if you fail, you will have to wear twice the weight you have been.

You will do the training that you just did for two months never removing the weights, not even to sit under the waterfall. Now are you ready?" Grivon nodded his head as Angela handed him a bokken.

Phoy handed his goddaughter a bokken, stepped back, and picked up a blindfold. Grivon cocked an eyebrow at Phoy.

"Is that for me?" Grivon asked

"Yes, it is," Phoy replied.

"With a blindfold on, how am I supposed to fight?"

"You have four other senses, use them."

Grivon raised two eyebrows this time, "What's her name?"

Phoy replied, "Why do you want to know?"

"Curiosity," answered Grivon, smirking.

"Curiosity killed the Pantherine."

"Huh?"

"Never mind, her name is Christy St. John."

Grivon nodded and looked at Christy one last time before Phoy put the blindfold on. When the blindfold was snug and Phoy made sure Grivon couldn't see, the sparring began.

Grivon stood with the bokken out in the ready position. He tried his best to hear only the sounds of Christy's footsteps on the sandy ground but was unable. The only way he knew the match was going to start was when he felt her tap her bokken against his.

They stood with bokkens crossed for what felt like an eternity. Grivon was having a tough time listening for her to make the slightest twitch, but all he could hear was birds and insects.

Then he felt Christy's bokken leave his. He tried to anticipate her attack but guarded where she wasn't even standing. He grunted in pain when the hardwood contacted his stomach.

Grivon stumbled forward and tried for a counterattack, but he was too slow. Christy was already moving away and preparing for another attack.

This time Grivon heard her soft footfalls on the sandy ground and blocked the blow meant for his head, but he was unsuccessful in keeping her from kicking him in the thigh.

Grivon stumbled forward two steps and was hit hard once more in his stomach. He was attempting to recover from the blow when he saw white stars outlined in red as his head exploded in pain. The next thing he knew, three concerned faces were looking down at him.

"What happened?" moaned Grivon.

"You lost faster than a Guild initiate on the first day of training," chided Angela.

"Very funny, could someone help me up?"

Phoy stretched out his hand and helped him to his feet. Grivon dusted himself off and said, "I guess sixty-four kilograms isn't so much."

Phoy started laughing and walked off with his goddaughter.

Chapter Nine
Splinter

"We all have demons that we must face and overcome. Some have more than others. Still others must face a single demon that holds them in the palm of its scaly charred hands,"-Chaos Guild Axiom

Five Years Later

I

Grivon ducked the bokken and thrust his forward. His bokken hit home against Christy's chest. She stepped back stunned and stood for a moment too long.

Grivon swung his bokken and knocked her feet out from underneath her. He stood with the point of the wooden sword up under her chin. Grivon heard clapping. Taking off his blind fold, he turned around to see Phoy and Angela smiling.

"Well done, Grivon," said Phoy with pride in his voice. "It only took you five years to do it."

"Five years of backbreaking weight training and reflection."

"Now you can begin the last leg of the training. It will take all your concentration and strength. I will try and teach you to use all five of the basic Magiah techniques. I know that you can do the Chaos technique, and Angela told me you that you used the Air technique.

Now, all that is left is the Water, Matter, and Fire techniques. I hope that we can get you to do all five. I can only do four and most people can only do one. If you can master all five, then that would make you the most powerful Kartah in Merkadiah."

Grivon nodded with a smile on his face. He hoped that the rest of his training would not be as difficult as the training leading up to the last task. For the last year, he pulled five massive boulders to the top of the mountain and back every day.

He beat Christy and now he could focus on the training he had originally come for. Once he completed it, he hoped that he could get back to Barbarah.

"When does it start?"

"Tomorrow."

Grivon nodded and sighed. Five years come and gone. His son, Terry would soon be seven. He hoped that he was being well taken care of. Grivon wished that he could be with his son. He wished Barbarah was with him. He wished.

That was all he seemed to do was wish to be somewhere else or was with other people. It was like there was a hole in his heart; some kind of deep, dark fire that could not be quenched deep within his soul.

It was a yearning for more than what this life was giving him. It seemed that his ultimate goal was a small light at the end of a long dark tunnel that never got any shorter.

He wanted to scream and lash out at all denizens of Merkadiah. Finally, he realized what it was he wanted and what would quench that fire in his soul, ultimate control.

He wanted to bring Merkadiah to its knees and watch the people's faces as he put forth his hand and destroyed them all. He would make sure that for the next century or two that his family was in total control.

At that moment deep within his heart, he ceased to be Grivon and became The Gryphon.

II

The rod hurt as it smacked Grivon's upper thighs. He stood on one foot on a small post three meters off the sand. There was a knife strapped under each armpit, and he was held a bucket of water in each hand.

All the while, he balanced a bucket of water on his head. To make it harder Phoy, Angela, and Christy were circling the post, smacking his leg with long thin rods every few minutes.

He had spent the last two hours standing like this. Now, he was glad that he had the strength training from hell. The only problem was that after an hour the water became heavier because his arms were outstretched, and if he wasn't careful his underarms would get stabbed. The sound of clapping almost sent him over the edge of the post.

"All right, that is enough of this. I have a couple of other things for you to do today," Phoy exclaimed.

The Chronicles of Merkadiah:
The Rise of the Gryphon

Grivon dropped the buckets and carefully pulled the harness down to his waist and unstrapped it. He jumped down off the post, landed in a kneeling position and handed Phoy the harness.

Phoy thanked him and asked him to follow him. Grivon, Angela, and Christy followed Phoy to an area that didn't look like it belonged on Ne-le. It was a beautiful grove of oak trees.

They were nestled at the bottom of a beautiful sloping hill and could only be seen if you were standing at the crest. Within the grove was a large square pit with twenty-five posts like the one he had been previously standing on jutting a few centimeters over the lip of the hole.

Above the center post was a small wooden dowel tied to a rope dangling from a strong limb high above. Grivon was looking at the setup and wondering exactly what was supposed to be accomplished at this station.

He was knocked out of his examination of the training course by a bokken gently hitting him on the head. He looked to the ground, picked up the wooden sword, and looked at Phoy with confusion.

"I want to see how agile you are. Go stand on any of the eight posts circling the center post and strike the dowel. Wherever the dowel swings, I want you to hop on the posts on the other side and hit again when it swings back toward you. Do this until I tell you to stop and watch out for surprises."

"What kind of surprises?"

Phoy only laughed and stroked his goatee. Grivon hit the dowel as hard as he could. It swung wildly away from him. He leapt to the opposite posts and as he steadied himself, the dowel came at him. Ducking, he struck the dowel on the downswing.

He kept leaping between posts and hitting the dowel for an hour. Phoy watched as Grivon tirelessly leapt back and forth with the agility of a Pantherine. The extreme weight training had been a good thing for him.

As Phoy watched Grivon, he pulled a small remote device out of a fold in his robes and pressed a button. The posts began to move up, down and vibrate. He immediately lost a little footing, and in the process of balancing, he was hit in the head by the dowel.

Grivon wobbled on the moving ground and fell into the pit. He landed in between the some of the outer posts and the dirt wall. The whine of the small engines that pushed and pulled the posts filled his ears.

His arms and legs were beginning to get splinters as the rough wood rubbed up against them. Much to Grivon's delight the posts stopped and a soon after a rope fell. Grivon grunted as he pulled himself out of the pit.

He laid in the soft dirt for several minutes trying to catch his breath. His arms and legs hurt where the posts either rubbed splinters into them or rubbed them raw.

He was pulling himself up to his feet when he was hit hard enough to taste blood. He fell, prostrate to the ground. When the daze wore off, he started to get up, and again he was hit to the ground. The cycle of trying to get up and being hit repeated itself for several minutes.

"Get up, you incompetent idiot. I would have hoped that a student as advanced as you would do better at my training, but apparently, I was wrong! Now get your sorry carcass up and assume your ready position.

I want to see what you really are." Phoy yelled.

Grivon grunted. He sparred with Phoy before and nearly killed him, but for some reason Phoy seemed a little stronger than he remembered. Grivon picked up the bokken and began to take a stance. But before he could, he was blocking attacks. He lost his footing and was on the ground with Phoy standing above him posed ready for a down stroke.

Grivon rolled away and as he did, he struck Phoy behind the left knee. Phoy's leg buckled and in a swift motion, Grivon brought his sword up to hit Phoy's back as he regained his footing.

The bokken glanced off Phoy's Aurora. Grivon grunted. This was more than a mere sparring match. Phoy was serious. Once Grivon gained a sure footing, he began to aggress toward Phoy. Each swing was parried at lightning speed. Then out of nowhere, Phoy began shouting questions.

"Who are you?"

Without thinking Grivon responded, "I am 'The Gryphon.'" Phoy blocked a blow, unaffected by Grivon's statement.

"What is your goal?"

"To rule with an iron fist!" Grivon roared, as he swung a mighty down stroke.

"Then your goal is self-serving?"

"Yes!"

"Then you no longer wish a better life for those you love?"

"No!"

"What do you really want, Gryphon?"

The Chronicles of Merkadiah:
The Rise of the Gryphon

"To bring this system to its knees. To watch the bureaucrats bleed. I want to use the trees of Rhokahl as torches. I want the fish of Baktüth to turn belly up. I want the Pantherines free of their ghettos. I want the head of The Autocrat as a trophy.

I want the head of Dahra Barrim beside it. I want to destroy the planet of Tühl. I want complete and utter control of everyone and everything. I want to see my children. I want to see Barbarah. I want you to die!"

As soon as the last words fell from his lips, he threw the bokken into the air and in a fluid, motion pushed out his hand and a large ball of electric blue fire shot from his right hand and engulfed Phoy. Christy and Angela screamed in unison. Grivon laughed like a mad man as the flames burned all around his master.

After the fire settled, Phoy was kneeling, breathing heavily, his bokken in his left hand, and his right arm over his stomach. He stayed like that for several minutes before he got up and said, "That was a stronger response than I thought you would have. Well done.

Now my question is, do I need to call you The Gryphon or Grivon?"

"Keep it Grivon for now. I am 'The Gryphon,' but until I kill the Autocrat, I am still just Grivon."

"Do you intend to burn down Rhokahl, or destroy the ecosystem of Baktüth?"

"I don't know. I was hoping to give Rhokahl to the Lepridis and Baktüth supplies over half the system with food. I was angry at you and my emotions came out in a fury. I'm sorry about the fireball."

"It's perfectly all right. Emotion is what gives the Magiah his abilities. The more passion you feel, the more natural the release of the body's natural electricity. I am glad that you can now do three of the techniques.

I hope you know that I will push you harder and harder until the point of breaking." Something suddenly seemed to occur to Phoy. "Speaking of passion. I know how often you use your rage and frustration to fuel your fights.

You should try to suppress it to a single bead of strength you can draw from. Does that make sense?" Grivon nodded wondering why Phoy thought to tell him that now.

"Now go get cleaned up or do whatever it is you want." Phoy patted Grivon on the shoulder. Grivon nodded, looked at Angela, and said, "I am going to the waterfall, do you want to come with me?"

"I will meet you up there."

Grivon regarded her for a moment and then turned and walked off.

"Phoy, I must speak with you. Alone," her eyes darted over to Christy.

"Leave us." Phoy commanded.

III

"You're what!" Phoy said almost screaming.

For several moments, the only sounds that could be heard were the chirps of insects in the trees.

"I'm pregnant," Angela said holding Phoy's gaze.

"Oh, good grief! What is he a freaking rabbit?"

"What?" Angela asked confused.

"Never mind that. Why? I thought that you of all people would know how to sleep with a man and not get pregnant. You are a trained assassin. How could you have let this happen? If he finds out he is going to have another child, he will stop the training.

Not to mention, he will become just another pawn in an unwinnable game of chess. What were you thinking?"

"I'm sorry to upset you, but I wasn't thinking about not getting pregnant. When I'm around him, I feel like my mind scatters to the corners of the universe. I want nothing more than to be constantly at his side cheering him along the way."

"The boy does seem to have that effect on people. You know I hope Christy does not get any ideas about him. That would be all I need. I hope I really do not end up regretting this, but I think it is time to step up the training, and I think it is time for you to leave.

I want you to go somewhere safe and have the baby. What do you plan on doing once the child is born?"

Angela blushed and said, "I would like for you to raise the child.

Teach the child everything. If you could please tell the child who the father is, but if by chance Grivon succeeds, don't tell the child that the father is The Gryphon."

"What makes you think I would be a good mentor to the child?" Phoy said stroking his mustache and goatee.

256

"The way you have handled Christy is excellent. I would want my child to be the same way. I know that he wouldn't want that, but it's what I want. Besides Grivon will never know."

"And what if any of Grivon's other children make their way here? Should I tell them that this child of yours is their brother or sister?"

"Only if you feel that is right. I would like to spend some time alone with Grivon before I leave. Do you think I could persuade you to let him have one week off from training to say goodbye? I think if I leave abruptly, he might spiral into a new depth of insanity."

"I fear he might anyway. He is extremely attached to you, and though he may not think it, he loves you the way he loves Barbarah, you can see it in the way he looks at you. I hope that it will give him more focus, but your charms seem to be what keeps him stable."

"I know, but I have to keep this a secret from him. I will probably go to the Assassin's Guild for the time being. Send word to The Chimera when Grivon has finished his training. I will bring the child here and then I will find Grivon.

I have this feeling deep down that he will still need me in some way. I think heartbreak awaits him when he sees his woman again."

"I fear that is the truth of it as well, for the man who is to look after her is a psychopath. He is also the leader of the Orsin crime family. I knew his ancestors.

They were honorable men, if you can call criminals honorable, but this one is deeply depraved. I hope that he hasn't killed her, or worse seduced her.

Barbarah is a very vulnerable woman and she is more attached to Grivon than Grivon is to you." Angela let out a long whistle.

"Phoy, I am going to go break the news to Grivon. I hope he takes it alright."

"You and me both my dear."

IV

Christy walked for several feet before teleporting to the top of the waterfall that Grivon was going to. She had been around men for most of her life, but she had never seen a man as driven and handsome as Grivon.

257

Something about him made something deep within her crazy. He had brought that pretty woman with him and long before she had ever met him formally, she had listened to them make love. It was hard not to hear them. The walls were made of paper and wood.

Even though they were on the other side of the compound, she still heard Angela's screams of passion. After several minutes of waiting, Christy decided not to wait at the top of the falls but to wait behind a large rock on the opposite side of the path and when he got into the water teleport over behind one of the rocks closer to the water.

It was a while still, but after an hour, Grivon finally crested the hill. He had a towel and soap with him. He was still only wearing a pair of black shorts.

Christy's stomach fluttered, if she was lucky, she might get to see him naked. It would be the first time in her life she had ever seen a naked man. She was three hundred years old and never been kissed.

She didn't know how Phoy would act if she brought up the things she had been feeling since well before her one hundredth year. She was only a child when Phoy took her in.

She loved the old man enough, that she didn't want to burden him with her feelings. Once Grivon was undressed and in the water, she teleported to the other side of the pool. Her face heated at seeing his nudity.

Shame washed over her for spying. But her curiosity had to be satiated. Now she knew. His physique was stunning. She gawked at him for several minutes, making a mental picture.

A familiar tingling washed over body and quickly turned into an agony that needed to be detonated. She was so engrossed that she almost didn't hear the footsteps behind her.

Christy suddenly came to her senses and teleported back to the top of the falls. She wanted to see who was walking up the mountain. When the person was in full view, she was surprised to see Angela.

She hoped that Angela hadn't seen her. Angela laid the towel on a dry rock near the pool and undressed before wading into the water with Grivon. It was all she could do to keep from laughing when she splashed him with water.

Laughing, Grivon splashed her back. As she was wiping the water from her face, he tackled her, and they began to kiss ferociously. Christy knew it wasn't right to watch, but after not being able to talk about her feelings and

258

thoughts with Phoy, she watched as Angela and Grivon made love on a rock on the side of the river.

V

Christy made sure to teleport into her room, but she was surprised to find Phoy sitting on her tatami. She lowered her eyes as Phoy's eyes bore holes in her.

"Where have you been?" asked Phoy.

"Training," Christy lied.

"Where?"

"Why does it matter?"

"I wished to have dinner with you, but you were nowhere to be found. I thought about going to the waterfall to see if Angela and Grivon had seen you, but I figured they would want some privacy.

I am going to ask you one more time, where were you?"

"I was on top of the mountain practicing forms. Away from the waterfall if you must know." She spat.

"I see. I guess I will tell you what I wanted to tell you at dinner.

Angela must leave in a week's time and Grivon will be very vulnerable. You are to proceed as you did when he first arrived, out of sight out of mind.

I am not saying that he would hurt you or anything, but I know that in two hundred ninety years you have never once said that any of my students were, 'handsome.'"

Christy blushed, her cheeks turning red as her hair.

"With that I will leave you, and the next time you spy on two people seeking privacy I will give you a sparring session you will not soon forget."

Christy nodded and let out a frustrated sighed as Phoy opened the door and walked out. Christy was shattered. Phoy never treated her like this before. She knew it was because of Grivon.

His presence drove Phoy into a frenzy. She supposed that whatever happened to Grivon on Tūhl was what had Phoy so frantic. She knew that Grivon was either still dealing with scars, or he was mad. Perhaps he was both.

Either way when Angela left things were going to be different.

VI

It was well after sunset when the slight knock came at Christy's door. "Come," she said.

Angela walked into her room and slid the door shut.

"What do I owe this visit from the consort of 'The Gryphon?'"

Angela laughed, "Cut the slag, you little voyeur."

"I don't know what you are talking about." Christy said, offhandedly while examined her nails.

"Oh, I believe you do. I saw you above the waterfall looking at us today. Did you learn anything? Did you like what you saw?"

Christy blushed and said, "I now know what a man looks like." Angela regarded Christy for a moment then said, "I think we need to talk elsewhere. These walls are thin."

Christy nodded and got up to leave. Angela walked behind her to the door. The two women walked out onto one of the porches and into the cool night air. Angela sighed and followed Christy to a small hovel several meters away from the main house and other huts.

"Phoy has never shown us this place. Why is it here?" asked Angela.

"It was my training quarters." said Christy. "I lived here while he taught me how to be the best Kartah in the system and the secrets of immorality. I also stayed here when you and Grivon arrived. Sadly, this is more my home than the main house."

The hovel was a small, square shack with a large bedroom and a smaller room with a showerhead, water dial and a hole in the floor directly under the showerhead. Christy shut the door to her bathroom and shut the wooden door to her hovel.

"What is it you wished to speak about?" asked Christy.

"As you probably already know, I am leaving at the end of the week. Phoy has told me that he knew you were spying and that he had talked to you about that, and that you are to stay away from Grivon for a while."

"I know. I am sorry that I violated your privacy. I was just curious. Phoy never taught me about delicate things. I hate to say it, but in three hundred years of life I have never been kissed, I've never seen a naked man and I burn with passion."

"I see. Who taught you about your moon cycle?"

"A female student came one time. She was here the year I began bleeding. I was hiding in the grove we were in earlier, bleeding through my training pants. I think I was about eleven years old.

She told me that it was normal and how to collect the blood and how to hide it from Phoy. Phoy knew I was becoming a woman, but I don't think that he realized he needed to teach me about womanly things."

"Okay, why is it that you never learned about more delicate matters?" Angela asked.

"She was killed soon after she arrived."

"By whom?"

"Revenants. They tore her limb from limb trying to get to her Aurora. I cried every day for a month. I wish she lived." A flash of despair shadowed Christy's face.

"I can teach you what she could not. I can show you how to make that burn go away. Be careful you do not become addicted to it.

"It is like the most powerful of drugs. I must also caution you about trying to sleep with Grivon. He is a good lover as you have seen, but he must not be pushed into the act or feel like he is being pushed into it.

If he does, he may kill you. He killed the woman on Tūhl that captured and brutalized him. He is a bomb waiting to go off. Personally, he is one bad day away from becoming one of those creatures you mentioned.

"You saw how he was today when Phoy was asking him those questions. Now I will instruct you how to give yourself what you seek. And you will find that after the first time you set yourself to the task, you will be much more relaxed."

VII

Grivon was laying on his tatami looking at the ceiling not really thinking about anything. Sleep's dark call was almost upon him, when the shoji slid open and in walked Angela.

She quickly disrobed to a pair of black shorts. He drank in her form making a memory of her near perfect frame. When Angela noticed, she blushed and giggled.

She lay down beside him and cuddled up close to him. Propping herself up on her left arm, she ran her soft right hand over his chest. She teased his nipple before letting her hand come to rest on an unscarred portion of his stomach.

Then, she spoke in a voice that demanded attention.

"Grivon, I have to leave. My sabbatical is over. I must resume my duties as an assassin. But don't worry. I will back as soon as I can. If I must, I will come and see you once you take over as The Autocrat.

You are a special person who can do whatever he sets his mind to." She kissed him on the forehead and laid her head on his chest.

"I hate you," he said flatly and looked up at the ceiling.

Angela was taken aback by what Grivon had just said. Flabbergasted, Angela stammered, "Surely you don't mean that?"

A cold, violent look came over his face as he stood up and shouted, "You said you loved me! You said that you wouldn't hurt me! I believed you, but I guess I should have expected that you would lie since that is your job! You never even granted me my freedom! I.

Hate. You! Stupid, sex-crazed whore!"

Tears poured down her face, "You Bastard!" she screamed. "I loved you more than anyone I have ever known! I thought that you were different, but I see that deep down you are nothing but a self-absorbed little boy who has a bitch fit when he can't have his way."

"You're damn right! I learned a lot about myself while Herrin Bebe had me. I learned that all people are disposable no matter how important they might be to you. You were a good distraction from my problems and heartache. Now that you are leaving, I realize I never needed you.

I never loved you. I hate you for making me betray the only woman who has ever loved me. I hate you! I HATE YOU!"

"Fine. I was staying until the end of the week, but since you hate me, I am leaving tomorrow. Now if you decide that you don't hate me, I will be in my room. I will be leaving tomorrow at dusk regardless. I love you and I am not just saying that. Goodbye!"

Grivon watched through hate-filled eyes as Angela slid the door shut and walked down the hall. He stood clenching his fists for a few minutes.

Then he fell to his knees and began to pull on his hair as he cried out in deep pain. Unable to do anything else he pounded the wooden floor until his hand was bloody.

She cut out his heart and then shredded it into pieces. It was like when he left Barbarah, except this time it was reversed. He hated that he lost his temper like that. Nevertheless, he knew that she was just paying lip service to his ego.

The Chronicles of Merkadiah:
The Rise of the Gryphon

She didn't really love him, and she was most likely planning on going back tomorrow anyway. Then a realization came to him. Phoy was doing this. He was sending her away, because he thought she was distracting him from the training.

It was time for Phoy to stop pulling peoples strings. Grivon dressed and walked to the indoor training room. Several students were sparring with live weapons.

Grivon found his saber and walked outside to where Phoy was meditating. Phoy was sitting in the lotus position at the edge of the rock garden.

He sat alone and undefended. Grivon smirked. It would be so easy to just kill the man, but it wouldn't be honorable.

"Phoy Yin. I challenge you to a duel. The loser can either yield or die. Do you accept the terms?" Grivon yelled.

"Is there no other way?" Phoy asked with exasperation.

"No!" screamed Grivon

"Very well Gryphon, I accept your terms."

Grivon watched Phoy stand up and turn to face him. He also became aware of Angela running out of the house wearing nothing but the shorts she was wearing earlier.

Christy came running from somewhere from behind the main house. She was completely naked. The rest of the students and servants of the compound soon followed. Grivon looked at the crowd for a minute and returned his attention to Phoy.

He energized his Aurora, and Phoy did the same. Then he took his favorite form, the High Thay're. Phoy stood with his wrists crossed in front of him. He was defenseless. A willing sacrifice for the new ruler of Merkadiah.

Impatiently, Grivon stood waiting for Phoy to make the first move. After several minutes, Grivon fed his furnace and cooled down. Without warning Grivon did something that Phoy never saw before.

He sheathed his weapon and put both hands with palms facing out toward Phoy. The ground underneath his hands trembled, and two large boulders came out of the ground leaving holes at least a meter in diameter and at least three meters deep.

Suddenly they caught on fire, and once they were on fire lightning began to orbit around the burning spheres. It was awe inspiring. With a mighty roar, Grivon hurled them at his mentor.

Phoy dodged the two flaming projectiles and was caught off guard by Grivon suddenly appearing and swinging his sword at his head. Phoy ducked just in time and Grivon only caught air.

Tumbling backwards, Phoy energized a katana from thin air. His strength drained, but he needed to be cautious, this time Grivon was out for blood. He did not know why, but it could not be good, whatever the reason.

Grivon dug into the high forms he memorized long ago, and Phoy barely parried each blow. Angela and Christy watched with open mouths as sparks flew from the blades glancing off one another.

Grivon was a blur and Phoy was having trouble keeping up. Then a sound that Angela heard from her various missions filled their ears. Grivon was no longer hitting blade on blade. He was hitting Phoy's Aurora field directly.

Angela watched in horror as Phoy's field weakened. If Grivon didn't come to his senses, Phoy was going to die. Knowing that he was going to die soon was not what bothered Phoy. It was the things coming from Grivon's mouth.

"Die, you stupid bitch!" Grivon screamed. "I hate you, Herrin Bebe!

I hope you die a horrible death. Why did you have to do this to me? Look what you made me do you little slut. I will kill you! I will destroy you!"

Tears came to Phoy and Angela's eyes as they realized that Grivon was traumatized worse than they thought. He was projecting his rage toward Bebe on Phoy. At this moment Phoy was Bebe, and the more primitive parts of Grivon's brain were in control.

"Grivon," yelled Angela, "that is Phoy! He is your friend, and mentor.

You wouldn't want to kill your friend, would you?"

"I want to see his guts strewn across the rock garden. I want to mount his head on my wall. He is my nemesis, and I will kill him!"

"But Phoy is your friend. Why do you feel this way?"

Grivon's voice cracked with emotion as he screamed, "He told you to leave me! He told you to go away because I wasn't learning fast enough. I need you Angela. I love you!"

Grivon dropped his sword, dropped to his knees, and gripped his head as white-hot pain surged through his temples. He pounded the dirt until his knuckles opened staining the white sand.

Phoy got up and walked over to Angela and Christy. He looked them over and without showing emotion he said, "You two get some clothes on. He does not need to see you indecent in his current state. The rest of you go back to your quarters!"

Christy nodded and walked back to her hovel. Angela turned and walked back into the main house. Phoy turned and went to Grivon. He sat pounding the dirt cursing the day he was born. He cursed the sky and the stars in it.

He cursed the sun and the moons and the planets. It seemed as if Grivon was regressing into himself. Phoy began rubbing his back, and after several minutes, he stopped pounding the dirt and let Phoy lead him to his room.

Grivon felt weak and powerless. His world was swirling down a black pit. Angela was leaving at the end of the week. He couldn't get in touch with Barbarah. It was almost like he was splitting into two different people.

Once Phoy got Grivon to his room, Grivon collapsed. Phoy yelled for Angela. She came running as fast as she could. Grivon opened his eyes, gurgled something unintelligible and fainted.

VIII

Grivon awoke to the sound of a drop of water dripping into a pool. He knew no matter what, when he opened his eyes, he would be in the stone room at Bebe's. Taking several deep breaths, he opened his eyes and looked around.

To his utmost surprise, he was lying on his back looking at a mirror image of himself. Out of the corner of his eye he could see the cavern he often retreated to during the time with Bebe, and as of late when he meditated. It cut the pain of the water pouring over his skin.

He couldn't move his arms or legs. The one thing he seemed able to move was his lips. Once he was able, he noticed that the face in the mirror was like his, but it wasn't him. It was the one who promised to help him so long ago.

"Who are you?" he asked the face.

"I am you. At least what you think of you anyway. I am the one you called The Gryphon."

"How did you come to be inside me?"

"You made me. I was without name and form until you met Phoy. I am what some people would call your subconscious, or what others would call your ego. I am the drive behind all your ambitions.

I am what makes you tick," the man said with a sinister sneer.

"That really doesn't answer my question. I guess what I want to know is, why you are so violent. I want to know what makes you dominate my thoughts and my mind."

"Ha! I did not receive those qualities until Herrin Bebe came into our life. I was around drifting within your consciousness the whole time.

Occasionally, I would whisper into your head an idea or action. Other times I simply took control and let you think you were some sort of freak.

How else could you kill all those clones of yourself?"

"I just needed a few seeds of destruction to come to full bloom. I am created when someone goes through what you did. Sometimes in young children, things happen to shape their thoughts and feelings.

Those thoughts and feelings do not always come to surface until later in life when moments of heartache or of extreme duress awaken them. Much like today.

"In your case I was made from not only the words and actions of the students of The Guild, but from your own self-hatred. I had yet to fully form within you when Herrin Bebe captured us.

As your body took the abuses, your mind couldn't. To keep you from totally losing yourself your mind made me, and this place. Oh, I and this cavern existed long before you left The Guild, but Bebe awakened me in you.

I was officially born the first time she brutalized you. I protected you from her. I took control of your mind until Angela came to us.

"Angela drew you back to the surface. Instead of your brain killing me, I fought hard to stay in the periphery of your conscious self. I broke through a couple of times and much to your pleasure I would think,"

The Gryphon said.

"You are the one that let me love Angela against all my better judgment. We are different you and me. I want the power of The Autocrat to help make this solar system a better place for everyone.

You want the power to dominate. You want nothing more than to lash out at everyone. You would have killed Phoy and then turned on Angela. She loves us. I don't know what you are, but you are not me!" yelled Grivon.

The Chronicles of Merkadiah:
The Rise of the Gryphon

"Oh, but I am. Remember the final day of The Guild Tournament. Remember how much you loathed and hated that slut Ubiroe? Even though I still lacked form within your consciousness I was there pushing you to ravage her, but I wasn't strong enough yet.

I wasn't fully formed until you killed Bebe. I once again wanted you to give her no less than what she deserved, but sadly, you have no stomach for torture.

"So, I bided my time. Then when Phoy gave us the second dose of neuropoison, and I came to the front of your consciousness. The effects of the Ayahuasca allowed me to slightly merge with you.

"Now that I have you where I want you, I will offer you a choice. We are more powerful together than apart. I want you to allow me to merge with your consciousness completely.

Together we would be the perfect combination of tyrant and benevolent ruler. We could be the ultimate demagogue. We are what this solar system needs, ruling duality.

You remember your history, right? 'The Purging' is what formed all of this.

You could have almost entire autonomous control. You would have to share your power with Barbarah and Steven, but that is not as bad as it seems if you really think about it.

"Not to mention you would have Aridaunts that have autonomous control over their fiefdoms. Then they would answer directly to our triumvirate. It is a beautiful thing that we can create, but you will have to get your hands dirty.

We will have to kill political opponents as soon as they make themselves known. You may even have to sleep with a few more women.

"What do you say? Do we have ourselves a deal?" asked The Gryphon.

"I will still have the most control over my own mind, right? Not you and your twisted outlooks?"

"You have my word. I will be nothing but a minor fracture of your personality that will help you through the times that require you to kill and or torture another human. Little do you know, but I enjoy that sort of thing.

I am good at turning you and your 'bad' feelings off and taking control when I need to. Although I will say, you have never actually killed anyone yourself. I just push, and you do it." The Gryphon said smiling.

"All right, I will allow this merging of my personality. Just don't make me into a womanizer."

"Perish the thought. Whatever chances you had with Christy are long gone now. She thinks you're insane for sure. If she still feels any passion towards you, I don't think you want to mess with her. Phoy will kill you for one, and two, I think she is still a virgin."

"What's wrong with that?"

"Three hundred years is a long time to go without ever having felt the warmth of another body, or the gentle caress of a lover's hand. That is a can of worms even I couldn't get us out of."

"Okay, so when can I get back to the land of the living?"

"Now."

IX

Grivon nimbly jumped around the tops of the moving posts striking the dowel. Phoy stood watching him go for over four hours. Just striking and dodging. He was amazed at how well Grivon had recovered.

After being out cold for nine days, he awoke with a tremendous hunger and a desire to hurry up and finish his training. Phoy had been trying to teach him how to use the water technique.

The water form was the most dangerous since it dehydrated the user. The theory behind the water technique was to depress the amount of water within your blood and expel it in a super-heated spray.

Most of the students that learned this drank at least eleven liters of water a day. He was also showing him the final form that allows the Magiah to pull the various metals from his blood to make a weapon and then fortify it into a fully functional sword of the Magiah's design.

Both forms caused tremendous loss to the Aurora Field of the person using them. Phoy stroked his long thin mustache. Grivon was more stable now and he seemed different somehow.

He was more mature than he was the night he went crazy. It was as if he somehow came to terms with himself, but he was still different. He had a look of both wisdom and petulance.

He was still Grivon, but at the same time, he wasn't. He gave Angela a passionate kiss when he awoke and once again, when she left the next evening.

The Chronicles of Merkadiah:
The Rise of the Gryphon

Phoy watched Grivon jump around for a while longer. He decided to let Grivon wear himself out and walked back inside to tend to his bonsai trees. The one simple pleasure he held dear.

Edgar Lewis

Political Interludes

Kossahk

Ormah was full of bustling people and vehicles. The largest city on the tiny planet of Nomah was also the capital of Merkadiah and was now Kossahk's home. Every night he wandered the streets hoping to find a good target.

This city was a lot different than Buthak. It had no sewer access that he could find and there were soldiers everywhere. Tonight, he was wandering the alley ways trying to find the elusive Orsin Merchants.

He came to the end of an alley and saw a large public board in the center of a large circle of buildings. Walking over to it he noticed several wanted posters. One of them was for him.

They were offering a million credits and special directorship to whomever captured him dead or alive. Kossahk tore down the wanted poster with his face on it. He tucked the paper into an inside breast pocket, pulled his cloak tighter against his body, and pulled the hood further down to cover his face better.

Looking both ways to see if anyone in the throng of humans saw him, he darted into another alley across the street. So far, the three months spent here were more productive than the three years spent on Merk.

That proved to be a horrible choice. There he met with the leaders of several Pantherine gangs, but they weren't interested in helping him send a message to the Senate. They were more interested in getting money.

He kept trying to talk them into it until he was told that if he didn't stop that they were going to turn him in, so he left Merk, and went to Dumas.

On Dumas, he stayed out of trouble except for destroying the military training center there. The Pantherines hiding out there did not appreciate what he did and secured him a trip to Nomah. Here, he found the capital and was going to send his final message.

First, he needed to meet with someone who could get him some explosives and a Network connection, so he could contact K'datra.

He wandered down the stinking alley hoping to find a pleasure house or some other seedy spot. Surely an Orsin Merchant would be there. As he came to the end of the dark passage, a lone purple door with a single spotlight above it shined in the night.

Walking up to it he rubbed his paws together and knocked. A small door in the top of the larger door opened and then slammed shut. Suddenly, the large purple door opened, and a burly man in a nice black suit ushered him in. He vaguely heard the man say, "Welcome to Twister."

Pushing past the guard, he noticed this was a rather upscale place. People were sitting at tables eating and drinking, naked women danced on a stage to the side, and others were gambling. Kossahk resisted covering his sensitive ears that were being assaulted by the loud music playing.

He walked up to the bar and sat down. The bartender walked over and looked him over for a few moments before asking, "What's your poison?" the man asked gruffly.

"I need information, how much does it cost?" asked Kossahk.

"I don't know, depends on the information."

"I need to find an Orsin Merchant."

"You came to the right place, my friend. This is an Orsin run pleasure house. Go to the back of the room, and go through the first door you see. Take the stairs and go up to the top room. There you will find what you are looking for." His gruff demeanor now all smiles.

"Thank you, here is something for your trouble," Kossahk laid down a golden coin the humans called a mark and walked to the back of the room.

He found the door and walked up the stairs. With his nerves out of sorts, he entered a posh private room. It was furnished with crimson carpet and white velvet curtains. There were several people gambling and a man sitting in a chair with two half-dressed women dancing in front of him.

There were several bald men with tattoos on their foreheads standing guard near him. They regarded Kossahk for a moment then motioned for him to walk over. He was greeted by a short, bald headed man with an M tattooed on his forehead, thin lips, and missing his right arm.

Kossahk wondered how he had lost his arm without going to rejuvenation, but thought it was better that he didn't stare.

"How can I help you?" the man asked narrowing his eyes.

"I am looking for an Orsin Merchant. Can you help me?" Kossahk asked.

The little man smiled and said, "I am one, how can I help you?"

"I need several timed selmar tubes and one AS-34 with enough darts to take on an army."

"Well that sounds interesting," He purred. "How many timed tubes will you need?"

"How many can you get me before the end of the week?"

The merchant put his hand to his chin for a moment, "Three thousand."

"How much will that cost?"

"That many tubes plus the AS-34, seven hundred thousand marks."

Kossahk hissed slightly, then said, "May I use your Network terminal?"

"Follow me."

Kossahk followed the strange man past the gambling tables and walked into a back room where the terminal was located. The merchant stood behind him as Kossahk typed in the address of the party he wished to contact.

Several white dots danced across the blue screen. After four or five cycles of dots scampering across the screen; it went black then showed a woolly looking Leonis giving the screen a weary gaze.

He had grey streaks in his mane, his whiskers were turning white as, and white fur was beginning to grow around his muzzle. Kossahk took off his hood to reveal his face to his master.

The Leonis' face flooded with surprise and then melted into joy.

"Kossahk, you bastard!" K'datra said, laughing. "You haven't checked in since that little maneuver on Dumas. That was a thing of beauty! Where have you been in the last five years?"

"Trying to lay low. I got separated from my unit and wound up on Merk. I tried to get our Pantherine cousins on Merk to help with the mission, but they wouldn't help so I came here a few months ago. I have no gear, and I have a target for this weekend.

I need you to wire this man standing behind me seven hundred thousand by tomorrow. Is that possible?" Kossahk pleaded.

"Marks or credits?" K'datra asked impatiently.

"My apologies. He wants it in marks."

"Hmm, well that is the real trick. Let me talk to your supplier."

Kossahk motioned for the merchant to walk over. They traded places and Kossahk listened as they talked and negotiated. Then when the merchant stepped back Kossahk went back to talk with K'datra.

"I was able to work him down quite a bit. I'm not sure why but he wants to help us. I suggest that you get some incendiary to put into those tubes as well. I will pay the extra expenditure. Contact me as soon as you can."

"Yes, my Lord."

The screen went blue and Kossahk turned to the merchant and said, "You heard the boss, add incendiary fluid to the order."

The merchant nodded and left the room. The shipment came in two days later. Kossahk spent several hours preparing for his last mission. Sitting in front of the mirror he prepared for the big event.

The Orsin Merchant spared no expense in his accommodations. They gave him the finest suite in the building, and a line of credit that could be used for all his wants and needs including gambling, women, and drinks. In the two days he partook in those things

he found he liked them all and wished he had found those pleasures sooner than later, but he made an oath to K'datra. Now his only focus was his final mission.

His goal was going to go down main street Ormah and light it up like a candle. He was hoping that for each building he threw a selmar tube into it would catch several other buildings on fire. By the time he was apprehended by SPA or the military, half the city would be in flames.

That was where the AS-34 came in. He wasn't going to go quietly, and he wasn't going to roll over either. This would be on his own terms. His mate dead, he had no cubs, and to top it all off, he would welcome the adventure called death.

When he finished making his explosives, he had three thousand timed tubes, an AS-34 and several cartridges holding a total of five hundred darts. It was time to watch the humans die like the vermin they were.

They invaded their home and took from them their ancestral grounds. They even tore down their sacred places and forced them into ghettos.

It was time for the humans to burn, and time to watch their leaders die. Kossahk started laughing. He stood up and strapped two bandoliers across his chest. Then he strapped on a belt containing a hundred of his selmar tubes and then secured two satchels full of the tubes to the belt, along with a holster holding his new sidearm.

He looked himself over in the mirror and smiled. He was ready for war. He walked over to his Network terminal and typed in the codes to contact K'datra. K'datra's face lit up with a smile when he saw Kossahk ready for battle.

"You are my crowning achievement, Kossahk," said K'datra with pride in his voice. "I have been training several thousand new Shadow Kat leaders.

The Chronicles of Merkadiah:
The Rise of the Gryphon

This operation will spread across the entire system. Our voice will resound throughout the Senate. Our name will be feared by all who whisper it. We will be admired by those that hate The Autocrat, and all because of you and your desire to watch them burn."

Kossahk knelt, genuflected and stood facing K'datra, "Thank you my lord. I will do as I have been instructed."

"Very good, now go forth and fulfill your oath. Your name will live on as a hero to our people. K'datra out."

The screen went blank, Kossahk put on his cloak, and left Twister forever. The streets were deserted, and the buildings were dark. The night reeked of stale sweat and urine in the alley ways leading to the main street of Ormah.

Sharp smells of stale vomit pierced Kossahk's nose for the fifth time in half an hour. He resisted the urge to retch as he stepped over a human passed out drunk in the street.

This was an aspect he hated about the pleasure districts of the towns he had been to. During his time on the human worlds, he found that he hated humans for three more reasons.

First, they were self-destructive, and there was the fact that they elevated their own pleasures and comforts over those of their fellow humans. Not to mention, they loved controlling their own kind and making them suffer.

Humans were worthless and disgusting creatures. You would think that a creature that claimed to be enlightened and tolerant would know how to respect a different species and their way of life. It was time to show them just how unenlightened and intolerant they really were.

Kossahk finally reached the end of the main street. At this early hour the streets weren't very crowded. Though he wished they could be, it was too risky to do this during the day.

He reached down into each satchel and pulled out a selmar tube. He preset the timers for three minutes. Now all he had to do was press the priming button and throw it through a window in a building.

With all his strength he threw the metal tube through a window and hurled another one into the window of a building across the street.

Kossahk moved on to the next two buildings and as he threw the explosives into the windows, he began to chant the Tigris War Mantra.

"Forever we march.
Unto the tides of war.
For queen and tribe,
Fires come to our door."
"They never can know,
The price we pay.
For our queens are fragile.
And wish us away."
"We march on to our resting place.
That gives us honor, glory and space.
We miss our queens as we march on.
We clear our minds for the horizon."
"And now it's time to say goodbye.
For the flames of battle on our right.
We fight this battle for queen and tribe.
May our deaths give them piece of mind."

He bellowed out the old chant the whole time he walked down the street. The sound of the first explosives detonating echoed like thunder in the distance. It made him laugh as he continued to blurt out the mantra, flinging more tubes into storefronts.

When he reached the end of the street, he turned to see that over half the city was burning. Cackling with glee, he raised his hands and began to conduct an invisible symphony.

By now he had stopped saying the chant and was humming an exquisite masterpiece of music that flowed through his head. Kossahk was brought out of his elation when he heard the snap-hiss of firearms being loaded.

He pulled out his new AS pistol and loaded it. When he turned around to see three Kartah leading an entire legion of Wergare troops. The Kartah had their Auroras activated, the Wergare wore top of the line battle armor, and each was armed with a RA-71 Peacekeeper. Every weapon was pointed at him.

Kossahk sighed. It was time for one last battle. Even though he had seen few, he was ready to be with his queen in the afterlife. It was time

to go out in a blaze of glory. He pulled out a group of selmar tubes that had been fastened around a single mortar shell. The Kartah's eyes grew wide when he primed the tubes. With a maddening cackle, he threw the device into the center of the crowd.

Kossahk ran away and took cover as quickly as possible. He loaded his pistol and pulled the trigger. The darts spilled from it and pierced the foreheads of countless clones. The Kartah that survived the explosion came running toward him.

For the first time in his life, Kossahk felt both fear and euphoria at the promise of death. He stood as the three surrounded him. The pain of the first sword running through his abdomen was the most incredible sensation.

The second sword stabbed through his left pectoral, bringing a smile to his face. He laughed as he stood in the center of a dying city. The screams of burning humans filled his ears, making him laugh as the third Kartah took his head.

Hannah

The slug barely missed Captain Hannah Mayleiah's head. She and her unit were sent to Semiramus to get trenches ready for the reclamation of the planet from Pantherine control.

Hannah was a graduate from the Fire Guild at the age of twenty-three. Instead of going to work for an Aridaunt, she went to combat school and graduated the head of her class.

Her teachers called her a prodigy of leadership. She also scored the highest of any student in seven years on the Freemont Tactical Exam. Hannah was proud of her abilities as a leader and as a tactician.

Unfortunately, she was under heavy fire from a squad of Tigris scouts. They were all armed and none of her troops could move from their current position. Her engineers kept digging away to try and form a trench and some foxholes for cover.

Hannah was lucky that her engineers were able to get a foxhole dug for her, even though it was too shallow. They kept digging away to make it deeper and from there try and make a command trench.

Hannah hoped that the scouts would soon run out of Carbon Dioxide capsules. The cats were shooting in short bursts trying to conserve resources, exactly which she didn't know. All she knew was that everyone was pinned down and a squad of four scouts was responsible.

They made sure to teleport the unit five kilometers outside of the ghettos and palace, which put Hannah and her unit out in the middle of an icy desert.

Her commanding officers had hoped to give them enough distance to make five kilometers of trenches and tunnels. The objective was to secure Lord Omar Bradley's former palace. The Pantherines had recently overpowered Lord Bradley and his garrison not three standard weeks prior.

Everyone involved in the battle, except Lord Bradley, died. Lord Bradley was lucky to lose a leg and was teleported to rejuvenation. Unfortunately, now the objective seemed a little out of reach.

All her soldiers were dead, and her engineers were being killed one by one, and for some reason, her medics were on the other side of the frozen wastes. She looked around her. In the confusion, she dropped her weapon.

Then she spotted a stock jutting out of the snow. Pulling herself from the foxhole, she charged for the weapon. The tips of her fingers were touching the stock, when a projectile severed her Achilles tendon.

She let out an unholy scream as pain the likes of which she never knew coursed through her left leg. Her legs buckled, and she rolled down a snowdrift and passed out as a her head smacked against a large boulder.

When Hannah awoke, she was in pain. She was hanging from a support beam in a dark room with no windows. Her wrists were encased in thick manacles, and her toes barely touched the floor. A single candle lit the small, brick room.

She assumed she was in the palace prison. It felt as if a thousand tiny needles were poking into her head, and searing pain ran from her ankle to her lower back. Trying to find an exit, her eyes darted wildly around the room, and she realized she was naked.

A deep embarrassment overcame her knowing that those bloodthirsty cat-men had seen her body. Time passed slowly. She didn't know how long she had been hanging there, but she watched the candle burn down. When the candle was just a stub, she heard hinges on a door creak and heard footsteps coming toward her.

Two figures stepped around the table with the candle, and she gasped. One was a tall Leonis, with a large well-kept mane, and smelled of lavender and lilac. The other was some sort of abomination.

He looked to be half Tigris and half human. Hannah gasped as the Leonis began to look her over.

"This is a good specimen. She will do well at our pleasure house," said the Leonis.

Then the abomination smiled and said, "Yes, she will. Thank you K'datra, she will fetch a pretty penny. You did make sure her entire unit was dead?" Martxapahn reached out and began squeezing her leg muscles.

He grabbed her jaw, inspecting her eyes and face. Martxapahn was impressed by her youth and beauty. She possessed a bob of jet-black hair, high cheek bones, slight olive complexion, and a set of fiery blue eyes that burned with anger and intelligence.

Yes, she would fetch quite the high price. Hannah cringed and let him poke and prod her, but she knew giving in would admit defeat. When he let her jaw go, she spat as hard as she could.

A thick glob of mucus and saliva hit the abomination directly in the eye. Martxapahn pulled out a dark handkerchief and wiped his face. Then he turned to the Leonis and said, "A feisty one. Are you sure she should be used as a common harlot?"

The Leonis chuckled, "She can be broken soon enough."

Martxapahn huffed, "Very well, do as you wish. The unit she was sent with is dead, correct?"

"Yes, Lord Martxapahn."

"Well done K'datra. Are the Lancers ready to deploy?"

"Yes sir. I have five battalions ready, along with another seven Shadow Kat units. I am training the Lepridis for a special assignment on Rhokahl."

"Very good, get her and the others ready for transport. I think the Pantherines of Hades will like her."

Hannah gulped and hoped that she could survive.

Alejandro

Doctor Susan Nguyen stood with her associate, Doctor Alejandro Suarez, looking at their first successful chimera, a human– snake-crocodile hybrid. It had the head of a crocodile, the torso of a man and the tail and tongue of a snake.

It possessed broad shoulders and long thin arms with three bone spikes and no hands. In the place of the hands were two holes that opened and closed in sync with its breathing.

Small green scales covered its back and face. A long and red ropey forked tongue flicked out of its mouth and sniffed the air. Its jaw opened exposing dozens of long razor-sharp teeth.

With large golden eyes, it stared imposingly at Doctor Suarez and Doctor Nguyen. Alejandro looked in wonder at the creature. It was the culmination of decades of research and development.

"What do you want to call it love?" Alejandro said.

Doctor Nguyen looked in her lover's coal eyes and said, "Alagasapien."

Alejandro nodded, "You said it had a special ability. Tell me about it?"

"The muscles in its arms contract with its breathing and when it is commanded by a scientist that wears a special device, it can spray a neurotoxin on an enemy that will automatically begin to eat away at the skin and slowly kill the person or Pantherine."

"Hmm, well that name is as good as any I suppose. Now what other projects have you been working on, my dear?"

"There is the human-cockroach hybrid and my human-ant hybrid.

What about you, my dear?"

"I have been perfecting an enhanced human. It will have supper strength, super senses, and super speed. The only drawback is that to sustain itself on enzymes found in white blood cells, so until I can come up with a synthetic form of the enzyme it can inject or drink the research will be on hold."

Susan nodded, "Well we can't all have our research come around so, quickly can we?"

"I suppose not. Anyway, you have your Alagasapiens, Blotella, and

Clavata to show The Autocrat and the rest of the Senate. Hopefully you will be able to get more funds for our research."

"Yes, that would be helpful to both of us," and as she spoke these words, she pulled Alejandro to her and kissed him.

Xianliang

Retreat!" Colonial Ruff shouted. Not needing to be told twice, Major Xianliang Chan ran into a retreat tunnel in the trench he was in. He had been put on the front lines of Hades to try and reclaim the planet. Unfortunately, the Pantherines were holed up in Arik's palace.

Somehow, they found someone to supply them with weapons that were on par with those of the newly formed military. They had added murder holes and turrets to the palace. Additionally, they teleported their cousins from the other ghetto and with them they brought their special tribal weapons.

The tribal weapons were primitive at best but still effective. The Lepridis brought composite bows that were over a meter tall and shot arrows just short of a meter long with six-centimeter-long serrated tips.

They could cut through the best battle armor and pierce flesh and bone. Xianliang ran as fast as he could as Lepridis arrows stuck in the ground behind him. One arrow got close and cut the side of his face.

A sudden mournful roar echoed through the trenches. It alone made the most prepared soldier's blood run cold. It was the howl of the Chisis Lancers.

They employed a long metal pole that tapered to a fine point and was serrated on either side. They could run at speeds up to forty kilometers an hour, with bursts up to seventy-five.

There was not going to be any escape for the security forces this time. It was a good day to die. For once, the ever-present snow clouds had cleared, away and the sun was a dull grey ball within the wisps of cloud. It was time for the short summer season to begin.

Instead of taking the tunnel that went back to the command center, he took a dirt ramp that led up to the ground between the first two trenches. He turned to see a squad of seventeen lancers running toward the first trench. If he wasn't quick, they would jump in and run to cut down the fleeing forces.

Xianliang got to the top, pulled his RA-71 to shoulder and pulled the trigger. The rapid snap hiss of the slugs firing calmed his nerves. Three lancers dropped to the ground. This made the remaining ones sprint faster as he finished off the cartridge in the weapon.

He dropped the firearm and pulled out two AS-31 service pistols. Gritting his teeth, he snapped the carbon dioxide cylinders into place on each one savoring the snap-hiss of the gas filling the chambers.

He dropped to one knee and shot all the darts out of the two weapons. By this point, he had managed to kill five lancers. Dropping his pistols to the ground, he noticed the remaining lancers closing the distance between the first trench and him.

It was time to put his Fire Guild training to use. He hated the fact that he had wasted his life in the Guild, and now was wasting it as a soldier. When he finished the gauntlet, he was told that there were no openings for Kartah and since he had been at the Fire Guild, he could go to Combat School and come out an officer.

After the grueling training and taking several tactical warfare classes, he graduated as a Major. He was given a detachment of security forces and sent to Tūhl to squelch the uprisings.

When they were forced to retreat, he and his detachment were sent to Baktüth. There, things went without incident. He was trained as a Baktüth Guard and was on Baktüth when the mad Tigris and his unit came and blew it all to Hell.

Now it was going to take several decades to rebuild from the ground up. After that slag show, he was sent to Hades to serve under Colonial Wilson Ruff, to try and retake the ghetto. It was almost like he was cursed.

Thankfully he hadn't been demoted yet. Xianliang quit his musings as he drew his saber. A shiver of pleasure run up his spine at the ring of metal-clearing wood. Leveling the sword at the approaching cats, he exhaled sharply and hoped that he would at least be teleported.

He was surprised when a Lepridis arrow struck the ground a millimeter from his foot. Squinting, he turned his gaze to the palace, and saw several Lepridis archers standing on one of the turrets.

A deep anger flared up from an unknown source. For the first time since his graduation from The Fire Guild, he charged up his Aurora. Flying into a sprint, he ran and jumped, barely clearing the two-meter-wide trench. Regaining his footing, he tapped into that reserve of rage, and ran headlong toward the Lancers.

The Chronicles of Merkadiah:
The Rise of the Gryphon

His sword raised he let out a battle cry and cackled as the arrows from the turret were dissolved by his Aurora. As he approached the two remaining lancers, he pressed the button to release a hidden stiletto dagger from the pommel of his sword.

Once the blade was ejected, he pushed his body to gain a small burst of speed and tumbled forward toward his targets. In a swift stroke, he severed a foot from each Chisis. They tripped and were impaled by the handles of their weapons.

After he finished rolling, he turned to look at the dead cats. Then turned around and looked to the turret. The rage still boiling, he extended his hand to shake a fist at the twelve archers.

Instead of shaking his fist, bright purple lightning arched from it and incinerated all the remaining targets on the other turrets. He smiled and passed out.

When Xianliang awoke, he was surrounded by several Special Protection Agents in a military tent. The familiar cold of Hades permeated his bones, and his head felt like an axe was buried in it.

His stomach shrank. and butterflies begin to flutter. Now he was going to be demoted, or worse court-martialed. All for disobeying a direct order from a superior officer.

At least he had saved what was left of his unit. If it meant charges of insubordination and treason, then so be it. It was better to face the chopping block young for saving one's comrades than to die a toothless old man wondering if he could have saved them.

Xianliang was just about to ask one of the agents what he was being charged with when four members of the Depublic Guard walked in with The Autocrat behind.

That explained the Special Protection Agency being there, but why would The Autocrat be coming to the arrest of a disobedient soldier? Surely, The Autocrat had more important things to do, unless his disobedience directly caused the death of the entire unit.

The only other thing he could figure was since it was during a time of war, he was going to execute him personally.

"Is this the coward?" growled the Autocrat as he glared at Xianliang.

"Yes sir," the agent closest to Xianliang said.

"Good. I have heard a lot about you Major Chang. You disobeyed a direct order of retreat; not only did you destroy an elite unit of Chisis Lancers, and somehow supernaturally defeat a battalion of Lepridis Snipers, but saved the lives of over fifty soldiers.

Your disobedience saved the lives of your unit. What do you have to say for yourself?"

"Sir, if I may speak freely?" Xianliang asked.

The Autocrat nodded.

"Sir, I would do it again just to make sure that no one had to die due to those beasts."

"Very good then." said the Autocrat smiling. "It seems that I have made the correct decision in giving you the highest honor in the military, the Platinum Star of Bravery.

Additionally, you will be promoted to an Aridaunt. You will be like the Baron D'Shovah or Lord Arik Small. You will not necessarily have a fief, but you will answer directly to me.

You will be put in charge of all military operations and management of all Special Interests that seem to be clogging up the Senate as of late."

"Will I have unilateral control of my duties?"

"If by that you mean you have direct control over military campaigns and funding for the various groups asking for money? Then, yes. If I have any questions, I will contact you."

"Thank you, sir, it will be an honor to serve you in this manner. When do I start?"

"Next week. Get some rest and be prepared to begin your duties in Gaul city."

"Sir if I may ask, why am I not starting duties in Ormah?"

Everyone in the tent seemed to wince at the question, and somehow the air seemed colder. Xianliang's heart pounded in anticipation as he waited for the answer to his question.

"The city burned to the ground because of that psychotic cat terrorist that destroyed Buthak," The Autocrat said with a red face. "The new Capital of Merkadiah will be Gaul City on Merk." With that, The Autocrat turned dramatically, and strode out the tent, his guards flanking him.

Xianliang lay back on his cot and put his hands behind his head. He stared at the drab color of the canvas and thought about his upcoming duties.

286

Martxapahn

Martxapahn stood in the common room of Dahra's boarding house. He looked around at the paintings of Dahra's female ancestors wondering who the sires of the women were.

Sighing, he turned around to face the ruling council of the Barrim Clan It was not going to be easy for them to give up their matriarchal self-government, but to fight a war Martxapahn needed men, not women who thought they were better than men.

He looked at the three women sitting in front of him in high backed blue velvet chairs. The chairs clashed with the brown wood of the floor and walls. Each woman wore a foul look on her face. This made him smile.

It would be hard to take their power, but for the other planets without the clan to support him. Family or not, he needed to rein them in.

The men on the planets around Tūhl feared and loathed the women of the Barrim Clan. It was imperative that the other planets he controlled gave him their support before he lost them to The Autocrat.

"I have called you here to tell you that you have one of two choices. Either you can elect a single male governor and pledge your fealty to me, or you can spurn me and be left independent until The Autocrat steps out and destroys all your efforts.

The choice is yours; choose wisely."

Dahra stood up and screamed at Martxapahn, "I'll be damned before I let a man tell me what to do again!" Her blue eyes were wide and full of malice.

"Men are the inferiors to women and must be shown the correct way to live. The only reason we have tolerated you has been due to who your father and mother were. We Barrims have always been loyal to Lord Xóa and The Empire.

"Now you are telling us that unless we submit to a man, that you will give us over to the Senate and the pirates that call themselves Kartah?

You would let them rape and pillage our villages and then set up several governors that will answer to either a puppet female Aridaunt or a male Aridaunt that will make sure our way of life is destroyed. No thank you."

She snorted and sat down. Martxapahn began laughing, "And I thought I was crazy," Then he pointed at Dahra and said, "You killed your husband during your coup, and your late daughter Bebe met her end after brutalizing a young man for almost a year.

You all know he did it. Grivon D'Gaul was the man that lived with you. Funny, weren't you his father's torture master?" he asked pointing to Dahra.

"You allowed an aspiring Kartah and possible benevolent leader to be tortured and then wondered why he killed your daughter. I had heard tales of how loyal you were to Daggot, but I guess those were wrong.

"Now, what is your choice? I must warn you that the man you choose must be unspoiled. He must not be a eunuch and he must still have his tongue. Tell me what you choose!" roared Martxapahn.

The three women pulled back in fear and talked amongst themselves before Dahra said, "Could we not have one of your sisters govern us?"

"No, and if you don't hurry up and make the right choice, my sisters will have all of your heads, and then all of your subjects will be managed by a man of my choosing."

The women conversed for several more minutes with Martxapahn watching. Then Dahra turned around and looked at Martxapahn, "We will submit to your terms. Is there anything else you need to discuss with us?"

"No, but my sisters have some business to discuss with you." Martxapahn leaned heavily on his cane as he walked out of Dahra's house. He looked at his five sisters and said, "They will be a problem in the future.

Kill them all except Dahra. Bring her to me. I will take care of her myself. I will be at my palace. Make sure Dahra doesn't know you killed the others."

Dahra entered Martxapahn's audience chamber. The heals of her shoes clicked on the white and black-checkered tile floor as she strode toward the end of the room. She didn't see anyone on the raised area at the end of the chamber.

What Martxapahn wanted with her was a mystery. She was ushered out of her home by one of his sisters and brought here. It seemed strange that he wanted her here, but she never could understand what Martxapahn's intentions were.

When she was at the other side of the room, she noticed a pole stretching up into higher levels. She stood looking at the opulence Martxapahn surrounded himself with. It was unlike anything she had ever seen.

The Chronicles of Merkadiah:
The Rise of the Gryphon

A new dimension of hatred for the Senate and The Autocrat burned inside her. Most of it was for Martxapahn, the great "savior" of the clan.

He was no better than the rest of the bastards in charge. Dahra's musings were interrupted by a mechanical sound. She looked up to see the bottom of Martxapahn's chair descending, and the pole disappearing into the floor. Stepping back off the platform, she watched as the chair clicked into place.

She stood looking at her oppressor with disgust and terror. For the first time in a long time she felt uncomfortable in the presence of a man. He sat smugly in his large chair wearing the look of a regal ruler and gripped a tall stone goblet in his left hand.

Her stomach dropped as Martxapahn leered at her. Averting her eyes, she blushed. Something horrible was about to happen to her, and she had no one to blame but herself.

"Do you know why I brought you here, Dahra?" asked Martxapahn with a slight purr to his voice.

"No, my lord," Dahra answered genuflecting.

He snorted. "You are going to have to answer for the murder and torture of the countless men of your world. As well as the brutalization of Grivon D'Gaul.

I know he said his name was Grey Sander, but he was not to be harmed under any circumstances." He paused to make sure she was still standing in terror. The misandrist was.

"I thought I made that clear. Had I known he was using a false name I would have told you his description. But still you allowed your sociopathic daughter to have her way with him. Now, he is probably a fractured schizophrenic at best.

God only knows, he could end up being a tyrant! I hoped to control him in the end, but since you disobeyed orders, you must be punished. I am a firm believer that the punishment should fit the crime. I am giving you over to my personal guards as their personal servant."

Martxapahn watched her quiver in fear for a few moments before he stood, gripping the goblet tight in his pawlike hand. He took several deliberate steps, savoring the amount of fear exuding from his new subordinate.

Her mind must have been running through several sick and twisted scenarios of what he or his guards were going to do. He had no intentions for her to be tortured or hurt by guards.

Only for her to know servitude, and pain, but not the kind she was most likely imagining at the present moment. When he was standing a half meter from her, he licked his lips as the color drained from her face.

Suddenly, he splashed the mild acid across her face. The flesh sizzled and frothed as the yellow liquid stole the sight of her left eye and marred the pretty face she once prized.

Her screams echoed through the empty chamber and were drowned by his laughing. When he gained possession of his palace, he made sure jammers were installed, so he could properly conduct business such as this.

After several minutes of her agonizing screams three medical technicians he hired came and took her to his medical floor. She would be fine but disfigured physically the same way Grivon was emotionally and psychologically.

If he could find that bastard, then maybe he could win this war, but the chances of that happening were looking more and more grim.

"Oh, and you need not worry about Shelah. She will be in good hands with your sister."

With that he turned and walked off relishing in her sobs.

Martxapahn

Martxapahn stood in the common room of Dahra's boarding house. He looked around at the paintings of Dahra's female ancestors wondering who the sires of the women were.

Sighing, he turned around to face the ruling council of the Barrim Clan It was not going to be easy for them to give up their matriarchal self-government, but to fight a war Martxapahn needed men, not women who thought they were better than men.

He looked at the three women sitting in front of him in high backed blue velvet chairs. The chairs clashed with the brown wood of the floor and walls. Each woman wore a foul look on her face. This made him smile.

It would be hard to take their power, but for the other planets without the clan to support him. Family or not, he needed to rein them in.

The men on the planets around Tūhl feared and loathed the women of the Barrim Clan. It was imperative that the other planets he controlled gave him their support before he lost them to The Autocrat.

"I have called you here to tell you that you have one of two choices. Either you can elect a single male governor and pledge your fealty to me, or you can spurn me and be left independent until The Autocrat steps out and destroys all your efforts.

The choice is yours; choose wisely."

Dahra stood up and screamed at Martxapahn, "I'll be damned before I let a man tell me what to do again!" Her blue eyes were wide and full of malice.

"Men are the inferiors to women and must be shown the correct way to live. The only reason we have tolerated you has been due to who your father and mother were. We Barrims have always been loyal to Lord Xóa and The Empire.

"Now you are telling us that unless we submit to a man, that you will give us over to the Senate and the pirates that call themselves Kartah?

You would let them rape and pillage our villages and then set up several governors that will answer to either a puppet female Aridaunt or a male Aridaunt that will make sure our way of life is destroyed. No thank you."

She snorted and sat down. Martxapahn began laughing, "And I thought I was crazy," Then he pointed at Dahra and said, "You killed your husband during your coup, and your late daughter Bebe met her end after brutalizing a young man for almost a year.

You all know he did it. Grivon D'Gaul was the man that lived with you. Funny, weren't you his father's torture master?" he asked pointing to Dahra.

"You allowed an aspiring Kartah and possible benevolent leader to be tortured and then wondered why he killed your daughter. I had heard tales of how loyal you were to Daggot, but I guess those were wrong.

"Now, what is your choice? I must warn you that the man you choose must be unspoiled. He must not be a eunuch and he must still have his tongue. Tell me what you choose!" roared Martxapahn.

The three women pulled back in fear and talked amongst themselves before Dahra said, "Could we not have one of your sisters govern us?"

"No, and if you don't hurry up and make the right choice, my sisters will have all of your heads, and then all of your subjects will be managed by a man of my choosing."

The women conversed for several more minutes with Martxapahn watching. Then Dahra turned around and looked at Martxapahn, "We will submit to your terms. Is there anything else you need to discuss with us?"

"No, but my sisters have some business to discuss with you." Martxapahn leaned heavily on his cane as he walked out of Dahra's house. He looked at his five sisters and said, "They will be a problem in the future.

Kill them all except Dahra. Bring her to me. I will take care of her myself. I will be at my palace. Make sure Dahra doesn't know you killed the others."

Dahra entered Martxapahn's audience chamber. The heals of her shoes clicked on the white and black-checkered tile floor as she strode toward the end of the room. She didn't see anyone on the raised area at the end of the chamber.

What Martxapahn wanted with her was a mystery. She was ushered out of her home by one of his sisters and brought here. It seemed strange that he wanted her here, but she never could understand what Martxapahn's intentions were.

When she was at the other side of the room, she noticed a pole stretching up into higher levels. She stood looking at the opulence Martxapahn surrounded himself with. It was unlike anything she had ever seen.

The Chronicles of Merkadiah:
The Rise of the Gryphon

A new dimension of hatred for the Senate and The Autocrat burned inside her. Most of it was for Martxapahn, the great "savior" of the clan.

He was no better than the rest of the bastards in charge. Dahra's musings were interrupted by a mechanical sound. She looked up to see the bottom of Martxapahn's chair descending, and the pole disappearing into the floor. Stepping back off the platform, she watched as the chair clicked into place.

She stood looking at her oppressor with disgust and terror. For the first time in a long time she felt uncomfortable in the presence of a man. He sat smugly in his large chair wearing the look of a regal ruler and gripped a tall stone goblet in his left hand.

Her stomach dropped as Martxapahn leered at her. Averting her eyes, she blushed. Something horrible was about to happen to her, and she had no one to blame but herself.

"Do you know why I brought you here, Dahra?" asked Martxapahn with a slight purr to his voice.

"No, my lord," Dahra answered genuflecting.

He snorted. "You are going to have to answer for the murder and torture of the countless men of your world. As well as the brutalization of Grivon D'Gaul.

I know he said his name was Grey Sander, but he was not to be harmed under any circumstances." He paused to make sure she was still standing in terror. The misandrist was.

"I thought I made that clear. Had I known he was using a false name I would have told you his description. But still you allowed your sociopathic daughter to have her way with him. Now, he is probably a fractured schizophrenic at best.

God only knows, he could end up being a tyrant! I hoped to control him in the end, but since you disobeyed orders, you must be punished. I am a firm believer that the punishment should fit the crime. I am giving you over to my personal guards as their personal servant."

Martxapahn watched her quiver in fear for a few moments before he stood, gripping the goblet tight in his pawlike hand. He took several deliberate steps, savoring the amount of fear exuding from his new subordinate.

Her mind must have been running through several sick and twisted scenarios of what he or his guards were going to do. He had no intentions for her to be tortured or hurt by guards.

Only for her to know servitude, and pain, but not the kind she was most likely imagining at the present moment. When he was standing a half meter from her, he licked his lips as the color drained from her face.

Suddenly, he splashed the mild acid across her face. The flesh sizzled and frothed as the yellow liquid stole the sight of her left eye and marred the pretty face she once prized.

Her screams echoed through the empty chamber and were drowned by his laughing. When he gained possession of his palace, he made sure jammers were installed, so he could properly conduct business such as this.

After several minutes of her agonizing screams three medical technicians he hired came and took her to his medical floor. She would be fine but disfigured physically the same way Grivon was emotionally and psychologically.

If he could find that bastard, then maybe he could win this war, but the chances of that happening were looking more and more grim.

"Oh, and you need not worry about Shelah. She will be in good hands with your sister."

With that he turned and walked off relishing in her sobs.

Martxapahn

Martxapahn stood in the common room of Dahra's boarding house. He looked around at the paintings of Dahra's female ancestors wondering who the sires of the women were.

Sighing, he turned around to face the ruling council of the Barrim Clan It was not going to be easy for them to give up their matriarchal self-government, but to fight a war Martxapahn needed men, not women who thought they were better than men.

He looked at the three women sitting in front of him in high backed blue velvet chairs. The chairs clashed with the brown wood of the floor and walls. Each woman wore a foul look on her face. This made him smile.

It would be hard to take their power, but for the other planets without the clan to support him. Family or not, he needed to rein them in.

The men on the planets around Tūhl feared and loathed the women of the Barrim Clan. It was imperative that the other planets he controlled gave him their support before he lost them to The Autocrat.

"I have called you here to tell you that you have one of two choices. Either you can elect a single male governor and pledge your fealty to me, or you can spurn me and be left independent until The Autocrat steps out and destroys all your efforts.

The choice is yours; choose wisely."

Dahra stood up and screamed at Martxapahn, "I'll be damned before I let a man tell me what to do again!" Her blue eyes were wide and full of malice.

"Men are the inferiors to women and must be shown the correct way to live. The only reason we have tolerated you has been due to who your father and mother were. We Barrims have always been loyal to Lord Xóa and The Empire.

"Now you are telling us that unless we submit to a man, that you will give us over to the Senate and the pirates that call themselves Kartah?

You would let them rape and pillage our villages and then set up several governors that will answer to either a puppet female Aridaunt or a male Aridaunt that will make sure our way of life is destroyed. No thank you."

She snorted and sat down. Martxapahn began laughing, "And I thought I was crazy," Then he pointed at Dahra and said, "You killed your husband during your coup, and your late daughter Bebe met her end after brutalizing a young man for almost a year.

You all know he did it. Grivon D'Gaul was the man that lived with you. Funny, weren't you his father's torture master?" he asked pointing to Dahra.

"You allowed an aspiring Kartah and possible benevolent leader to be tortured and then wondered why he killed your daughter. I had heard tales of how loyal you were to Daggot, but I guess those were wrong.

"Now, what is your choice? I must warn you that the man you choose must be unspoiled. He must not be a eunuch and he must still have his tongue. Tell me what you choose!" roared Martxapahn.

The three women pulled back in fear and talked amongst themselves before Dahra said, "Could we not have one of your sisters govern us?"

"No, and if you don't hurry up and make the right choice, my sisters will have all of your heads, and then all of your subjects will be managed by a man of my choosing."

The women conversed for several more minutes with Martxapahn watching. Then Dahra turned around and looked at Martxapahn, "We will submit to your terms. Is there anything else you need to discuss with us?"

"No, but my sisters have some business to discuss with you." Martxapahn leaned heavily on his cane as he walked out of Dahra's house. He looked at his five sisters and said, "They will be a problem in the future.

Kill them all except Dahra. Bring her to me. I will take care of her myself. I will be at my palace. Make sure Dahra doesn't know you killed the others."

Dahra entered Martxapahn's audience chamber. The heals of her shoes clicked on the white and black-checkered tile floor as she strode toward the end of the room. She didn't see anyone on the raised area at the end of the chamber.

What Martxapahn wanted with her was a mystery. She was ushered out of her home by one of his sisters and brought here. It seemed strange that he wanted her here, but she never could understand what Martxapahn's intentions were.

When she was at the other side of the room, she noticed a pole stretching up into higher levels. She stood looking at the opulence Martxapahn surrounded himself with. It was unlike anything she had ever seen.

The Chronicles of Merkadiah:
The Rise of the Gryphon

A new dimension of hatred for the Senate and The Autocrat burned inside her. Most of it was for Martxapahn, the great "savior" of the clan.

He was no better than the rest of the bastards in charge. Dahra's musings were interrupted by a mechanical sound. She looked up to see the bottom of Martxapahn's chair descending, and the pole disappearing into the floor. Stepping back off the platform, she watched as the chair clicked into place.

She stood looking at her oppressor with disgust and terror. For the first time in a long time she felt uncomfortable in the presence of a man. He sat smugly in his large chair wearing the look of a regal ruler and gripped a tall stone goblet in his left hand.

Her stomach dropped as Martxapahn leered at her. Averting her eyes, she blushed. Something horrible was about to happen to her, and she had no one to blame but herself.

"Do you know why I brought you here, Dahra?" asked Martxapahn with a slight purr to his voice.

"No, my lord," Dahra answered genuflecting.

He snorted. "You are going to have to answer for the murder and torture of the countless men of your world. As well as the brutalization of Grivon D'Gaul.

I know he said his name was Grey Sander, but he was not to be harmed under any circumstances." He paused to make sure she was still standing in terror. The misandrist was.

"I thought I made that clear. Had I known he was using a false name I would have told you his description. But still you allowed your sociopathic daughter to have her way with him. Now, he is probably a fractured schizophrenic at best.

God only knows, he could end up being a tyrant! I hoped to control him in the end, but since you disobeyed orders, you must be punished. I am a firm believer that the punishment should fit the crime. I am giving you over to my personal guards as their personal servant."

Martxapahn watched her quiver in fear for a few moments before he stood, gripping the goblet tight in his pawlike hand. He took several deliberate steps, savoring the amount of fear exuding from his new subordinate.

Her mind must have been running through several sick and twisted scenarios of what he or his guards were going to do. He had no intentions for her to be tortured or hurt by guards.

Only for her to know servitude, and pain, but not the kind she was most likely imagining at the present moment. When he was standing a half meter from her, he licked his lips as the color drained from her face.

Suddenly, he splashed the mild acid across her face. The flesh sizzled and frothed as the yellow liquid stole the sight of her left eye and marred the pretty face she once prized.

Her screams echoed through the empty chamber and were drowned by his laughing. When he gained possession of his palace, he made sure jammers were installed, so he could properly conduct business such as this.

After several minutes of her agonizing screams three medical technicians he hired came and took her to his medical floor. She would be fine but disfigured physically the same way Grivon was emotionally and psychologically.

If he could find that bastard, then maybe he could win this war, but the chances of that happening were looking more and more grim.

"Oh, and you need not worry about Shelah. She will be in good hands with your sister."

With that he turned and walked off relishing in her sobs.

Xianliang

Xianliang sat in his posh, furnished office looking over the lates reports from Semiramus, Hades, Felion and Rhokahl. The Pantherines still held an ironclad grip on those worlds. The human citizens ushered into ghettos.

There the men were subjected to torture, and the women were put in pleasure houses to dance for and copulate with Pantherine males. They were doing what Arik did in reverse.

Down to eating them and keeping leathers made from their skin. He slammed his fists on his desk and swore profusely. Frustrated with his efforts, he reached into the bottom desk drawer and pulled out a bottle of chamomile brandy and a glass.

Quickly, he poured himself a glass and downed it. A sudden belch rattled some loose papers on his desk. Feeling refreshed, he wiped his mouth and picked up another report. This one was from the Chaos Guild.

It detailed the last ten years of a student named Terry Sander. He was a natural swordsman and already achieved level twenty. Xianliang let out a long whistle. This Terry was some kind of prodigy.

He constantly won every monthly tournament among the students. This man was as impressive as the fugitive Grivon D'Gaul. He realized that The Autocrat had stopped looking for him several years ago.

Maybe he died, or perhaps it was because he went to Tūhl after he passed The Gauntlet, and he met his end there. Xianliang shook his head. Either way it was a waste of talent. Just because he was the son of the great Daggot D'Gaul, he was prevented from excelling.

Xianliang reckoned that this Terry fellow was what Grivon would have been like if The Autocrat hadn't been so hellbent on keeping him from becoming a Kartah. He knew that if he ordered Terry to run The Gauntlet that he would succeed, but it might draw attention from The Autocrat.

That didn't really matter, did it? The Autocrat put him in charge of all military and special interest affairs. He could use this kid as his own personal Kartah.

The Autocrat or Depublics hadn't ever assigned any, and it was a known fact that Lord Arik once employed seven and that the Baron D'Shovah had eight.

He pressed a button summoning his Network terminal from a hidden compartment in his large wooden desk. A couple of quick keystrokes brought up a program that he installed to keep track of his budget.

There was enough money to pay ten Kartah decent salaries for ten years or he could just get an elite few and put them on a higher payroll. After several minutes of thought, he realized that it would be more impressive if he could get the top student from each Guild and put them on the payroll.

Not to mention, he still had his war funding he was giving to Dr. Nguyen and Dr. Suarez. Their armies of experiments were horrific to look at, and they were effective against Pantherines.

The only downside was that their makeup became unstable after a standard week, and they melted on the battlefield. That was part of the reason the Pantherines had been able to hold their worlds so well.

Every time any units made of these chimeras were sent out to battle after a week they were melting, and their controllers killed. Xianliang shook his head. If only Pantherines could adhere to the civilized rules of the Senate.

A report he once read said they did believe in some sort champion combat, but it was too iffy to know if it was good idea. His frustration was really starting to get the best of him. In ten years, the budget for this uprising cost them seven hundred million credits.

The everyday man in a fief couldn't make ends meet just from the tax and tribute burdens this was causing. No one in The Senate seemed to care as long as they were the ones standing when it was all said and done.

Letting out another sigh, he poured himself another glass of liquor. He downed it in a swallow and quickly put the Pantherine campaign out of his mind. Right now, he wanted to draft a request for Terry and the other top students of the Guilds.

He knew that the Air Guild, Water Guild and the Matter Guild might give him political students, but it was a risk he was willing to take. Then he decided that if he wanted the best Kartah, he would request the top combat students.

Xianliang hummed tunelessly as he typed his drafts and sent them to the respective Guild Masters. He sighed and drank another glass. With that out of the way, it was time to read the report that he had dreaded the most, The Martxapahn Report. Or as he affectionally called it, "The Candy Report."

What the Pantherines lacked in technology and weapons, Martxapahn possessed. The Therian now held Odin, Nomah, Tūhl, Z'Quial, Jude, Dumas and several other planets and moons. The Autocrat's fiefdoms now included less than half the Solar System's planets and moons.

To make matters worse, The Barrim Clan seemed capable of sending thousands upon thousands of well-trained peasants to the front lines to defend against the Wergare Clones the military was using.

A loose paper fell from the stack of papers and floated to the desk. It caught his attention, and the information on it made him do a double take.

Martxapahn was now allied with The Barrims. Xianliang's temper flared, and without thinking, he crumpled the paper. Now he definitely needed a drink.

Pouring another glass of liquor, he swirled it for a moment before downing it in a gulp. This was the only thing keeping him from pounding on his desk and breaking things.

He shook his head and popped his neck. It felt good and it put him a better frame of mind. An idea popped into his head. He could send the experiments to fight the Barrim Clan, and recent guild graduates to the Pantherine front.

They would be hot-headed and ready for a good fight. It was crazy enough it just might work. He picked up the brandy bottle and kissed the picture of its namesake, Vincent Van Gough.

If he could subjugate The Barrims, then he could slowly but surely gain back fiefdoms, and maybe keep from losing more in the process. It was a brilliant plan, now if he could find a General to lead them.

That was when he noticed another report under the Martxapahn report. It was about a young Captain named Hannah Mayleia. Attached to it were her records from the military academy and her service record.

He immediately was impressed by her grasp of tactics and scant use of resources. He was also taken aback by her skill with adaption and improvisation.

Up until recently, she was a prisoner of war for the better part of the last decade. She had been part of an advanced force to recapture Semiramus but was captured and forced to work as a Pantherine pleasure girl.

The report gave unnecessary graphic detail on her experiences. After years of being subjected to these tortures, she finally escaped in a heroic dash from a pleasure booth.

She decided the next time one of the higher up Pantherine officials came to her, she would try and get a knife or sword from them and kill them with it and escape.

Biding her time, she waited, and when the moment was right, she killed a Tigris General with his own Kadar and escaped. She was able to teleport to Merk and from there was taken to the hospital on Niriah.

Xianliang wanted to make the girl a General to help him fight against the Barrim Clan. Then he looked at the date on the report. It was from last month. It was concerning that he overlooked it and then saw his bottle of liquor was over three quarters gone.

He shook his head and signed out of the terminal. It was time to go home. Tomorrow, he was going to head to the hospital on Niriah to talk with this Hannah girl and see if she was fit for command.

Hannah

Hannah lay in bed with tormented memories of being shot and locked up in the Pantherine hellhole. She could still remember their smell as they ravaged her. It was the same thing day in and day out for almost a decade.

The feel of their coarse fur rubbing her skin raw was still very real, and the memories poisoned her sleep every night. Hannah shivered, trying to get rid of the memories. Her skin crawled and moved on its own, signaling time for her daily dose of medication.

Reaching over to a hovering tray beside her bed, she grabbed a glass of water and a packet of taka powder. Taka was the root of a beautiful flower on the planet Jude. When dried and ground into a powder, it made a powerful pain killer and sleep aide.

She gently opened the silver packet and stirred the grey-white powder into the water. Swirling it for a moment to make sure it was dissolved, she groaned.

The flavor was a bitter one and when she awoke after taking it, her tongue was often stuck to the roof of her mouth. There must be a better way to take this slag, she thought.

Knowing it wasn't going to magically find its way into her system; she resisted the urge to just lay awake forever and downed it in a gulp. Soon it would take effect, and she would be in a deep dreamless sleep.

When she first arrived, she was taking the powders seven or eight times a day. It helped, even if she had become addicted to it. Hopefully, they would help wean her off it when the time was right.

She lay back in her bed waiting for the cold feeling that began in the extremities and spread to her core. The cold would be followed by the most extreme ecstasy, and then the sweet release of sleep would take over.

Each dose was better than the last and the hospital didn't seem to mind giving her all the taka she could take. Sleep's black fingers were invading her vision when the door to her room slid open.

The sight of what came walking through somehow counteracted her journey to oblivion. In strode eight Depublic Guards. They flanked the door and drew their swords into an arbor of steel.

A tall olive-skinned man with slanted eyes strode in under the arbor. He wore a navy-blue robe with golden epaulets. The pommel of a saber stuck up from a baldric strapped to his back.

He motioned for the men to lower their weapons. In flawless unison, the guard sheathed their swords. Hannah looked the man over and then observed the service and rank patches.

He was a graduate of both the Fire Guild and the Combat School. He was an Aridaunt and what looked like a marksman. He wore three other service and rank patches creating a large diamond shape over his heart, with The Platinum Star of Bravery in the center.

He was a war hero. She even saw several patches that she had never seen before. Hannah's eyes got wide and she placed her right fist over her heart, bowed at the waist and then brought her hand out with her fingers extended toward the man.

He simply smiled and said, "As you were."

Hannah sat back in her bed, sighed and said, "What do I owe the honor of this visit Lord…Baron…Count…"

"I have no honorific. I am just Xianliang. I am the Special Aridaunt in charge of all military and special interest affairs. I have received a report of your exploits General Mayleiah."

"With all due respect, I am no general."

Xianliang laughed, "That's because I recently promoted you. You will be working for me as long as you wish, that is if you are up to it."

Hannah raised an eyebrow, "How much will my commission be?"

"Double the normal for someone of your rank, is that acceptable?"

"That is more than generous sir. I will need taka to sleep at night, will that be a problem?"

"I don't think so. How soon will your leg be ready?"

"I am on the mend for several more weeks. The doctors said that since I was not able to teleport to a rejuvenation facility that it healed naturally, so I may have a slight limp for the rest of my life."

"That is fine I don't expect you to be leading from the front. That is, unless you want to." Xianliang said smiling.

"If I feel the need, I will."

"Very good," Xianliang said. "I will be leaving you now. When you finish your stay just teleport to the Senate building. They will direct you to my office." He gave her a slight wave and walked out the door.

The Chronicles of Merkadiah:
The Rise of the Gryphon

Hannah watched as the Depublic Guards followed Xianliang as he walked out the door. She assumed he must have been a very important man if he had that many of the Depublic Guards. She lay back down.

Her head felt like it weighed five times what it normally did. Soon the freedom of deep sleep would be upon her.

Part III

In Decennium

Chapter One
The Final Task

"Time flies on silken wings." -Pantherine Poet

I

Grivon concentrated on the image of a katana in the black behind his eyes. Once he saw the weapon, he imagined holding the weapon in his hand. After several minutes, he felt something in his right hand.

He opened his eyes and there was a fully made katana. Flourishing it, he laughed at the accomplishment, then scraped the edge along his arm hair and watched the blade sheer off hair.

A sudden weakness overcame him along with a bout of dizziness. Fearing something was wrong he asked Phoy what was happening.

"When doing this technique, it uses the metals in your blood to form a brittle version of the weapon. It is then fortified into a useable weapon with a razor edge.

This will lower the amount of direct hits your Aurora Field can take, but from the look of things, yours may be able to hold up under stress.

Of course, your body may not be able to. However, with time, a diet rich in iron, magnesium, zinc, and training on an individual level, your body can hold up during prolonged combat.

Today's session is over. I have other students I need to teach." Grivon nodded, and the katana dissolved back into his hand. He

bowed to Phoy who returned the gesture. Then he took his leave. He walked to his room ready to lie down. He had been trying for several hours to get the form right, and finally, he did.

When he reached his room, he took off his shirt and lay flat looking up at the ceiling of the house. Letting out a discontented sigh, his eyes roved the ceiling, as memories of Barbarah and Angela filled his mind.

He missed them both; he loved them both. His head began to hurt and, his eyes begin to tear up. Then he heard The Gryphon's voice deep within his head.

"Crying will not help us," The Gryphon said.

"My heart is breaking. Angela had to leave and Barbarah is somewhere with Steven. I really need to see at least one of them. I long for their touch. My chest aches and I want to leave and at least find Barbarah," Grivon said.

"I wish I could tell you I know how it feels, but I have no emotions. It's what gives me my irresistible charm. Besides, I am still you and part of me misses both as well. Just not the same part you miss them with,"

The Gryphon chuckled.

"You're a pervert!"

"What? I'm a man of simple needs. Besides you can't say that you don't like it."

"I went eighteen years without the desire of knowing a woman, and then when Barbarah and I made love the first time I felt at peace with myself. I could never make love with Angela or Barbarah ever again and be perfectly happy."

"Let's get off this topic, you hopeless romantic. I am trying to make you feel better. You could always try to seduce Christy, if you're interested."

"You said not to even think about her that way, what made you change your mind?"

The Gryphon chuckled and said, "I know, but she sure is hot, isn't she?"

"You're sick, you know that?" Grivon groaned.

"The best parts of people are always their sickest." The Gryphon cackled.

"I should have known, but I always believed that you're only as sick as your secrets."

"That statement is very true for you, isn't it?"

Feeling hurt Grivon said, "I hate you. I don't even know why I put up with your constant carnal desires and your insults."

"Just remember if I die you die. I am a part of you whether you like it or not, and if I were to withdraw from your personality you would probably never be anything more than a blathering puddle of goop wanting his mother. We. Are. One."

"I know," Grivon said putting his hand over his face. "Just lay off for a while. I need some time to myself, and you don't help."

"I know I don't. That's not my job. I'm not supposed to help you feel better about yourself. I am just supposed to help you function and get along in this life. Believe me if I could split from you and have my own body I would in an instant."

Grivon was brought out of his conversation by a furious knock on his door.

"Who's there?"

"Christy. I wanted to know if you would like to practice against me using what you learned today."

Grivon paused and before he could answer, he heard The Gryphon say, "Yes, we would like that, maybe we could…"

"Shut up!" whispered Grivon.

"What's that?" Christy said at the muffled reply.

"Sounds great." Grivon said trying to be cheerful.

He got up from his mat, put on his shirt and slid open his door. There stood Christy in her purple bodysuit. Grivon looked her over and motioned for her to lead. She led him out to a sandy area at the edge of the compound.

They stood looking at each other. Each energized their Aurora, both formed katanas, and took their favorite stance. For several minutes, they just stood looking at each other. Becoming restless, Grivon short jumped behind Christy and let out a downstroke.

Christy sidestepped the attack, parried, and in a reversal swung her sword in a horizontal cut at Grivon's neck. He short jumped several feet away. Christy yelled in frustration and charged at Grivon. Forcing his katana back into his body, he held out both hands and, in an instant, a cloud of super-heated steam shot from the palms of his hands.

Christy screamed as she was engulfed by the vapor. She came out the other side of the cloud, swinging her katana wildly. Her Aurora was a crimson red. Grivon quickly appeared in front of Christy and pointed a saber he had formed at her throat.

Grivon heard clapping. He turned and saw Phoy standing behind him. He was sporting a smile a kilometer long. Christy was smiling as well.

"Did I miss something?"

"You have finished your training," Phoy said.

"What!" Grivon asked surprised.

"That's right, you little bastard," said Christy with a smile on her face.

"You can go fulfill your dream. This was just to see if you had been able to master all five Magiah forms and the weapon form. Tomorrow, we are going to have a feast, and then you can leave when you're ready."

Grivon stood, feeling numb. It was so hard to believe. He spent the last fifteen years training. It was one of those things that hits you and takes away your breath. It was wonderful. It was magical. Suddenly the spark of rage that he kept smoldering flared. It was time to kill The Autocrat.

II

Grivon awoke early the next morning. He ran to the waterfall and washed up. Then sat underneath the icy water to center himself. As he let his mind go blank, he watched the sun break over the desolate valley beneath him.

The purple clouds looked majestic as they were blown away by the winds. The sight was enough to make a blind man see for the first time. His eyes began to fill with tears. He thought about Barbarah and how very soon he would see her again.

Closing his eyes, he drew up a fantasy of seeing her. She ran and jump into his arms and kissed him. She would tell him how much she missed him and was glad that he was alive.

Once he was ready, he teleported back to his room and dressed in his black guild robes with the single rank and service patch. He strapped his saber to his lower back in a horizontal position with the hilt in an easy to grab position, drew it, and began to practice simple forms until he heard a small knock at his door.

He slid it open to see Christy standing at the door in a purple kimono with golden chrysanthemums, looking at Grivon. She gave him a large toothy smile. Grivon returned the smile and stepped out of his room, following her to the indoor training room.

The large square room in the center of the house. The floor was like the rest of the house with hardwood slats. The walls were decorated with an assortment of weapons, and a large thatch mat took up most of the floor.

On the back wall of the room sat Phoy on a dais. In his lap sat a long metal pole. His hands rested on it and he wore a stern look on his face.

Christy walked to the side of the room where the servants and other students stood. Grivon walked over to Phoy and knelt on both knees before him. He placed his fists to either side of his legs and bowed his head. Phoy looked down at Grivon and smiled.

"Normally, before a student graduates, I have them fashion a weapon that they can call their own, but this time I have something that was given to me by your father. It was a weapon passed down the D'Gaul line.

It once belonged to Darrian D'Gaul. This weapon is called a carbon command rod. It responds to your thoughts. It can morph into any type of melee weapon you can think of. It is an invaluable tool.

The technology for it was lost a long time ago, but I think you might be able to duplicate it if you so choose."

The whole time Phoy was speaking Grivon kept his head bowed and listened. Then Phoy said, "I present to you this weapon of your father's."

Grivon looked up at Phoy and put his hands out like a supplicant. Phoy placed the meter-long metal staff in Grivon's open hands. He gripped and bowed his head in silent gratitude.

"Rise a Magiah, my friend." Phoy said smiling.

Grivon arose, holding the new weapon tightly. He looked at Phoy, who returned his gaze with a nod. Having permission to leave, he went back down to his room. Once he was there, he put the weapon on his bed mat.

Rubbing his hands together, he ran to the dining room. There laid out before him were countless plates of all his favorite foods that Phoy fed him over the last fifteen years. Grivon sat down next to Christy, and they all began to eat.

The chamomile brandy flowed, and when a plate ran out of food, another was quickly brought in its place. They all talked about things that had happened over the years and about those crazy nights Grivon and Angela would make love and how it could be heard all through the compound.

Phoy laughed as he told about a time, he was sure that the two had gone to sleep.

"So, in the quiet of the night, I began pruning my bonsai trees. Then right as I was about to make a difficult cut on my favorite tree, I heard a woman scream in ecstasy. My hand slipped and instead of cutting off a single branch, I ended up cutting the trunk in half! That's when I told him that if he were going to copulate, he had to do it at the waterfall.

That way people could sleep, and I would keep from almost killing any more of my trees!"

The story was followed by round of horselaughs from everyone but Grivon. At first, he blushed; then he began laughing as well.

"I remember that day," Grivon said with a smile on his face. "You brought me the bonsai and told me to 'care for it.' Then you turned and walked away. I cared for that little tree until it sprouted new growth. That was the most taxing thing I've ever done."

Everyone then started exchanging stories about Grivon and his exploits. Even Grivon told some crazy stories about dragging the boulders up to the water fall every day then trying to sit under the falls with the giant rocks still shackled to his arms, legs and torso.

The night wore on until the cooks couldn't cook anymore and the liquor reserves were gone. Grivon felt drunk for the first time in his life.

He had to lean on Christy to walk back to his room. She lay him down on his mat after moving his new weapon. When Grivon lay down, he fell right to sleep.

Christy moved some of his hair out of his face and kissed him on the forehead. Christy slid the door shut and walked down the hall. As she rounded a corner, she ran into Phoy.

"Why does it seem like every woman in Merkadiah wants to fall in love with that man? Can you tell me?" Phoy asked while stroking his mustache.

"I'm not in love with him. I just think he's attractive. You know dad, I am three hundred years old. Don't you think it's time I at least had a boyfriend?"

"I know it is hard, but I just do not want you to waste what you have to give on just anyone. There will be a special person for you one day.

I know it seems like I am not being fair, but a hardened fighter, like the ones you meet here, are no good for a woman like you. I know you can hold your own and I have taught you all I know, but the sort of life that comes from being the partner of a Kartah is one of strife and worry. You do not need that."

Christy hung her head and nodded. Phoy hugged her and sent her back to her hovel. She enjoyed living there more than in the main house.

It was quiet. The walls were not thin, and sounds didn't reverberate. She could sit around naked or just sleep all day. She didn't have any students, since Phoy didn't think she possessed the ability to teach.

Christy opened the door to her hovel, disrobed, and went into her water closet. She turned on the faucet and let the warm water run over her body. She melted into the tension-releasing heat. Once she showered, she lay down for the night.

As she fell asleep, the last thing on her mind was Grivon. While she couldn't call it love, she did care for him. A single tear fell from her eye and ran onto her pillow. What she wanted from him, he could never return, and she would have to live with that fact.

Chapter Two
Home Coming

"Sometimes rejoining those you love isn't the best of ideas," -Kossahk's Journal

I

Steven was on the prowl. The warm night air of Gaul city was filled with may smells he found intoxicating. Though most people didn't find the same set of smells intoxicating.

Most people found the foul smells of a city disgusting, but he was more enlightened than most people. Gaul had proven to be a far better city than Ormah.

He was glad that he funded that Tigris to burn down that pitiful place. The planet that mined the most valuable resource in Merkadiah seemed a much better fit, and he told Theo as much. So, when Ormah went up in flames everyone moved to the new city he picked out.

Rounding a corner into an alley brought more of the filthy smells he enjoyed. He was headed toward a particularly seedy pleasure house he owned called Willsin's. This was now his twice-weekly routine.

In the last ten years he spent with Barbarah, he had to adopt a normal way of living. He couldn't perpetuate his predilections with her around. It was difficult to find a new way to feed his addiction to violence, but he found a way.

The first thing he did was create a signet ring with the Orsin family crest stamped on it. The crest was a shield divided in half with red on the left and gold on the right. In the center was a white tau cross.

This ring replaced the ridiculous outfit his ancestors once wore. When he wore it, he felt like a giant walking dog. A humiliating costume to say the least.

However, he kept the mask to communicate with the rest of his organization via the Network. To make his ring effective, he sent out a bulletin that if a person came into a casino or pleasure house wearing the new ring; they were to be given whatever he or she wanted.

The Chronicles of Merkadiah:
The Rise of the Gryphon

Steven was happy about that, because in the last ten years he had gone out twice a month to find a woman he liked at one of his pleasure houses. They were all beautiful, and they were all dead.

After a few hours of intense pleasures, he killed them in the most painful and violent ways he could think of. They were all honored and it was time for another.

After all, Barbarah was the mother of his child, and he was quickly losing interest in her. Steven walked into Willsin's. He sauntered back to the bar past the dancers and gambling tables.

Flopping down on a barstool, he ordered a drink, Wenda Rum. The bartender noticed his ring and brought him an entire bottle of the liquor he ordered.

Steven thanked the man by laying down three marks on the bar. Then turned around, took a swig from the bottle, and leered at the dancing women on the stage.

It was going to be a tough decision tonight. In his later years, he wasn't so picky as far as looks went, and why should he be? He had Barbarah at the mansion, so in ten years it had been about the violence.

His desires had always been about power and control. The kind he couldn't demonstrate toward Barbarah anymore. Too many doses of the memory wipe drug could cause long term memory loss, dementia, and other unsavory side effects.

Learning to maintain control was hard and even harder when your patience was tested on a daily basis. He watched several of the women give personal dances, and some took men to back room arcades for a private moment or two.

After an hour and drinking the full bottle of rum, he found a girl he liked. She had raven hair down to her bottom, soft brown eyes and a near perfect body.

Steven was immediately aroused. He motioned for the bartender and said, "Who is that?" pointing to the woman he had just seen.

"She's a new girl, her name is Angela, I think. Do you wish to take her to your apartments, my lord?"

"Yes, I think I will. Make sure to send a cleanup crew after six hours."

"Yes, my lord," answered the bartender.

II

Steven opened the door to a private apartment he owned in the middle of the city. They walked in and the lights came on. He told Angela to make herself comfortable. She wasted no time in disrobing right in front of him.

This level of brazenness made him happy. His eyes roved over her angelic body. He reached out and grabbed one of her breasts. After letting him touch her for a few minutes, she pulled his hand off her and motioned for him to follow her.

Surprised about how well she knew the place, Steven followed without hesitation. His mind already filling with the fantastic ideas of what he was going to do.

III

Three hours later, Angela awoke to find Steven was standing over her with a long knife and a sadistic smile on his face. She raised an eyebrow and said, "What are you going to do with that, lover boy?"

"Oh, you'll find out. Considering I took exceptional care to have this building wired with teleportation jammers, I can do with you as I wish." Steven said menacingly.

"Is that so?" Angela said, and lunged hard at Steven. Caught off guard Steven was forced to the ground and disarmed. He attempted to crawl for the knife, but Angela was quicker. She had the knife in her hand for only a few moments before she was tackled by him.

They wrestled around in the dark each trying to subdue the other. In the tussle Steven got scratched on the inside of his thigh. With glee in his voice Steven said, "I think I kind of like this sort of thing!"

The words weren't even off his lips when Angela rolled him over and pressed her knee into his solar plexus. With the knife held to Steven's throat Angela said, "My name is Angela Simone. I'm a friend of Grivon D'Gaul's. I haven't seen him in ten years, but I know where he is, and he is looking for you now.

I am going to send him a message tomorrow and I need to know where your mansion is located."

"How did you find me?" stammered Steven.

"I'm an assassin, and I know a few Kartah moves as well," she leaned forward and put her left forearm on his Adam's apple. "Now, are you going

316

to tell me what I want to know Orsin Steven Anthony, or am I going to have to remove your fingers one at a time?"

"I'll tell you whatever you want to know, just don't hurt me," Steven gurgled.

"What a sniveling little whelp you are. I'm surprised; I expected more out of an Orsin Godfather."

Steven blurted out the location of the mansion and before he could try and gain control over Angela, she knocked him out.

IV

Grivon closed his eyes as Phoy shut the door to the teleportation device. Thankfully, this one would take him to another device in the capital city on Merk. Grivon waved a final farewell to Phoy, Christy and the rest of the students and servants of Phoy's compound.

As the device charged up Grivon closed his eyes and began to count the seconds until he was in the city of Gaul. It was the name of the capital city of the entire system.

V

Phoy and his entourage watched as the blue light in the chamber faded and Grivon was gone. Phoy sighed and turned around to walk away from his teleportation device.

As he was walking into his house, the door to Christy's room opened and Angela walked out with a ten-year-old girl walking behind her. The girl had Grivon's platinum hair and Angela's large brown eyes.

The girl held her head high, and despite her shy demeanor Phoy could see some of that cold burning fire that lay within both of her parents.

"She has spirit," he muttered under his breath.

"Phoy, I'd like you to meet my daughter, Angelica D'Gaul."

"Hmm, what an interesting name. Are you a hundred percent sure that you want me to take her and train her?"

"Yes, she has already learned some things with The Chimera," said Angela with a wink.

"Taking over for her mother?"

Angela smiled, "Maybe."

Phoy smiled, shook his head and motioned for Christy. Christy walked over and ushered the girl into the dining room. Angela and Phoy watched, smiling, until Christy and Angelica were inside and the door to the house slid shut.

As soon as the door shut, the smiles fell from their faces. They each held the other's gaze for several minutes before Phoy embraced her in a hug.

"Be careful," he said.

"Yeah, Yeah. I will, you grumpy old man."

Phoy cocked back his head and laughed. Angela winked at the man as she stepped away. Phoy blinked, and she was gone. All he could do was shake his head.

The ability to teleport without a device was one that he had taught her in the first stages of Grivon's training. He was happy that most of his knowledge had been imparted upon Grivon and Angela, but still there were a few things that only the right person could know, and that person would be his successor.

VI

Grivon was counting for seventeen seconds when he arrived in the teleportation station in Gaul. He walked out into the large room with gates and people. He walked to the clearance counter and stood in front of a young olive-skinned man.

The man looked him over. Grivon was wearing his Guild robes with the Kartah patch, the Chaos patch and Phoy's patch. The man looked him over and checked something on his screen.

Grivon watched as the man's eyes widened. He looked at Grivon and then glanced back at his screen before saying, "You are free to enter Gaul City, Mr. D'Gaul."

Grivon nodded to the man. Then as he was walking off, he turned, looked at the man, and said, "Where is Anthony Manor?"

"It's in the middle of the city. It's the second biggest building in Gaul, next to the Senate building."

"Thank you."

Grivon walked out into the warm setting sun and looked around at the people walking on the streets of the city. He stared in awe at the height of the buildings, but only two stood out.

The Chronicles of Merkadiah:
The Rise of the Gryphon

A very tall tower with hundreds of floors stood to the south and in the middle, stood Anthony Manor. It was amazing how Steven was able to obtain so much money, but that was not important. What was important was that he hurry to the mansion.

VII

Grivon was exhausted when he arrived at Anthony Manor. He was broke, and unable to hire a rickshaw or carriage, so he had to walk the fifteen kilometers to the center of the city. Once he caught his breath, he took in the sight of his friend's house. It looked bigger up close than it had far away.

The house was over fifty floors tall and sat in a large square in the center of a circular patch of grass and trees. A tall iron fence circled the mansion with only a single gate at the north side.

Grivon walked around the perimeter of the yard until he came to the gate. There was a small Network terminal on a rock pillar holding half the gate.

He pressed a button that said talk and said, "I am Grivon D'Gaul; I am a friend of Barbarah and Stevens, please let me in." It seemed like an eternity before there was an answer.

"What is your name?" asked a man on the terminal.

"Grivon D'Gaul. May I come in?"

After what seemed like hours, the gates opened, and Grivon began his journey towards finding his friends.

Chapter Three

Preparing for Greatness

"The River of Battle frothed and foamed as the loan warrior prepared to enter," -
Excerpt from "The Journey of Shadows," Pantherine Folk Tale

I

Barbarah's heart was trembling with excitement, and her stomach lurched with uncertainty. It was the first time in sixteen years that she had seen her lover. She stood primping herself in front of her mirror.

Wanting to make sure she wore the perfect ensemble for him, she changed clothes again. Searching through her closet, she found a long flowing red dress. Rushing to put it on, she smeared her makeup.

Letting out a frustrated grunt, she quickly reapplied it. She pursed her lips to make sure her lipstick was applied correctly. A nagging thought about Keith suddenly reared its head. Telling Grivon about him was going to be difficult.

Even though she shared the bed of Steven for eleven of those years, she hoped that Grivon would forgive her for her lack of strength. This evening would bring about either some sort of good or some sort of evil.

It was all so surreal, and that was what scared her more than anything. With a heavy sigh, she walked out of her room to meet Grivon.

II

Grivon stood in the foyer of the mansion waiting for someone to come down the stairs on either side of him and greet him. The weapon Phoy had given him was starting to get heavy. Then he had an idea.

He took the rod from his back and formed it into a katana. The weapon he felt suited him best, and he sheathed it in the cloth that he had wrapped the rod in.

Just as he had secured the lighter weapon to his back and breathed a sigh of relief, he heard heavy footsteps coming down the left stair.

Turning to see the owner of such heavy footsteps, he saw Barbarah. She wore a flowing red dress tied at the waist by a silver chain. She laughed as she charged toward him and leapt into his arms.

Grivon's heart leapt into his throat at the sight her. He laughed, embraced her tightly, and before he could look her over, she forced her lips against his in a kiss that made him go numb. It was euphoric.

Once he could pull her from his lips, he was able to look at her for the first time in seventeen years. She gained some weight; her muscle tone was diminished, and she was showing a few wrinkles around her eyes.

Barbarah looked Grivon over for the first time as well. He was much more muscular, if that was possible, and carried a jaded look in his eyes.

She looked in his eyes, hoping to see that old fire she always loved, but it seemed to be combined with age and suffering. Otherwise, he still looked handsome and as if, he hadn't aged a day. That part was strange.

It was almost as if time hadn't touched his eighteen-year-old features.

She sighed and hugged him once more before Steven came sauntering down the stairs.

"It has been almost twenty years since we last spoke, my old friend," said Steven, as he got closer. "I figured you would be dead by now or arrested. Where have you been?"

"Yes, please tell us where," Barbarah asked with sparkling eyes.

"I would love to, but right now, I am starving. Is there any way we could eat?"

Steven made a funny face and nodded before saying, "Follow me."

Barbarah stood beside Grivon as Steven led the way into a dining room. The room was larger than the Guilds mess hall and was lit with crystal chandeliers.

The dining table looked large enough to seat an army and at each chair was a place mat, silverware, and two glasses, one for liquor and one for water.

Much to Grivon's relief they did not stop there and continued to walk through the room until they reached a small stone room with a single round table and four chairs.

Sitting at one of the chairs was a boy barely twelve. Grivon noticed right away that the boy bore a striking resemblance to both Barbarah and Steven.

"It looks like she's been productive since you last saw her," chided the Gryphon.

"Not now!" said Grivon in a hushed tone.

"What was that?" Barbarah asked.

"Nothing."

Barbarah shrugged as she sat down between Steven and the young boy. As Grivon sat down across from Barbarah, several servants brought in plates of food and set them down in front of each person.

Each person was given a glass of water and a glass of brandy. Grivon looked down at the plate. There was a fire roasted meat he had never seen chopped up and mixed with a combination of mushrooms, onions and peppers.

Then on the side were some white mashed roots. He didn't hesitate to begin eating. After everyone finished, Grivon polished off six plates and drank twice that many glasses of water and two glasses of brandy.

Steven, Barbarah and the child only ate a plate each. They looked at Grivon in awe at how much he had eaten. Barbarah could count on one hand every time she had ever eaten like that.

She thought back to the little restaurant that she used to eat at in Ormah with the noodles and muscles.

"So where have you been all these long years Grivon?" Steven asked.

"At first, I went to Tūhl to try and find Phoy. That was the biggest mistake of my life," said Grivon with a slight bit of malice in his voice. From there he began to tell the story of Bebe.

When he was finished, Steven took the child from the room and left Barbarah and Grivon alone. Grivon had to chuckle at the look on Steven's face as he left. It was one of disgust mixed with horror.

Barbarah, on the other hand, just looked at him with compassion and understanding. Then, without thinking she said, "Let's go take a walk around the city. We can talk some more about your adventures." Grivon nodded his agreement.

III

The warm night air was a relief compared to the chilly night air on Ne-Le. Before they left, Barbarah took Grivon to a guest room. There he locked up his new weapon, showered and dressed in some of Steven's extra clothes.

Grivon was happy to be in the company of Barbarah again. He kept himself from asking the question that was burning in the back of his mind, if that child at dinner was Steven and Barbarah's. He knew that he was their child, but at this point, it wasn't worth getting upset over.

At this point, he was just happy to be with the one he loved again, even though his heart pulled to see Angela again too. Barbarah helped him realize who he was, and Angela nursed him back to health so many times.

As they walked, Grivon told her about Phoy's training and about all the crazy things he was made to do. He left out certain parts about him and Angela that he knew would hurt her.

When they finished talking, they found their way back to Steven's mansion and were in the room where they ate dinner. They sat sipping wine and laughing.

Then what seemed at the drop of a hat Barbarah's face grew serious. Sitting the fluted glass down, she said, "There is something I have to tell you."

Grivon's stomach fell to his knees. This wasn't an enjoyable way to start a conversation.

"What do you have to tell me?" Grivon stammered.

"That she's a..." The Gryphon hissed.

Grivon pushed his sinister alter-ego's voice out of his mind.

"I need to tell you that even though I love you and have missed you all these years, I had Steven's son about eleven years ago. He said that I was the only woman he ever trusted and that he loved me.

At that time, I felt so weak of mind, and thought you were dead. I embraced his kindness and took his bed."

Grivon felt his heart begin to ache and pound harder. His breath became short and he wanted so bad to lash out her, but he knew the words that came out of her mouth weren't hers. He could tell that something had happened over the years and that she was not who she used to be. She never would have betrayed him like that, would she?

"There is more," she began. "Now that you are back, I realize that in all these years I never stopped loving you even though I do love Steven now as well. I know that you said we would wed when you came back, but I just don't think I could choose between you two.

It would devastate Steven, and I just couldn't do that to a man like him. He really is a good man. I know you don't fully trust him even though he is your friend.

Right now, I think that if we all could just be friends like we were in the beginning, that would be the best thing."

"I told you she had been productive in your absence," chided The Gryphon. Once again, Grivon forced the voice out of his mind.

"I don't know where to begin with that statement," Grivon said trying hard not to show any emotion in his voice. "I feel like you betrayed me.

You said you loved me and only me, but just because I lose contact with you, what is the first thing you do? You hop in the bed with my best friend and have his kid!" By this time, Grivon was screaming and Barbarah was cowering in fear.

She never saw Grivon like this before. It was unnerving to see him express so much anger. Then she heard him say something she never thought she would hear.

"I wasn't going to tell you, but, yeah, I missed you too. I missed you so much I took the bed of the assassin who was trying to kill me!"

Barbarah felt like her heart was sucked from her chest and was replaced with the most agonizing pain she ever felt. She started crying and became short of breath.

Then she yelled out words that she never thought she would hear herself say.

"I hate you! You egotistical bastard. As much as you claim to love me, and I find out that some of my suspicions were true! I wish you never came back!"

"I wasn't going to tell you about it, because I didn't really love her the same way I love you. But you, you just spread your legs as soon as you get lonely and have a kid. I understand the pain you have gone through.

But if you must know why I slept with my assassin was because for some reason she loved me as much as you did. I needed that love to make me sane after the brutalities Bebe made me suffer.

"I'll tell you something else. I have learned to punish those who have wronged me! I have learned that mercy is a weakness. I have learned personal justice is strength, and I will punish the one responsible for our troubles," at this point The Gryphon had taken over Grivon's mind.

Barbarah whimpered and flinched, thinking it was going to be her. Then Grivon turned and stalked out of the small dining room. Barbarah breathed a small sigh of relief, but then realized that Grivon was either going after Steven or maybe even Keith.

IV

The Chronicles of Merkadiah:
The Rise of the Gryphon

Steven sat at the battleship-sized desk in his war room. He leafed through reports from his underlings in the organization. He was unhappy that Grivon was back in his life. As far as he was concerned, Grivon should have stayed on Ne-Le, or better yet, died.

Now his years of planning and control were going to unravel in a matter of moments. Of course, he could try and convince Grivon that since he "managed" the money of several key Aridaunts, the Kofahs, and the Depublics, he was instrumental in killing off the old Autocrat.

Additionally, he was controlling many of the actions of the new one, Grivon could just take control. He leaned back in his chair and scratched his chin. Perhaps he would buy that. Whatever it took to keep him from learning the truth. Then again, Barbarah could tell him, but that was unlikely.

Just as Steven was, feeling good about his musings, his Network terminal beeped. Rolling his eyes, he hit the button and Theo's face appeared on the screen.

"Good evening my Lord," said Theo bowing.

"What's good about it?" Steven growled.

"Am I bothering you?"

Steven sighed, "No it's been a stressful couple of days. What do you need?"

"I wanted to tell you that Martxapahn has consented to a tournament tomorrow, but only if he and I are fighting." There was a hint of worry to Theo's voice. Steven realized that he might be able to make Grivon happy and deal with both Martxapahn and the incompetent Theo.

"Good, where will it be held?"

"It will be held in the tournament hall of the senate building. The Depublics and Kofahs will be there to preserve decorum and to make sure if I die, there will be someone to take over."

"Is your First Depublic loyal to me?" Steven snarled.

"Yes."

At least that was a bit of good news, "Very good, you can think for yourself."

Theo put his index finger up to make a comment when a loud din came from the hall.

A loud banging came from Steven's door. He looked over to see a sword blade pierce the wood. Theo watched as the color drained from his master's face, and without being told, Theo ended the conversation leaving only a blue screen in his place.

Steven ran and grabbed a sword off the wall. It wasn't a saber, but it would help. He assumed Barbarah told Grivon about Keith. This was not going to be good. It looked like Grivon was going to try and kill him.

If there were some way he could keep his life, and let Theo and Martxapahn die, then he would be lucky. Steven could get Barbarah to kill Grivon as he slept. Then he would be in control of the system.

The door splintered and Grivon strode in. He was holding an odd-looking weapon. It was a saber but was made from different metals.

Grivon was also shinning with an Aurora the likes of which Steven never seen. Steven took a stance and grinned. This was going to be a tough fight. He hadn't even so much as practiced a basic form in fifteen years and Grivon was a more dedicated person than himself.

Grivon didn't even take a stance. He ran headlong at Steven and swung the sword. Steven tried to parry but his sword was easily pushed aside. Grivon stopped with the blade of the sword against Steven's neck.

"Tell me one reason why I shouldn't cut off your ugly head?" Grivon growled.

"Because you can kill The Autocrat and Martxapahn," Steven whimpered.

"I can kill The Autocrat and a candy?"

"No!" Steven shouted. "Martxapahn is the name of a Therian who successfully took over half the fiefs in the system and then seceded. The system has been in conflict ever since. Those damnable Barrims are also part of the problem. They keep killing Kartah, and our military forces can't stop millions of angry peasants."

Grivon lowered the blade and said, "I'm listening."

"I own several companies that have been in my family for generations. One manages the prominent politician's money. This gives me direct access to The Autocrat. He told me that there is going to be a tournament tomorrow between him and Martxapahn. If you want, you can kill them both to realize your dream. In order to do that, you have to keep me alive."

The saber melted into Grivon's hand and the Aurora dissipated. Steven breathed a sigh of relief. Grivon had taken the bait. Before anything else could be said, a breathless Barbarah ran into the room.

The Chronicles of Merkadiah:
The Rise of the Gryphon

"Good you're both okay," she said huffing.

Grivon gave her a sad smile and then turned back to Steven with an unsettling look on his face.

"Tell me what I need to know!"

V

Grivon was tired. Between all the walking and the almost duel with Steven, he was ready to sit in a nice hot bath and let the tensions of the day melt away. After all the things he learned, he was happy to be alone.

Quickly, he disrobed, walked into the large bathroom, and started running a steaming hot bath. Walking down into the basin, he sat watching the hot water flow up and over his legs. Goosebumps arose on his arms, neck, and back. Suddenly, he heard a sound. He opened his eyes and looked up to see a naked Barbarah.

Surprised Grivon stammered, "What are you doing here?"

"One last fling. I've always known deep down that somehow our love was doomed and that it would end up being my fault. Here I am to show you one last time how much I love you and that I can't choose between you and Steven. That after you and I have each other one last time, that will be it."

Grivon nodded. At least when all was said and done Angela would come and comfort him. He was heartbroken and making love to her would only be a consolation, but at least he would be happy with her one last time.

Chapter Four
Greatness Realized

"Atop the pillar of power everything is yellow dust." -Pantherine Proverb

I

Grivon walked through the arch into the room where the tournament was going to take place. His eyes surveyed the room, drinking in the scene. The grounds were in the basement of the Senate building. The floor was made of hardpacked dirt with benches surrounding it.

Grivon was wearing his Chaos robes, and he had his father's weapon tied to his back. He walked into the arena and was stopped by a barrier of crossed swords. Two Depublic guards stopped him in his tracks.

Not wanting to cause problems, Grivon nodded and turned to walk out. Then without warning, he ran as hard and as fast as he could. Before the guards could stop him, he was on the other side of them looking up at a ceiling that clearly didn't belong in the arena.

As he studied the walls, he noticed an area that looked like some sort of enclave with three seats. Then he realized that The Autocrat and his two Depublics normally sat there and watched the tournaments. Once Grivon had finished taking in his surroundings he looked around at all the faces of government surrounding the room.

He picked out governors, Aridaunts, Kofahs and The First and Second Depublics. Then he laid eyes on The Autocrat and Martxapahn standing across from him, staring.

Grivon looked on in revulsion at Martxapahn. Then he turned, looked at Theo and said, "My name is Grivon D'Gaul, and you are going to die."

"Did you say Grivon D'Gaul?" stammered The Autocrat.

"Yes, and you killed my parents. Now I am going to kill you and that thing over there!" shouted Grivon pointing at Martxapahn.

"Look. I didn't kill your parents," The Autocrat stammered.

"Yes, you did! Do not lie!" Grivon screamed.

"If there is no reasoning with you, then I guess I have no choice than to let you try and kill us. After all, I did try and kill you, so I guess I do owe you that much."

"I will kill you!" Grivon shouted.

"You will try, and you will fail," answered The Autocrat.

"I will take you both on at once!"

"Let the boy try," Martxapahn said laughing.

The Autocrat nodded his agreement. Then each man took the stance of their favorite forms. Grivon morphed his father's weapon into a saber and took the High Thay're stance. In the blink of an eye, Grivon short-jumped, and cut off the Autocrats head.

Martxapahn and the surrounding bureaucrats gasped at the brutality of Theo's death. Grivon smirked and short-jumped in front of Martxapahn. Martxapahn's face reflected fear for only a moment.

Then he reversed his stance and struck out with his sword. Grivon parried the blow with the guard of his saber and kicked Martxapahn squarely in the jaw.

Martxapahn stumbled back only to regain his footing. Grivon grinned. This was what he had been waiting for. A worthy opponent, and with that realization he energized his Aurora. This brought on a rash of whispers among the onlooking politicians.

Even Martxapahn let his guard down for a moment to gawk at his Aurora. Grivon smirked and touched the bead of smoldering rage he had learned to control.

He fed it with the stinging words of his peers, he fed it with Ubiroe's flamboyance, he fed it with Bebe's brash brutalities, he fed it with Barbarah's betrayal, and finally he fed it with his own self- hatred.

His arms and hands were a blur as he relentlessly attacked Martxapahn. Martxapahn's heart beat faster with each passing moment. Grivon's barrage left no room for any sort of counterattack.

He didn't even try to energize his Aurora, because the moment he focused on something other than Grivon's cold green eye's; he was dead. At this moment, it was safer to try and parry each blow and find some stable footing.

Then the unthinkable happened. His back was against the wall of the arena. He looked as Grivon raised his sword for the coup de grace. Suddenly his wits came about him; he short jumped from his current location to five meters behind Grivon.

Growling, Grivon turned to see Martxapahn activate an aquamarine Aurora. Grivon grinned. Now it gets really interesting. He licked his lips, flourished his sword and took a High Kathagah form, and shaped his saber into a katana.

There was a gasp among the audience. This made Grivon smile and grip the new sword with both hands, as he steadied himself. He finally met his equal in combat. This was the thing that he was searching for. Not the love he had found with Angela and Barbarah, but the sheer violence, terror, and elation that came with combat.

The passion that came from fighting a worthy opponent. Grivon waited for Martxapahn to make his next move. It seemed like an eternity but, Martxapahn finally twitched ever so slightly and Grivon short jumped behind him.

Martxapahn blocked Grivon's cut with his sword raised barely above his head. Then in a fluid motion thrust Grivon's blade back and turned around into a swift counterattack from the Natchi form.

Grivon saw the counterattack and blocked it. This cost him some momentum, but that was a small price to pay to keep his head. Martxapahn tried to withdraw the sword for a new attack, but found that the force he had struck with had caused the blade to bury in the soft metal of Grivon's.

Grivon saw the opening and took his left hand off the sword, which caused him to be bent over slightly more than was comfortable, and blasted Martxapahn's Aurora with a spray of super-heated vapor.

Martxapahn's Aurora turned red for just a few seconds as Grivon's went to a black-grey color. Martxapahn screamed as he looked down at his right leg. There was a large red hole and he could see the bone.

Roaring, Martxapahn pulled his sword free from Grivon's and took a step to the left, to try and force Grivon off balance. But Grivon remembered Phoy's first task about the path of least resistance and saw the opening he needed.

Right as Martxapahn raised his saber for the attack, Grivon cut him off at the thighs. Martxapahn fell over onto his back, screaming in pain. Grivon stood over him with the blade of his sword up under Martxapahn's chin.

He gazed into the eyes of the mad Therian and nodded. Before he could cut off his head, what was left of Martxapahn's body began to glow blue in a cocoon of light and was teleported to rejuvenation.

The Chronicles of Merkadiah:
The Rise of the Gryphon

The whole affair was over in less than five minutes. The Kofahs and Depublics all kneeled in front of the new Autocrat. Grivon stood looking as the other politicians and Kartah followed suit. It was almost over.

All he needed to do now was to make sure he would stay in power for a long time to come, and that Angela, Barbarah, and Steven had their respective places of authority in his new government.

II

Grivon stood at a podium at the base of the high seat in the Senate Chamber. His mouth was dry and his palms sweaty. This would be the first time he ever addressed a large crowd. He scratched at his cheek; the amethyst mask was proving hard to get used to.

After he was sure everyone was seated and listening, he began his first speech as ruler of Merkadiah.

"The first order of business is that I am giving the first of my two annual decrees. The first thing is that as of this moment, there are no more Depublics or Kofahs, and I will reassign all fiefs and interest groups," He paused to quickly swallow some water.

Licking his lips, he started again.

"Any unassigned Aridaunts will be returned to the rank of Governor or be given a regional office of the Special Protection Agency, a new police force being commissioned in the next six months.

Anyone who objects can come and talk to me in my personal office. Now my second decree." This time he paused to let what he said sink in.

"I now have autonomous control over all laws and persons in this system. We will now have a new form of the feudal system we used to have. Aridaunts will oversee fiefs with governors under you and Kartah under all of them with the addition of the Special Protection Agency."

There were several murmurs and disgruntled comments coming from the chamber. This only strengthened Grivon's resolve.

"Now that I have everyone's attention, you will no longer call my position The Autocrat. I am now and everyone who takes my place after me will be known as The Gryphon, and now I present to you the new face of the Depublics."

Grivon motioned and two people clad in robes came into the Senate chambers. The audience could tell one was male and the other was female. They wore bright green robes, and each wore a mask made of garnet.

Grivon raised his hands palms facing up and said, "I give you The Unicorn," motioning to the woman standing at his right. "And the Pegasus!" Grivon motioned to the man on his left. "If they give an order or say something to anyone in this system, it is as if I said it."

"Now for the final thing before you are all dismissed to your fiefs to spread the word about the new order of things, I have an answer to all your burning questions about certain rebellions.

The Pantherine ghettos are to be closed as of this moment. Their tribes will be split up and each given their very own planet. The Leonis will be given the planet of Tygrano. The Tigris will be given the planet of Felion.

The Lepridis will be given the planet of Rhokahl, and the Chisis will be given the planet Felonius. All Aridaunts with holdings on those planets will be reassigned as governors or some other useful job. I call this session closed."

The Aridaunts and other politicians began to file out of the room speaking to one another with words like, "Tyrant. Blue Blood," amongst other things. They were unhappy that the son of Daggot D'Gaul was now in charge, and that he was just like his father.

Once out of ear hot some began discussing secession, others talked about assassination plots, and others still were conspiring to kill him themselves.

Grivon, Steven, and Barbarah just watched their smiles hidden behind their new masks. It was going to take a lot of work to finish suppressing the Barrims, but at least the Pantherines would be happy with the news that Sekhet was going to give them that evening.

After the politicians dispersed, the door from Grivon's new office opened and Phoy walked up to him. His arms behind his back he looked up at him, "You know they will defy you at every turn and label you a tyrant in the histories after your time as ruler."

Grivon chuckled, "It will be fine. Let them think what they want. After all I am the one in control and they will agree or be made to agree."

Phoy shook his head, "You still have a lot to learn."

The End of
The Rise of the Gryphon

About the Author

Edgar lives in the mountains of North Carolina with his lovely wife and four beautiful children. Edgar has been a retail flunky, factory worker, government employee, fast food manager, and is a certified pharmacy technician. An avid gamer, Edgar can be found behind the game master screen any given Saturday night running a game for his friends.

www.ingramcontent.com/pod-product-compliance
Lightning Source LLC
Chambersburg PA
CBHW051232260626
47162CB00002B/385